Nina Dufort

Nina Dufort has worked as a secretary, a junk dealer, a theatrical dresser and a gofer in an avant-garde art gallery but is now a successful painter who sells her work through the Portal and Rye Art Galleries. She lives with her family in Kent. This is her first novel.

∫

SCEPTRE

Defrosting Edmund

NINA DUFORT

SCEPTRE

First published in 1998 by Hodder and Stoughton
A division of Hodder Headline PLC
A Sceptre Book

10 9 8 7 6 5 4 3

British Library Cataloguing in Publication Data

Dufort, Nina
   Defrosting Edmund
   1. English fiction – 20th century
   I. Title
   823.9'14 [F]

   ISBN 0 340 71682 7

Typeset by Palimpsest Book Production Limited,
Polmont, Stirlingshire
Printed and bound in Great Britain by
Clays Ltd, St Ives PLC, Bungay, Suffolk

Hodder and Stoughton
A division of Hodder Headline PLC
338 Euston Road
London NW1 3BH

To Sophie and Isobel

'Tis very warm weather when one's in bed.

Jonathan Swift

Upstairs in her Kent farmhouse, Xenia Whitby unfolded a pillowcase and sharply shook out its crisp folds before seizing a feather pillow and stuffing it vigorously inside. Having just telephoned her brother Edmund to invite him down from London for the weekend, she was preparing the spare bedroom for the poor betrayed darling.

Outside the window was the dark expanse of Romney Marsh, a view which she found uninteresting and sparse, preferring the tree-covered hills behind the house, where the land rose up billowing from the levels. Tonight a thin moon shone through a narrow gap in the curtains and she twitched them together to shut it out. The curtains were thick and white, and heavily lace-edged, which infuriated the more discriminating guests as they fumbled through the flounces to lean and stare at that mysterious chequerboard flatness, a world invented for the Red Queen and Alice to run across, leaping ditches and windblown hawthorn hedges in an effort to stay in the same place. Bed and cushions were smothered with pristine antique cutwork, crisp broderie anglaise and embroidered net, so that guests were frequently entrapped by button or heel and cursed the prettiness as they fought their way free from the lacy entanglements, and were deeply worried when drips from early-morning tea spattered brown spots on the arctic white sheets. However the pink sofa was comfortable and the bookcase well-stocked, surprisingly so since Xenia had no reading habit. Her husband Johnnie, together with Edmund, had unfortunately something to do with its catholic contents, ranging from Kipling to Karl Popper, via Mungo Park, Rose Macaulay and Julian Barnes. Knowing that Xenia never examined the shelves and giggling tipsily one evening prior to a visit by Johnnie's censorious and stuffy Aunt Bea, they had inserted various volumes of light pornography. Aunt Bea had breakfasted on Sunday morning with a very guarded look on her face, and the hint of a rose-coloured blush on her weatherbeaten cheeks; the books were forgotten after the childish joke and had remained unnoticed on the shelves for years.

Sniffing appreciatively, Xenia adjusted a small vase of *Viburnum farreri* and then left the room, pausing on the landing to straighten a watercolour which she had bought not long after her marriage to Johnnie. It had at first been hung in the drawing room but had been relegated to the upstairs after she had discovered that there were a great number of versions of Rhee Almshouses in the Snow by the same artist in many other people's houses. As she started down the stairs she heard the click of the telephone receiver being replaced and through the banisters could see Johnnie standing motionless on the flagstones beside the oak table where the telephone stood. He had his hands deep in his pockets and his shoulders were hunched. From her height she could see, as he turned and retreated to the drawing room, the small bald patch in the otherwise thick grey hair, and felt a rush of both suspicion and love. Her lips narrowed for an instant before she proceeded down the stairs and followed him with a cheerful smile firmly attached to her face.

She folded herself into her conventionally small arm-chair opposite Johnnie who sat, apparently immersed in his father's old Sussex cattle stock record book, snug in the vasty deeps of his father's huge battered shed of an armchair. Xenia was a tall woman, and the smallness of her chair exaggerated her length and long slim legs sloping out across the silky Turkish hearthrug, almost meeting Johnnie's on the other side of the fire.

'I've just been getting poor Edmund's room ready,' she said.

Johnnie looked up at the apparently calm, regularly beautiful face.

'Why do you always refer to him as "poor" Edmund? His book business is going along very nicely now he's got that Charlie Parrott fellow in on the antiquarian side, and he seems to have completely recovered from the Sylvestra debacle.'

'Of course he hasn't got over Sylvestra!' she almost snapped, startling him. 'How could he, so quickly? She was his entire life!'

'Well, he never shows his distress to me,' replied Johnnie, who privately thought that three years was quite long enough to get over someone like Sylvestra. 'He seems perfectly well balanced and in control of his affairs.'

'He hasn't had any affairs since Sylvestra!' she replied indignantly. Johnnie looked hard at her again, wondering if she was wilfully misunderstanding him, or whether he needed to explain what he meant. In either case, she was mistaken.

'I hope he won't be bored this weekend. Apart from the bonfire tomorrow night, I've nothing in particular for him to do, though I thought we might perhaps go over and have a drink at the Eeldyke pub, Sunday lunchtime.'

As far as Xenia was concerned, drinks at Sunday lunchtime meant a late, probably spoiled lunch. It had never occurred to her to shift the time of the meal so that she did not have to wait irritably for the men, trying to prevent pheasants from overcooking and parsnips from being blackened to charcoal. As she hid her irritation so successfully, they repeated the offence time and time again.

'But isn't that the awful pub where the police arrested all those druggies?'

'No, it certainly isn't. You're thinking of the Bell and Hatchet in Fingle,' said Johnnie shortly.

'Well, I'm sure it's not poor Edmund's sort of place,' she replied lamely.

'Let me be the judge of that. I think he'll enjoy the Eeldyke Inn.'

She waited until he had started reading again, and then said: 'Phil Johnson is dropping off the chair and trunk I bought in the auction up at Hilary's last week.'

'That's very good of him,' replied Johnnie patiently. 'It seems an awful long way for him to come just to deliver a bit of furniture.'

'He was coming anyway. He has a girlfriend near Fingle, apparently.'

'It's time for bed, I think,' said Johnnie, shutting up the book. He leant forward to nudge her foot with his. 'Come along, my old darling.' He held out his hand and pulled her to her feet. 'Where are all these bits of furniture to go, then?' he asked.

'I thought the trunk would be good for Rupert's room, beneath the window, to keep all his old toys in. All the rubbish he simply will not throw away. Don't forget he's out on exeat the weekend after next.'

She went to the kitchen to make some hot chocolate and he to his ritual door-locking and alarm-setting. He had just completed this when he discovered one of the farm cats crouching craftily beneath a chair, so he had to unbolt to put her out, relock and reset the alarm. The cat stared at him with great wide-apart pale eyes: like Xenia's, he thought briefly, before consigning it gently to the chilly dark. They stared at him with a strange lack of contact, as if focusing on the space between his own eyes.

Once in bed he picked up an old paperback copy of *Poets in a Landscape* by Gilbert Highet and amused himself with Catullus while Xenia fiddled with face-cream and brushed her streaked tawny bob. She took a long time so he put the book down and watched her uptilted face in the mirror, remembering her mother, who was about the same age when he had first met her as Xenia was now. The same deep voice, the same startling slanted blue eyes. But what a difference in personality! He had wondered sometimes if he had not been dazzled and confused by the mother, Sofia; bewitched, no less, into marrying the equally beautiful long-legged daughter.

Xenia's father had met her half-French, half-Russian mother in 1938 in Paris, when she was in her late teens, and had fallen in love, only to lose contact during the war. At the Liberation he had gone immediately to the flat where she had lived with her mother and elder brother before the war, hoping against hope that she might still be there. She was, and Xenia's family tradition had it that Sofia had calmly asked him: 'Darlink, what kept you so long?' Sofia had packed herself up and together with her *maman* had returned to England with him, marrying him a year later after they had had time to pick up the pieces.

Sofia had been delightful, supercharged company, Johnnie remembered fondly. She still was, but Xenia had always found her mother a hard act to follow and had retreated into as conventional a style as she had been allowed. Xenia had regaled Johnnie with the embarrassments she had suffered in her childhood when her mother had essayed to be the perfect parent visiting her at boarding school. She had turned up on Sports Day in trousers. 'Darlink, I thought you said it was picnic and games?' she had said, as she stared dumbfounded at the array of hats and pretty flowery dresses *de rigueur* for such an occasion. The school concert had also produced a sartorial misunderstanding. Sofia had worn an elegant black silk dress, proudly surmounted by her grandmother's diamonds. 'So lucky we were to 'ave saved them!' she had said, glancing curiously at the assembled neat blouses and tweed suits decorated with safe little regimental brooches on their lapels. She had not made the same mistakes again, but Xenia had been perpetually terrified of further examples of inapt behaviour and had mistaken for censure her schoolfriends' lively and eager inquisition about this glamorous parent.

Xenia had at last finished the remedial work on her face and neck and slipped into bed beside him in her white lace nightdress. Johnnie was suddenly aware of her tense boniness, which he found emotionally touching but, that night, also physically unsettling. He smiled at her as he put out the light, knowing that he was able to cure the tension, at least temporarily, but was unwilling.

Outside a deep and penetrating frost had begun to bite into the soft leaves of the remaining annual weeds, destroying their tissue so that they drooped, wilting on their stalks.

Edmund Yearne was mugged by the smell of his flat as he unlocked the door and, stooping down to retrieve the box of books with which he had staggered upstairs, nudged the light switch expertly with his chin. The major participants in the olfactory party were soot, engine-oil, orange peel and something near-indefinable which reminded him vaguely of old ladies' face powder. In spite of having had the carpets and curtains cleaned when he first moved in three years ago, the smell still lingered, annoying him each time he returned home. He dumped the books on a table, threw his keys into a chipped china bowl full of fluffy pocket jetsam and eased himself into the microscopic kitchen to make tea.

Once back in the sitting room he sorted through his haul, the result of a house sale in an unpromising part of Hackney where he had discovered a number of saleable books, although nothing too exciting. A first edition, in torn dust-wrapper, of Graham Greene's *Ministry of Fear*, 1943, very nice copy, he noted as he listed them. A first edition of Iris Murdoch's *Under the Net*, 1954. William Boyd's *An Ice-Cream War*, slightly fly-spotted dust-wrapper, and a brown paperback uncorrected proof copy of Elizabeth Jennings's poetry collection *Recoveries*, 1964. He paused with his pencil in mid-air. The titles of the first books to come from the box were disturbingly coincidental to the steps down which he and Sylvestra had slipped towards the death of their marriage, a series of events he had yet again been giving a mental dusting that afternoon while waiting to make a bid. He had not quite reached the 'recovery' stage. He rose and went to draw the curtains, shutting out the November night. Lukewarm air filtered upwards behind the dusty beige Dralon and escaped through the thin panes into the dark.

'There should be a proper tea-tray, with a teapot and a plate of crumpets,' he thought moodily, knowing that his own laziness had prevented him from getting the two former items out of the cupboard and forgetfulness had stopped him buying the latter on the way home from work. The unfinished mug of tea had cooled so he padded back to the kitchen for a refill; the kettle was the same grubby shade of cream as the mug, with identical sad brown flowers printed on it. He knew that scarlet, green and blue kettles were available and he liked strong colours, but it had not occurred to him to buy one for his own pleasure. He hadn't made the slightest attempt to change the rented flat which had most probably last been redecorated while Elizabeth Jennings was writing *Recoveries*. The wall lights were in themselves period pieces now: lacquered brass torches with white glass shades, etched with flame designs and backed with irrationally-shaped pieces of dirty teak.

He finished his list, repacked the books, ate an unappealing plate of fried black pudding for supper and then sat down to a recently discovered method of keeping unwanted thoughts at bay: having spent several years dealing in books he had decided it was time he wrote one himself and had started haphazardly to write a novel. The plot had been easy but when it had come to fleshing out the narrative he had found himself irritatingly sidetracked by details and this evening was held back by a search for a name for a minor character. Nimrod Bolt was the most recent favourite but was a touch too unbelievable even for a work of fiction. Another contender was Wisley Drizzel, but this too was out of bounds since it was not only too Dickensian but the name of one of his regular bookshop customers.

He was almost immediately interrupted by the telephone's ephemeral bleating and in reaching out for it knocked the flimsy apparatus to the floor from where he could hear his sister's fruity voice beaming up from beneath the table.

'Hello? Hello? Edmund? Whatever are you doing?'

'Xenia! I was on the point of calling you.' He lied glibly – he really had been meaning to, over the last six weeks.

Xenia was two years his senior and, since his divorce, had taken him over in a proprietorial manner, and been very kind indeed. Far too kind, in fact, and Edmund had occasionally been forced to fight off her good intentions with a metaphorical baseball bat.

Her name had been imposed by their mother, Sofia, who had refused to countenance either the Jane or Susannah suggested by their English father. The poor man had gamely fought and retired hurt, but rallied and won the second round with Edmund. Their mother had added a touch of

surrealism to their otherwise conventional country childhood in Hertfordshire, sparkling dangerously at Sunday
lunchtime drinks parties and meeting her husband off the
six thirty train in her grandmother's floor-length wolfskin
coat.

'Come down and see us, darling,' commanded Xenia.
'You've not visited for weeks and weeks.'

Edmund was suddenly aware that he needed to get out
of London for a bit quite urgently, more particularly out of
the flat.

'I'd love to. I can't get away till tomorrow lunchtime
though . . . If I turned up at about two thirty? Would that
be all right?'

'That'll be perfect,' Xenia replied, pleased by his alacrity.
'We're having pike for supper tomorrow.'

'Sounds wonderful. Sort of deep, dark and muddy.'

'Actually, it's delicate, white, and you won't even think
of mud when you taste it. See you tomorrow.'

''Bye, Xenia, and thanks.'

He was temporarily cheered by the thought of leaving
London for the comfortable country time-warp in which
the Whitbys lived and he returned to the novel, having
to resort to the back pages of Chambers' Dictionary where,
between Musical Terms and the Greek Alphabet, was an
entry entitled 'Some English Personal Names'. Running
his finger down the lists and marvelling at the unlikeli-
hood of ever meeting anyone named Adalbert, Eusebius
or Oughtred, he finally settled for Crispin Hemp, which
suggested the required scratchy roughness for the character
that was slowly forming in his head. He finally achieved
two short-but-perfectly-formed sentences before becoming
entangled in the difficulties of arranging a realistic meeting
between Hemp and heroine in Pollock's toyshop.

By ten o'clock he was ready for bed. The bed in question
was a lumpy double divan with both casters missing on one

side and therefore propped up on book-club copies of those evergreen inhabitants of charity bookshop shelves, Pearl S. Buck and Dennis Wheatley. He had not shared the bed, or anyone else's, for some time now. His wife Sylvestra had left both him and London to go and live with a coracle-maker in Somerset, and after a lot of confabulation his two teenage children had gone with her.

Xenia had been deeply shocked by the divorce, being a person who saw other people and events only in terms of good or evil, black or white with no soft pigeon-backed shades of grey or beigy-fawn allowed existence. The word 'perhaps' rarely came to her lips. She also prided herself on her ability to judge character, which was why, Edmund thought, she was so very shocked.

'I simply do not understand!' she had kept on repeating. 'What nightmares for you, poor Edmund.'

Edmund had understood only too well. Sylvestra, having what was once termed a 'flighty' temperament, had ceased to love him and started to love someone else. She had gone, and had eventually been awarded half his assets. He had been lucky, he thought, as he pulled his jersey over his head together with his shirt, that he had been able to find a partner to buy into the business and had been able to continue with the shop at all. He was on 'good terms' with Sylvestra, that often hypocritical euphemism which meant merely that there was a polite refusal on his part to admit to any resentment.

The figure that was reflected in the wall mirror as it bent and stretched over the bed, twitching an extra blanket into position, was slim but solid, and just below average height, though not in any way out of proportion. A dark furred triangle on his chest was echoed by an arrow of dark hair which sped down his stomach as if determined to draw attention to his genitals. He was not much interested in his own appearance but imagined it to be average for his age, forty-eight, and he knew, but did not care, that grey hairs were beginning to appear in the thick, straight, brown hair, though he had recently been startled while shaving by the appearance of an enormous white hair emerging like a rocket from his left eyebrow. The clear, pale blue eyes slanted very slightly upwards. His nose was composed by genes with a penchant for architecture and was now a trifle pinched, giving a look of gentle austerity.

Edmund had got out of the way of seeking specifically female company, though he was not at all unpleased when it occurred in the natural course of his work, but he rarely now followed up any promising beginnings. There had been one or two modest attempts to kick-start his love life a year or so ago, with women who had eventually sensed his confusion and lack of real commitment and who had shrugged their shoulders philosophically, put aside their hoes and ceased scratching for those pent-up emotions which they had expected to uncover with ease and assuage with a great deal of self-congratulation.

He draped his jeans over the arm of the chair and got into bed with a sigh of relief, having become suddenly very low.

'All our bodies are made up of similar chemicals,' he thought. 'All our bodies, all over the world. And all our lives,' leaning over to turn out the light, 'all our lives are filled, all over the world, with the same events. There's a sameness to our condition which defies us to find any interest in it at all. It's only the little details that are different – and the little details are really similar to other little details all over the world, just doled out in different proportions.'

With this somewhat muddled and unoriginal thought he fell asleep suddenly and without warning before he was able to depress himself any further by the effort of thinking. The room grew cooler, and a draught from the window whistled softly in his ear, so that in his sleep he pulled the bedclothes over his head and dreamed he was in a dark and stuffy cave with wolves staring at him with their bright close-together eyes.

Edmund awoke, sharply aware of the cold. His legs had been bicycling subconsciously for some time in an effort to keep warm and he leant from the bed to feel the heater. Stone cold. Cursing a little, he rolled over the other way and reached for his jersey and jeans. His last dressing gown had started to shed little tufts of green towelling on the carpet, and then had abruptly fallen apart in despairing shreds. The smell was there again in the mornings, as it always was, but his nostrils were anaesthetized by the cold and it seemed fainter than usual. 'Jesus!' he swore as the stiff denim slid icy-cold over his thighs. The lights did not work either. A power cut. He lit the gas stove and put on three saucepans of water, for coffee and washing. The sky was clearing and brightening as he stood with his fingers tucked into his armpits, watching the tiny bubbles form and steam begin to rise from the pans.

Outside the car roofs were whitened and he looked across to the small garden in Paddington Street, a long-since ex-graveyard with the tombstones now neatly lined up against the low walls, where in the summer children played, lovers picnicked with Persian rugs and white wine, and other alcoholics sat muttering in dark brown groups in the evening, drinking cider. The grass was also white with frost. Surely it was unreasonably cold for November? A man walked slowly down the road with his hands deep in the pockets of his black leather jacket, his breath puffing out in front of him. His head was shaved and he appeared to be wearing some sort of narrow yellow hat. Edmund leant closer to the glass and stared hard to confirm what his eyes were telling his numb brain. The man had a banana stuck lengthwise, fore-and-aft, to his skull. Edmund grinned, then started to laugh hopelessly and immoderately, infinitely cheered by the utterly flamboyant ridiculousness of the gesture. What the concept behind it was he had no inkling, but the idea of getting out a tube of glue, carefully reading the instructions for gumming bananas to brain, and then proceeding to do so, gave him enormous pleasure. He was not alone. Two young women in thin jackets, hunched with the sudden cold, stopped and gaped as banana-man passed, then doubled up screeching and nudging each other.

Edmund intended to spend the morning in the shop before returning to collect his things and his car and running for the country. Searching in a dusty carrier bag he discovered a scarlet cashmere scarf which Sylvestra had once given him for Christmas, and a pair of over-large leather gloves which he had borrowed from Johnnie and forgotten to return. Encasing himself in his long black winter coat he set off for Baker Street station, carrying his box of books and whistling a marching phrase of 'The British Grenadiers' over and over again in time with his steps up Luxborough Street.

The glass door of the shop was newly painted with neat gold lettering, very upmarket, Edmund thought. 'Parrot and Yearne' above, 'Antiquarian and Modern First Editions' written smaller beneath. As he shouldered open the door, he experienced a tiny twinge of regret that he should have to share what had once been his own little kingdom which he had fought and sweated to establish, but the sight of his partner Charlie already behind his desk, wrapping up a parcel, immediately made him feel guilty.

'Morning, Eddie!' said Charlie, siting the address label neatly in the centre and rubber-stamping the shop's name and address across one corner.

'Morning, Charlie. Why are you doing parcels? Where's our Treasure?'

'Treasure has another bloody hangover. I've sent him out,

out of kindness, to buy the coffee and get some fresh air. He looks a bit ill so we'd better keep him in the back room this morning, with a bucket and towel handy, so he doesn't frighten anyone off.'

Tom Treasure was a student at London University, reading Russian. He was very impoverished and very useful, working generally Wednesday afternoons and all day Saturday. He dealt with mail-orders and the computer, effortlessly dealing with a system that had taken Edmund many painstaking hours of familiarization. Tom's abilities had lightened the workload considerably and Edmund and Charlie were prepared to put up with his occasional binges and frequently anarchic demeanour for the sake of his competence between times.

Edmund peered over Charlie's shoulder at the parcel.

'Ah-ha! Your erotic-sounding New Yorker, who thinks she's Helene Hanff.'

'Yes, except that she's no poor struggling writer, is she? These are very hard to come by, copies of Murgatroyd's *Waking Dreams*.'

'He seems to have done rather a lot of daydreaming. How many books in the parcel?'

'Four vols, half-calf, fifty pounds each,' said Charlie, cheerfully patting the parcel. 'I can't imagine that she really wants to read them.'

Charlie was tall, slim and dressed like a less confident version of one of those romantic-looking male models who so casually dispose themselves across the pages of *Vogue* as accessories to girls of aching thinness with hard-child faces. He was however quite hopeless with women, becoming idiotically tongue-tied in their presence, and the more he fancied them the worse he was at talking.

Treasure struggled through the door carrying three polystyrene beakers of coffee. His face was grey and his fingers puce with cold. 'She's only ordering those books to impress you. It must be lust, no one could possibly want to read them,' said Treasure.

'You are feeling a bit better, I take it?' replied Charlie. 'You're just jealous of my superior physical attractions, you burnt-out dissolute.'

'I've got to leave at twelve thirty,' announced Edmund, starting to sift through the mail. 'I'm off to the comforts of Kent.'

'Your sister?' asked Charlie.

'Yes. I've been neglecting her a bit recently.'

Edmund had once been lyrical about Xenia's cooking, which had caused Charlie to develop a curiosity about Edmund's private life that had surprisingly not been deadened by the odd visit to Edmund's Marylebone flat.

The morning passed busily enough with more browsers than usual, refugees from the cold, and enough buyers to keep the till bleeping regularly. Two or three people came in with books to sell. Edmund stayed till Charlie returned from a swift lunch at the pub round the corner and then re-scarved and coated himself, and set off back to the flat to collect his overnight bag. His car, a green Volkswagen estate in the evening of its life, was a mess inside. Dog-eared catalogues with muddy footprints on them and rolling tins of WD-40 littered the floor and a nest of discarded unlucky scratchcards occupied the glove compartment. Edmund drove off in the best mood he had been in for some time. It was odd, he thought, how the lethargic miasma occasionally lifted, enabling him to see, albeit temporarily, far into the distance, once more a man with keen sight and an appetite for life.

The traffic was heavy, and Christmas decorations were already, worryingly, in the shops. He did not wish to think about Christmas yet, and switched on the radio, but had to negotiate a right turn and left it for a minute on a country and western station while trying to cross the oncoming

traffic. The songs seemed a procession of repetitions of a sin-
gularly small vocabulary, endlessly rearranged around one
emotion to melodies indistinguishable from one another.

> 'My pore ol' heart's a-breakin',
> 'Cos my sweet lurve . . . went away-ay-ay . . .'

He tuned to another station but was already thinking about
Sylvestra. Bugger it all, he thought. How does one stop
going on and on about it? How does one stop examining
one's behaviour for causes, mourning the effects? Edmund
had not dammed Sylvestra's torrential temperament, nor
thrown buckets of cold water over the pyrotechnical dis-
plays of rage; he was now unable to turn off the memory
of the tiny blonde Fury, shrieking and throwing teacups
and tomatoes at him. She had found their children less
than fulfilling, and he couldn't stop himself from grinning
momentarily when remembering her annoyance when they
decided to go with her to Somerset. At some point in their
life together he had ceased, perhaps through overuse of his
exiguous faculty for enjoying high drama, to automatically
believe all she said. His responses had become deadened,
and he had been unable, for instance, to realize that her
desire to leave London was urgent and real.

Via punk revival and Euro-pop he achieved some calming
Brahms and managed to switch his attention to his novel.
He interviewed himself, set an exam paper on the subject.

> Q. Why are you writing it in the first place?
> A. Something to do? To see if I can?
> Q. I see. Not because you have anything to say?
> A. I won't know if I've got anything to say till I've said
>   it.
> Q. Is it about ideas, or behaviour?

A. Hadn't thought.

Q. Stop wasting time then, and think.

He paused in a minor traffic jam near Brixton. A red-haired woman in a Metro next to him was staring, and he realized that he had been talking aloud.

Q. Are you happy?

A. I don't think so. I'm not very unhappy at the moment though, which seems like a great advance to me. I even laughed aloud when I was on my own.

Q. Did you turn the gas off?

A. Don't spoil everything!

He tuned in to a talk on the invasion of Britain by the Romans, which interested him enough not to notice the miles, and suddenly found himself turning off the motorway at Parden, an unlovely sprawl of business parks, out-of-town superstores and warehousing. There were miles of interlocking by-passes weaving around builders' housing estates designed, in an attempt to relieve the monotony, to look as if each house came from a different part of the country: toy-houses with a muddle of red brick and gables, pink or yellow rendering, blue-grey slate roofs, tiled roofs, round windows, square windows, mock-Tudor beams and Georgian porticoes. Sometimes an ancient farmhouse stood suffocating amongst its brasher neighbours. Around all this was poor, marshy-looking land with little clumps of rushes and the occasional skinny pony grazing sadly beside redundant or broken stock-bridges.

'I wonder if the Celts thought the Romans' new buildings looked so hideous?' thought Edmund, circling a roundabout twice in an effort to find the right exit. 'Were they seduced by the plumbing and warm floors, delighted by the sparkling white and gold of the new temples in the new town centres? Did the Cantii feel diminished by the stone roads searing across their own ancient trackways, flattening sacred groves on their way to newly important towns?' He imagined, in cartoon-form, two Celts standing doubtfully beside a new road.

'It's a great wonder, Beric. It's what they call progress,' said one.

'It's just going to increase the number of carts and chariots,' said the other. 'More and more congestion. And we'll be inundated with tourists from Gaul.'

Another twenty minutes and he was into rural surroundings, pulling off a B road into a narrow lane running south through ancient coppiced woodland, at the end of which was the Whitbys' farm. Preferring to arrive at the back of the house rather than the chillingly elegant Georgian front, he turned through the iron farm gates with the brick cowsheds and modern barns to his left and rattled up a narrow track over a cattle grid to the back. This was considerably older than the front and had an organic look to it, as if it had heaved itself out of the ground, sprouted without any human help. The low afternoon sun shone on the brickwork, turning it pinky-gold and highlighting the tortuously twisted branches of the weeping ash beside it. There were unthawed patches of frost in the shade of the wash-house wall, where Meg and Flit the sheepdogs now slept. Edmund opened the heavy green-painted kitchen door, entered the back hall with its brick floor, muddy boots, dog leads, and derelict jackets that Johnnie wore around the farm. Hearing noises from the kitchen beyond, he called out, gingerly patting the ancient labrador that rose off its blanket in the corner and came to sniff him, farting and tail-waving.

'Edmund? Is that you? I'm in the kitchen!' Xenia called. 'Why do you always come round the back?'

It was wonderfully warm in the kitchen and Edmund put his bag down on a chair and gave his sister a hug.

'I like to surprise you. Is there anything left to eat?'

'I'll make you some lamb and lettuce sandwiches in a moment, and there's some choccy pud. I was just going to take the coffee into the drawing room. Johnnie's in there, but he has to go out soon to help set up the fireworks at Holy Hill.'

'Of course. I'd forgotten, it's Guy Fawkes.'

Xenia sliced neatly at the remains of a small leg of lamb while the kettle boiled, dabbing redcurrant jelly on to the slices before tucking them up between crisp lettuce sheets in thick brown bread.

'Here, you take this, and I'll take the coffee.' She picked up the tray and led the way, saying over her shoulder: 'As soon as Johnnie's gone we can sit by the fire and have a nice chat.' Edmund knew that a nice chat was code for a serious interrogation about his social activities since she had last seen him, and he began rapidly to invent a list of interesting events to keep her happy. In the hall they had to skirt round a large elm seaman's chest and chair placed in the middle of the flagstones.

'What are these doing here? Are they new?'

'Just been delivered. I've been naughty and gone mad at an auction.'

Edmund, knowing that money was rarely one of Xenia's problems, smiled to himself at her fake concern at her own extravagance and, not for the first time, found himself wondering why she was five feet eleven inches tall and he was only five feet eight.

Johnnie put down his newspaper and grinned at him with enthusiasm. 'Very good to see you!' He smacked the sofa beside him, inviting Edmund to sit down, and raising a puff of dust which mortified Xenia. She had not been allowed to rearrange the room at all, Johnnie being deeply wounded whenever she suggested refurbishments, and apart from one or two new chaircovers and cushions and a coat of paint, it was very much as it had been when his father had lived there, full of ancient and battered furniture and books. Edmund sank into the sofa beside Johnnie, eating his sandwiches in the light and warmth of the great log fire while Xenia poured coffee, stirring sugar into Johnnie's with concentrated devotion.

'Steady on, darling! You'll wear the pattern off the bottom,' Johnnie said.

'Xenia says you're on bonfire duty this afternoon. When's it to be lit?' asked Edmund.

'Oh, around six thirty. We like an early kick-off because of people not wanting to keep the small children out too late. It looks as if it will be a cold evening. Very clear sky again. Bound to be a sharp frost.'

'I don't think I'll come,' said Xenia, 'I'm going to cook the pike and watch a rerun of *Inspector Morse*. I've been to too many bonfire nights with the boys, and it really is getting slightly out of hand now, rather rough. I don't want to get cold feet – standing about.'

Edmund had never attended the Holy Hill bonfire rite through simply never having been staying at the house at the right time. He knew Johnnie considered it a chore, but was himself quite excited by the prospect of flames against the dark sky, loud explosions and the smell of smoke.

As soon as Johnnie had left the house Xenia started her questioning, hopeful for signs of improvement in his social life, but he fended her off admirably. No, he hadn't been eating takeaways. Yes, he had seen the Portley-Talls, and had taken Mary Portley-Tall's sister out to dinner at a Japanese restaurant in Fulham. He had eaten last Sunday lunch with old friends Seb and Fennel and had telephoned Uncle Serge in Paris. This last was true. He had, he said, his inventions gathering speed, been to a good party in

Islington, but as he saw her expression change from gentle concern to dissatisfaction at her own recent lack of social stimuli, he decided not to over-egg the cake.

'Well, you do appear to have been very busy. I'm so glad you are beginning to cheer up, and take notice of people again. Johnnie and I have been very dull these last few weeks. Everyone is holding fire till Christmas. Johnnie is always so busy with the farm, and with the boys away . . . and . . .' Her voice tailed away, almost suggestively, as if he should enquire further.

'And?'

'Well, he seems to find every excuse to go off on his own these days.'

Edmund sensed trouble. Xenia so rarely confided in him, but she had once or twice hinted that she suspected Johnnie was, well, not being faithful to her. There had once been an unfortunate affair with a farm secretary. That was long in the past, but Xenia had remained continuously and sharply suspicious. Edmund thought it unlikely that Johnnie would be straying again, although he could not entirely dismiss the idea out of hand. He tried to reassure her.

'But, Edmund, I'm sure he is up to something.'

'I doubt it. I'm sure that's all in the past. He's not really that sort of person.'

'You're all that sort of person, aren't you?' she said, hoping to provoke confessions.

'Nonsense. I resent being lumped in with everyone else in that sweeping way. And besides, both Johnnie and I are getting old and grey, and the luscious ladies we both so frequently meet behind every hedge are appalled by our old-fashioned clothes and fat tums.'

Xenia frowned.

'I suppose you think I'm past it too?'

'You, darling Xen, definitely don't look your age, and you certainly haven't got a fat tum.'

'Neither have you.'

'Well, Johnnie has, a bit, and I'm sure you're letting your imagination run amok.' Edmund hated the idea of discord between his sister and brother-in-law, the thought of friction in what he had come, since the divorce, to think of as his own family home too.

'It's just something Rosy Pressing said last week . . .'

Edmund got up and stood in front of the fire, warming his behind and selfishly trying to forestall any further confidences.

'Let's go and get that furniture out of the way. Where did you want the chest?'

'It's for Rupert's room. Johnnie helped bring it in, and said it was rather heavy.'

'Perhaps we could manage it between us.'

They went out into the hall and Xenia lifted the lid, giving a moan of annoyance.

'Oh what a nuisance! It's full of rubbish. No wonder it was so heavy. I'll fetch a bin-bag and we'll get rid of it.'

Edmund knelt on the stone flags and rifled through the contents. There was a layer of grubby newspapers dating from the year before, interleaved with plastic carrier bags, and beneath that a single layer of children's paperback books, two large Jiffy bags stuffed with odd sheets of paper, some covered in handwriting, others typed. Then there was a battered flat Kodak box, bright yellow and filled with old photographs and some drawings.

'I hope whoever sold the chest intended to part with these. It all looks as if it's been put away carefully, on purpose.'

Xenia waved the open mouth of the black plastic sack.

'Tough. They should be more careful. Come on. Start filling up.'

'I suppose they may be dead. I can't see any names anywhere, nor an address.' The bulging Jiffy bags were newish and previously unused. 'Don't you think we ought to check . . .' he started, but Xenia had already commenced whisking papers into the bag.

'They're only children's things. Do come on. We'll never get this upstairs if you start to read it all now.'

She dragged the bag out and left it in the back hall, where the contents sidled and settled, rustling the plastic and making the dog raise its muzzle and stare with a flicker of interest.

Together they lifted the chest and manoeuvred it up the stairs, past Henry's room, empty since he was at university, to Rupert's, empty because he was at school. Edmund noticed that although it had been untenanted for several weeks, it still had that smell of dirty socks and pubescent sweat that lingers even when the owner of the socks is far away. A large black and white pop poster was stuck to the sloping ceiling with red-topped pins. It showed three posturing young men with shaven heads and inexpertly applied eye makeup, waving their rudely gesturing Struwelpeter hands. Thick black lettering announced them as 'The Dark Entry'. Xenia saw his glance.

'Grim, aren't they? They were all in the sixth form with Henry when Rupert started there, and the whole school is besotted with them. I think they're what's called an "indie" band.'

Outside the sky was already darkening and the soft mist of condensation on the windows was like the bloom on a plum. They heard the back door slam, followed by rattling in the kitchen.

'Johnnie's back. I'd better go and start the tea.'

Johnnie had already put on the huge kettle and was ferreting in a tin, searching for cake. Edmund went back to the drawing room and stoked up the fire, making flurries of sparks fly up the chimney. Tea was substantial, with buttered toast and thick, juicy fruitcake. Edmund gave a little sigh of pleasure as he bit into the toast. Johnnie watched him with amusement.

'You'll need to be properly stoked up before going out. I'm collecting the Ovenden children and Freda on the way. Lucky's already over there, setting up rockets.'

Lucky was Johnnie's cowman and lived half a mile down the lane in one of the new cottages that had been built by his father in a burst of altruism in the 1960s.

Hunting for warm clothes in the back hall, Edmund chanced upon an old black fedora hat hanging dustily on a wooden peg by the door, and happily slapped it on his head, an ancient friend which he had left behind and forgotten about some years before. They set out in the Land Rover to collect the Ovendens, three of whom were already hopping and bouncing about at their front gate in a frenzy of anticipation, kitted out in identical red knitted woolly hats and reminding Edmund of a gang of garden gnomes up to no good. They tumbled into the back of the Land Rover squeaking and yapping like puppies, and Freda came out of the house carrying a fourth small person; calling for order, she settled them down on plastic fertilizer sacks.

Other groups of people were converging on the meeting point as the Ovenden-Whitby contingent arrived. They came on foot, by bicycle and by car from all directions and the pub yard was already tightly packed with people milling about an old tractor and flat farm cart on which two stools and a couple of chairs were placed. Johnnie had to park some way past the pub, so they all got out and walked back, the Ovendens melting away into the throng. Yet more people came, torches flashing, swarming down the hill from the houses round Rhee church, and a welcoming roar went up as the pub door opened and four elderly men tumbled out carrying brass instruments and a huge drum. They were heaved on to the cart with a great deal of teasing and good-natured complaints, and settled down on their seats. The drum started to thump regularly, its beat signalling the lighting of oily rags wound round staves, held, Edmund saw, by a group of hairy giants in bikers' leathers, to whose massive beer-bellied frames the harsh flaring light gave the grotesque appearance of Norse berserkers intent on setting the village afire.

'That's the local chapter of Hell's Angels,' remarked Johnnie. 'It was their turn to organize it this year.'

The trumpets tootled and the Hell's Angels surged forwards in a disorderly column, the cart lurching along behind the chugging and backfiring tractor, and following them came the crowd, their breath steaming, their boots crunching along the road. It was an impressive sight, Edmund thought, as he followed Johnnie to the bonfire field. The short walk was enlivened by an inebriated torch-bearer stumbling and setting fire to the hair of his brother-in-arms ahead of him. There were shrieks of laughter and howls of fright as he was rolled in the grass verge and extinguished, dusted down and set on his feet again, unharmed. The procession turned into a field where those without torches tripped on frozen ruts and stumbled over anthills and Edmund saw they were in that part of the land where the hills ceased to undulate downwards and became the Marsh, and that straight ahead in the flatness one lone irrational conical hill stood, a last outpost of the higher land, at the base of which was piled the most massive bonfire he had ever seen. It was the size of a house, composed of uprooted thorn hedgerow, an entire hut, old shed doors, pallets and a broken chicken coop. Surmounting it was a superb Guy which, as they got closer, Edmund saw was wearing what appeared to be a rather good pinstripe suit. Its face had been painted with skill, a monstrously malevolent expression on its mask. They pressed forwards, torches were tossed into the pile and flames started to crackle. 'There she goes!'

The flames caught hold and raced up into the night air,

roaring and hissing, and Edmund was jostled and pushed from behind, the crowd fanning out over the grass, long shadows leaping and jiggling. He lost sight of Johnnie and could now feel the immense heat from the flames on his face, see fountains of sparks rising up. The crowd quietened, absorbed in communal atavistic homage; then the Guy, burning fiercely, slipped downwards as the ropes which bound it to the stake were consumed and another shout went up: 'There he goes!'

Two boys alongside him, their faces shiny pork-pink in the firelight, unzipped their jackets and brought out bottles, swigging from them enthusiastically, their heads tilting right back, the light flickering across their gulping throats. A man in front of Edmund slid his arm round his companion, twisting his hand into the thick ginger hair that streamed down her back.

Was this still really a celebration of the discovery of the Gunpowder Plot? Of Guy Fawkes' agonizing death? Of the vanquishing of the threat of popery? Edmund wondered if it might not be some deep communal remembrance of ritual sacrifice and his skin crept into goose-pimples as he imagined the realities of being burnt alive. Surely he could smell burning flesh? Torches were now flashing up the side of Holy Hill, lighting from beneath the branches of the single tree which stood on its summit, and picking out three gallows-like constructions beside it.

Smoke from the fire drifted round the base of the hill, mingling with the greasy steam from a barbecue taking place across the field, at which a queue was already forming. The smell explained, the hairs on Edmund's arms subsided and he returned to gazing up the hill. His feet were numb and he took his gloves off to blow on his fingers.

The firebrands had been extinguished and ghostly figures flitted back and forth on the summit. Up there somewhere was Lucky Ovenden, waiting for the fire to die down a little more before he set light to the fuse and started off the display with a giant rocket.

It burst with a shattering bang that startled Edmund in spite of his anticipation. He was feeling distinctly disorientated and was wondering if he had not slipped back a few hundred years. The huge symmetrical cloud of golden stars which had been released drifted gracefully down, sparkling and twisting, some even hovering, caught in the massive updraught of heat from the fire at the base of the hill. Three more rockets were loosed to deliver their screaming, corkscrewing squibs into the atmosphere, wailing like tormented souls in hell. Someone nudged him on the arm and he looked aside to see a pale woman's face, with immense dark eyes, her hair lit with an aureole of gold flecks from behind.

'Edmund Yearne?'

'Yes?'

'Johnnie sent me over with this.' She held out a hip flask, which he took gratefully.

'It's brandy,' she said. 'He's down by the fire, watching out for any idiots who may have brought their own bangers.' She smiled, turned and slipped away before he could thank her.

The crowd had spread out across the grass and up the lower slopes. Three huge Catherine wheels now spun on their wooden uprights, a Crucifixion scene. Edmund sipped the brandy. It occurred to him that the woman might just possibly be the cause of Xenia's little misgivings. How had she discovered him in this mêlée? His neck was becoming stiff with staring upwards, and the show was flashing its way to a climax. An incongruous tank was now outlined in fireworks, spitting blue sparks from its gun, a final set-piece. One more earth-shaking explosion from a rocket and it was all over.

The fire still burnt fiercely at the centre, and was surrounded by people seeking its warmth after standing so still watching the fireworks. Duffel coats, windcheaters, Barbours, bright synthetic ski-jackets, old tweed coats. Children wove in and out of the crowd screaming and shedding bits of burger and bun, their faces streaked bloodily with tomato sauce. Edmund remembered taking his own children, Hatty and Jerome, to bonfires when they were small and held a picture of them in his mind, of their straight little figures outlined against the light, jerkily waving sparklers. Although he saw a few faces he knew from visits going back over the years, and smiled back at the nods and greetings he received, he was feeling lonely and not part of the crowd. He'd been disturbed by the clarity of his recollection of the children.

The row of willow trees which marked the boundary of the field was uplit, bare branches highlighted with gold streaming upwards into the night. A group of youths, stripped down to sweatshirts, had linked arms and were dancing a rowdy can-can, circling the fire and kicking at its outer rim, sending embers spinning red-hot into its fierce heart. Edmund had been exhilarated by the anarchic quality of the evening and wondered if the more ordered civic events, where people were so herded, guarded and taped off in an understandable desire to avert accidents, were, by denying the common need to experience the occasional exposure to danger, also denying the next generation the love and understanding of the power of fire, along with any feeling of actual participation.

Johnnie suddenly loomed up beside him, his fine, rather Roman features decorated with smuts.

'Sorry we got parted. Good show, wasn't it?'

'Very, very impressive.' Edmund waved the hip flask. 'Thanks for the brandy. It was very welcome, but I'm at a loss to understand how your messenger found me?'

'I told her to look out for the Guy Fawkes hat and red scarf,' said Johnnie, 'but I didn't think she'd find you. She wanted to go home early and said she'd deliver it on her way out if she saw anyone answering your description.'

'Who is she?'

'Amelia Sailor.' Johnnie's voice had a trace of feeling in it that made Edmund wonder if his surmise was correct. 'Lovely woman,' Johnnie continued. 'She made the Guy.'

2 ∫

Amelia Sailor's husband, Nick, had jumped off Beachy Head, leaving a note on the first page of a shiny new red notebook. 'I've become boring. Time to go.' This had been read out at the inquest, and there had been an inadvertently amused murmur at the Coroner's Court. Sympathy was extended more generously than it might have been had the note been more self-indulgent.

Amelia always preferred to say that he had 'killed himself' rather than that he had 'committed suicide', since the former had more immediacy than the ritualistic, considered connotations of the latter. During the first year of the eighteen months since it had happened she had endured mourning 'in the English style', when some people had looked consideringly at her as if wondering whether it was her fault, or considerately left her to herself in order for her to 'grieve in peace', 'to give her time to get over it'. She found that it was she who crossed the road to save them from embarrassment and would rather have been surrounded by wailing women in black, would rather have beaten her breast and put ashes on her head and have had it all over with a funeral the next day. Her marriage had been volatile, and, at times, worrying, since Nick had an unstable streak, but it had not been unloving and she had initially felt more anger than grief that he should leave her so flippantly. There had been months of wrangling with banks, solicitors, insurance and house-agents, leaving her in the end homeless and with a very small income from her work as a jeweller. There had been a few real friends who had not let her run away from them, who had sat with her in the evenings, brought her bottles of wine but seen to it that she didn't drink too much, who had put her to bed, taken her shopping and who had helped comfort not only her but her daughter Josie, who cried, and cried, and cried.

The house and land sold, leaving her a ridiculously tiny amount of capital, she and Josie had moved into a series of rented houses and cottages, all on short leases until this last one, which had been promised for three years. It stood in a lane between Eeldyke and Rhee, and there was an outhouse that she had contrived to turn into a jeweller's workshop where she'd worked furiously with great speed and concentration once she had settled in. Josie was still at school and unable to contribute much to the finances except in the holidays when she managed to get much-sought-after jobs picking raspberries, sorting potatoes, waitressing in pubs.

One autumn evening, running short of tobacco, Amelia had gone to the Eeldyke pub and Johnnie Whitby had been standing at the bar in his dirty work overalls, having a quiet pint. He greeted her in such a friendly and courteous way that her rather grim mood had melted. They sat far apart in the window under the eye of the landlord Seth, and chatted at first of commonplaces and then, discovering mutual interests and concerns, most enjoyably. She took great care to keep her distance however, and although she found him both likeable and attractive, and although she was mourning no longer, was very careful indeed not to appear to flirt or try to be too interesting. A couple of farmworkers and the mechanic who serviced her ancient

Peugeot were sitting in the corner. She could feel the odd glance from their direction, although they appeared to be deeply involved in talk of tractors and sprockets. One could not hiccup on the Marsh without its being reported.

When she had previously met him, casually at drinks parties in the past, he'd seemed a man of great calm and confidence, and a little unapproachable. She had also noticed and, on occasions, spoken to his elegant wife, who had never ceased to watch her husband, making sure that he didn't talk too long to any one person, particularly if they were female, and Amelia had found her overbearing and cool.

She met Johnnie several times by accident after the first drink in the pub, and he had lent her a biography of William Blake which she had enjoyed and returned after reading with a note of thanks, via Seth. The next time she had visited the pub there was another book waiting for her and slipped into the rubber band about its cover was an open note: 'We need a Guy for Bonfire Night. Could you possibly help out?'

Amelia was grateful to him for trying to draw her into local activities and set about the task assiduously, making a huge and lifelike body and a splendid head, well-stuffed with straw and newspaper. Josie had donated an armful of laddered black tights and they had made an extravagant wig from them, and stuffed old pigskin gloves for his hands. The face had been painted with an over-dramatic expression, to make an impression at a distance. Having consulted Josie first, and feeling rather strange about it, she forced the body into Nick's last surviving suit, one she had always hated but which had somehow escaped all the trips to Oxfam with his other clothes. They had been stern with themselves about these, keeping only really useful things like socks and jerseys which they could wear themselves, and the odd shirt.

'I don't think I want to come tomorrow,' Josie said.

'But why not, sweetheart? We've been before, and it's always such a good evening.' Amelia wondered if it might have something to do with the suit.

'Ruffles wants me to go out with her, to go to a gig. We've got a lift from her house into Parden.'

'And what about getting back?'

'Ruffles' Pa says he'll collect us. They're going out to dinner in Parden anyway and'll meet us outside the club.'

'Well, I suppose that's all right then. What time will you be back?'

'Oh, midnightish I should think. Don't *worry*, Mum. I'll be safe, it's door-to-door service!'

Parden being the only source of bright lights and incipient danger available, Amelia had occasionally to concede requests of this sort, in order not to seem overprotective. She was quite certain that as soon as her back was turned Josie would leap into a rundown car full of boys called Spliff, Kite and Spud and disappear into the roughest pub they could find. She was sure because that was what she had done when she was the same age as Josie.

Later that evening Johnnie had called to ask if she'd been able to make the Guy.

'Yes, I have indeed! It's been fun. What shall I do with him? Come early on the night, or do you want him before then?'

'Best if you could bring him around, say about three o'clock tomorrow afternoon? Is that OK, or would you like me to fetch him?'

Amelia didn't want him to see the inside of her house, squashed and cramped as they still were with too much large furniture and unopened packing cases. She didn't want him so close.

'No, don't worry, I'll bring him over. See you then.'

*   *   *

Amelia took the Guy over the next afternoon, putting him in the front seat and fastening a seat belt about him. Josie sat in the back, picking nail polish from her fingernails and wondering what to wear that evening. She didn't really have much choice. She could either go as herself, in jeans or leggings and a T-shirt, or dress up in her only party gear and high heels; she didn't have much in between. Or she could wear her scarlet party dress over her leggings and wear trainers . . .

They stood in the cold sunshine watching as a young man shinned up a ladder with the Guy over his shoulder, both silently judging the breadth of shoulder under the quilted checked shirt, the narrowness of hip, the mop of black hair. Johnnie pulled up in a Land Rover and trailer bringing a load of old fenceposts and pallets to add to the pile.

'Hey, that is a masterpiece! Many thanks, Amelia.'

'I think the whole thing is barbaric,' said Josie.

'Well, I suppose it is. Sometimes our civilization has a very thin skin,' said Johnnie, watching as the Guy was made fast to its stake.

'I *always* think it has a thin skin,' said Amelia. 'Perhaps there being too many people stretches it.'

Josie shivered. 'I'm getting cold.'

'Not surprising. You've never got enough clothes on. Winter's coming,' said Amelia automatically, finding that she sounded exactly like her own mother.

'Anyway, do you think we could go soon? I've got to get ready.'

Getting ready, Amelia knew, could take up to two hours and Josie was due at Ruffles' house by six.

'I'll see you tonight, then?' said Johnnie hopefully. 'I'm bringing my brother-in-law – Xenia doesn't want to come.'

As soon as they got out of earshot and had got in the car, Josie said, in a teasing, mock-whiny schoolgirl voice: 'Mr Whitby likes you, Mum.'

'Yes, I believe he does. And I like him too. Only not in the way you're insinuating, you sordid little beast!'

Josie tossed her head, flicking her goldy-red hair over her shoulder and out of her eyes and giggling. 'I was only teasing!'

'Well stop it at once. I hate being made to feel I ought to blush.'

Later, having delivered Josie, Amelia drove back to the cottage through the lane where her old house stood. She had not done this intentionally and automatically indicated left and turned into the drive, almost immediately realizing her mistake and braking. Through the leafless trees which surrounded it she could see that the study shutters had not been fastened and that the room was now painted a bright yellow; a large gilt-framed mirror hung over the fireplace. Upstairs, where their bedroom had been, the curtains were drawn, but she could see the silhouette of a figure walking to and fro. A wave of regret rose up in her throat like heartburn and suddenly she was dripping tears. Reversing sharply, driving down the road out on to the Marsh, she pulled up with a jerk on the verge beside a dyke, in whose black water was reflected a fingernail-paring of new moon. Amelia felt in her pocket for a handkerchief – she loathed paper tissues – and blotted her face with the thin cotton. She sat quietly and rolled a cigarette, leaning back, puffing, staring at the moon and trying to regain control of herself.

'You will go back to the cottage,' she ordered, 'and you will tidy your face. You will then go to the bonfire.' She took a long, last drag on the cigarette. 'That house was once my peaceable kingdom. Well, peaceable some of the time. I've been cast out of Eden, and although it wasn't all my fault, I've got to get on with things.'

She drove on to the cottage, grabbed a cold sausage from

the fridge and made up her eyes sketchily, leaving for Holy
Hill too late to catch the procession but just in time to see
the fire lit. 'There's a new bogeyman for the end of the
century – the man in a suit,' she said to herself as the
flames licked round the bottoms of the Guy's trousers,
having become more aware since Nick's death of obstructive
officialdom and soulless managements. 'Bonfire – bone fire
– no smoke without fire . . .' Her nose was scorching and
her back freezing, but she had seen Mary Beaton who had
been one of her chief comforters and suppliers of wine and
friendship when she had been grieving, and started to push
her way through the crowd to say hello. A loud explosion
close by made everyone jump – there followed a bit of a
scuffle and some swearing before she heard Johnnie's voice
raised, demanding a young boy turn out his pockets.

'Give me that banger. Thank you. We don't want any
silly accidents here.' Amelia saw him, and saw the boy
slink off, muttering brave retreating abuse. 'We can't let
them start doing that now while there are so many small
children about.' He stood by her, watching the furnace with
an expression of satisfaction. Then he turned to her. 'You
look a bit . . . well, um . . . a bit down,' he said.

'No, not really,' she assured him, then suddenly: 'That
was one of my husband's old suits, on the Guy.'

'Oh God! Was it a case of getting it out of sight, or an act
of revenge?'

She was surprised by his directness, and looked sharply
at him. 'A bit of both, in a way.'

'How does it feel?'

'Flat, actually.'

'Here, have a nip of this,' he said, diving inside his coat
and producing a hip flask. She took off her glove to undo the
stopper and had a sip, then another, and coughed a bit.

'Thanks. I can feel it going all the way down.' He noticed
her neat long-fingered hand and found himself wondering

who it was she reminded him of – perhaps a very small Queen Elizabeth the First?

'Don't get too close to the fire, you might self-ignite! Look, I've got to hang around here, wander around the fire, trouble-shooting, sort of. Could you take the flask and see if you can find my brother-in-law? His name's Edmund Yearne and he's a small man in a big black hat and red scarf.'

'Oh, I see. Very easy. There's only about five hundred people here. Well, I'll try, though I can't see how in this crowd . . . and I want to go straight after the fireworks.'

'You won't join us for a drink then, afterwards?'

'No, I'd like to go home, but thanks for the offer.'

'Well, you might see him on your way out. If you don't, you can keep on sipping, and give the flask back to me some other time.' He instantly felt silly, like a man being caught playing on his own with a toy car. But she appeared not to have noticed his spur-of-the-moment ruse, intended to engineer another meeting, and went, picking her way through the illuminated faces and dark, swaddled bodies, stepping gracefully in her long black skirt and boots over a comatose Hell's Angel who had been drinking all afternoon and was not even awakened by the first of the rockets. Contrary to Johnnie's expectations, Amelia miraculously found the owner of the hat who, with his red scarf, brought to mind the Lautrec poster of Aristide Bruant so popular in kitchens in the early 1960s, delivered the brandy and left the scene.

A police car cruised by, the last rocket scorched to its zenith and exploded, leaving a brief pink and green after-glow as its stick drifted quivering down through the dark air, landing on the back of, and startling, a Suffolk ram put in amongst a flock of Kent ewes that evening to start his duties.

Amelia caught the ice-green marbles of the cat's eyes in

the beam of the torch as it turned to lope ahead, racing her up the path to the back door. A little owl called out sharp and ringing, 'Qui-ick, qui-ick!' She struggled with the key, cursing, and the cat lost patience and reluctantly used the catflap. Her kitchen ran the length of the house beneath the catslide peg-tiled roof. Ancient Rayburn at one end, sink awkwardly placed at the other, and in between, ranged against the wall, there was a long row of modern cupboards – 'units' the agent had called them while showing her disdainfully around the place, trying to find something about which to be enthusiastic in a house which had already been spurned by other would-be renters, in spite of the shortage of available properties.

Amelia went straight to the far left-hand cupboard and took out her last bottle of the previous year's sloe gin; she shut the cupboard doors firmly, since they had an eerie knack of springing open by themselves when her back was turned, making her jump. There was no central heating, no washing machine or dryer, no lack of mould, blackly spreading across the bathroom ceiling, and she had found on her first day there the skeleton of a cat in the coal shed, beside something which she had taken at first in the dim light to be a sheep's blackened, decapitated head, but which resolved itself, after being poked with a stick, into an old bicycle saddle coated in dust.

She poured herself a generous splash of gin, and leant up against the stove warming her thighs, easing off her boots. This year's sloes were seeping precious juices out into the gin in two bottles in the wash-house. The sloes had been picked only two days before, and the gin would not be drinkable until the end of January at the earliest. Only two bottles this year. She admired the rich amethyst-ruby colour, the plum-almond scent, the winter taste. She also noticed that her socks, Nick's socks, had holes in them, and that there was a small acid burn hole on her skirt where she had carelessly splattered spirits of salt while working on a gold ring. She must not let herself become too scruffy and careless of her apppearance; that would send out signals of defeat, or even signs of an insouciance she did not possess. She wondered if the thought had come to her because she was aware that someone fancied her, and that she could have fancied him back, had he not been married. She vividly remembered Nick had once been obsessed with a terrible little trollop of a waitress. If she were herself to indulge in adultery, the wife in question would refer to her as a terrible little trollop, and she would find that distasteful, nor would she like to upset anyone, even Johnnie's icy spouse, for the sake of her own satisfaction although she was increasingly feeling the need for male company. She preferred the term strumpet to trollop, she thought, taking another sip of the gin: strumpet sounded ringing and brassy, like a besmirched angel; trollop sounded lollopy and bosomy, like those overcooked kitchen wenches at pseudo-mediaeval dinners, with their tits hanging out of anachronistic white blouses and corsets. She finished the gin, stoked up the coal stove and boiled a kettle to make herself a hot-water bottle, then leaving the light on to guide Josie in, she went up to bed.

Her bedroom was the best room in the house, although it was on the lane side which meant she was often woken early in the mornings by tractors and lorries off on their day's work. The thin door had a delicately cut eighteenth-century iron latch and the rooms had a higher ceiling than those downstairs. It had a large sash window and in the late summer, when they had moved in, it had been light and airy with a view across acres of sunny wheat, flat greenness dotted with sheep, and sky, sky and more sky. It was also on the leeward side of the house, calmer and less buffeted by the prevailing southwesterly winds. Josie's room was to the windward, and in September they had hung out of her window watching approaching storms, the vast cumulo-nimbus clouds boiling and bursting like giant cauliflowers on the horizon, waiting till the last minute before slamming down the sash as the sky darkened and the first fierce raindrops dashed against their faces. Amelia enjoyed the weather and its inescapable inevitability on the Marsh, where there was no shelter and she felt at one with the elements and could take and love whatever they threw at her. As winter had come in, she had piled on the blankets, lit the paraffin stove and listened snugly while the rain pattered on the Kent peg tiles above and gurgled in the gutters, and the nights had become longer and longer.

She slipped off her skirt, then, good intentions thwarted by the cold, removed only her tights and knickers, tucking her long and rather grubby cotton petticoat around her pale legs as she leapt into bed wearing the two jerseys in which she had attended the bonfire. She could smell the smoke in them as she huddled under the bedclothes, waiting for her body heat and the hot-water bottle to make a bubble of warm air. Tomorrow was Sunday, so she could stay in bed as long as she liked, but in practice would get up and go out to her shed to get some work done, having a batch of silver earrings to make for a craft gallery in Canterbury.

She drifted off to sleep while planning the next morning's work, only to reawaken almost immediately, her subconscious ear hearing the click of a door being quietly closed as Josie crept in at one a.m. She was now unable to get back to sleep, and lay there stirring the immortal soup of worries and frets common to those awake at that time of the morning.

'This is the wrong way round,' she thought crossly, 'I should have stayed awake worrying because she wasn't yet back, not woken up and started worrying because she was.' She proceeded to fret about having enough sheet silver in hand to complete the job, and whether her stock of saw blades needed replenishing, and the risks involved in liking Johnnie, and who was Aristide Bruant, and what shall I do, what shall I do?

Even though orders had picked up a bit over the last two months, things looked a bit bleak. Last month, after having paid off all the bills and allowed for food and extras like firewood, she had had only ten pounds spare. The woodman had brought the logs too big. She would have to split them all. 'I'll get Josie a black velvet hat for Christmas. But there's nothing now, till Christmas. Halloween, Bonfire Night over. Just approaching winter and Advent, and that's a period of mourning. They take all the flowers out of churches in Advent. A silver, reusable Advent calendar would be fun to make, like a Russian icon, covered with small silver doors to open, with tiny bolts, and inside each a golden thing, apple, rabbit, bird, something different for each day . . .'

She slept again, the fat little cat curled up in the small of her back. Outside the water in the dykes started to solidify around the reeds, an icy skin spreading across the dark surfaces.

Three miles away, up beyond the half-moon of old degenerated cliff-face that rims the inside edge of the Marsh, Johnnie poured out three brandies, toasting Xenia's successful pike with *beurre blanc*, and put on John Lee Hooker while they settled down to roast themselves by the fire and play a round or two of cribbage. They retired to bed at eleven, Edmund relaxing into the warmth of his bed, cup of tea at elbow and book in hand, reading only a paragraph or two before slipping away on a tide of comfort and security. But he awoke during the night, his book having dropped to the floor with a thud. He was a light sleeper and he had left the bedside light on. It was three a.m. and he felt thirsty –

too much wine at dinner – and also surprisingly peckish. A navy towelling dressing gown hung on the back of the door, so he slipped it on and tiptoed out on to the landing and down the stairs to search out a biscuit or two, or perhaps a bowl of cereal. The kitchen was warm, but intimidating, having been the subject of one of Xenia's recent improving sessions. Beautiful deep cupboards, drawers that slid in and out like silk, all paint-stained a soft bluey-green. Immaculately tidy lists and neatly marked calendars hung on the wall beside the vast new refrigerator. A dark green bowl was filled with eggs, to remove one of which would have destroyed the impossible symmetry of their arrangement. The black and white tiled floor was spotless and all the supper dishes were neatly stacked in the dishwasher. It seemed quite difficult to know where to look for anything edible, but Edmund remembered the cake tin, took a plate from the wooden drainer above the sink, and cut himself a slice, careful not to leave crumbs all over the table. Too tidy, he thought as he looked about, inhumanly tidy. He appreciated order, but liked to be able to see the things that had been ordered. There was not a cup or a wooden spoon in sight. He was still not sleepy, so he searched for hot-chocolate powder, but couldn't find any. At least the milk was in the fridge and he warmed a cupful, added some sugar and sat thinking. The dog sighed in its sleep in the back hall, and Edmund remembered the sack of papers they had taken from the chest that afternoon and went in search of it. The house was immensely silent, so quiet that he could only hear the soft hum of the fridge and himself and the dog breathing.

He rootled through the sack, pleased that it hadn't yet been put out to be burnt, found the things he was looking for and returned to the kitchen table, opening up the yellow photographic paper box. On top lay a child's wax crayon drawing, much creased. It showed a boy sitting on a swing, with a girl standing behind him, her hands on her hips, looking unmistakably cross. At the bottom was written, in young child's writing, 'My trun naw' and beneath this, in sprawling capitals, IMIM. The tree from which the swing was suspended was a child's tree, but drawn with knowledge of trees and the way their branches sprang from the trunk, sloping upwards and away, not stuck on like horizontal afterthoughts. The leaves were real leaves, amongst which was a plum. The children's bodies, although square with legs and arms at each corner, had the appearance of volume. It seemed almost the work of an adult trying to be naive, but Edmund knew it wasn't.

Beneath this, a pile of black and white snapshots of picnics in rocky places, some beside the sea, and a larger photograph of a girl in a dark swimsuit, her head held self-consciously as if staring at her outstretched feet, her face almost obscured by a panama hat. Then there was a scruffy watercolour painting of cyclamen leaves, their marbled surfaces delicately but loosely done, a professional piece of work. On the back was a shopping list. 'Bread, bacon, biscuits. Cabbages and Kings. Deodorant, loo paper, toothbrush. Something for supper. Kippers? Ring Percy and get him to sort out the hedge.' This was followed by a doodle of a flower in a jug. Next came three or four letters on thin airmail paper, with no envelopes, from school friends, he thought, as he read the neat round English handwriting.

Dear Imim,

I hope you are well and having a lovely time. How is your new school? Do you have to speak French all the time how gharstly. Chooky is well and the farrier has just been to do his new shoes Mummy says I'm getting too big for him and we will have to get a new pony next year. Can you do any riding in Lebanon?

There followed more in the same vein. 'What a boring child!' thought Edmund, putting the letter down. 'But at least I know they once lived in Lebanon.' The letter was dated 1957. He felt it was probably addressed to a girl, little boys not writing letters to each other much. The other letters were much the same, except the last which came from a child with a livelier mind, detailing a birthday party and a visit to Cornwall. There was a PS: 'I've found out all about you know what and it's all revolting.' It was signed Helen, with an exaggerated amount of kisses round it.

Imim was a strange name, but perhaps it was Lebanese, though the drawing appeared to show essentially English children, the boy in long grey shorts and socks, the girl in a Fair Isle jersey. He turned to the exercise books, one of which had a name on the thin foreign cover. Beneath the black printed picture of Minerva, surrounded by a classically scrolled border, was written 'M. A. Anderson', and beneath that, less confidently, 'M. A. Fleury'. He opened the first one and found it to be a book of poetry, each poem carefully copied out on the right-hand page, while a drawing in crayons illustrated it on the left.

'Automne' par Victor Hugo
L'aube est moins claire, l'air moins chaud, le ciel moins pure . . .

Here a scarlet pen had ferociously underlined the final 'e'.

Le soir brumeux ternit les astres de l'azure . . .

Again the energetic pen had underlined the 'e' of azure.

Les longs jours sont passés, les mois charmants finissent
Hélàs! déjà les arbres qui jaunissent!

There were two or three more verses and at the end the red pen had admonished: *Vu. A récopier en écrivant mieux.*

The writing was indeed poor, sloping this way and that, the writer struggling to come to terms with all the French curlicues and flowerinesses. The drawing opposite was of a path through a wood, the influence of Arthur Rackham strongly felt, though clumsily applied. The trees bearing yellow leaves encircled a lone figure in the centre of the path, struggling with an umbrella while a positive whirlwind of yellow leaves whipped round her.

More poems, Anne de Noailles, Verlaine, Valéry. Other drawings all done with a delightful careless energy and feeling of movement. The red pen had been at it again, more approving of the drawings. '*Très bien*' was written large across the bottom of most of them. Hard to guess how old the artist was – perhaps nine or ten?

He ploughed on. He pulled out the contents of one of the Jiffy bags. Miss Anderson/Fleury had been a prolific note-maker and writer. It was full of mismatched sheets of paper, some pages torn from different exercise books, some brown-edged sheets of typing paper held together with rusty staples, some in manuscript, some typed on what had probably been an old-fashioned portable typewriter. The clock on the wall of Xenia's kitchen said four a.m, but he read on, picking out a couple of sheets at random.

I saw someone murdered once, when we lived abroad with my stepfather. The sun was hot and hard as I left school, so I put my satchel on my head to protect it, carrying it as I'd seen the Kurdish women carrying their bundles down the hill, over the stony ground where the bare rock poked through the reddish earth and scraggy goats grazed, their bells tinkling softly in the heat haze. I needed both hands free to eat the bag of green almonds sprinkled with coarse salt that I'd bought at the school gates. A tall, friendly Sudanese stood there every day at lunchtime, when we were sent home for the rest of the day, it being too hot for schoolwork. He sold almonds, and little crescents of hollow bread, which he would open and sprinkle with dried thyme and more salt. He only had one hand. I knew that this was because he had been caught stealing in his own country and had it chopped off as a punishment.

My mother would not be at home since she had a bridge morning at the St George's Club, and would stay for lunch afterwards. Georges, my stepfather, was away in Jordan on business. Nadia, the maid, would be at home in the fourth-floor apartment, and would have lunch ready. But there was a shop in rue Hamra, only four minutes or so past our apartment, which sold American comics, and I decided to pay a visit there for a quick browse before going home. The comics were frowned on by my mother. Ice-cream was also forbidden on health grounds, as was playing with the concierge's little boy, Nabil, because Georges said he had TB. Rue Hamra was noisy and dusty with traffic: mule-carts, buses, Mercedes taxis, larger American cars, pedestrians walking slowly, slowly in the 100° F humid air, on their way home to lunch and the afternoon sleep. Gently dripping with sweat and just about to turn into the cool, dark newspaper shop, I saw two men leaving the building two doors ahead. They wore unremarkable white shirts and light drill trousers, sunglasses, and both carried black briefcases, and were arguing nervously. A black car screamed to a halt just past me and suddenly from the rear side window came cracks and flashes. One man threw himself to the ground, but the other, as the car roared off, had leapt backwards against the white wall, slowly sliding down the cement, leaving a snail's trail of scarlet behind him. He lay on the ground, jerking horribly, and then was still, with a red pool slowly spreading beside him.

There was pandemonium. Jabbering, shrieking people closed around me. I was incapable of moving, legs jelly-like, stomach heaving. The proprietor of the shop which sold the American comics, the reason for my presence there, grabbed me by the shoulders, gave me a little shake before turning me round the other way and giving a little push.

'Va! Va chez ta mère. Yallah!' I fought my way back through the crowd, the heavy satchel banging against my legs.

Up in the lift, unlocking the door with my own key, I subsided on to the cool stone floor in the hall. Nadia came out of the kitchen. *'Qu'est-ce-que tu as, ma petite? Tu es malade?'* I told her it was just the heat. She fetched a glass of water and put her hand to my head. 'Come and have your lunch. I've made *sambousek* for you.' Out on the balcony, at the cool green marble table in the shade, I listened to the ice-cubes tinkling in the glass as I put it to my lips, heard a faraway hubbub of shouting and hooting cars. Beyond the red-roofed houses and tall apartment blocks the sun shone on the brilliant sea with a malicious sparkle. I ate the *sambousek*, peeled a peach and ate that too, then went to my room to tackle the grammar, the metric system, and learn by heart the weekly paragraph of French history which had to be recited aloud every Friday.

My mother looked in later, a beading of sweat curdling her face powder and dark blood-red Elizabeth Arden lipstick.

'All right, my sweet? Doing your prep? I'm just going off for my rest. So, so hot today.'

I waited, hearing her high-heeled shoes ticking across the stone-floored hall, her door shutting. I waited still, until quite sure she was asleep, then crept out into the sitting room to telephone Eugenie, who was the daughter of an official at the Russian Embassy, and who lived in the next street.

'Can you come over, after you've finished your home-work?'

'I'll ask Papa. He's just off for his snooze.' There was rapid conversation in Russian, then: 'Yes, it's OK. I'll see you in half an hour. Watch for me from the balcony. I don't want to ring the doorbell and wake your parents.'

She came in due course, still wearing her blue school overall with its little white collar. Her hair was tied up in complicated pigtails finished with crisp bows of white nylon ribbon. She beamed at me and flopped down on the bed, her chin held in her hand in what she imagined to be a sophisticated manner.

'You'll never guess what! I've a secret! Shall I tell you?' said Eugenie.

'If you like.'

'Well, I've found out all about sex from Samia! Listen, this is what men and women do when they go to bed . . .' There followed a highly imaginative, and to me totally unbelievably ridiculous account, and we sat there shaking with laughter at the preposterousness of it, certain that we would never submit to such an idiotic chain of actions in order to have babies. But I was also doubtful.

'Are you sure she's telling the truth?' I asked sus-piciously. Samia, their maid, was only fifteen, and a renowned fibber.

'But yes! She says she has seen grown-ups doing it when she was younger, and they thought she was asleep!'

Outside, the sun was on its downward path. Soon the world, the adult world, would wake up again, and return to work as the air cooled and the frangipani smells from the gardens grew stronger. I never told anyone what I had seen that day, in the street, and it was for a long time muddled in my mind with Eugenie's hilarious story of men with their trousers down, bouncing up and down on top of women.

Edmund was quite transfixed by this. Amused, horrified and interested all at once, he wondered if this was a fragment of an autobiography, or just a single reminiscence. He flipped through the pile of papers and found there appeared to be some order to them. First a few pages torn from an exercise book, probably used as a diary and written in immature handwriting. Then perhaps a letter or two, and then a typewritten account, then again more handwritten diary-like jottings, again followed by a rewriting in more adult language. It was as if someone had sorted through their diaries, discarding much of the material, and then reassessed, making a précis, in an effort to make sense of their life, a tidying up of the past.

He stuffed all the pages back and took everything up to his room. He was truly tired now, and would look at the rest when he returned to his flat. He slept, his ruffled dark hair and incipient stubble incongruous on the white lace-edged pillow.

'Xen? Where did that chest come from?' Edmund tried to get her attention as she fried eggs and turned rashers of bacon. She was neatly dressed that morning in clean, new-looking jeans and a navy guernsey, and was concentrating on getting the eggs just perfect.

'I told you. At an auction.'

'But where? Down here? In London?'

'Norfolk. I went to stay with Hilary. We drove over to an auction in a place called Bolt.'

'Could you give me the address of the auctioneers?'

'I've got the catalogue somewhere. Try the hall table. Why all the fuss?'

'You know those papers we found? I rescued them. I'm quite sure they were put away, hoarded on purpose. I thought I'd try to trace the owner.' He hadn't really thought of it, until that moment. 'It's just that I don't think they were *meant* to be thrown away. They are really quite interesting. There's a name on one of the exercise books. M. A. Anderson. She writes very well.'

He went off to look for the catalogue.

'Can I keep this?'

'Yes, of course. Now here's your breakfast, fusspot. *Do* get started.'

Johnnie was sitting at the table, reading the newspaper, but folded it up crisply and stretched. He had finished his breakfast before Edmund had come downstairs.

'I've got to go and talk to Lucky.'

'All right, Johnnie. Edmund and I are going to the beach.'

'Then as I'm busy all morning, I suggest Edmund and I meet up at the Eeldyke pub for a drink before lunch.'

Edmund wasn't keen on the idea of the beach, thinking that he would probably die of hypothermia, and anyway, Xenia hadn't asked him if he wanted to go, but he liked the idea of a drink before lunch.

'Don't look so miserable, Edmund. The beach will do you good. Then I can drop you off at this awful Eeldyke hole and I can get on with the lunch. I've got this wonderful lamb dish to try out.'

Being treated like a child had a curiously comforting effect on Edmund, who did as he was told, ate up his breakfast, happy enough not to have to think what to do, although he would have liked to sit and sift through the papers they had found. But it was too much to hope that Xenia would let him do anything he wanted.

Later they took the old labrador, smelly and grinning

in the back of the car, and drove to Jury's Gap, where they drove up a steep slope on to the sea wall, just past the army firing ranges. The tide was far out and the only soul in sight was a solitary shrimper, pushing his net across the still-receding tide. It was a little warmer here than it had been inland and they scrambled down the shingle past the high-tide line of jumbled seaweed and gulls' feathers, down on to the miles of scoured clean, shining wet sand, with its little runnels and channels and flocks of sparkling white birds, standing all facing one way, admiring their own reflections in the shallows. Edmund thought this must be one of the best beaches in Europe, and was instantly off, searching for something interesting . . . a stone with a hole in it, a perfect cockleshell. Xenia watched the neat, self-contained shape, hair flopping about as he stooped and examined first this, then that. She thought he really should get married again. In the year after Sylvestra had left she had often asked lone women to lunch whenever he came to stay, with the result that he came less frequently. These women had found him attractive, but puzzling. He had either had too much to drink and talked maniacally about matters which confused them, or had smiled benignly and hardly spoken at all. She had given up, at last, after he had patiently explained to her that he was not on the market for the highest bidder to snap up like some slightly scratched Regency table. He had said that he came down to see her and Johnnie, to get briefly away from work, and to wallow in her wonderful food. He had not added that the women she fished up out of her pool of acquaintances, the acquaintances of acquaintances, neither the tough Sloanes with their thin lips and thinner legs, nor the soft, fumbly women with ill-defined features and frilly shirts, were not in any way his type. Most of them were too young, in any case. He had no intention of being trapped into another family. But Xenia, who hated untidy ends hanging out all over the place, had been hard to convince. She would prefer to see him tied up, a neat package of brown paper and string, firmly sealed at both ends with emotional and physical responsibilities.

Xenia tied a scarf round her head to prevent herself from getting earache in the cold wind and bent to unleash the dog. He plodded over to the nearest pool and stood there, hoping he wasn't required to frisk about. She stepped out after Edmund, now a speck on the shoreline. When she had caught up they walked in quite comfortable silence in the direction of Rye for a while, passing a small fishing boat beached in the earlier autumn storms and already smothered in weed as it lay askew on the sand. This was the beach they had come to when their children were small, picnicking beside one of the wooden groins, and Xenia had busied herself pouring out coffees and orange squashes, setting out plates on sandy rugs, drying their damp swimming costumes on the wooden bars of the groin, and running after the children, joining in their games in an effort to avoid talking to Sylvestra, who kept on asking her what she thought of such and such a book, which she had not read, or whether she had liked a particular performance in a film she had not seen. Xenia preferred to talk about real people, their triumphs and misdeeds, and to pass judgement on their ways of bringing up children. Once Johnnie had said that she really must drag herself out of the Jane Austen era, and she had spent a whole week trying to read *Mansfield Park*, to see what he meant. She often pulled the conversation away from things that she knew nothing about, or which might be controversial. She skillfully prevented Sylvestra from talking politics to Johnnie, Edmund from arguing with Sylvestra over the rightness or wrongness of positive discrimination.

She'd so much been his guardian angel when they were children that it had taken Edmund some time to realize her chief fault was mental laziness. He preferred to think it was laziness rather than a real deficiency. She had been his champion when their father had ranted at him about leaving university, his English degree only one-third completed, and he had gratefully hidden behind her then, for the last time. He hadn't cared for academic life at all, wanting to be out and doing, earning money, not sitting endlessly pulling apart what seemed to him perfectly made novels, looking for the signs of prejudice and influence that his tutors always ferreted out, to his own amazement. He had then hated the drastic surgical operations carried out upon poetry, snipping and slicing at it so that it fell apart in his head, cut to tatters and worthless, all the immediate pleasure in reading it dissipated.

He had also become involved with the daughter of a Labour politician, whose very name was anathema to his father, not because of his politics but because of his personal offensiveness. He had, under her wing, joined in student protests, in the days when students actually did such things. Xenia, by then already married, had seemed glamorously adult, and their father had been bulldozed into acquiescence as she pleaded, night and day, for his reinstatement in their father's good books. But the poor man was already weighing up the con of Edmund abandoning his degree with the pro of his being parted from the undesirable acquaintance to whom he seemed in danger of becoming seriously attached.

Edmund had in fact only been attached by lust. Carrie had been a gorgeous girl, with beautiful breasts which she flaunted, un-bra'd in the fashion of the time, at every opportunity. He'd rarely been able to drag his eyes up to her face, with its petulant expression as if permanently waiting for an overdue compliment. She had treated him kindly enough when he was with her, but he had eventually tumbled to the fact that he was one amongst many. She explained her sudden disappearances as party commitments, but he had dismally discovered the truth one afternoon when he had been due to meet her at a friend's flat, had arrived too eagerly early and, the door being on the latch, had walked straight into the sitting room at high speed almost falling over Carrie, rolling stark naked on the floor with the friend. Her eyes were so hazed by overindulgence in Lebanese Gold that she barely recognized him and lay there giggling. Betrayed, he had lashed out at the friend unnecessarily hard, and had been told coldly, once she had recovered her clothes and senses, that jealousy was deeply uncool. He often caught sight of Carrie on the television where she presented a pretentious late-night chat show with great poise and considerably more weight than she had carried in her Cambridge days. She still looked gorgeous, and petulant.

Xenia was now complaining about cold toes, and Edmund had had enough fresh air blown into him to last till the end of the century. They turned their backs to the wind and went back to the car, driving to the Eeldyke Inn where they had arranged to meet Johnnie. They drew up amidst a bevy of motorbikes, pick-up trucks and cars ranging from a new scarlet Saab to a Morris Minor held together with baler twine. Xenia agreed reluctantly to come and have a quick drink with them before going back to get lunch ready, stepped inside with a disdainful smile on her face and was almost instantly knocked sideways as a large man, with an equally large ginger beard, lurched towards the door, belching as he went. Seth's wife, Phylly, was looking somewhat distracted behind the bar.

'You go on off home now!' she called out after the weaving giant. 'I'm not serving you again today!' She turned to Edmund. 'He's been drunk for three days now. Sorry, what would you like?'

Edmund bought Xenia a gin and tonic and himself a

pint of Goachers, nearly spilling the beer as a cream cat pranced and wove in and out among the bottles of brightly coloured squashes and cordials and jars of pickled eggs and onions. Several men had now followed the flatulent giant outside and were clapping his helmet on his head, manhandling him on to the bike and pointing it in the right direction. He rode off, sitting very upright and glassy-eyed, the bike presumably knowing its own way home.

'I'd like some ice,' said Xenia curtly.

'I've got no ice,' said Phylly, bending down to draw a pint from the barrel behind her. The cream cat leapt on to her back and she let out a screech, whereupon it jumped casually on to the shelf above her head and knocked down a glass.

'Ooh! That cat! He's getting downright familiar!'

Xenia's face was now frozen in disbelief. In the back room the piano was being played and a group of noisy young men were playing toad-in-the-hole, an ancient game of skill in which brass weights are pitched on to a low, lead-topped table with a hole in the middle. Land the brass flat on the table top and you score a point. Getting it to slither down the central hole, whereupon it rings a bell in the drawer beneath, earns you two points. Great fun for the very young or very inebriated. The ringing of the bell was accompanied by cheering and a lot of back-slapping.

It was Johnnie playing the piano, sitting in a haze of cigarette smoke which eddied about as he stood up to greet them. A woodstove pumped out a comforting heat and at a table nearby two couples sat with a baby gurgling and gurning in a basket between them. Xenia was appalled and had to be restrained from making loud remarks about health hazards and the NSPCC. Edmund was relieved to find a pub which did not smell of fried onion rings and chip fat and that had no music other than that provided by the customers. He had been shaken out of his rather frosty

London persona by the frequent changes of scene over the weekend and was considerably more relaxed, finding that he was not dreading the return to London as he usually did by Sunday lunchtime, when the thought of the dreary mess he had made of his life usually loomed up at him like an attack of indigestion. He had his work, the novel, and now there were the papers to explore, the author to uncover.

Xenia interrupted his train of thought by announcing that she had finished her drink and no longer wanted to stay in this hell-hole. Lunch would be ready at one thirty. Would they please not be late. She pushed and shoved her way to the door, her head grazing the nicotine-stained ceiling. She narrowly missed being mown down by a shaven-headed young man with seven earrings who was ruthlessly rolling a barrel through the customers to set it up behind the bar. Two young women sat chatting nearby, inexpertly smoking, drawing in too long and puffing out noisily, sliding aggressive glances about them as they spoke as if waiting to be reprimanded. 'Still at school,' thought Edmund. The barrel-roller leant over to them.

'Have a good time last night, Josie?'

'Ooh yes! Dark Entry's a really great band. You should have come.'

'Nah, couldn't get away. We had our bonfire do here, see?'

Johnnie stopped playing the piano, to expressions of regret from an elderly couple squashed into the corner.

'Good pub, isn't it? I never came here till a few months ago, and now I drop in fairly regularly for a pint after work.'

Xenia suddenly reappeared and fought her way back to the bar.

'I think you should know,' she said officiously, as if getting her own back for the lack of ice, 'that there is a toad under the washbasin in the Ladies'.' Her deep voice bounced off the ceiling, silencing the nearest customers.

'I know,' said Phylly calmly. 'Isn't he a pet? He's been there two or three days. I'll get round to putting him out this afternoon.'

Xenia left again, and Edmund and Johnnie, once they had stopped laughing, got into conversation with a professor of classics and her husband, were then joined by a farmer whose land adjoined Johnnie's, and his wife, and then by a friend of the wife's, who was a singer with the National Opera.

They noticed the time and had to make an emergency exit in order not to be late for Xenia's lamb and parsnip stew, her apple pie with cheese pastry. Amelia and her friend Mary Beaton were just arriving on the back of Mary's motorbike as they were leaving, and Johnnie paused, his hand on the roof of the car, watching Amelia's bright hair bounce back into place as she removed her helmet, and Mary's black hair slide shining out of hers. Amelia smiled at Johnnie. Johnnie felt he was beginning to slip on the oilslick of middle-aged concupiscence, but could not forbear asking her if she had enjoyed the book he'd lent her.

'I'm afraid I haven't finished it yet,' she said politely, shoving her gloves into the borrowed helmet, undoing her jacket at the neck and trying to avoid his too-fond gaze with some embarrassment. The man with him was staring at her too, with interest. Recognizing him, she thought he looked less forbidding without his hat.

'We'd better get inside – see you soon,' she said, more warmly than she intended. They entered the pub, Amelia acutely conscious of Johnnie's eyes following her, eating her up, she thought crossly. Perhaps someone was right when they said that true friendship between a man and a woman was only possible if there was a certain mutual physical antipathy.

They found a space to sit just by the door.

'So, Mr God-Almighty Whitby has the hots for you?' said Mary.

'Keep your damn voice down, you idiot! Yes, I've got a problem. But I'm not sure how to sort it out, if I want to even, just yet.'

'You've got to, you're crucifying the poor man.'

'Nonsense. We only met a few weeks ago, and *nothing* other than a little book-lending, a couple of quiet drinks, and a lot of good conversation has been going on,' said Amelia defensively.

'All right, I believe you!' said Mary. 'You may have started off with the purest of motives, but he definitely yearns for you.'

'That was the other man's name,' said Amelia. 'His brother-in-law.'

'What?'

'Yearne. Edmund Yearne.'

'Then he must be Xenia's brother. She's an airhead, seriously stunning for her age though.'

'I know, I've met her once or twice at parties. She seemed overprotective, bullying even. But he is very fond of her.'

'I'm sure he is. That doesn't mean that he isn't on the look-out, however subtly. He had a salty look to me.'

'Don't be ridiculous,' said Amelia, 'And please don't let's go on talking about it in here. Even the chairs have ears.'

'I can hardly hear you myself. Didn't you say Josie would be here?'

'Yes, she was going to walk down here to meet her friend Ruffles, so they can post-mortemize last night's gig.'

'I expect she's in the back, chatting up Mikey.'

'Oh Lord. I knew she was up to something,' said Amelia, looking around anxiously.

'You can't keep her in purdah. Life's different for both of you now. Get what happiness you can.'

'Do you seriously see me as Johnnie Whitby's bit on the side?' asked Amelia, put out by the prospect.

'No. Not really. You're not mistress material. You're too honest. Think how tiresome it would be, all that secrecy, and covering up tracks, notes in haystacks and screwing in barns.' Mary doubled up laughing.

'You're quite right.' Amelia had to laugh too, and made up her mind at last that she would allow it to go no further.

'I'll nip it in the bud,' she said, 'but it has been nice, being fancied. It's so long since that happened.'

'What about Eric?'

Amelia managed to blush and look smug at the same time. Eric had come to buy her bantams when she was selling up the house, an energetic and friendly young man who had tracked her down six months later, ostensibly to ask her advice about broody hens. He had, quite unbelievably to Amelia now, stayed the night, and come on other nights for the next month. She had been ridiculously easily seduced and, briefly, very happy, knowing that it must somehow be short-term, like a visit to a magical theatre, and it had indeed died a sudden death, as things do sometimes when they flare up too fast. She had discovered that he had a wife, and a small baby, at his smallholding near Hythe, and ended the affair at once. She frequently warmed her hands on remembrances of the physical conflagration, and had no regrets at all. She sipped her strong cider.

'Yes. That was fun. I never thought I would do anything like that.'

'I don't know why you are so shy. You've got a very strong physical presence.'

'Do you mean I smell, or that I'm an obese weight-lifter?'

'Neither! Don't be silly. I'm serious. I've seen men watching you, but because you aren't a big-chested dumbo, they don't understand why they are watching you.'

'Well, I'm so flattered and boosted by that assessment, but I've never noticed all this attention you think I attract.'

'Did you notice the brother-in-law, though? Now he had what I call physical presence, too, although he's not much taller than you.'

'Yes, I noticed him. A comfortable-in-his-own-skin sort of man,' said Amelia.

Josie appeared with Ruffles in tow, emerging from the back room. Ruffles had dark rings of slipped eye makeup, giving her a panda-like appearance.

'May Ruffles come and have lunch with us?'

'Of course you can. I hope you like mince on toast, because that's all we've got.'

Ruffles indicated that she was very happy with mince on toast, not keen to have lunch at home because her father was on the warpath about her smoking, her lack of enthusiasm for her A levels and her and Josie not being standing waiting outside the club last night on the dot of midnight.

3

Edmund went back to London late that evening, the 'boring old rubbish', as Xenia had called it, in a Peter Jones carrier bag on the passenger seat. Peter Jones, he recalled, had been Xenia's spiritual home when she first married. 'I'm going to try and visit Peter Jones,' she'd declare at breakfast, as if announcing a treacherously difficult journey to Westminster Abbey.

His flat greeted him drably, seeming even bleaker than when he had left it on Saturday. Johnnie had pressed a brace of pheasants on him when he had left and their copper-coloured plumage looked exotically out of place lying on the brawn-jelly patterned Formica surface of the kitchen worktop. They were already well hung and he fetched a bin-bag, switched on the radio and started plucking. The feathers drifted to the floor, floated up to the ceiling, got into the cupboards and clung to his eyebrows. The long barred tail-feathers he stuck in a jug like a bunch of flowers and, holding his breath, he cleaned the birds, avoiding touching their stretched scaly feet and legs which stuck out pathetically like bunches of tiny lizards.

That done, he hoovered up the remaining fluffy bits and put the birds in the fridge, and should have gone to bed, but went to sit, sifting through the papers in the Jiffy bags till well after one o'clock. He felt a twinge of guilt at his curiosity, prurience even. There were things here that weren't meant to be read by other people. Or were they? Why write down all these adolescent miseries, why edit them, keep them, if you don't want them to be read, eventually? He thought of Oscar Wilde's young lady who kept a diary in order to have something sensational to read on journeys and the guilt vanished. He read:

I was bereft in the convent's parlour amongst the ugly Edwardian furniture and lace mats. The clothes which I had felt quite proud of that morning were stiffly new and uncomfortable. Once on, they had looked laughable, as if I had been sent back two or three years and become a little girl again. Apparently it was not permitted to wear stockings until the lower fifth form and the fawn kneesocks considred suitable for twelve-year-olds were held up by elastic garters, which bit into the skin beneath the knees.

My mother had just left and now I was unable to stop crying. An elderly nun came to collect me and take me to the dormitory, and was too gentle, too understanding for me to cope with and I howled hopelessly under the weight of her kindness. The building was old, with large early-Victorian additions, and a well-preserved Victorian garden with giant yew trees and terraces, walled hide-aways, orchards and surrounding woodland. Florid yellow roses climbed over archways, releasing showers of hoarded raindrops and petals down one's neck. There were long, brown corridors, rooms named after saints and biblical places. There were lawns on which only the sixth formers were allowed, and the nuns whisked about the place in their greenish-grey habits and black veils, seemingly intent on catching one out in yet another forbidden area. It was cold that first term, and we were only allowed to light the gas fires for one hour on hair-washing days, Tuesdays and Fridays, in order to dry our hair, and we knelt, three at a time, in front of the hissing flames, our heads hanging down in a row: curly ginger, tangled black, sleekit mouse. Baths were also twice a week, with a nun on hand to check the hot water level with a ruler before we undressed and got in. What she would have done if they had been overfilled I can't imagine, since to let it out would have also been a waste, and waste was one of the greatest offences.

In the mornings a nun stood ringing a bell, bed by bed, waiting till each occupant showed signs of life. 'God bless you, my darlings. Time to get washed and dressed.' We were belled to breakfast, clappered out of classes to lunch. The chapel bell tolled continuously, it seemed to me, and for this we had to wear thin white cotton veils, tied with grubby white tapes on the napes of our necks.

I was given Latin coaching by an unctuous chaplain in swishing black soutane, who sat too close and left the convent not long after I had arrived, 'under a cloud'. I was unsure what 'under a cloud' meant, but took it to mean that he had gone to Hell, since in Heaven one was allegedly permitted to sit on them.

I waited for letters like a vigilant sparrow-hawk, alert for the thin, red-white-and-blue-edged airmail envelopes hiding amongst the fat, white, crisp English ones. But there were many other girls with parents abroad, so I had to search hard for my weekly epistle from my mother, who, amongst loving enquiries as to my health and progress, and much love and kisses, often simply listed things they had been doing, never describing them. There had been a riot, they had been over to Amman, they had lunched with so-and-so, been to a party at the Embassy, the Royal Navy was in port. But why there had been a riot, what they had eaten for lunch, was rarely mentioned, which was odd because she sometimes had stories published in magazines.

I suffered, as did many other children, from loneliness and dreadful homesickness. Homesickness is a wasting, falling disease, when one seems to be lost deep inside one's head and the eyes take in nothing, the ears do not hear and every smell is alien. No matter how kind and interesting other people are, one cannot let go the ache and join in. I grieved for my hot, dry, habitual landscape, missing out on the beauty of the surrounding thick woodlands and lush greenness that covered the clayey soil. When I had last left England, it had been from the flinty East Anglian countryside, flat and wide open to the sky. I had been to so many schools, this being the eighth, that I had lost the knack of making friends, not bothering too much, knowing that I would soon be moved on and the effort would be wasted.

Eventually, feigning a more jolly personality than I possessed, I joined in the summer evening games of cricket on the sloping lawn beneath the terraces, did handstands against the wall with the others, our striped dresses hanging limply over our heads, vests and navy knickers exposed. I wept water-marks over algebra, loved history and tolerated the rest. Toleration crept up gradually, to the point where the homesickness eased and I rediscovered my early habit of pretending to be someone else. The place had its romantic aspects, after all, and it was quite enjoyable to sit melancholic under an apple tree in the nuns' graveyard, a pre-Raphaelite prisoner, Rapunzel in her tower or the Lady of Shalott, and mope mum along the passages with my hair hanging down my back and a moody pout on my lips, looking completely idiotic. I ignored the laughter and rock and roll coming from the common room on Saturday evenings after Chapel, and hung out of the windows, brushing my hair in the twilight. But in the end I fitted in somehow. We all did, misfits all.

Edmund read the description of homesickness with a sinking sensation in the pit of his stomach, feeling a twinge of the loss he had felt at being left for the first time at prep school when he was nine. He searched for a torn-out exercise-book page he had seen earlier, which seemed to have been written at the time described, in a definite development of the sloping French script he'd noticed in the poems.

Today is the worst day this term. Uncle Theo was supposed to come and take me out as it's visiting day, but I sat all morning in the hall by the window and he never came. I suppose he must have forgotten. I checked his letter and it did say Saturday the 21st, and all the others were fetched and I wasn't. I hate him! They've all forgotten I'm here. Sister Madeleine came and made me spend the afternoon tidying up the art room to take my mind off it, she said, but it wasn't much fun compared to being taken out to lunch in Hastings. She speaks French to me in a funny accent. She says she comes from Yorkshire. She let me do some painting after I'd finished all the drawers and shelves, and washed out all the paint pots. We have to use poster paints here, and they make one's fingers feel scratchy and dry, like touching flowerpots. There is a new gardener and Carol nearly fell out of the window trying to look at him, but he's not even good-looking.

There followed three signatures, all slightly different as if she'd been practising them, and the address of the school:

Mimi Anderson   M.A. Anderson   Mimi Anderson

St Cecilia's Convent
Hatton Hoo
Hastings
Sussex

So, there she was, back in England and having difficulty in adapting to English boarding school life. The name Imim, he could see now, was merely a childish aberration, mirror-writing taken up as a nickname, and she appeared to have dropped the use of the name Fleury. She didn't sound too seriously unhappy, and he liked the slightly wistful, mocking tone of the typewritten piece. He yawned. In the morning he would telephone the auctioneers in Norfolk and get her address. Unpacking his bag his thoughts turned back to the uncertain undercurrents he had sensed between Xenia and Johnnie. All did not seem quite as it should be and he imagined he had picked up a certain pent-up frustration in Johnnie, particularly after they'd met the two women outside the Eeldyke pub. The fair-haired one, Amelia the brandy-bearer, hadn't seemed more than lightly friendly, so if something was going on between them, she was a very good actress. He had a natural brotherly interest in Xenia's welfare, but didn't see how he could interfere and supposed hopefully that it would all blow over.

'I'm afraid we cannot disclose the identity of the vendor,' said the business-like voice of the woman speaking for the auction house.

'But I'd really like to return these papers. I'm certain they were left in the trunk by accident,' pleaded Edmund.

'If you give me the lot number, and the description of the item, I can find the name and address, and if you would care to write to us, explaining the situation, we will forward it to her. Then she'll be at liberty to contact you if she wants the papers returned.'

This seemed reasonable, if tortuously slow.

'OK,' he said, reluctantly, rapidly flipping through the pages of the catalogue till he found a Biro mark against one of the entries. 'Here it is. Antique elm seaman's chest. Rope handles. Lot Number 231.'

'Thank you, sir, and your name please?'

He spelled out Yearne and told the woman to await a letter.

'Dear Madam,' he wrote on his firm's headed writing paper, 'I have accidentally come into possession of some papers which were, I feel sure, inadvertently left in the seaman's chest you sent for auction a few weeks ago. The only names I have managed to discover are on an exercise book and are M. A. Anderson and M. A. Fleury. I would very much like to send . . .' he crossed out 'send' and wrote 'deliver them to you . . . as they appear to be of a personal nature. Perhaps you would care to get in touch with me, and we could arrange the transfer?' He added his home address and phone number, and signed it, wondering if he could justify a business trip to Norfolk.

Charlie Parrott looked at him suspiciously.

'What are you up to?'

Edmund explained the story as best he could, and Charlie's face registered exaggerated disappointment.

'Oh, I thought you'd found something really exciting, like long-lost love letters from Lytton Strachey to Nancy Mitford.'

'You oaf! No, nothing like that. But these letters are sort of intriguing. Odd, and it's rather interesting, being inside the mind of a thirteen-year-old girl. She seems to have had a rather bizarre life.'

*   *   *

In the hiatus which followed the despatch of his letter, Edmund grew increasingly anxious, thinking that maybe the auctioneers had not passed on his letter, or perhaps had not even received it. He would have to write again. He tried to trace the Sussex convent but it had closed down, been turned into a retreat or nursing home of some sort and all the nuns who might have known Mimi were, he was told, either dead or gaga. He had made this call from his flat, not wanting to let Charlie know that he was becoming just a little obsessed and fidgety. He tried to keep his mind off the girl, about whom he was beginning to feel possessive, busying himself buying and selling, listing, answering queries, consulting catalogues, searching for elusive first editions of first novels by long-forgotten authors and matching bare volumes to near-pristine original dust-wrappers. He was on the verge of abandoning hope when the letter came, with a London postmark and an address in Camden, but the contents were deeply disappointing.

Dear Mr Yearne,

Thank you for the letter which Manson and West have passed on to me. I'm afraid I don't know anyone of the name Anderson or Fleury. The trunk belonged to my aunt, Helen Strood, and after she died in a road accident in September I, as her heir, had to clear out all her possessions and put her house on the market. There was a lot of muddle at the time, and I didn't realize there was anything in the trunk when I sent it to auction. I don't actually remember having seen it on previous visits to my aunt, but perhaps she had recently bought it herself? I'm sorry not to be able to help further.

Yours sincerely,
Marianne Strood

Edmund worked that morning in a mood of frustration,

barking needlessly at Tom Treasure and causing him to sulk mutinously in the back room, thinking up seriously funny and biting ripostes which it was too late for him to use.

After shutting up shop he took Charlie for a drink at the French pub as an apology for his foul mood.

'I'm sorry. It's just these papers. I didn't get the response to my letter that I'd been hoping for.' He outlined the problem, adding, 'I don't see how I can trace her now, at all.'

'Perhaps the aunt had an address book. It might be possible to ring up all her friends and see if they knew anyone called Mimi Anderson. You did say she'd lived in East Anglia as a child?'

'Yes, she mentions it.'

'Well, try that then. I don't really know why you're so keen on returning them.'

'Nor do I, but I just feel I have to make an effort of some sort. I've become quite attached to the writer. She was a funny, almost sombre little person as a child. She must be about the same age as me.'

'She might very well be dead.'

'I know you think I'm one-hundred-and-one. Yes, I suppose she might be. But you're right. I'll see if Miss Marianne Strood has her address book.'

They turned to talk of other things, being joined by a mutual friend who was waiting for his girlfriend to turn up for a pre-theatre drink, but, five minutes to curtain-up, she had still not put in an appearance.

'Sod it. I'm not wasting these tickets. Charlie, do you fancy the spare?'

Charlie was agreeable, having nothing better to do that evening, and they left Edmund to break the news to the girlfriend, should she arrive. At a quarter to eight, there being no sign of anyone answering her description, he finished his pint and set off home on foot, eager to telephone Marianne Strood and see if an address book existed. He'd recalled that one of the early children's letters had been signed 'Helen'. It was just possible that the childhood friend might be Aunt Helen.

The printed letter-heading of Marianne Strood's letter included a telephone number, and he rang, sitting on the sofa, pulling his ear nervously. He was answered by someone with a young, rather breathy voice.

'Um, yes. I'm sure there is one. But I've had huge bonfires of all her letters and things. I did bring the business ones back, in case of having to sort out anything serious. But I was going to write to her friends, to tell them of her death, only my mother put it in *The Times* and the *Telegraph*, and said I needn't bother. Would you like me to see if I can find the address book for you? Only I can't look now, I'm expecting friends for supper in a few minutes.'

'That would be very kind. I really do want to get to the bottom of it. Sorry to be such a nuisance – can I ask one more thing? How old was your aunt when she died?'

'About forty-six or forty-seven,' the girl replied, with a slight impatience in her tone, so he thanked her again and rang off, going straight back to the papers for further delving into Mimi's childhood and adolescent years.

I've been told over and over again that being shy is a way of drawing attention to oneself. This is unfair, and untrue, in my case anyway. I'm *not* shy, but I am a bit nervous of making a fool of myself by saying the wrong thing and being laughed at. But I do wish people would leave me alone and stop trying to 'draw one out' as my mother puts it, making it sound as if I'm a thorn in the sole of her foot. There's nothing to draw out, I'm just not given enough time on my own to sit and think. At school we were hardly ever alone and I thought it would be wonderful to leave, to be allowed just to *sit*, or paint, on one's own. But Mum keeps dragging me out to lunches, and drinks parties, which are horrible things where no one listens to anyone else, and they all gabble at the same time about absolutely nothing. I hoped they were going to talk about interesting, grown-up, important things, but they just bore on about what jolly times their daughters are having being skivvies in Switzerland, or learning Italian in Florence. They only ever ask me what parties I've been to and if I have lots of interesting young men hanging around me. (No – not one. I don't actually seem to have met any interesting young men.) I suppose I'll have something to talk about when I go up to London to art school in September.

Poor child, Edmund thought sympathetically, wondering if his Hatty suffered from the same problem. He could remember with agony those parties where one was paraded, in one's best grey flannel suit, and expected to fall into line, say all the right things to complete strangers, not to put one's foot in one's mouth and to suddenly appear to be an adult without having had enough practice. Mimi's mother was back in England but where was the stepfather Georges Fleury? The next handwritten diary entry made it clear that they were back in Norfolk – he looked up Salthouse and found it was not far from Bolt, where Xenia had bought the trunk, and was presumably close to where Aunt Helen lived.

I've met one interesting man at last. But he's quite old. He's up here birdwatching, but he's writing a book about a man whose wife keeps on having babies and they can't use contraception because they're Roman Catholics. I can't see how one could write a whole book about that, but he made it seem very funny. At least I laughed because I knew it was funny, but felt I ought not to, because I haven't a clue about contraception. I think

I must be the only person that doesn't. Helen laughed at me when I asked her, but I believe *she* doesn't know either. She came over this afternoon and we went by bus to Salthouse and wandered about the beach, watching the terns dipping and hovering over the seashore. I was looking for amber, but didn't find any. Helen says it needs a good storm to bring it up, churned up from the sea-bottom. We did find some fossils, belemnites, which people call thunderbolts. We also found a dead coypu which had tangerine-coloured front teeth and stank terribly. That's where we met the man, sitting on a bank with a notebook and binoculars, and Helen asked him if he had seen anything rare, and we got chatting. Helen's like that. She doesn't have any problems talking to people. Then it turned out that he was staying with friends of Helen's parents nearby, and we went and had tea with them. Afterwards he drove us home to save us the bus fare. I wouldn't have talked to him, of course, if I'd been on my own. I think he may have thought we were older than we were. He asked me what I was reading at the moment and I said *Lolita*, and he laughed and laughed. Helen is staying on at school to do A levels, then going to university to do Eng. Lit. I do wish I hadn't been to so many different schools. I've done the Norman Conquest five times, once in French which was a quite different story. I do read a lot but Helen says I'm reading all the wrong books. I don't really choose them though, I just read whatever comes to hand. It's a habit and I panic when I've nothing to read when I'm waiting for something to happen or am going on a journey. I found the copy of *Lolita* on the bus coming home from Norwich. It had been left on the seat with a purple chocolate wrapper as a bookmark.

Edmund was entranced by this child, and the adult self that

was beginning to emerge, but he was abruptly disturbed by consecutive letters in the pile, from a man signing himself Phillip. Starting to read them, he felt his hackles rise and then a sense of shame. The cheap writing paper almost ignited in his hands – they were full of deranged hate, paradoxically sprinkled with adoration, devotion, intentions to marry her and make her his forever. They were also the written equivalent of what he imagined an obscene phone-call to contain. They detailed what this Phillip would do to her next time he met her, what he would like to do, now, sitting thinking about her in the next room. Insanity leapt from the pages, dancing in front of his eyes. He felt sick, imagining his Hatty being the recipient of such hideous letters. His picture of a funny little schoolgirl evaporated. But why had she kept such filth? The answer was in her own cool reassessment of the situation, a sad hindsight.

I settled in the small room in Oakley Street with enormous enthusiasm. Liberation at last! Upstairs were a couple with a small baby who cried a lot, and beneath me a couple of merry lesbians, who dressed up in kimonos and gave rowdy parties on Saturdays, playing a song called 'The Seventh Son' over and over again, and a lot of Rachmaninov. On the same floor as me was another room, and a bathroom between us, but I hardly ever saw the occupant. We occasionally met on the landing, both moving to the same side to let each other pass, dancing from side to side in that English way as if terrified of touching each other. He had a long, thin body and well-structured face and greeny-blue eyes with a slight tic beneath his left eye, as if he was perpetually nervous, or very tired. I was deep in my first year at art school, and although I was feeling my work didn't fit in with current conceptions, too figurative and academic for the time, I was happy, having abandoned a lot of the alleged shyness and made friends, dredged London for all that was fun and free, and there was a lot going on. I wore high black vinyl boots and very short skirts. We drank, when any of us had any money, in King's Road pubs and sat endlessly in coffee houses, talking, talking, talking. We travelled in gangs to each other's lodgings, drank bad red wine and smoked a lot. I started to meet my neighbour on the stairs more and more frequently. Now I can see that he was waiting to hear the front door open and came out when he thought it was me, pretending to be going somewhere.

Coming up the stairs one evening after having been to the pub with two friends, we were just about to go into my room to continue the session when he came up the stairs behind us, looking rather sad, so we asked him to come and join us. He sat on the floor by the gas fire, and seemed nice enough, told us he was writing a thesis on gnosticism, which I had to go and look up in the dictionary. He was erudite, good company and laughed a great deal at all our bad jokes. From then on, he latched on to me. I was flattered at first. He was considerably older than us. I won't say I fancied him because I was still a virgin, and curious, not knowing who or what I did fancy then, because I was unaware of what was on offer. The main reason most women sleep with their first man seems to be just plain curiosity, which explains why they often go to bed with people who their friends think are complete creeps. His name was Phillip, and he took to knocking on my door, standing there looking lanky and eager, and began to take up time I hadn't got to give him.

One night I let him in after he had arrived clutching a bottle of wine and explaining that he had finished his thesis and wanted someone to celebrate with. I made a disastrous mistake, since I drank too much wine and went to bed with him, in a sleepwalking sort of way, and was horribly disappointed. His bones stuck into me and I felt absolutely nothing but pain, and afterwards got up immediately, feeling dizzy, shaking and distressed, but stone-cold sober. There had been something about him which had revolted me when it was too late to stop. I think it was his hands which felt rough, scaly and cold, like a lizard. I wanted him to go. It was a mistake, I told him, but he ignored me, kept telling me how lovely I was, came after me, forced me back. I felt hot, sticky and filthy and he lay there on my sheets, with an overturned ashtray beside his arm, laughing at me. I was in a fog of anger, almost speechless with rage, but managed to get him to leave, protesting his undying love, carrying his horrible shoes in his scaly hand, saying he'd see me tomorrow when I'd calmed down, was less upset.

'No, not tomorrow. Not ever again!' I squawked at him and slammed the door, bolting it.

Out of embarrassment I didn't dare leave the room all next morning till I heard him go downstairs, and then ran to the window to make sure he had really left. I bathed, cleaned up my room in a frenzy of distaste and sat there wondering what on earth had possessed me. I mean possessed literally, since he had had a distinctly sinister feel to him. But that night he stood outside the door, knocking, rattling the door handle, swearing. I had so little experience, no knowledge of excuses, gentle dismissals. The telephone was in the hall downstairs, unreachable without going past his door. A letter was poked under the door. I was terribly shocked by it, and stayed in my room all the next day, terrified. The next night was the same, and the next, and the next. But then I watched him leave the house and I managed to get myself out to the art school, where I was asked why I looked so grey and frightened. I couldn't say, since it all seemed such an unlikely nightmare.

He was waiting on the landing when I returned at six that evening, blocking the way, his eyes quite manic. I turned and fled to the telephone at the end of the road, gibbering with fright, and managed to explain roughly what was happening to a friend who promised to be round with reinforcements in twenty minutes, telling me to wait by the telephone box. She arrived with two hefty male colleagues who escorted me back to the house and up the stairs where Phillip bounced out of his room again.

'Get into your room,' said Nails (as in 'hard as'). 'I'll deal with this.'

Once inside I couldn't hear what was being said, at first, but then there was a great deal of shouting and pushing. Phillip was screeching that he loved me: 'She's mine, I tell you, mine! I know you're going in there to screw her. She's mine.' I don't know quite what happened, but someone had fetched the landlady, the police were mentioned, and the boys sat with me all night listening to him crashing about in his room. In the morning he left. I never saw him again, but it took weeks of his absence before I could sleep properly, so frightened was I by the ugliness of what I'd brought to the surface by my own fault. I had merely been curious, and drunk, but felt that one of my nine lives had gone.

Edmund searched his past anxiously, wondering if he had ever caused such a storm of revulsion in any of his one-night stands in the sixties. He did hope not, but could see how such a thing might happen, particularly with a young girl involved with a near-psychopath. The man obviously had a severe mental problem as well as scaly hands. He hoped she had got over it and gone on to better nights with better men – but he couldn't understand why she had hung on to the repellent letters. As a warning to herself perhaps, or as proof of some sort in case he approached her again? In the sixties few people would have done other than blame her for getting into the situation in the first place, but she'd been so young, so obviously inexperienced. Sleepwalking, she had called it. Sad, very sad. But she had not really been asking for sympathy, just telling the story. An exorcism of some sort. He went on reading, looking for evidence that she had recovered herself and her physical integrity, and her pleasure in being an art student in the big city, but he was haunted by the image of the scaly, pheasant-foot hands.

4

The ice on the Royal Military Canal began to melt reluctantly, the wind blowing ripples on the newly exposed watery stretches. The sky was grey and heavy and a pair of fieldfares hung about in a hawthorn bush, flashing their pale wingpits. Amelia lit the woodstove in her workshop and set about the latest batch of earrings with the electric polisher before finishing them off with a cloth and fitting the long gold hooks for pierced ears. She checked her order book and neatly packaged them up in green tissue paper. They were very pretty, gold hoops with small jade or amethyst birds hanging in their centres as if on swings. Not particularly original, but very saleable. Six silver bangles of intricately twisted and knotted silver strands, five gold rings set with moonstones . . . '. . . and a partridge in a pear tree . . .' she sang, wrapping them up in red tissue this time, pleased with the Christmassy effect. She slipped them into little silver boxes of various sizes, each having her name printed on the lid. She wrote out a delivery note, having to stop and start all over again after having noticed that she had put 'five pears' instead of 'five rings'. They were to be delivered to Rye that afternoon, and with any luck the shop would have a cheque ready for last month's sales, enough to start off the Christmas shopping by buying Josie's hat. But she knew she had to go easy with the cash, although there was other money due in soon. It was very difficult to budget for anything with such a haphazard income.

The window darkened for an instant as a figure passed by, coming to knock on the door of the shed, making her jump nervously before she realized that it was Johnnie with a brace of pheasants in his hand. She was perpetually on the look-out for strangers, having to keep a certain amount of gold and silver on the premises; she always took it up to bed with her at night. She went to the door and he stood there, almost sheepishly, holding out the birds.

'I've brought you a present.'

'But how wonderful! That's very kind of you.'

Her resolve not to take advantage of his now rather obvious taking for her wavered. She could not churlishly refuse pheasants and make them both look ridiculous. She would have to ask him in.

'I've finished for the morning. Can I make you a cup of coffee?' she said.

'That would be very nice.'

She locked up the shed and he followed her across the yard, watching her skirt twitch from side to side, as hopelessly enthralled as a Victorian gentleman at the sight of pale stocking above a neat kid boot.

In the long kitchen the cat sat rocking and nodding in front of the old Rayburn stove and they sat on either side with their mugs, sipping, and sliding in their intentions. He noticed the poor state of the ceiling, the basket of vegetables on the floor, the brown paper sack of potatoes and the ancient, moulting piece of cut-up carpet on which the cat sat yawning and washing itself.

There was a framed painting on the wall between the windows which attracted his attention. It showed a walled garden with a woman standing naked in a bower, looking modestly surprised and covering herself inadequately with a small book. Johnnie got up to take a closer look. There was a man seated on a stool on the grass, also naked, looking across his shoulder at the viewer, holding out a book as if he had just been interrupted between lines. A lush fig tree filled in the background below a golden sky – in fact the whole picture was executed in golden tones – like a late afternoon in London, hazy with dust.

'Mr and Mrs William Blake?' he asked, delighted to have found out the subject matter without having to be told.

'. . . in their garden in Lambeth, surprised by a visitor while re-enacting a scene from Milton! Rather a long title for such a little painting,' she said, very pleased that he had recognized it.

'It's a lovely little painting.' He bent closer to look at the fine detail of the plants, the soft blue shadows on the skin. 'You painted this?'

'Yes. A long time ago, when I had more time – that's why I so enjoyed the Blake biography – I've been fascinated by him for as long as I can remember.'

He sat down again. He hoped that she had not found the pheasant present patronizing, but she was a sensible woman and surely wouldn't take such a small gift amiss, however independent she had had to become, and he hoped . . . He watched as she leant back in her basket chair and stretched her legs out, putting her feet up on the stove, her normal way of warming them up. She had not intended it as a provocative gesture, but she saw as soon as she had done it that it could be interpreted as such, implying complete ease and familiarity with his company, and cursed herself. Her skirt was long, and he could still see no more than her worn red shoes. A clock ticked on the dresser.

'I hadn't realized you had such a professional set-up, out there.' He nodded in the direction of the shed, intrigued by what he had seen behind her as she stood at the door. The glimpse of tools neatly hanging up, the gas bottles and burner, the appearance of a miniature blacksmith's forge with tiny anvils set in vices and what looked suspiciously like a dentist's drill hanging from the wall.

'I have to be particularly professional now.'

'Yes, I'm sure you do. But you enjoy it?'

'Oh yes! I love it. It only gets a bit boring when I have to do a large amount of one thing for an order. Then one has to grit one's teeth to get through all the repetitions.'

'And where do you sell them, or is it all on commission?'

'Oh, craft galleries, enlightened jewellers, craft fairs, that sort of thing.'

Johnnie thought it was odd that he met so few professional women. Most of his acquaintances' wives either did nothing or were immersed in charity work. Of the few that had trained for a particular occupation, even fewer seemed to take it up again once they had children. Of course none of them needed to work, or showed any burning desire to do so. Need was something he knew he had been buttressed against all his life. His financial problems, such as they were, were caused by the stock market, the EC and CAP, and were as nothing compared with the daily counting of pennies, the carefully rationed drink and tobacco with which Amelia wrestled. He did not feel guilt, since such matters were in the lap of the gods, he felt; but he was, in the best sense, a charitable man, and certainly put his money generously and willingly where he felt it would do most good, whether collecting boxes or into more practical and close-to-home ventures such as making sure that a certain amount of money was spent each week at the village shop. He tried to employ the maximum amount of people consistent with modern farming practices, but his father had employed seven regular farmhands, and he could find work for only two, with extra part-timers when needed. His mother had employed both cook and cleaner and two gardeners. Xenia made do with a cleaning woman two days a week. Amelia had nothing to fall back on . . . To fall back on . . . to throw up one's arms in surrender and lean back into the comforting embrace of a massive insurance policy, or yet another legacy. Insured up to the hilt, the other upper-middle-classes of his age, who believed in their own existence even if nobody else did, were mostly still as snug and smug at the end of the twentieth century as they had been at its start. There were of course exceptions to this, he remembered. Two or three people he knew had been severely discommoded by the Lloyd's disaster and sent their children to state schools, pretending that the accents they proceeded to develop for reasons of protective colouring were rather fun, really, and kept quiet that their clothes now frequently originated in charity shops. Amelia looked as if she had never been able to shop anywhere else.

'Would you care for a few more pheasants? We seem to have a glut this year.'

'Yes, indeed I would. But I have no freezer, so not until we've eaten these.'

'No, of course. I was wondering. Would you take a small commission from me?'

'Yes. What is it? Cufflinks?'

'No, I want . . .' he struggled to think of something relatively expensive, but not too obviously over the top, '. . . a bracelet for Xenia. Like the one you're wearing, or something like it. In gold.'

Amelia gulped. A small commission indeed! She wore a solid silver bangle, square in section but tapering to a gap at the back, the top flat surface covered in a writhing gold thread pattern, with golden beads set in between. It made him think of drifting seaweed, with gilded bubbles caught up in it.

'Well, yes, certainly. Is it for Christmas? I'll work out a price for you and telephone . . . no, you call me, tomorrow afternoon perhaps? What colour gold, and what carat?'

He looked at her helplessly. Did gold come in different colours?

'There's red gold, yellow, white, and nine carat, or eighteen carat. Nine would be best for a bangle, I think, and cheaper.'

'How about yellow gold, with the beady bits in another colour?'

'Yes. Well that's settled then,' she laughed. It had been a good day so far, even if it had started to rain. Work completed, new work coming in. Outside a car went past, slowed as if the occupant was looking in at the gate, then speeded up again with a great spray, soaking a young man walking his deerhound up the lane.

They relapsed into silence and the cat settled closer to the stove, assuming a meringue shape.

'I've got to deliver some work to Rye, this afternoon,' she said.

'Well, I mustn't hold you up – thanks for the coffee.' He stood up reluctantly and hit his head on a beam. He noticed a small pile of her business cards on the table.

'Can I have one of these?'

'Of course.'

He wondered if he could risk a kiss on the cheek, or even both cheeks, but decided against it.

''Bye.'

After he had left, she accused herself, unnecessarily, of rudeness. But how to cope with this enormously tall man who had turned suddenly into a jumpy schoolboy once in her house? She was as aware of his thoughts as she was aware of his height, and didn't know what to do with either of them, and had failed to send out the negative signals she had intended to. Now he had seen the scruffy interior of the cottage and would feel sorry for her. However, it was nice to be given pheasants and she was grateful for both them and the commission. If the pheasants had been shot at the weekend, they'd be ready for eating by the next, and she went to hang them in the icy pantry at the end of the kitchen. She quite often came by game, occasionally potting a rabbit out of the upstairs back window of the cottage with Nick's old four-ten. Mary had given her a hare a couple of weeks ago, which she had accidentally run over in a lane near Fingle. 'Waste not, want not,' she had said to herself as, having discovered it was not damaged, she threw it into the back of her car. 'He just leapt across in front of me,' she said sorrowfully, handing Amelia the poor, draggle-furred corpse. 'It's rather sickening, but he will make a good stew – he's not at all squashed.'

Mary was a GP with a local group practice in Rhee. She was a few years younger than Amelia, and had ripped through an inheritance and two husbands before taking a serious look at her life, whereupon she decided to become a doctor at the age of thirty-two. The years of study, examinations and training she had taken in her stride like an acrobat rushing towards a paper hoop, bursting out the other side triumphantly with a whoop and a bow. She rarely moaned about stress, and was ecstatically happy about her work, tending colds and cancer victims with equal devotion.

Amelia thought about the hare, and grinned to herself. She fetched the remains of an apple pie from the fridge, poured brown sugar and milk on it and sat down by the stove again, the plate on her lap, with a battered copy of the *Ingoldsby Legends*. Johnnie had told her that the author, Richard Harris Barham, had lived in the area in the 1820s and that there were several local stories in it. 'Try "The Knight and the Lady",' he had suggested. 'It's surprisingly risqué for the period.' She had at first found the jocular verse form irritating but soon got used to it, and enjoyed the fun-poking at contemporary enthusiasms. The illustrations by Leech and Cruikshank were rather dull, she thought, but those by Tenniel were excellent, outshining the stories themselves. 'The Knight and the Lady' was a tale of a wife with a wandering eye, left alone for too long while her elderly husband went out bug-hunting and botanizing, and who was not unnaturally soon comforted by a nice young man. The husband disappeared into a pond and was discovered dead some days afterwards, his coat-pockets full of eels. His wife had the eels cooked for supper, and ordered her husband's body be popped 'again in the pond – Poor dear – He'll catch us some more.'

Amelia rather enjoyed this, and was just starting on 'The Witches' Frolic' When she noticed that time was pressing on her and she ought to set out for Rye to deliver the jewellery. She marked the page with a jay's feather, made a shopping list, collected her stock and business cards and went off to town, taking the zig-zagging Military Road, splashing through puddles and humming a song. A heron flew up in the drifting rain, heading for Holy Hill, its neck tucked in and legs trailing, great wings slowly beating, as compact and heavy in flight as it was ethereally tall and spiky-thin on the ground. Like lapwings, thought Amelia, so elegant and slim on the fields but once in the air plunging club-winged about the sky – it being hard to imagine that they were the same bird.

Having delivered her treasure, collected and banked a cheque, she spent some time in a bookshop and there met Mary, who was chatting to a boy with dreadlocks, admonishing him jokily about not having a coat.

'Hello! I was just ticking off Steve. He's just got over pleurisy, and there he is, wandering about in the rain without a coat. What are you up to?'

'I've just been paid, and thought I'd get Josie's Christmas present – she hankers after a black velvet hat.'

'Oh great! Can I come too? I've got an hour before surgery

starts. We can try things on. It's what our mothers used to do, isn't it? Try on hats to cheer themselves up?'

'Are you down, then? What's up?'

'Not a lot, really. That's the problem. I suddenly felt an attack of winter coming on. Let's go and find these hats of yours.'

They went down one of the cobbled lanes which run between the High Street and Cinq Port Street, with a fine mizzle of rain blowing down their necks, and entered a small shop which sold, apart from velvet hats, swishing skirts in dark-dyed jewel colours, cheap embroidered bags from Chile, indigo shirts from China, and peacock-patchwork jackets from God-knows-where, all to the accompaniment of loud music. Mary thrust one of the hats on her head and posed in front of the mirror, her face a mockery of her mother, thoughtful and considering, cheeks sucked in, eyes half-shut, head turned this way and that a fraction. *'Wonderful.* I want it! She took it off and tried on another in pink, and poutingly applied imaginary lipstick. 'Listen, they're playing that song that Josie likes – "Liquid Lady, Shady Lady." Do I look like a shady lady?'

'Nothing on earth would make you look like a shady lady!' said Amelia, trying on first the black one, then the green. Mary had an open, clear-complexioned face, with wide light hazel eyes and a lightly freckled nose.

'That's my trouble, I think. I look like one of the children from the Secret Seven. Tuck your hair in under that, there. That's good.'

'I know for Josie it has to be the black one. It's just that the green looks better with my hair, and hers is the same colour as mine, only, I suppose, more so. I feel rather faded beside her.'

'Dye it then,' said Mary, looking back over her shoulder to take in the side view. 'I've been dyeing mine for years.'

She pulled off the pink hat and shook her dark locks. 'I'm really mouse, or perhaps, at a pinch, rich rat.'

'I've got to get back soon – I like to be there when Josie comes home,' said Amelia, paying for the black hat. 'And I've got to get out of here before I buy something for myself.'

Xenia caught sight of them through the window as she passed on her way to the hairdresser's, saw them giggling like children and was annoyed by the sight.

'What *do* they think they look like!' she thought patronizingly, having spotted Amelia's worn old corduroy coat, her head tipped back laughing at the sight of Dr Beaton in biker's leathers, sucking in her cheeks and pulling faces. A tiny pulse beat in her forehead, suppressed rage, which was not soothed by the process of having her hair washed, snipped and blow-dried. Emerging an hour later, neck muscles taut, she went into an expensive clothes shop and bought herself a little scarlet wool jacket with Tyrolean buttons. When she got back to the farm, Rosy Pressing was in the kitchen, ironing. A little appeased by her purchase, and the clean smell of freshly pressed shirts, she made a cup of tea for them both, and watched Rosy for a moment or two, recalling what Rosy had said a few weeks ago: 'I've just passed Mr Johnnie when I was bicycling up here. He was helping Mrs Sailor with a bag of coal. Poor lady. She's had a rough old time of it these past few months.' Xenia had seen his Land Rover outside Amelia's cottage that morning. How often, she wondered, did Johnnie help poor Mrs Sailor with her coal? Perhaps he helped her to do other things as well. He had never mentioned Amelia to her, which was in itself suspicious, wasn't it?

'If anything is going on, I'm not going to be the last to know this time. I'll have to keep a close eye on him, like watching a kettle to stop it boiling.' Her grasp of proverbs, as with so many other things, was inexact.

She admired her haircut in the hall looking-glass and ran her hand over her forehead. Her skin was getting rather dry, which in turn would lead to wrinkles. Johnnie could not have been at Amelia's house for long, because he had returned soon after her, but he had gone out again immediately after lunch with Fred Turtle to start work on the fencing at Hoppits Shaw. But was that where he still was? She picked up a magazine and flicked through it, then put her coat on again, and her Wellington boots and a hat to keep her hair from being ruined. 'Come on, Fatty.' She waved the lead enticingly in front of the old labrador. 'We're going for a walk.'

It was still drizzling steadily when she left the house, slamming the door behind her. They walked up the garden, through the white iron gate into a little spinney behind the house, following a path that in the spring would be thick with bluebells, but was now muddy and smelt of rotting leaves and fruity fungus. Amelia Sailor, stupid bloody name. Arty-farty, scruffy, and so irritatingly composed. She drew herself up and stalked along, elegant and worried. The labrador plodded behind her, hating the wet and wondering why, after several days in the warm, he was being dragged out in this appalling weather. He was her only excuse for walking up there in the rain, with her hair just done, should Johnnie see her.

She approached the edge of the wood and looked across the field that adjoined it, to where Johnnie and Fred should have been repairing the fence. She could see Fred in the distance, bending over a roll of wire. Of Johnnie she could see no sign, nor could she see the Land Rover. She watched for a few minutes more, the rain beginning to drip from the edge of her waxed cotton hat, bedraggling the feathers in the band, and then, jerking away, called the dog and set off back to the farm, where she dumped the dog and took the car, driving down past Amelia's cottage slowly. She could see Amelia's car tucked into the little driveway, but not Johnnie's Land Rover, so she speeded up and went on to the village shop at Rhee where she got out and bought a newspaper. She turned the car round too fast and Josie, who had got off the school bus at the shop so she could buy a packet of ten cigarettes, had to leap for her life.

Xenia drove back more carefully, ashamed of herself. The Land Rover was just turning into the drive ahead of her as she arrived.

'And where have you been?' she asked Johnnie peremptorily.

'Oh, just had to go and fetch some more wire. There was more to do than we thought, so I left Fred up there doing the posts. It'll be dark soon, I'd better go and fetch him and the tools. What's up?'

'Nothing. Nothing at all.'

He noticed the *Telegraph* tucked under her arm. 'We've already got the paper, I was looking at it this morning.'

'I couldn't find it.'

'Well, tea would be nice. I'll just fetch Fred.' He drove off up the rutted miry track to Hoppits Shaw, wondering if she'd gone soft in the head.

She felt deeply silly. But the suspicion still nagged at her, through tea, the six o'clock news, and supper, which was a dish of lambs' tongues cooked with apricots. After supper she sat rifling through her address book, making out a list of guests for a Boxing Day lunchtime drinks party. She hemmed a skirt, put buttons on a shirt, lost her thimble, fidgeted and then was finally unable to stop herself from asking Johnnie if he thought they should invite Amelia Sailor. She did this purely to see his reaction.

'Invite her to what?' he said cautiously.

'Invite her to the Boxing Day party, I was just talking to you about it.'

'If you like, darling.'

No reaction at all, not even a flicker.

She put the needle and thread back into the faded red velvet needlecase that had been her grandmother's, found the thimble where it had rolled up against the fender, folded up the shirt so neatly that it looked as if it had come straight from a shop. Johnnie sat there reading, as he usually did after supper, a look of calm innocence on his face.

'Well, perhaps not. After all, she won't know anyone, will she?' she said.

'I thought that was the whole idea of a party, meeting people one didn't know?' said Johnnie, looking at her with irritation. 'Anyway, she'll know lots of them. I've seen both her and her husband at the Emsleys on several occasions in the past, and at the Appletons, and she's friends with Dr Beaton. Being widowed doesn't mean she has to be avoided like a dangerous predator escaped from the zoo.'

Xenia's thermal imaging equipment picked up on the warmth of his reply.

'I wasn't thinking of asking Mary Beaton either.'

'Well you certainly should. I will, if you won't.'

Xenia found all these unattached women floating around unsettling, and she unwisely continued. 'I wonder what made Amelia's husband commit suicide? Perhaps she was playing around . . .'

'Xenia, you must not speculate like that! There are other reasons for killing oneself. Depression, loss of dignity . . . the poor man had lost his job, had no income. And he had a reputation for being a bit unsteady. Bill Emsley says he once heard that Nick was involved with a barmaid from the Bell and Hatchet. Kept on seeing them together.'

'Now who's speculating?' she pounced. 'I swear men are worse gossips than women.'

'Probably. But we're not so malicious.'

'I'm not being malicious! I will invite Amelia if you want me to.'

'I didn't say you were malicious. I was speaking generally – and can I please finish this chapter before bedtime?' He could think of one or two other reasons for suicide after this conversation. Perhaps he had defended Amelia too overtly, for Xenia appeared annoyed at being lectured and got up, sharply unfolding herself from her chair and picked up the mending, saying stiffly that she would go up to bed.

'All right, I'll be up in a minute or two. I'll bring you some tea, if you'd like it?'

'I expect I shall be asleep by then,' she said fractiously, and loped out of the room.

Johnnie immediately got up and stood in front of the fire, hands in pockets. Xenia was like a borzoi in pursuit of . . . whatever it was borzois pursued. She was definitely sniffing about, but he was damned if he could see how she had picked it up. He had not been indiscreet in any way. For God's sake, nothing *was* going on, except in his imagination, and that was a faded faculty nowadays. But he was annoyed with Xenia, unfairly so, for finding his bone before he had had time to bury it safely. *If* she had found it. Perhaps these were just scaring-off tactics; she had a habit of wheeling people around and away from whatever it was they fancied, sometimes before they knew they fancied it, in case the satisfaction of the fancy affected her adversely. He retrieved his book and settled down again, not to read to the end of the chapter but to finish the whole book.

5

Edmund daily expected the Strood address book to arrive in the post, but five days had elapsed since he had spoken to Marianne, and he was dealing with a call from a woman enquiring whether he stocked first editions of any of Barbara Cartland's *oeuvres* when a striking-looking girl pushed open the glass door of the shop and wandered in confidently, glancing first at Charlie, then at him. Edmund looked up and smiled and she quietly waited for him to finish talking, glancing about the shop without much curiosity.

'I'll be with you in a minute,' he promised, his hand momentarily covering the receiver. 'No, I'm afraid we don't have any in stock – yes, perhaps we should, yes, we do deal in modern literature.' He raised his eyebrows in conspiratorial mock-annoyance at the girl. 'Well, not quite all. Romantic fiction isn't one of our specialities. Yes, I'd be delighted to try . . . yes, yes, now which titles . . . I see . . . and your name and address? Thank you. We'll be in touch as soon as I can locate them. Goodbye.' He turned back to her. 'Sorry to keep you waiting – can I help?'

She opened her bag and produced a small packet. 'Mr Yearne?'

He nodded.

'I've been meaning to post this for the last three days. I thought I'd bring it round in my lunch hour.'

'Aunt Helen's address book? Oh wonderful, wonderful!' He was beaming at her. At last he might be able to achieve a result. She passed it over. Her face had the neat, almost featureless perfection of a photographic model, her eyelids heavy with soft grey eyeshadow, artfully ruffled short shiny haircut; Edmund could feel Tom Treasure's eyes boring into the back of his head through the glass window from the back room, and could also sense a certain interest from the other desk, where Charlie stood, having stopped whatever it was he had been doing; now he stared in their direction in a most unprofessional fashion.

'It's very kind of you to have gone to this trouble. No Andersons or Fleurys in it, I suppose?'

'I did look, but no. It's quite exciting, this Find the Lady game you're playing, isn't it?'

Edmund could detect no signs of excitement in her face.

'Well, it would be if I could get anywhere with this. I'm sure that your aunt was at least a childhood friend of the person I'm looking for. She certainly visited, or lived in, that part of Norfolk in her teens.'

Tom Treasure popped up beside him like a glove-puppet, and Edmund took pity on him, leaving him to search for some imaginary pen on the desk for a moment, before giving him the Barbara Cartland enquiry to deal with. Tom took it, but lingered, ostentatiously dusting the shelf nearest to him with his elbow.

'I'm going up to Norfolk in a week or so – I have to see the house-agents and clear up one or two more things. Let me know if there's anything I can find out for you, up there.' She smiled her perfect little smile at Edmund, turned and swung out of the shop, mission accomplished, all long legs and little flame-coloured jacket. Tom Treasure let out a moan and clutched himself.

'Don't make a nuisance of yourself, Treasure,' said Charlie in a threatening whisper. 'Go back to your cell if you can't behave. We do have other customers in here, you know.'

These other customers, a man in a long mac with grey hair in a ponytail and a diminutive Dr Crippen look-alike, had both halted in their leisurely grazing of the shelves, and had turned, gazing dreamily after the girl.

'What very well-stocked shelves,' said Tom, forcing Charlie to giggle childishly.

Edmund was already turning over the pages of the address book, which had an unpromising soppy puppy on the cover. It looked almost new, and inside were few crossings out, no addresses changed. He would start telephoning at once. No, better wait till he got home. Aunt Helen appeared to have known a vast number of people and it was going to take a very long time if he had to go through all of them. He hoped he struck lucky before getting to C.

On his way home that evening, Edmund bought a bottle of Irish whiskey and a selection of packeted sandwiches from a Croatian-run supermarket in Marylebone High Street, preparing for a lengthy session. He made a crib sheet: 'Good evening. I'm sorry to bother you [how apologetic he always sounded] but I believe you were a friend of Helen Strood? I'm trying to trace another friend of hers called Mimi Anderson, or Fleury. I've come by some papers of hers which should be returned. Marianne, Helen's niece, gave me your address.' He poured himself a whiskey and got dialling.

Half an hour later he'd got halfway through the A's, had three no-replies which he noted down to try again later, poured himself another drink and opened a packet of sandwiches which turned out to be curried chicken. By nine o'clock he was at the end of C, and rather drunk. Feeling he might start slurring his speech, and rather disheartened, he decided to call it a day. He'd got so used to hearing 'Sorry,

No, Sorry, Can't help you, How interesting, So sorry', that he no longer knew how to spell the word sorry, felt that it was an alien word, probably from some Balinese dialect, and that it meant absolutely nothing. He ate the last half of a salami sandwich and lay back on the sofa, staring at the ceiling.

'I am undoubtedly mad, have almost lost my voice and will certainly have a huge phone bill. All in order to give back these wretched papers, which I feel are mine now anyway.' 'But,' said his quiz-master voice, 'it's no longer just returning them, is it? You want to *meet* the woman, admit it. She may be a female orang-outan married to a circus strongman for all you know. Have you thought of that? You feel attracted to her, and every simple sentence of hers you turn over, examine, pick at like a vulture. You think you know her, but you only know what she chose to let you know. You're guilty of reading other people's letters, which is a heinous crime. You're guilty of secretly opening wardrobes and examining their clothes, pawing over their mental underwear like a miserable pervert.' He was bemused by this tirade from his alter ego, but delighted with the idea of mental underwear, starting to imagine the intellectual underclothes of various people he knew. Charlie Parrott, for instance, would wear shiny black plastic boxer shorts. Tom Treasure, a leopardskin posing pouch, with a grubby, cigarette-burn-covered singlet. Xenia would have a boned corset of prejudicial steel, and long lace-edged Victorian drawers. He was entranced by this variant on the old game, poured another drink and had A.S. Byatt in a dark green and scarlet tapestry liberty bodice made by Vivienne Westwood, and Albert Einstein in graph-paper-patterned long combinations.

He went to run himself a bath, pouring an ancient and unused bottle of Floris aftershave into the steaming water. 'That'll drown the smell, if nothing else,' he muttered, getting in and lying there, wallowing. The soap flew through his fingers and he could not be bothered to retrieve it, lay there gazing at the little black hairs on his big toes.

> 'Albert Einstein,
> Had a fine time,
> In the jungle with a chimpanzee,
> Who taught him all there was to know,
> About their relativitee!'

He chuckled at this a little, but wasn't it Albert Schweitzer who had sat in the jungle in Africa? He dozed off for a minute or so and awoke with a jerk as he slid down in the water, his foot connecting sharply with the cold tap. Splashing, he heaved himself out and rubbed down with a hideous towel covered with orange parrots. Sylvestra had left him all the nastiest towels. He was slightly dizzy, and a little cross with himself for having drunk so much. He wrapped the towel about his waist and headed for the kitchen where he made himself, with great precision, a proper pot of coffee, found a blue and white cup with a saucer that matched and returned crookedly to the sofa, picking up his black hat from a chair and stuffing it on his head on the way. His brain was slowly clearing, so he started where he had left off the night before, with a couple of Mimi's handwritten sheets from the pile on his table.

He came round to the flat this evening, but I was so busy with some new designs I had to make him wait. If they weren't finished they would weigh on the mind all over Christmas, and they had to be got in to Franks the day after Boxing Day. He sat very patiently, reading *Magister Ludi*, and didn't lose my page marker. I had to keep turning round to look at him – he's so beautiful and has these long fingers, like Lytton Strachey in the Carrington portrait. I finished at nine o'clock and changed fast into red dress, but it's very cold, so had to put on old coat over it which spoilt the effect rather. We went off to the Queen's Elm where we'd arranged to meet R., and the RCA crowd. R. is celebrating not only Christmas Eve, but the fact that he hasn't touched a drop since starting his new book, and feels he can be allowed a break now he's reached Chapter Five. He was wearing his Mr Freedom satin jacket and was pissed already when we arrived, bellowing out funny stories, lighting one fag after another, so that he sometimes had three burning in the ashtray all at once, and one in his hand as well. But since he never gets belligerent when drunk, or, miraculously, boring, and everyone else was pretty much the same way, it didn't matter. I hope this book does as well as the last; he must surely have eaten up all his advance already? Sean came in saying that it was snowing and everyone rushed out to see, very excited as everyone is when it first snows; one can almost smell the change of mood, the pleasure at the initial sight of it. We left with R., he to his bed, and us to search out a church in which to go to Midnight Mass, to make sure it really was Christmas. R. fell over a cat on the way out, hugged us hugely and said he'd catch up with us on Boxing Day. There were some old Polo mints in the pocket of my coat which we sucked to take away the beery smell, sitting close together in a back pew. We needn't have worried. There were a lot of old gentlemen wearing black velvet-collared overcoats, snoring their way through the service, and you could almost see cartoon brandy fumes rising up into the air. I got an attack of morbid religiosity and felt I shouldn't take communion as I was living in sin, sort of.

'I thought you were living in Kensington, sort of.' He was convulsed at his own old joke. We fairly bellowed out 'Hark the Herald Angels' and there was an excellent choir, beautiful descants. Christmas again. I got quite choked, red-nosed with tears flinging themselves from my eyes. I know it's cheap emotion, but can't help it. When we got out it was quite white everywhere and still snowing. Quite quiet, footsteps muffled. Even the congregation coming out of church sounded snuffed out as they wished each other happy Christmas. We ran, skidding and slipping, all the way back to the flat, and wrote our names huge in the snow outside the front door. I suddenly felt I was acting in a film and nearly spoilt the moment.

There was another half-sheet stapled to this, which read:

R. was found dead in his flat yesterday afternoon. Boxing Day. I simply cannot believe that we won't see him again, *ever*. We were going to meet in the pub that night. They think it may have been a heart attack, but he was only thirty-six – not so very old, and he didn't take dope or LSD, ever. We both feel shattered and cannot let go of each other for long, reassuring each other that we are still here, I suppose. Tonight there will be a wake for him at the Q.E. It's what he would have liked – such a shame that he'll miss it. The funeral isn't for some time because there has to be a post-mortem. I remember his great width, both physical and mental; his cracking smile, his tremendous interest in everyone and everything about him, and his constant encouragement. 'Go on, my love, do it now, before you're too old to enjoy it.' Everyone who knew him loved him.

Edmund almost burst into tears himself, still sitting there in the orange parrot towel and hat. Cars slooshed past in the street, and he shivered, sobering up fast. His girl was with someone she loved, even if he did make poor jokes in church. It was most odd that she didn't mention his name, had in fact carefully avoided doing so; her intentional concealment pointing perhaps to the fact that she was no longer with that person when she wrote or rewrote the entry? As usual, no dates, no nothing.

He marked the name where he had finished phoning that night, and went to bed after drinking a precautionary pint of water. He lay there imagining himself arriving at Mimi's front door, ringing the bell and it being opened by . . . the imagining ceased to be imagining and he dreamed . . . a woman wearing a red dress, with Marianne Strood's beautiful impersonal little face, stood on the step. 'Yes,' she said. 'I am Mimi Anderson. But the papers are not mine. I never wrote them. But you are expected to stay for dinner.' He followed her into the house, whose walls were all painted yellow, with a black and white tiled floor, decorated with an armoury of swords. She turned to him, and said: 'We often do a little fencing after pudding.' And he replied: 'I'm afraid I didn't bring mine,' and the consequence was that all the other guests challenged him to a duel after dinner. Dinner was only baked beans, served on dirty cream plates with chips and cracks, and he told the faceless people that he had only come to deliver some papers, but they said he was a wimp, and made him stand on the table, flicking beans at him from the tips of their knives. 'Where are the papers?' they chanted, 'Where are the papers?', subjecting him to a cannonade of beans. He didn't know where they were but he was sure he had them when he arrived. Had he left them on the bus? Panic seized him and he was suddenly out in the street, running, miraculously not covered in tomato sauce as he'd feared. He shouted out 'My God! My God! They're persecuting me!' and he was followed by a rabble singing 'Hark the Herald Angels Sing', chasing him into Baker Street Underground station, waving machetes and kukris, hatchets and halberds. Then Marianne Strood appeared beside him at the ticket machine and bought him a ticket, but started to kiss him goodbye, which was quite exciting. She wrapped a long black leg around him, rubbed her foot on the back of his knee and he felt, well, very excited indeed, and then he woke up with the inevitable consequences.

'I really am too old for this,' he said crossly, padding off to the bathroom. He had not let the water out of the bath earlier, and he watched the soapy soup flowing sluggishly away, leaving a light tidemark behind it. He felt compelled to get the bath cleaner out and scrub.

'Here I am, cleaning the bath at two a.m. Here I am having wet dreams at the thought of an unknown woman. It's Mimi I want, not Marianne. Although I know a lot about her past, she knows nothing of me whatsoever and cares not a jot. She probably doesn't even know she's lost the damn writing anyway.' At which point the doorbell rang, so he tied the hideous towel around him again and went cautiously to see who it was, almost expecting a host of vengeful dinner party guests in evening dress.

His son, Jerome, stood there, looking both hopeful and apologetic. 'Hello, Dad. I'm sorry it's so late, and I know I've woken you up, but I wondered if you could put me up for a couple of nights?' He stepped inside, eyeing the towel with distaste, putting his knapsack down on the sofa. 'You see, I was supposed to go to a party tonight, but the train from Manchester was delayed because of the snow, and now it's too late. The others went off to somewhere in Shepherd's Bush, but I thought I'd try here.'

'Snow?' said Edmund, trying to clear his aching head.

'Yeah. It's been snowing all day up there, and got really hard just as we were about to jump on the nine o'clock train. We've been held up for hours and hours. I was quite surprised to find there wasn't any snow here.'

'Well, it's good to see you, even at this time of the

morning. I was awake anyway, just had a nightmare. How about something hot to drink?'

'Great, that'd be really good. I'll make it, shall I?' Jerome dived into the kitchen and rattled about, chatting. 'Is there any bread? I haven't eaten much since lunch. Ah, here it is. Marmite? Jam? That'll do. How's Aunt Xenia and Uncle Johnnie? Have you been down to see them recently? I've hardly seen anything of Stuffy Henry in Manchester.'

He came out of the kitchen with two cups of hot chocolate and half a loaf of bread smothered in Xenia's best raspberry jam, sat down beside his father and tucked in. He resembled Edmund not at all, except in height, for which Edmund was grateful. He had golden curls like a pre-Raphaelite angel, a small sharply turned-up nose and a chin with a cleft in it. Both girls and boys thought him rather pretty, and he was a popular member of his archaeology course.

'How's your mother?' asked Edmund.

'Oh, fine, fine. She's "doing" American Indians, at the moment.'

'Oh, I thought it was carpentry.'

'No, that was the last enthusiasm. She made a wonderful dining table, but when we tried to have lunch on it, it sort of lurched sideways and we had to take evasive action as it all slid to the floor.'

He chuckled engagingly, and polished off the bread and jam. 'Well, I suppose you'd like to get back to bed. Have you got a couple of spare blankets?'

Edmund felt delicate the next morning but arranged to meet Jerome for a drink and a meal after shutting up shop. Jerome fancied dim sum, which was handy as Chinatown was close by. He was lyrical about his first term at university and his archaeology course.

'You'll never guess what,' he said, his mouth full of sticky rice, 'we're doing a field trip at Easter, a dig near Holy Hill! Isn't that a coincidence? The field-walk round the base turned up quite a bit of first-century Roman stuff, sherds, bits of mortars. They think it's possible there might have been an army post there, and a small settlement.'

'You could stay with Uncle Johnnie. I'm sure he'd be glad to put you up.'

'Well, I'd rather do whatever the rest of the gang are doing, really. I mean I don't want to miss out on anything.'

'No, I suppose not. But it'd be useful for the odd hot bath to wash off all the mud and I daresay one of Xenia's suppers wouldn't come amiss, either.'

'Oh, yes, that'd be great.' Jerome paused. 'Pass those little cakey things, please. Stuffy Henry will be there, too, I suppose.'

'Why? Don't you two get along so well now?'

Jerome and Stuffy Henry, so named because of the prim expression on his face when teased as a small boy, had been friendly as children, in the way that cousins are when thrown together because of their parents' relationship rather than through choice, but when Jerome had moved to Somerset with Hatty and their mother, their interests and outlook had diverged naturally, and Henry had gone up to university the year before Jerome.

'He's got some very odd friends in Manchester.'

'What do you mean, odd?' asked Edmund, pouring himself another glass of beer.

'Well, I'm not sure. It's just that I thought I'd see quite a lot of him. I know he's a second-year and all that, but he wanders around looking as if he's on something. You wouldn't recognize him from last year. He was still very much the rich farmer's son then. You know, like all checked Viyella shirts and moleskin trousers? The last few times I've seen him, he looked as if he'd spent three nights on the trot raving.'

'What! Henry at a rave? Are you sure?' Edmund recalled

the boy, pink-cheeked and shining with health, as with sleeves rolled up he helped Johnnie dose the sheep. More "Hireling Shepherd" than "Death of Chatterton".

'No. I mean I don't know. I was exaggerating. But he definitely isn't the same person at all. He looks a bit pasty and out of it. Definitely going downhill. Can I finish these too? You're sure you've had enough?'

'Go ahead. Is this something I should pass on to Johnnie?'

'Good Lord, no! It's not that serious. He'll see for himself when Henry comes down.'

'Well, I'm terribly glad to see *you* so cheerful. You've obviously made the right decision about what course to take.'

'Oh yes. I am absolutely sure. It's *the* most interesting thing.'

'Lucky you, then. Now let's have a cup of green tea and then go back to the flat. I really must get an early night.' Edmund tried unsuccessfully to attract the attention of a waiter who was leaning against the wall, gazing into infinity with the appearance of a monk meditating on a mantra.

Jerome left the next morning for Somerset, with a birthday card for Hatty from Edmund tucked into his pack. 'Tell her not to forget to visit me when she's up in London next time.'

'As if,' said Jerome, giving his father a hug. 'We'll be up quite soon, before Christmas. I'll ring you.'

They were alert, friendly and demonstrative children, thought Edmund, gratefully, although he realized they were not children any longer.

'And *you* are OK, Dad?' asked Jerome, giving a final look round the dingy flat. 'Perhaps Hatt and I could give this a coat of paint, in the summer vac?'

'That would be wonderful. I've been very lazy about it and it *is* a bit grubby.'

'Speak to you soon then, Dad, and love to Uncle J. and Aunt Xenia.'

Edmund was very pleased to have been visited. He enjoyed his children's company very much and was glad that they enjoyed his enough to make contact regularly out of their own choice. Edmund had, in the early days of the divorce, been careful never to criticize their mother or stepfather, left them out of battles and always tried to consider their opinions but it had been hard work never to appear miserable or hurt in front of them and to strike the right emotional balance when in their company. They had seen straight through his well-meant dissimulations, he had found out later, when the dust had settled, but they seemed to him to have come to terms with the split-up in an unusually well-balanced fashion. Jerome had a strong practical streak in him. All for the best, in the best of all possible worlds, he thought, a trifle bitterly.

That evening he eschewed the whiskey and telephoned from C to F and struck lucky with a Mr Fuller from Sheringham, who thought the name Anderson rang a bell. 'I don't think I ever *met* anyone called either Fleury or Anderson, but interestingly I bought some books from Marianne, Helen's niece. I spent some time with the ink-eradicator on the fly-leaves. There were certainly some volumes of Napoleonic history with the name Fleury in them. If you'd care to hold on, I'll go and check.'

Edmund held his breath.

When he returned, Mr Fuller announced that two of the books were signed G. Fleury, and that the address was still faintly visible, despite his efforts with the eradicator. 'No 6, rue Flaubert, Annecy. Then there are two more, *Le Procès Verbal* by le Clézio, and an anthology of French fairy tales. The first is inscribed "Syrie Anderson", and the second "M.A. Anderson, The Flower House, Kettleham". Kettleham, by the way, is just a few miles from here.'

'That's very helpful indeed,' said Edmund, writing down

the address in excitement. 'I'm very grateful to you. Did you know Helen Strood well?'

'She wrote articles on ornithology in the parish magazine,' said Mr Fuller. 'We used to go birdwatching as part of a group. She'd give me lifts sometimes, in her beautiful car. I was very sorry to hear about her accident. She was knocked down by a truck, I believe.'

Edmund thanked him again, profusely, and felt that he was at last getting somewhere. Someone, a neighbour perhaps, must know of the Andersons, and a visit to Norfolk was now imperative. He triumphantly telephoned Marianne Strood.

'Guess what? I've got an address from a Mr Fuller. You sold him your aunt's books? Well, one of them had M. A. Anderson on the fly-leaf, and an address. It's in Kettleham, apparently quite near Bolt.'

'Yes, just down the road from there. I was going up on Saturday. I've this lovely car, courtesy of my aunt, and I quite fancy a long drive in it. Why don't you come up with me, and you can go and see if there's any sign of the Andersons?' She sounded friendly, more interested than when he'd last met her.

'That would be an excellent idea.' The thought of being driven up to Norfolk by Marianne was quite attractive, ego-boosting even.

'Where do you live?' she asked. 'Ah, yes . . . well, I may as well pick you up then. How about seven thirty, or is that too early?'

'That'll be fine. I'll be ready.'

'OK, I just hope it isn't a wild goose chase for you.'

He couldn't resist telling Charlie of his success, and his arrangements with Marianne, when he went in to work on Thursday morning.

'I don't believe it. You jammy dodger!'

'What a very strange expression. Yes, I'm quite looking forward to the experience. Driving with her, I mean.' Edmund recalled his dream rather uneasily. She couldn't be much older than Jerome. He picked up an order and went into the back room to do some work on his new section on illustrators' books, there being a lot of cross-referencing to be done. An hour later he had got as far as PEAKE, Mervyn, and entered the brothers Grimm's *Household Tales*, black and white and some colour, 1946, and Lewis Carroll's *The Hunting of the Snark*.

Charlie called out to him: 'Edmund, as you're already there, could you run a check to see if we've got anything illustrated by Tenniel, apart from the two *Alice*'s? I've a customer here who is interested.'

Edmund did so, but found nothing in stock. He glanced through the little window into the shop, but Charlie's desk was half-hidden by a jutting shelving unit. He came out into the shop and came face to face with a person, a woman, who seemed oddly familiar to him, but was, for an instant, nameless.

'Hello!' he said, confident that the name would come to him in a second or two.

'Hello!' she replied, also momentarily perplexed. They were both out of their contexts, London life and country visits being in separate compartments of Edmund's brain; Amelia, having no idea of his profession, was certainly not expecting to find him there.

'Amelia,' he said at last, making the connection.

'Yes. How clever of you, and you're Edmund, only minus the hat.' She stared at him, still fazed by the coincidence. 'I didn't know this is what you worked at,' she continued, suddenly confused, hoping he didn't think she had sought him out on purpose, which she had not. She had been to visit a bullion dealer a couple of streets away, and now had a small packet safely stowed in her bag. Nine carat red gold, a piece of eighteen carat yellow, and several ounces of sheet silver. Having completed this part of her business, she was filling in time before an appointment with the Victoria and Albert Museum's craft shop. If she could get her work on display and on sale there, she would begin to do very nicely indeed. Her samples and a book of designs and photographs were in a little black briefcase tucked under her arm. She'd just been wandering around the area, looking in at shop windows. She had been intrigued by the strength of the Tenniel illustrations when reading the *Ingoldsby Legends* and had idly wondered what else, apart from *Alice* was illustrated by him, and thought a smart antiquarian bookshop was just the place to ask.

Edmund introduced her to Charlie, who was beginning to wonder what on earth there was about Edmund that brought a succession of desirable women to his desk. What was it that women fell for? He'd once read the result of a survey in a tabloid newspaper, searching for the qualities that women find most desirable in a man, and seemed to remember that the result was a six-footer with a tight bum, huge bank balance and an improbably large penis. He could discern none of these qualities in Edmund, yet in a short space of time two very pullable women had entered the shop to search him out. This one was a lot older than the delectable Miss Strood, definitely forty, but she had something sexy about her, in spite of her rather tired clothes. The face was fine, pointed, pretty. He glanced at her neck, that being where age usually first makes an appearance, but it was swathed in a green silk scarf, wound round several times. He couldn't see the rest of her, since she was enveloped in a coat, but she looked as if she might be rather shapely beneath it. And the hair, a waving mass of dark gold, neither short nor long, nor apparently styled in any way. Lively hair . . .

He gave up, shot Edmund a suspicious glance and went

back to his catalogues. Edmund was coming to the same conclusions as Charlie as he chatted to Amelia, wondering if he could offer her a lunchtime drink. He looked at the clock on the wall behind Charlie's desk. Nearly midday. Charlie wanted a late lunch.

'I'm on the point of popping out for a pint and a sandwich. Would you care to join me, if you have the time?'

'Yes, I'd like that. I've got an appointment at two o'clock and nothing much to do in between, although I was going to have a look in the Portrait Gallery, as it's not far from here.'

'You could do both. I've got to be back by one.' He fetched his coat, leaving Amelia a moment to stand and take in the terracotta walls and the sheer weight of books lining them: the ancient leather-bound, the newer cloth, the brightly jacketed volumes of knowledge both empirical and ideological, novels imaginative, novels pretentious, learned and self-indulgent. The many millions of words poured out in the English language, most to no great effect, in the centuries since printing was invented.

'See you at one, Charlie.'

'Sure. Don't be late though, will you? I'm lunching with Rich Uncle.'

No one had ever seen Charlie's Rich Uncle, but he indubitably existed since he had, Edmund learnt, been the backer when Charlie bought into the business.

Out in the street an icy wind whipped up scrumpled chocolate wrappers and bus tickets, and a McDonald's carton flew snapping at Edmund's ankles.

'There's quite a good place just round the corner. It's full of thespians and porn-merchants, but does a decent ham sandwich.' He steered Amelia, hand beneath her elbow, through the etched glass door and to a round table by the window.

'What would you like to drink?'

'I'll have a Jameson's please, if they've got it.' Edmund was pleased she shared his taste in whiskey, and went off to get it and order sandwiches.

Amelia, her briefcase and bag tightly wedged between her ankles beneath the table, watched him with interest. He had no trouble getting the barman's attention immediately, in spite of the already busy bar. He certainly did have physical presence, but now, instead of Aristide Bruant, she saw that a slimmer, slightly taller version of Napoleon Bonaparte was nearer the mark.

He returned, bearing the drinks, which he carefully set down on the sticky brown table-top. 'They'll bring the food in a minute. So, now tell me. What's the interest in Tenniel?'

'I came across some illustrations in a book your brother-in-law lent me. One of them was of two horsemen going over a cliff – one of the horses is a ghost horse and has amazing, car-headlight eyes and glows in the dark. I was intrigued by the composition and force of it. The story's quite good, too. I found out the origin of the expression "A flash in the pan". Shall I tell you, or do you know?'

'I thought it came from those photographers with their old plate cameras, holding up magnesium flashes.'

'No, it's earlier than that. The smuggler is being chased by an exciseman and draws a pistol . . . Oh, thank you . . . what lovely thick sandwiches . . . a horse pistol, whatever that is, and fires a shot at the exciseman's horse, which is the ghost horse, and only flame, not blood, jets out of the hole in the horse! Then he fires again, this time at the rider, but the horse pistol "flashed in the pan". I suppose what we'd call a misfire.'

She set about her ham and mustard sandwich with gusto, searching in his face for resemblances to the Xenia she had met. Just the eyes perhaps, that rather piercing light blue, and the slight slant upwards.

Edmund was delighted with her company, and could see that Johnnie, if he was indeed interested in her, had reason to be so.

'I think the *Ingoldsby Legends* were published around the 1830s,' he said.

'So you know the book! Have you actually read it?'

'Yes, but ages ago, when I was a child. I think the story you described is called "The Smuggler's Leap", am I right? I may have read the copy you've been lent, because I can remember the picture! My father had a copy. I believe they were incredibly popular to start off with. Every-house-had-one sort of popular. But later Victorians thought some of them, well, perhaps not quite the sort of thing young ladies should read in the drawing room. The moral climate started to change quite fast after the end of the Regency period.'

'Yes, I've only read a few of them so far, and I can imagine that infidelity and boredom with one's aged husband would be considered unsuitable for Victorian misses, however amusingly described.'

'Isn't it a pity that more modern novels aren't illustrated?', Edmund said, thinking of his growing collection of books illustrated by Rex Whistler, whose Rococo pastiches delighted him.

'Yes, I suppose it is. But on the other hand, illustrations do stop people using their imaginations. I used to get so cross when I came across the first illustration of the hero with quite a different face to the one I had envisaged. And now we have the "film of the book" to help out those with no visual imagination – but that can be irritating too, for the same reasons.'

'What did you like to read, as a child?'

'Everything I could get hold of. When I was quite young I loved Kipling, and C.S. Lewis of course, and all those historical novels by Rosemary Sutcliffe about Roman Britain. At school I read a lot of old children's books, the kind our parents read. Henty, D.K.Broster, John Buchan, Saki, Conan Doyle ... then came Jane Austen and Charlotte Brontë and Dickens. Then Lawrence Durrell, William Golding. I remember a book we weren't allowed to read at school, in fact there were lots of books we weren't allowed to read at school, but this particular one had a supposedly over-explicit description of childbirth in it. So of course we read it, but remained none the wiser about how the heroine had got herself into that condition in the first place.'

The buzz of the crowd around them, the warmth and the alcohol loosened their tongues, and they carried on, and on, discovering similarities in adult reading and discrepancies and dislikes, pet hates and loves. Amelia admitted that she had got so desperate once on holiday in Greece, bookless, that she had been reduced to reading the back of a detergent packet, followed by the instructions on a roll of Kodak film, and started to teach herself Greek by translating the advertising in a local newspaper and the bilingual instructions on a bottle of shampoo.

'I've got to get back', said Edmund, suddenly remembering the Rich Uncle. It was five to one.

'Oh, goodness, yes. And I've got to get over to Kensington.'

'We'll meet again, perhaps, next time I come down to stay with Xenia?'

'I'll search you out – and we can carry on the conversation,' she promised.

They went their different ways, Amelia to the Victoria and Albert, and Edmund in some haste back to the shop. He felt warm, well nourished and philanthropic. He bought an *Evening Standard* from the bad-tempered newspaper seller on the corner, next door to whom, in a doorway, was a large cardboard box, from which a pair of boots protruded. This was unusual, since Edmund walked past that way every morning and the owner of the boots was usually rolling up his blanket and flat-packing his box at that time of the day. It was lunchtime and yet he had not got up and gone off on his rounds. Edmund paused.

'Do you think he's all right?' he asked the newspaper seller, who huddled himself deeper into his dandruff-covered, greasy duffel coat, sucking in his cheeks and blowing out steaming, malodorous breath.

'Don't see why not,' he said.

'Well, usually he's up and about by now, isn't he, by lunchtime?' said Edmund. He turned and tapped on the box. 'You all right, in there?' The boots did not stir and Edmund had a sudden sinking sensation. He bent down and shouted into the box. 'Come on! I just want to know if you're OK.'

'He's probably pissed,' said the newspaperman, flipping a newspaper neatly in half with a flick of his wrist and holding it out to a customer, palm upwards ready for the money.

'What's wrong?' said a man in a pinstripe suit and expensive camel-hair overcoat.

'I think he may be ill. I pass every day, and he's usually up and about by now, or at least sitting there begging. I've never seen him asleep at this time of day.'

The man looked about him, as if searching for help, then twitched his trouser legs up an inch and squatted beside Edmund. 'His legs are stone cold,' he said, removing his hand from the ankle above the boot. They looked at each other uncertainly but a girl came up, a girl whose clothes, face and hair were all uniformly grey.

'What's up with Gareth?'

'We don't know. We think he might be ill.'

'Pissed,' said the newspaperman, selling another newspaper.

'Gareth? Gareth!' shouted the girl, tugging at his feet.

It was awkward, trying to get him out of the box. Edmund and Pinstripe had to haul from one end, while the girl pulled at the box from the other, gradually exposing the rest of the man called Gareth. His arms were tightly folded over his chest, the hands stuck in his armpits, and he was stiff. He was quite definitely dead, and the putty-coloured face stared up into their own, unconcerned, no longer there.

'You've been selling newspapers for the past hour, standing next door to a corpse!' said Edmund heatedly to the newspaper vendor.

'Serve him bloody well right. Put off the customers, he did. You going to get someone to come for the stiff, then?'

A teenage police constable appeared, pimples standing out scarlet on his pinched face. The girl sat, stone-faced, beside the body. An ambulance was called and Pinstripe and Edmund drifted discreetly away.

Charlie, already in his overcoat, was pacing up and down behind his desk.

'You rat! I'm going to be bloody late!'

'A man died in the street,' said Edmund.

'Did you have to stay and bury him? No, I'm sorry, I'll get off. See you later.'

Edmund had been shaken out of his previous convivial mood. He'd got used to the man in the box over the past few weeks; they'd even started to greet one another.

'Morning.'

'Morning, mate, spare a fiver?'

Now he was extinguished: by the cold, disease, alcohol? He did not know. The man had had a set routine. The blanket was always placed just so on top of the flattened box. Routine keeps one going when things are bad, Edmund was aware. He'd once been obsessed with it for a short period just after he'd moved into the Marylebone flat. He'd followed a strict formula, as if that would prevent any further bouts of disaster; his talismanic behaviour including counting the steps up to his flat, placing his things in exact preordained places, and always leaving the place at eight fifteen a.m.

exactly, not a moment before or later, standing by the door staring at his watch as if waiting for a supernatural command to lift off. He had walked up the same side of the street each day, drunk one pint of beer standing in exactly the same spot of worn carpet at the bar of his local pub, and become distressed and fretful if anyone else happened to be standing there when he wished to avail himself of its particular prophylactic properties. It had all sorted itself out, eventually, when his depersonalized mind had decided for itself that this type of behaviour was a nail no longer needed to hold itself together.

He heard the ambulance coming, and went to the door, staring down the street. Then he got on with his work. The head of cheerfulness which had built up while sitting in the warm pub with the pretty, intelligent Amelia had been dissipated. Life was short, life was sweet, and he'd better get on with living it. He helped a customer with a query, sold two first-edition copies of a 1930s novel which had recently been televised, and typed up stock cards. He rearranged a shelf, made lists and was serving another customer when Charlie returned, glowing with alcohol and red meat.

'He was late too, I just beat him to it. I'm sorry about your brush with death. Now who was that incandescent lady?'

'She's from the darkest depths of Romney Marsh. I don't know what she does, or who she is really, except that my sister thinks her husband is chasing after her.'

'Don't blame him. So you didn't find out anything about her over lunch? Whatever did you talk about?'

'Oh, books, and things.' Edmund was suddenly irritated by Charlie's curiosity.

Charlie raised his eyebrows to heaven.

Later on that afternoon he received a call from Xenia, who rarely rang him at work, and who appeared to desire his company yet again for the following weekend.

'Xenia, I can't. I'm off to Norfolk this weekend. I've

got a lead on Mimi Anderson at last, and I've got to follow it up.'

'Mimi?'

'You remember! I've told you all about her. The papers in the seaman's chest?'

'Oh, that rubbish. Yes. You're getting very boring about her.'

'Well I'm sorry – but I could come down the weekend after, if you'd like, only that's getting very close to Christmas. You do still want me to come for Christmas?'

'Of course, darling Edmund. Where else would you go? I just need to . . . it's Johnnie, again. I want you to talk to him.'

'Oh, Xen! I do think you should ask him yourself, outright, if you're so worried – I really do think you may have got things out of proportion. But I will be there the weekend after next, I promise. Take care of yourself.'

He put the phone down, anxious. She had sounded a little shrill, unbalanced even, and that was unusual.

6

Edmund was washed, shaved and dressed by seven o'clock on Saturday morning. He packed Mimi's exercise books and writings into a carrier bag, just in case he might be lucky enough to be directed straight to her, although he was not too hopeful of this, having checked out through directory enquiries that there were no Andersons in Kettleham. Judging by the negative response from Helen Strood's friends – he had got no further than Mr Fuller – she had most probably left the area a long time ago. A fiendishly icy east wind sliced through the cracks and gaps in the window frames, the sky was an indeterminate grey; he shoved an extra sweater into the bag.

Marianne rang the bell at seven thirty precisely, causing him to gulp down the rest of his coffee and sending him tumbling downstairs and into the street like a Jack Russell after a rabbit. The car was a complete surprise – a long, mean, navy-blue Bristol 401, and Marianne, dressed in a black leather jacket and trousers, a white cashmere shawl draped round her shoulders, looked set to raise a few eyebrows in Bolt. Her face was a beautifully painted little mask, with a small neat smile. He settled back in the red leather seat, feeling for the belt.

'There aren't any, I'm afraid. There's nothing strong enough to bolt them to. As it's a classic car, it's exempt.

You'll just have to trust me. Right? Off we go.'

The engine hummed throatily as they slid through London on their way to the M11. It was a car that was much stared at, and Edmund covertly watched Marianne enjoying the attention. She was a good driver and he relaxed sufficiently to start chatting to her, interested in the car, asking her about her job. She was pleased by his eagerness and enthusiasm, being more accustomed to dispiriting young men who were acutely, self-consciously laid-back, determined to remain unimpressed by anything in case they should seem naive. Edmund discovered that she worked for an independent TV production company, that she was twenty-five, older than he had supposed. She lived alone, she said, but had a man, which last fact she divulged without being asked, as if it were a much-practised warning. She called the man her 'partner', an expression which still jarred on Edmund. A partner, to him, was someone with whom one worked in business, an equal shareholder, or someone with whom one played tennis. He must be careful how he introduced Charlie in future.

They stopped at a service station just before joining the motorway and Edmund went halves with the petrol and bought a large bar of plain chocolate which seemed to please Marianne, who ate most of it, holding out her left hand for another piece every five minutes or so, like a child. The sun had come through the cloud and hung low in the sky like a blood orange over a landscape browned and silvered by wind and frost. Marianne did a little questioning too, in between mouthfuls of chocolate, asking about the bookshop and Charlie Parrott's place in it, and he asked her more about Helen Strood. Had she been married? No, she had not. Would Marianne's father perhaps remember some of his sister's friends? He had died, quite a few years ago, she said, which was why she had inherited the house, and the car, which had originally been her grandfather's.

Had she kept any of the private letters belonging to her aunt, he asked hopefully. She replied that she'd had an enormous bonfire of everything like that. He thought it lucky that she had not discovered Mimi's outpourings, or they would certainly have met the same fate.

They turned off and headed for Newmarket, where they eventually stopped for a short break, to stretch their legs and have a cup of coffee. Edmund had been rather aware of her legs as they drove, their leather encasements alternately creasing and straining over her kneecaps as she changed gear. When they came out of the coffee-shop, a few flakes of snow were floating down, which caused Marianne to look slightly anxiously at the yellowing sky. It was the first hint of any emotion on her face that Edmund had seen.

'That could be a real drag,' she said, getting back into the car. 'The windscreen wipers aren't exactly brilliant and the windscreen itself is a bit difficult to see through.' Edmund had noticed that it was small, and in two parts, with a central bar, but the snow seemed light enough as they drove on, more sedately. But soon there were increasingly heavy flurries, causing Marianne to lean forward in her seat, straining to see. They passed through Swaffham, then Fakenham. 'Bolt's next,' said Marianne, with relief in her voice.

On reaching Bolt, a red-brick and flint townlet, they drew up outside a pub where they had a beer and a lager, pâté, with not quite enough toast, served with a garnish of rock-hard onion rings, cress, leather-skinned tomato and the tasteless ribs of an iceberg lettuce. Marianne followed this up with a chocolate fudge pudding, which, she said, made up for the awful pâté. Edmund was now finding it harder to find subjects for conversation. She was quite hard work, he decided, as he wandered about while she did her business with the house-agents.

The snow was beginning to settle on the pavements and

the inhabitants hastened their steps as they went about their Saturday business. A tiny woman in a yellow headscarf crossed the road towards him as he loitered in front of the church, her arms overflowing with a great sheaf of funeral lilies and florist's greenery. Edmund tried to be patient, but Marianne seemed to be taking an inordinate amount of time. He stamped his boots in the snow, batting his arms up and down to try and keep warm, nearly decapitating an ancient gentleman coming up behind him in macintosh and beret, head down and semi-blinded by the snow.

She emerged at last, and leaving the car where it was they walked down a side street to Aunt Helen's house. This was also of porridgy flint, with red-brick quoins and a range of green-doored outbuildings inside a low flint wall. A black and white cat was sitting alone in the garden surrounded by clumps of blackened dead chrysanthemums and upturned flowerpots; it opened its pink mouth and miaowed silently, picking its way over the snow-dusted dark earth towards them.

'That's Tache, Aunt Helen's cat,' said Marianne. 'Don't let him get in as I unlock the door. He's got a new home now, next door with the Watkinses.'

There was a pile of letters on the floor inside, which Marianne bent to retrieve and, putting her gloves and shoulder bag on the nearest chair, started to look through.

'I have to arrange with the Watkinses to readdress the post for me, and to come and check the heating's going on and off all right. I'm worried about burst pipes.' Edmund looked round the sparsely furnished room, low-ceilinged, long, with its two Ercol chairs and pine coffee table on a great expanse of pale grey carpet, like three lonely peas on a plate. 'Most of her things are sold. I just keep the basics here, plus bedlinen and pots and pans.' Marianne sat down and started to open the letters, throwing junk mail and circulars to the floor beside her. 'So much for putting her death in the paper. There seems to be a vast amount of people who didn't see it. Look!' She held out a handful of Christmas cards. 'I'll have to get her address book back as soon as you've finished with it, and try to sort out who they are all from. Pity people only put their Christian names in cards. How am I supposed to know who Hilary and Siegfried are?'

Edmund was standing by the window, a determined figure who looked as if he were plotting to escape from Elba. Uncharacteristic impatience rising, unable to help himself, he asked when they might think of setting out for Kettleham?

'Soon,' said Marianne, opening another card and reading it before slipping it back in its envelope and putting it with the others. She joined him at the window and Tache leapt for the sill, skidding in the snow and scrabbling at the glass, his paws leaving dirty streaks. 'Of course. Kettleham and your mysterious Mimi. I'll just check everything is OK upstairs, go and visit the Watkinses and we'll be off. There's coffee and longlife milk in the kitchen if you'd like some.'

While she was away he sat in the chair by the empty hearth, sniffing the cold and musty air and wishing he had a book to read. The shelves had been emptied, leaving dark tidemarks on their cream paint. There were a few red drawing-pins stuck into the beam above his head, and by the door. Relics perhaps of long-ago Christmas decorations. A dead geranium in a cracked terracotta pot. One watercolour, of an ancient building in the snow, which somehow looked familiar. There was a little cupboard beside the fireplace, with a brass handle. He bent and looked inside it. A chessboard and box of men, a Monopoly set and a book, *Card Tricks for Beginners*, a dog-eared and sticky pack of cards. He shut the door again and leant back in the chair. There was something about Marianne that he could not quite put his finger on. She was undoubtedly remarkable visually, seemed intelligent enough, had hardly been unfriendly, in fact very pleasant . . . the outside door slammed.

'Hi, I'm back. Shall we go off then?'

In Kettleham, which consisted of only a dozen houses, they knocked on a door at random. Edmund had ready his prepared questions and explanations, but the woman who came to the door, all tightly curled mauve hair and velvety pink tracksuit, was brusque, shivering meaningfully on her door step.

'I've only recently retired here with my husband. But the Flower House is first right, a hundred yards up the lane on the left.' She whipped back inside and the door slammed behind her.

They found it immediately, and Edmund stood staring at it, his hand on the gate, his hopes shattered. It was an upright, red-brick doll's house, with Dutch gables. Its door hung from its hinges and the windows were blind, boarded up.

'Oh, shit!' said Edmund. His imagination had run away with him on the way between Bolt and Kettleham – he thought he might meet, if not Mimi herself, then at least people who knew of her, would direct him to her.

'Cheer up!' said Marianne, her teeth chattering. 'We'll go back to the other houses and knock on all the doors till we get somewhere.' She went back to the car, leant into the back seat and opened the boot by means of a button hidden beneath the armrest. She produced a pair of impossibly shiny clean Wellingtons, and Edmund discovered what it was that worried him most about her – she was too perfect, too neat, too clean and tidy. He had an overwhelming desire to roll her in the snow.

'The only problem is', she said, brushing snow out of her plucked eyebrows, 'that in this area most of the cottages are owned by weekenders, which means they are only occupied for a week or two a year. A lot of the villages round here are ghost-towns in the winter.'

The first two cottages seemed to prove her point, there being no reply from either of them. They saw a man in a flat cap, splitting logs in his front garden further down the road, a cape of snowflakes across the shoulders of his jacket, and approached him. He remembered Mrs Anderson and her daughter.

'That'll be a good while ago,' he said. 'You'd best ask the old vicar, he's retired now. Yes, the old boy'll remember.' He directed them to a white house across the road. By this time they were getting very cold indeed, the snow falling even thicker, getting down their necks. Edmund began to worry about the possibility of not being able to get back to London that night.

The vicar was at home and listened politely to Edmund's by now thoroughly confused explanation, delivered through clenched teeth, of the reason for their arrival on his doorstep, unscrambled it and invited them in. They were begged to take seats in his study, beside a coal fire which fairly belched out heat.

'Now I think I might be able to help you a little.' Edmund sighed with relief. 'I do indeed remember the Andersons. She was a *very* charming woman, but I don't know what happened to the daughter, after she married.'

'Married?' asked Edmund.

'Yes. I had the pleasure of officiating. I could find out her married name if that would help?'

It would not, unless it was something incredibly unusual, like Wisley Drizzel, but Edmund nodded enthusiastically.

'Then I'll go and and put the kettle on as you're both obviously near frozen to death, and I'll telephone the present incumbent. He's got the parish registers since nineteen fifty in his study. There's too much vandalism about to keep them in the church.'

He disappeared and they heard him using the telephone in the hall.

The warmth began to rush agonizingly back into Edmund's fingers and he watched Marianne sitting there quietly, snow melting off her boots on to the hearthrug. Her cheeks were pinker now, and she appeared a little less made-up, less immaculate than she had earlier. The window was darkened by falling snow, hypnotizing as it drifted past the panes. Out of professional interest he turned his eyes to the bookshelves, but they were overflowing with heavy theological works, aged green Penguin crime novels and learned volumes on the correct pruning of fruit trees. There was an ivory crucifix on an ebony stand on the cluttered desk, beside a shockingly flippant pink cyclamen in a pot. Edmund felt his eyes begin to close in the stuffy warmth.

The vicar returned with a rattling tea-tray on which was a motley collection of cups and saucers, placing it at his elbow on a shaky little table. He was a small, thin man, with a large Adam's apple that shot up and down in his wrinkly, mottled throat as he spoke.

'I've remembered one or two things about the Andersons while making the tea. They came here from the Middle East, although I believe they lived in Suffolk before they went out there. They rented the Flower House for a long time. Have you seen the state it's been allowed to get into? So sad, such a waste when there are such housing problems everywhere. I know two families who'd give their eye-teeth to get in there.'

He poured out the tea and handed Marianne a blue and white Spode cup, trembling in a red and gold Derby saucer, and Edmund caught the smoky smell of Lapsang Souchong.

'The child, Mimi, was an attractive little baggage. I can remember the wedding because the bridegroom wore such an astonishing velvet suit. But then it was in the nineteen seventies. I've contacted the present vicar and he will ring back shortly, as soon as he finds the entry. Poor man, so much busier than I used to be. He cares for four parishes now. Do have a biscuit.' He passed Edmund a little pink plate with a few soggy gingernuts on it, and Edmund gratefully took one and put it in his turquoise blue-rimmed Minton saucer. His cup, he noticed, was probably stolen from a railway café. Thick, white and heavy.

'My wife, who sadly died twelve years ago,' continued the vicar, dipping his biscuit in his tea, 'used to keep in touch with Mrs Anderson after she went back to London. Syrie, her name was, I think. She was some sort of journalist. It's all coming back to me now. Syrie was the daughter of the writer, Connaught Marvel.'

The telephone rang in the hall and he rose to answer it before Edmund could express surprise at such an eminent grandparent for Mimi. When he returned he handed Edmund a piece of paper with the details of Mimi's marriage on it, written in pale, wavering pencil.

Taylor – Anderson – Nicholas Charles to Miranda Amélie. June 27th 1974 – witnesses were Syrie Anderson, J. McGinnis and Helen Strood. 'I do hope that that is of assistance to you? You could perhaps look up their marriage certificate in London, which will give you their addresses at the time of their marriage. I seem to remember they came down from London for the wedding.'

The old man was so courteous, so kind, that they didn't rush immediately away, Edmund shooting Marianne a pleading glance as she started to rise from her chair, making her subside. They finished their tea, discussed Connaught Marvel, had another cup of tea and another biscuit. Edmund then thanked him profusely. 'We must, however, be getting back. We've got to return to London tonight.'

'I think that might be foolhardy,' said the vicar, waving at the window, 'it seems to be what they call a white-out.'

It was indeed a proper blizzard when they left.

'Christ! Are you going to be able to drive in this?' said Edmund, trying to wipe some of the snow off the windscreen, then going round to the sloping rear of the car.

'I'll manage. It's not dark yet . . . we'll have to go back to Bolt, and then I'll ring the AA to find out what the roads are like.'

'It's pretty obvious what they're like here. I feel I ought to be walking in front of the car with a flaming torch,' said Edmund, as they crawled forwards, the heavy car slithering. The flakes came towards them like speeding grey sparks and the wretched little windscreen wipers moaned and whined, unable to cope with the onslaught.

'I haven't a fucking clue where we are,' said Marianne. 'Could you stick your head out of the window, and see if I'm still on any sort of road?'

'I'll try.' Edmund removed his hat and leant out into the whiteness. 'Right a bit, right a bit more, that looks OK. I think there's a stop sign coming up.'

'That'll be the main road then. Thank God! I turn left there, and then we're back in Bolt.'

Edmund withdrew his head, banging his chin on the lower edge of the window. Marianne looked at him and smiled.

'Do keep your eyes on the road!' he implored.

'I can't actually see the road. I'm just guessing anyway. You look like Father Christmas.'

'I think I've got frostbite,' said Edmund, his teeth clattering together. The car chasséed round the corner and they then turned into the side street at the bottom of which was Aunt Helen's house.

'I won't try to get it into the garage – I might not be able to get it out again. There's a little supermarket just up the street. Shall we go and get in some supplies, do you think?'

They filled a wire basket with emergency rations: bread, bacon, butter and biscuits, more milk and two tins of Baxter's game soup and some marmalade which Marianne said she couldn't face life without, and a bottle of Jameson's. When they returned to the house, Tache flew through the door and sat down in front of the empty fireplace, looking huffy. Marianne flopped down in a chair and threw her head back, her once-perfect shiny hair now rats'-tailed and wild. Edmund felt that he should take charge of the evening; she'd been driving all day and must be tired.

'We'll get a fire going, that is if there's any wood?'

'Yes, there's a whole shedful.' She showed no signs of moving.

'Well, you see if you can get the heating going, override the time-switch or whatever, and get down some blankets. I'll go out and get the wood.'

'You'll need a key. It's the second shed. Here, it's on the ring with the Yale.' She passed it to him, and he made his sortie into the horizontally blowing snow. The shed was indeed full of logs, and dry kindling, and there was also a log-basket, covered in cobwebs. He made two trips across the garden with this on his back, feeling like King Wenceslas, taking enough to last the whole evening, or the night if things got worse. The night . . . he really did not want to get snowed in with Marianne. He'd run out of things to say to her. It might of course stop snowing, at any time, and he would telephone the AA at once. But he must check in the address book for any Taylors. Marianne was still sitting in the chair when he returned with the second load, looking very glum.

'What's the matter?' he asked, feeling he should be looking after her.

'No electricity, so the boiler won't fire. And there's no way you can do it manually. There are no lights, no nothing. I've tried. Power cut.'

'Well, never mind. The cooker's gas, isn't it? I'll soon get the fire going. Go on. Go and get those blankets, and then you can wrap yourself up in a rug and tell me your life story.'

She gave him an odd, almost pathetic look, but went upstairs, where he could hear her footsteps, cupboards opening, floorboards creaking.

He tore and scrumpled up the junk mail, overlaid his kindling and set a match to it. Mercifully it took flame at once, and he sat back on his heels, ready with some small pieces of ashwood to build it up. Tache rubbed his head up and down on his knee, as if scent-marking him as an appreciated piece of personal property. Edmund was relieved, there being only one thing more destructive to the male ego than failure with fire, or indeed, being obviously disliked by other people's pets. Marianne returned, wrapped in a pink paisley eiderdown, with four blankets and another blue eiderdown in her arms.

'Have we got any candles?' asked Edmund.

'Yes, a whole boxful. I'll get them.' She fetched them from the kitchen and stuck them in a line across the chimneypiece and Edmund put one in a little green enamel chamberstick he'd found in the downstairs lavatory.

'Shall we light them? I can hardly see what I'm doing.' It was dark now, and Marianne drew the curtains and struck a match, lighting the candles with some awkwardness and a lot of 'ouches', her fingers cold and stiff. The fire started to give out a breath of heat, and the room became less severely empty, all light focused around the fireplace, their shadows curtseying and bowing up the bare walls.

Edmund rang the AA, who expected the snow to ease off by midnight but meanwhile would advise everyone not to drive unless it was absolutely necessary. He relayed this message to Marianne, who had taken off her damp socks and was holding out her bare feet to the fire, her face inscrutable. He also removed his boots, hoping his socks didn't smell, and set them to dry by the fire. There was a tension between them; neither knew what to do or say next. He peered through the curtains and could dimly see a few flickering lights in windows and imagined other people digging out camping stoves, and Tilly lamps, bemoaning the lack of television. He had not got a television at home in his flat and so did not miss it, but could see how useful they were when one didn't have anything to say to one's companion.

'What about a game of chess?' he suggested. There didn't appear to be a book in the house.

She leant forward, clutching the eiderdown closer around her, and opened the fireside cupboard, pulling out the board and box.

'You've obviously looked in here – there are cards as well, if you'd rather?'

'I think I prefer chess. I'm not very good at it though. How about you?'

'I'm not too good at it either.'

'That's OK then.'

They pulled the little table closer to the fire and sat down cross-legged on either side of it. Edmund stoked up the fire, and they set out the chessmen. The pieces were tacky to the touch, lightly mottled with mildew, and they played rather cautiously at first till she, gaining confidence, started to skate about the board with a bishop with such success that Edmund decided it needed to be unfrocked immediately before it did any more damage. It took him a long time to checkmate her, and they had a cup of coffee before playing a return match. There were no sounds except the infinitely soft flutterings of the driven snow on the windows.

'There's no traffic at all, had you noticed?' she said.

'I thought I heard a tractor a little while ago.'

'My hands are still cold.' She looked at him, then held them out, tentatively. He took them, equally uncertainly, and rubbed the icy fingers, unwillingly at first, as if the familiarity might be dangerous.

'There,' he said, giving them back to her. 'I'll get us some whiskey. You can tell me about your Aunt Helen.' He returned with the bottle and a couple of tumblers and watched her as she set out the chessmen again.

'I'm white, this time. What about Aunt Helen?'

'Well, tell me what she did, what she looked like, how well you knew her . . . that sort of thing,' he said, taking a gulp of his drink, and moving a pawn in response to her opening.

'She was very clever. She read endlessly, and she took a lot of trouble with me. But I used to be made to come and stay by my parents, whenever they wanted to go off abroad, which was quite often. I think she thought I wasn't being properly educated because she kept on giving me books to read. I hate reading. I'd rather be doing something practical. And concerts, she took me to concerts whenever I stayed, driving down to Norwich or wherever, in the Bristol. She thought I was musical, but I'm not. I'd just learnt to play the piano very easily. I didn't know what I was supposed to feel about the music, how to emphasize the right bits. I just played, accurately, what was written down. I'd rather have sneaked off to a rock band.' She suddenly shifted a knight in a move which Edmund had prayed she would miss, wrecking his rather short-term strategy. She was beginning to play better and better, as if slowly rediscovering the possibilities.

'What else?' asked Edmund, who, having got her talking, was determined to keep her at it.

'She was mad about birds. She had her own income, but taught at the local grammar school, English. She was tallish, slim, quite a good figure really. But she never took any trouble with her hair or face, and had absolutely no taste in clothes or anything. No eye. I used to shop with her in Norwich, hoping to brighten her up a bit, but it was no good. We always came back with a replica of whatever it was we had gone out to replace. She was the same age as my mother, but she looked older. She made friends easily, Mother said. Very talkative. She was supposed to have had this long affair with a writer, but when it ended she never looked at anyone else. I think she put a lot of her affection into me, which was rather overpowering. It suited my parents because of their travelling. It was nice for them not to always have me tagging along.'

Edmund felt pity for her immediately, although her voice had not suggested she felt any for herself.

'How odd, then, if she was so interested in birds, that she should keep a cat.'

'Yes, I suppose it was. But she was more of an out-and-about, long-walks-and-binoculars sort of birdwatcher. And she always swore that Tache was too fat and lazy to catch any. Hey! What are you doing?'

'I'm castling.'

'Well, I don't know how to do that. It's not fair.'

He showed her the principle, and found himself, ten minutes later, to be checkmated.

'That's one-all. Shall we go and visit the pub? It's seven o'clock. Have you got a torch?'

'No. Don't let's go out again, not into all that miserable cold. I've just got nice and warm. We've got everything we need here.' She poured herself another drink, and threw another log on the fire, which by now was sending out real heat, having built up a good base of embers. 'Let's play one more game,' she suggested, 'and then we can start on the card tricks.'

Edmund was already beginning to feel fuddled, and Marianne seemed to have speeded up, not taking so long over her moves, annihilating his pawns and sending his bishops scuttling for cover whenever they dared to stick out their episcopal noses. However, he rallied and adroitly tempted her queen into danger, giving a whoop of delight as she fell into the clutches of one of his knights.

They sat back and surveyed each other in the flickering, guttering candlelight. She seemed to Edmund immensely more human, less of the supermodel. She pushed the table back towards the middle of the room, and moved closer to him, still enveloped in the pink paisley eiderdown.

'I'm bored with chess,' she said, putting her hand on his thigh.

Curious, curious, very, very curious. He could hear his own heart beating, surprised at being moved on so swiftly, surprised at his own physical response. Something was definitely stirring. A beat was missed, a lurch as he felt her body pressing closely into his, put his arms round her, feeling. He stared into her expressionless, inky-grey eyes, which had closed as he started to remove her jacket. Oh, hell! He jerked himself away, and her eyes opened sharply, read his thoughts with speed, and smiled.

'Don't worry, I've got some. Here.' She fumbled in the pocket of her jacket. So she had come prepared? The thought that she had planned this, had wilfully conjured up a snowstorm in order to entrap him fled across his mind, but he was unable to arrest it. He was not of the 'women are whores or madonnas' mentality, although he occasionally had sneaking suspicions that a great many of them were witches and possibly dangerous. They removed from each other whatever else seemed reasonable under the circumstances. She was thin, but definitely not unattractively so, very white, and seemed to know what she was doing. Yes, she did indeed. After a while he sank into her with a little gasp, instantly back into the dream of a few nights past. Any minute now a ravening horde would hammer down the door and demand his blood. He was determined to finish what he had started before he was caught and hacked to death. Her face was still, sensuously serious, and she made small encouraging sounds, her long legs wrapped about him.

'How long since . . . ?' she asked, her eyes open again, each reflecting a tiny candle.

'A very long time.'

'I thought so. Me too.'

'Why not?'

'I just haven't wanted to.'

'You said you had a man – a partner?' he said, lying back on the blue eiderdown, his arm beneath her neck, uncomfortably, his feet on the fender.

'I lied then. It was just in case you pounced and I didn't want you to. But I did want you to, and you didn't, so I had to pounce instead.'

'Oh, I see.'

She sat up and retrieved a pawn from the hearth. She was staring at him, taking in the compactness of his body, the slightly puzzled expression in his eyes, the tangled thatch of dark hair, greying near the ears, and smaller details, such as the small scar on his shoulder where he had been hit by an airgun pellet as a child, the already burgeoning dark stubble round his jaw, the lines round his eyes. He felt her scrutiny, felt as if he were being assessed for signs of age, and did not care. He also felt hungry.

'This is all very peculiar,' he said.

'Isn't it just.'

They were on neutral ground, equally balanced, and there was no more between them than that. Yellow and pink light flittered across the walls and their faces. She got up suddenly and went to her bag, taking out a green envelope which had the words 'Happy Birthday Marianne' written across it in white marker.

'Today? It's your birthday today?'

'Yes. But I had my party last night, after work. Someone gave me this as a present.' She had opened the envelope and taken out a tiny plastic packet.

'Have you ever tried it?' She poured the contents out in a neat line on the table top, made a small tube with a piece of the envelope and looked up at him. 'Want some?' He shook his head, vaguely appalled.

'No, no. It's not my sort of thing. I'll stick to the alcohol, if you don't mind. You seem rather expert at it.'

'No. I've never touched it before. I've seen others do it, of course.'

He wondered. Had he led such a sheltered life that he had never come across a nest of coke-sniffers before? No, not a nest . . . what would the collective noun be, for such a gathering? A snort, a sniffle?

She bent forward and drew it up, sneezed and wiped her nose, smiling. 'I always try everything once. Don't you?'

'Well no, not everything. How do you feel?'

'It's better than pudding.'

She eased her way back across to him, scattering chess-men.

'Supercharged. My turn now.' She pushed him gently in the chest, back into the blankets. 'We probably won't meet again, will we? We might as well make the most of it.' She laughed, rather high-pitched and clear, and talked, and talked, asking questions, which Edmund, considering his position and an almost total lack of breath, found hard to answer. He was convinced he was lying on the white king and queen, felt he was perhaps going through a mirror, as in the opening pages of *Alice Through the Looking Glass*.

'I'm so glad you bought the marmalade . . .' she said, 'I'm miserable in the morning without marmalade.'

'That's . . . that's a nice . . . oah . . . alliteration.'

'Oh, one of them. Like Caroline being continuously contented with cunnilingus?'

'Yes, I suppose so.'

He rolled, exhausted, into a blanket and watched her while she sat up and swept the chess pieces that remained upright to the floor. She pulled out the cards and set about playing clock patience, her movements fast and precise.

'Aren't you cold?'

'No, not at all.'

This, he thought, is a fairy tale without a point, without a moral. Certainly without a moral.

'Beautiful girl kisses frog. I'm afraid I'm still a frog.'

'And you can't have three wishes either,' she said, shuffling the pack with card-sharper's skill. 'It's a shame – isn't it? But I do feel as if I'd woken up,' he said.

Edmund felt starvingly hungry and rose, found his trousers and went into the cold kitchen where he opened a tin of soup and made some toast bringing it back to the fireside on a tray. She drank some of the soup, but left half of it for Tache, who had sat quietly by the fire throughout, only occasionally having to take evasive action from the flying feet and arms.

They made a makeshift bed, restacked the fire, and pinched out the candles. She tucked herself tidily up against him and they fell, both of them, into silence; warm, fairly comfortable, but somehow uncomforted, and from thence into an unsettled sleep. The snow slackened, the wind dropped, and all outside was quiet as the grave.

Not having slept on the floor for a good many years, Edmund woke that morning a bundle of bad-tempered cramps and aches, some of which he suspected had little to do with the hardness of the floor. A cold white lightness came through a crack in the curtains and Marianne was kneeling, fully dressed, by the fire, blowing hopefully on some kindling, raising a cloud of ash. She stood up when she saw he was awake.

'I've made us some breakfast – I'll bring it in. The power's back on again.'

Edmund found his clothes and tidied up the bedding. They were back to their polite communications of the day before, all possibility of anything more seemingly removed from the agenda. He felt that he had been one of those birthday presents women give to themselves in case no one else buys them what they want. 'A rather seedy, second-hand birthday present,' he thought on seeing himself in the bathroom mirror, unshaven and hair on end, with bags beneath his eyes. He rubbed a bruise on his elbow. The light was mercilessly hard. His alter ego suddenly kicked in: 'You ungrateful, self-pitying old has-been,' it said, 'you had a very nice time indeed. She's half your age and you are extremely lucky that she even looked at you.'

She returned with a tray piled with toast, coffee and marmalade. She had remade her face – it had returned to the blank geisha-girl mask, the 'I-speak-no-English' face that had so disconcerted him yesterday, held him back from searching for a definition of the person behind it. Someone was there, he was sure, but not his kind of someone, any more than he was hers.

'The road's been snow-ploughed and gritted. The Watkinses say it's not too bad at all to Swaffham, and almost clear after that. I think we should go soon.'

'You must have been awake for a long time.'

'I didn't sleep much. The cat kept shoving his whiskers into my face. I think he's starved of affection.'

'Like you and me, for instance?' he said, watching her eyes slide away from him. Edmund was confused by his own behaviour. Her motives seemed obscure and he was not sure that he wished to uncover them.

They drove back to London without incident and without any more than lightly general conversation, stopping as before in Newmarket. She treated the incident as never having occurred, which he thought was for the best. The further they travelled south, the less snow there was, and by the time they reached London there was none at all, which inclined him to think that he had invented the whole thing, so distanced did he feel from the previous night. Marianne dropped him off at his flat, offering her cheek to be kissed, which he did, thanking her for her help. He gave her a hopeless sort of hug.

'Good-bye, Marianne.'

She put her hand in her pocket and pulled out an envelope which he assumed was a Christmas card.

'You might like this.' He took it and waved, idiotically, as she drove away.

He let himself into his flat, still carrying his precious cargo of manuscripts, mission unaccomplished and aware that his trail had gone almost cold. The happenings of last night were a blurred fantasy which he had conjured up as one conjures up a fire, from tinderwood and dead twigs; all the accumulated desiccated matter that had hung around in his brain gone in one cleansing act of arson. In spite of a lingering hangover and in spite of the smell of the flat, which had risen rapturously to greet him on his arrival, he felt fresher, cleaner mentally. He pulled the card from his pocket, but saw that it had already been opened, and was addressed to Helen Strood. He sat down, winded with excitement. The writing bore a strong resemblance to Mimi's. He tore the card from its envelope and read:

Dearest Helen,

So sorry not have been in touch for so many months. The move went smoothly, and we are quite settled here now. Will see you very soon, I hope, and will relieve you of all my junk. Happy Christmas, lots of love, Mimi.

There was a PS: 'Here is the new address: Jarvis Cottage, Eeldyke, Romney Marsh, Kent' and a telephone number. 'I've lots to tell you, saving it for long letter in the New Year.'

He turned the card over, in amazement. It was hand-drawn in pen and ink, a gloriously triumphant little angel sitting in a tree, blowing a trumpet, delicately washed with blue and yellow watercolours.

7

Edmund did not call the number. He sat on the sofa, and, as if suddenly released from a sandbar by the turn of the tide, mentally sprinted for dry land. The sense of relief was dampened by a little splash of disappointment and he realized he had been enjoying the search itself. He needed to think hard before acting. If he rang the number, he might be told to put the papers in the post, and that would be that. Best to arrive on the doorstep.

That she lived barely four miles away from Johnnie and Xenia was a ludicrous coincidence. That she said in the card *'we're* quite settled' implied she was with someone, a husband probably, children most likely. He had always known she might have one – but he had to admit that he had been harbouring a sneaking, hackneyed Romantic vision of this woman, seeing himself arriving at her house as a knight errant, pulling up with a flourish and restoring her lost papers – she would of course have received him with loving gratitude.

It would be best to avoid involving Xenia, she had always shown impatience and boredom with the subject, and Johnnie too had not been interested in the slightest. He would keep the whole thing to himself from now on. He would be there on Friday night and could surely absent himself from the farm for an hour or two, for a long walk, or some other excuse, find her on his own and hand over the parcel.

He took out the yellow box of photographs again, and looked at the girl in the panama hat. She was what he wanted to remember about this odd phase of his life, not some greying, fatly-happy wife. Of course the photograph could be of Aunt Helen, although from Marianne's description he could not imagine that she would wear such a distinctly rakish panama; he imagined she would wear one of the garishly coloured coolie hats worn by the cardboard cut-out pin-up models advertising photographic film in chemists' shops in the 1950s.

Marianne rose up in his mind like a bubble. The card had obviously been amongst the others on the doormat, so why hadn't she given it to him at once? Perhaps she *had* planned to kidnap him for the night? He hadn't been good kidnapping material. He resolved to put his nose to the grindstone again, attend the scheduled book sales in Oxford on Tuesday, Tunbridge Wells on Thursday, assiduously hunt for desirable volumes in houses in Hampstead and try not to think of, nor read any more of, Mimi Anderson, or Fleury, or Taylor. He remembered her name was Miranda on the marriage lines in the parish register, Imim in her earliest persona. How many more names had she got? Unless Helen knew two people by the name of Mimi, but no, the handwriting had emphatically been the same on the card as on the papers. It was as if she had set out to cause confusion as soon as she was old enough to put pen to paper. And her mother, Syrie Anderson, Connaught Marvel's daughter. She had been a writer of short stories under the pen-name of McGinnis – one of those writers of great promise who had sunk into obscurity in the 1960s.

While Edmund was trying so hard to rein in his imagination and put all his energies into his work, Xenia was in a fury of suspicion. She camouflaged this under a heavy battery of smiles, force-feeding Johnnie enormous and delicious meals, polishing all his father's furniture into a state of shock. She kept up an unsubtle surveillance operation, asking aloud, while folding sheets with Rosy Pressing, where on earth Johnnie could have got to, he'd been so late for lunch, so long at the fair, so held up at the market, and Rosy's lack of response to these questionings she had taken as an admission of knowledge followed by dumb insolence. Rosy had been unfooled by the apparent casualness of the interrogation, and of course sussed that something was up; which suspicion she passed on to her brother's sister-in-law in the village shop.

On finding Johnnie's work-gloves on the kitchen table after he'd left to go and check on the sitting of a new footbridge over a dyke, she had made a special trip, trailing the labrador along with her, to where he had said he would be. He had been astonished to see her coming bravely through the drenching rain, a good mile from the house, and even more astounded by her errand.

'But darling, how kind of you. But I keep another pair in the Land Rover.'

'Oh, I just thought you might need them, and anyway, the dog and I both needed a walk. He's getting very fat.'

Lucky Ovenden had observed her at an upstairs window, peering through binoculars, and wondered uneasily if she were checking up on him, although he had merely been standing in the yard with the vet, having an invigorating exchange of views about badgers.

When Johnnie attended his annual get-together with fellow-golfers at an hotel in Parden, she had telephoned reception, asking him to ring her back over an unbelievably minor problem that could perfectly well have waited until he returned.

She patrolled the wintry lanes, particularly past Amelia's

cottage, and one late morning appeared in the Eeldyke pub, having spotted the Land Rover outside. She found Johnnie sitting quietly in the window seat with his pint, alone, apart from Phylly, who was furiously knitting a pink teddy-bear for her grandchild.

'I saw you through the window,' she announced, perching nonchalantly on a stool. 'I really felt like a drink, and thought how nice it would be to join you.'

He was a little amazed, particularly when she knocked back the gin and tonic he bought her and announced that they had both better be getting back for lunch. As it was only twelve fifteen and lunch was always at one, he felt a bit miffed. He liked to sit on his own, passing the time of day with Seth or Phylly, or just thinking about things . . . Amelia in particular.

In spite of not getting so much as a whiff of anything untoward, she was not reassured. On Wednesday morning she drove into Canterbury to complete her Christmas shopping, hoping her toes would not start hurting and hating to abandon Johnnie to his own devices, which freedom she was convinced would be abused. Avoiding groups of noisy French teenagers ganging up and down St Peter's Street and disregarding the charming group of musicians playing carols in the Buttermarket, she bought Johnnie two exorbitantly expensive jerseys, which he did not need, and a Liberty's red and blue silk dressing gown. Each Christmas they usually wrote out modest lists of things they would like for Christmas, exchanged the lists and then chose things from them for each other. This ensured little excitement on Christmas Day, but no nasty surprises either. After she had bought the dressing gown, she suddenly remembered the list in her bag, and bought him the new pair of secateurs that he wanted. Feeling a little calmer at having disposed of so much money, she headed for Marks and Spencer to buy her niece Hatty a pretty silky nightdress.

*　　*　　*

'Hello! Xenia!'

She looked up from the stand where hung sheaves of sugared-almond coloured nightdresses, and there stood Allie Snodland, arms festooned with artificial satin slips and lacy knickers.

'Allie! I haven't seen you for ages.' The standard greeting, whether one had met three months or three weeks before, signifying neglect on the part of the one addressed.

'Shall we pay for these and go and have a little something together? Or have you had lunch?' asked Allie. 'That is, if you've finished your shopping?'

Xenia felt quite tired, and the idea was tempting. She needed to talk to someone. They queued to pay and then headed for a small café round behind the Cathedral precincts which served delicious little fruit tartlets.

'No smoking here, I see,' said Allie crossly, replacing her packet and gold lighter in a tiny leather bag. 'Oh well! I shall just have to have two cakes instead of one. I'm sure that's why they ban smoking in these places – it makes one eat twice as much.' She ran her fingers through her faded blonde hair with a gesture of mock-resignation. She had not aged nearly so well as Xenia, was over-plump and had let her hands get quite coarse with fanatical gardening; the nails, haphazardly decorated with bright red polish, were split and stained. She sipped her coffee and looked at Xenia with an expression of affection, while thinking that she looked a bit peaky and anxious. She leant forward, bulging out of the small green velvet-seated chair.

'Now tell me all the news, Xen darling. You weren't at Smudgie's birthday luncheon last week – I was so disappointed. I was sure you'd be there?'

'I was . . .' said Xenia, desperately trying to think how she could have missed the lunch – she must telephone Smudgie and apologize – '. . . dreadfully busy – shooting lunches two weekends running, Christmas coming – you know how it is. It must have gone clean out of my mind.'

Allie knew that to Xenia a shooting lunch was like preparing a picnic for a couple of toddlers, and raised her eyebrows. Xenia really did look rattled. Allie probed and prised, poured more coffee, extracting the cause as a dentist draws a tooth. She had much experience in men's inability to control themselves and sensed that a soothing hand was needed.

'But you poor thing . . . of course, you must be worried sick.' She put one earth-stained hand on top of Xenia's immaculately manicured fingers and with the other forked up her second fruit tart. 'But are you really certain? Amelia Sailor isn't exactly the glamour-puss, is she? Hardly Johnnie's type, I would have thought. But of course, there was all that scandal about her husband Nick . . . I used to get along with her well enough at school, but she never struck *me* as being a femme fatale, although I did hear rumours that she was mixed up with some young man . . . not long after Nick died as a matter of fact.' She looked smug, having neatly contradicted her previous soothing words.

'I can't bear it! Poor Edmund says he's met her, and he's sure there's nothing in it – but you know how they all stick together. He's been off on some ridiculous romantic hunt for some woman called Mimi Anderson or something. All the way up to Norfolk to find her. It's been Mimi this, Mimi that for weeks . . . very boring, and he simply doesn't understand how much I need his support . . .' Xenia broke off as part of Allie's announcement sank in. She stared at Allie, dumbstruck. 'You were at school with Amelia?'

'Yes, at St Cecilia's. But Xenia, Mimi . . .'

Xenia interrupted. 'No, tell me all about this Amelia!'

Allie forgot what it was she had been going to say, and put her mind to recalling her days at St Cecilia's.

'Well, she was quite pretty, I suppose, and rather vague.

Her parents were abroad, I think, like so many of us. Daddy was in the Army and we kept on moving about, so I got sent back. It's a convent you know, such sweet nuns . . .'

'About Amelia?' reminded Xenia irritably. 'Know thine enemy' said a little voice in her head, though how school reminiscences would help her to de-escalate Johnnie's interest in the woman, she had no idea.

'I can't remember that much. She was good at art, used to do all the posters for plays and things. Oh, and she was one of those irritating people who never get caught. She used to get the gardener to buy her fags, and smoke in the woods, and go into Hastings by bus to see films we weren't allowed to see. That sort of thing.'

Xenia sat and digested all this unwelcome news. Allie continued: 'But, I was going to tell you before. Xenia, Amelia Sailor *is* Mimi Anderson. That's what she was called at school. I don't know when she dropped the silly nickname.'

Xenia let out a growl of rage and despair. Both the men in her life after the same woman! But Edmund could not know that it was the same person – or he wouldn't have had to chase off up to Norfolk. Did Johnnie know that Edmund was after her too? Perhaps they were already sharing her? She couldn't take in the implications of this. The horrible little trollop was obviously after anything in trousers. And the wretched woman had been invited to her Boxing Day party!

'I do wish I hadn't told you,' she said to Allie, 'I didn't mean to bore you with all this.'

Allie was not the least bit bored, she was riveted. And so were the other customers sitting near by. Xenia and Allie both had loud voices, and even their whispers had a penetrating audibility at the next table. Poor Xenia, it did not occur to her to use Edmund's interest in Mimi-Amelia to head off Johnnie's infatuation. And sadly it never occurred to her either to confront Johnnie with her suspicions. She had nothing in the way of evidence to confront him with. Allie was getting very interested indeed. Xenia, so elegant, so in control of her life, so slim, sitting white and angry in front of her, her coffee half drunk, her dear little cake uneaten . . . 'May I? Oh thanks. I do get so hungry when I'm shopping, and there was no time for a proper lunch . . . but darling Xen, I'm sure all this will blow over. Johnnie would never be so blatant and unfeeling.'

'It happened once before,' said Xenia doggedly, 'only I never actually caught him. It was going on though. I know it was . . .' She stopped.

Allie was unable to winkle out of her with whom and when, and gave up, thinking wistfully of her comfortable drawing room at her house in Chillingden, where she could put her feet up, and perhaps have one or two of those chocolate Bath Olivers which she had intended to keep for Christmas. Anyway, Xenia had been delightfully indiscreet, quite uncharacteristically so. Their younger sons both being at the same school, she would probably see Xenia at the end of term carol service on Friday. Then she could inspect Johnnie for herself to see if he bore the marks of an adulterer.

'Don't breathe a word, will you?' said Xenia again as they left the café together, causing some annoyance as crackling carrier bags bumped and jostled the other seated customers, their shoulder bags swinging indiscriminately and scattering little packets of sugar and teaspoons as they went.

Xenia drove home too fast, shooting a red light, and worrying for at least five miles that she could hear police sirens wailing after her. The road dipped down, running for a while beside the River Stour, past flooded water meadows, old water mills and ancient moated farmsteads, but she was not looking at the scenery. She was excruciatingly aware that she should never have disclosed her problem to Allie. But Allie had never appeared indiscreet, or had she? They'd not seen so much of each other since their children were older, but they frequented the same dinner party circuit, the same lunches, joined up parties for Glyndebourne. Was it Allie who had whispered to her once that something was going on between Jim Pierce-Hadstock and that sly-looking Anna Strachan? Oh God! She feared it was. What had she done? She slowed down on the outskirts of Parden, stopping to go to the supermarket. Aware of her overspending on the Christmas presents for Johnnie, she stuck rigidly to her list, not being tempted to right or left as she passed up and down the aisles with a wayward trolley, all wheels bent on going round and round in circles.

Once at home she hid her presents away in the bottom of the landing cupboard, where she had always hidden them and where everyone knew they were secreted. She took a paracetamol tablet and lay down on her bed, her head throbbing. She could think no further than trying to keep her men away from Amelia. Edmund would hardly be likely to bump into her while he stayed with them over this weekend, but he would see her at the drinks party. She could however keep him pretty busy handing around drinks and food, could make sure he was introduced to other people, led away from her. She tried to remember what else was happening this weekend that she had to take care of. Rupert's carol service, then bringing him home for the holidays. Henry back on Monday from Manchester. She had to prevent Edmund and Johnnie going down to the pub together, they might meet Amelia. She looked like the sort of woman who spent time in pubs, undoubtedly ensnaring other unsuspecting married men. She must plan carefully. And where *was* Johnnie at this moment? There had been no sign of his having come in to lunch when she'd looked in at the

kitchen. And she'd left him such a dear little pigeon casserole.

She couldn't lie here forever. She got up and changed
her skirt and went down to the drawing room to light
the fire, pausing to rearrange the Christmas cards on the
scarlet ribbons that hung vertically in rows on either side
of the fireplace. She then sat opening a new batch that
had arrived after she'd left for Canterbury. One from Uncle
Serge in Paris. Just a plain white card embossed in gold with
'*Joyeux Nöel et Bonne Année*' – a bit dull, but then the French
didn't care for Christmas the way the English did. One from
Allie, one from Amelia and Josie. She inspected this very
thoroughly, holding it with distaste. It was home-made, on
thick drawing paper, torn, not cut straight around the edges,
and showed an angel sitting in a tree with a trumpet. It was
drawn in black with blue and yellow watercolour carelessly
splashed over the robe and wings. She nearly threw it on
the fire, but on second thoughts pinned the card right at
the bottom of the ribbon, where it dangled unseen behind
the log-basket, and she felt her eyes and nose fill with tears.
Her whole life was becoming untidy, unravelling round the
cuffs, and her beloveds were blowing away from her, like
ten-pound notes in the wind.

Johnnie found her at teatime in the kitchen in the midst
of an orgy of whisked egg whites, bowls of creams and
custards spread out over the kitchen table, small saucepans
of melting chocolate and of caramelizing sugar on the stove,
dishes of toasted almonds and chopped candied peel on
the worktops. There was a smell of vanilla in the air. He
took a deep breath of it, and furtively nobbled a couple of
almonds.

'Shall I make the tea, as you're busy? It all looks very
scrumptious.'

'No! No! I'll do it! It's the ice-creams for Christmas.
I've got to get everything done in advance.' She wiped

her fingers distractedly on her skirt and rushed to take a saucepan off the stove, switched on the kettle and laid out a tea-tray, while continuing to dash back and forth between chocolate pan and eggs, whisking a bit here, blending a bit there, finding teaspoons and measuring tea into the pot with such speed that Johnnie felt queasy.

'Slow down, slow down! Let it all wait and come and have some tea.'

'I can't, I can't! There's so much to do. I'm nearly there.'

She combined several bowls and continued whisking the contents together as if driven by some alien force, splashing cream on to herself and all over the table. Johnnie took the tray and went off to the drawing room. The fire had gone out, and there were torn opened envelopes all over the floor. He looked for the newspaper and found only the front pages which were in the log-basket. She must have used today's paper for lighting the fire, he thought, uneasily, since such disasters did not normally occur.

'You've burnt the crossword,' he said when she eventually put in an appearance. 'And you've got custard on your chin.' He leant forward to chuck it away, but she shied back.

'So what have you been up to all day, apart from the ice-creams?' he asked, making an effort to try and draw her out.

'Christmas shopping,' she replied, almost curtly.

'That sounds like fun. Have you got everything now? I'm still waiting for those books we ordered for Henry.'

She did not reply, but sat cradling her teacup and staring at him suspiciously.

'You didn't eat the pigeon casserole.'

'No, I didn't have time to get back. I had a sandwich at the Woolpack.'

She could surely not be cross because he hadn't come back for lunch, when she hadn't even been there herself?

He shrugged and gave up; her edginess came as a shock after the over-eager desire to please which she had displayed during the last few days, and baffled him. Most unsettling. He wondered if it might be the wrong time of the month, but had never detected much change in her behaviour at these times before, apart from an irrational desire to scrub the kitchen floor herself, when she could perfectly well leave it to Rosy. Perhaps everything would calm down a bit when Edmund came down for the weekend, she was more relaxed when he was about. He had no Christmas shopping to do, having always left everything to her, apart from her own present of course, and that was in hand. When he had dropped in on Amelia that morning she had shown him the gold waiting to be transformed, and promised to have it ready by next week. He definitely still felt the same way about her – but was happy enough with the way things were, for the time being. Although she was neither encouraging nor dismissive, he enjoyed spending a few minutes with her, an hour here, once a week, once a fortnight, it didn't matter. He knew he would succeed in the end. The possibility of something more satisfying developing was enjoyable in itself; he was a hopeful traveller and was taking pleasure in the scenery en route.

However Xenia travelled badly. She was in any case a static person, deeply planted in her marriage and all that entailed – the children, who were ceasing to be children, the big house and its garden. She was frightened of venturing outside it. She was at this moment a sealed and overturned beehive of buzzing worries. Her energies had been perhaps unimaginatively directed at times, but who but a truly creative person could have summoned up an image of a burning, passionate affair out of such a gentle and well-behaved flirtation? Who could have been so mistrustful in the face of such minuscule evidence? Her intellect had been stunted because she suffered from an anorexia of the brain, refusing to allow it to be fed, nervous of the ridicule which she was certain would follow her admissions of ignorance, refusing to take an interest in any but the most superficial of arguments.

8

The brooding clouds which had hung over the Marsh all day began to shift as a northeasterly wind rose up, rustling the sedges and rattling the elder twigs. Lights were appearing along with the evening stars in the darkening dampness. They sparkled in the necklace of villages hung around the ancient inner shoreline, shone out singly in the empty expanse below. People were returning from work, putting on their kettles, lighting their fires, preparing their teas. Herds were milked, chickens and geese locked up against mink and fox, curtains were drawn, televisions switched on. Amelia shivered at the sudden change of temperature as she emerged from her warm workshop. Between the willows she could see the dumpy illuminated caterpillar that was the Marsh train riding along the causeway across the flatness, on its way to Hastings. She went to the washing line and felt the still-wet socks and sheets, and left them to take their chances in the wind, gliding back over the damp grass into the cottage. Josie would be home soon, so she busied herself with tidying up and washing dishes, having left all the housework till after she had completed her day's schedule of sawing, soldering and polishing. The hair dryer lay on one of the worktops and she switched it on, blow-dusting the row of glasses that sat on top of the cupboards, thinking that that alone was worth a mention in a slut's handbook. She had been relieved that Johnnie had not stayed long enough to become a pressing presence. He had seemed quite happy just watching her, and she was glad of this since she was so acutely physically lonely at times that a move in her direction would have been hard to repel.

Her sitting room was low-ceilinged, a small square room which had been the kitchen when the house was built, and in it she and Josie had put all their favourite things from their old house, so that it was full to bursting with unlikely objects and bright colours – a snug cave in which to lurk during the winter months. A wallful of books, arranged by subject or category, the dividing lines between biography and history, modern novels and anthropology, travel and gardening being drawn by a stuffed owl, a *famille verte* teapot, a box of Kleenex, a copper lustre jug, Amelia's silver christening mug and a deed-box with a broken lock. It was easier, when asked the whereabouts of the *Dictionary of Quotations*, to shout out 'Beside the cotton-reel box!' than 'Second shelf on the right-hand side, about halfway along.' There were pictures on the walls not taken up with the giant fireplace and the window: an early nineteenth-century naive portrait of a child in a low-cut white dress and a coral necklace, a painting of Amelia's of a girl riding a zebra, an architectural study of the interior of St Eanswith's church, a print of an Edward Lear landscape of the Lebanon mountains. All were framed identically in plain broad gold.

The walls were painted a soft pumpkin colour and the floor was covered by a large scarlet, blue and golden-green kelim. The curtains, cut down from the size needed to curtain the huge windows of the old house, were of faded thundercloud-blue velvet, sewn round the borders with a pattern of pearl buttons. On her desk, Amelia kept three brass globes, inscribed with intersecting lines and Arabic script – parts of an astronomical device of some sort, she had been told. She and Josie professed to believe they had magical properties, touching them when fate had been tempted, as people touch wood. They were also dented in places where Josie had once played bowls with them on the lawn when she was six. When she sat at her desk, Amelia used Nick's grandfather's country Chippendale chair, of walnut with a tapestry seat, and she placed her feet on a Stony George – a brown pottery hot-water bottle which she remembered using as a child before her mother had introduced the rubber variety. They had been gratefully discarded then, since they slipped out of the bed at night with a crash, waking up not only the user but the rest of the household.

The coal was kept in a green-painted fire bucket and the wood in an old copper boiler – polished to mirror status, reflecting the patterns of the kelim in its pink-gold silken surface. There were two scarlet painted wooden chairs on either side of the tip-up mahogany breakfast table where Josie sat and did her homework in the evenings, and Amelia drew or sewed. They had decided to put all their best things into one room since scattering them about the house had given such a meagre effect, Amelia having sold or farmed out so many of their other possessions. There was another small room on the ground floor, apart from the sitting room and kitchen, but in the winter it was very dark, and there were damp-stains on the walls, and both of them felt uneasy in there. It would once have been the parlour, with a bright fire burning in the grate and polished chairs for receiving visitors, but now they had filled it with packing cases and empty boxes and things broken but waiting to be mended when there was time to do so.

Amelia tidied up the newspapers and books, straightened the rug, ran a duster over the table and returned to the kitchen to make the tea. The cat lay on its back by the stove, its fluffy stomach exposed, daring her to tickle it. She stood and rubbed it absent-mindedly with her foot, rereading a letter from the bank. She was overdrawn, and would she kindly deposit enough funds immediately to cover the discrepancy. They were, she noticed with considerable annoyance, charging her twenty pounds for the privilege of being informed of this. She would have to telephone them and have a little shout, since she had two days before paid in a cheque which should see them into the New Year. And there was the money coming from Johnnie for the bracelet for his wife. She was still not sure whether the commission had come because he felt sorry for her, or because it was intended as a guilt-assuaging device for Xenia. But the poor man was not really guilty of anything. But then, she remembered, grinning, she had known what was on his mind. At school they had been taught that an evil thought was almost as bad as the sin itself, and she wondered if his conscience was quite clear. The cat yawned monstrously, showing all its dangerous needle fangs, and Amelia remembered the agonies of some of the girls at school when writing out a list of their sins for confession, for, in spite of it being an Anglican convent, they had all been made to attend confession the day before their confirmations. She had herself spent at least half an hour on her list, decided that she would hold everyone up in a queue if she went through them all and scrubbed out at least half her misdemeanours and laxities, not waiting for absolution. Was uprooting carrots in the convent vegetable patch gluttony or theft? She'd spent an anxious night worrying that she might have caught a disease from the pond water in which she had rinsed off the mud. And was sitting behind the curtains in the hall window seat secretly reading yet another banned book slothful, or was it something worse? Children had such an easy time of it now that most of the seven deadly sins had been transformed into matters of personal choice or 'rights', the majority of them being actively encouraged as a means of self-expression.

She heard Josie's footsteps running up the path, and the cat leapt to its feet in fright as the girl hurtled through the door, throwing her bag to the floor and asking all at once if tea was ready and was the man with the long hair and the deerhound actually living near here?

'Yes, to the first,' said Amelia, 'and I don't know what you're talking about to the second.'

'Well, it's a beautiful shaggy dog, and the man has long hair, plaited down the back like in the eighteenth century, tied with black ribbon – a queue I think it's called, and I've seen him twice before, walking past at the weekend. I saw him again just now as I got off the bus.'

'Darling Jo, calm down and pour the tea – have a bun.'

'OK, but he is *gorgeous*! How does one get to meet people like that?'

'Well, I suppose you could stand at the gate, and smile sweetly at him as he passes, or you could try dropping your handkerchief, or pretending you are lost . . .'

'No! Seriously!'

'You could ask at the Post Office . . . Do you mean to say that Ruffles hasn't found out who he is?'

'I did ask her, but she hasn't a clue. She lives even more out in the sticks than we do – she'd not seen him at all. But she's on the look-out now.'

'What's happened to Mikey? I thought *he* was man of the moment?'

'I did use to think he had this interesting mouth, and he has got a motorbike,' said Josie, eating her second bun and putting a second spoonful of sugar in her tea, 'but he'll be off to university in September, doing engineering, so it's not worth getting involved, is it? Oh well, I suppose I shall have to start going for walks as well. When does it start to get lighter in the evenings?'

'After the twenty-second, I think, that's the solstice. But winter's only just begun.'

'I can't wait for the summer then, all those long evenings after school, sitting out in the garden. I *loathe* the winter. I seem to spend all my time waiting for buses and lifts and freezing to death.'

'You could try wearing a coat.'

'But my coat is so awful.'

'I'm sorry, darling. It'll just have to do this year.'

Josie leant against the stove, then held on to the rail and bobbed up and down in a series of cursory pliés.

'Are my thighs getting fat, do you think?'

'No, they look the same as they did yesterday to me,' said Amelia, seriously inspecting them. 'What shall we have for supper, do you think?'

'I'll make it tonight. We could have a beautiful omelette and finish up all those bantam eggs. The woman at the farmshop says they've gone off lay now, and there won't be any more till it starts getting lighter. And I could do an apple crumble? School lunch was totally disgusting today – what they call curry, only it's sweet with horrid fat sultanas in it, like rabbit droppings.'

Amelia was pleased with the offer, and went back to the sitting room to read, until it was time for the six o'clock news. Josie went upstairs to change, and play a tape that had been lent to her. 'Liquid lady . . . shady lady . . . all I need is you . . . ooo . . .' she warbled, throwing her school skirt into the corner and putting on leggings and two pairs of socks. 'Admit it Sadie . . . you know deep down, you wan' it too . . . oo.' She stood by her window, opened it a crack and lit a cigarette, puffing the smoke out into the dark. There was no hedge in front of the house and she had a clear view of the lane, so she would surely see him, even in the darkness, as he walked back with his dog.

Mikey's motorbike was a serious attraction, the answer to getting out and about when marooned on the Marsh without a driving licence. But the young man with the plaited hair, a bit old hat, perhaps, but what a perfect face, and what long legs. Probably a bit pretentious. But he'd had a wonderful leather jacket, and his jeans were a good cut . . . She finished the cigarette and opened the window further, flinging it as far away as she could.

'Direct hit!' called out a voice, and a shadowy figure waved at her, walking past without slowing down. She nearly leapt out of her skin. Well, that was one way of making contact. She'd scored a hit with the butt, but he wouldn't be able to see her in the dark. She closed the window softly and went downstairs to start her homework.

Amelia was kneeling on a cushion by the fire, her book on her lap, a favoured reading position. She had taken Geoffrey of Monmouth's *History of the Kings of Britain* from where it had been resting beside the stuffed owl, and was now deep into the story of King Lier and his daughters.

'Mum?' Amelia did not appear to hear. 'Mum? Amelia!'

Amelia started and looked up anxiously, her hair in her eyes. Josie had had to resort to her Christian name in an effort to attract her attention. Shock tactics were needed when she was immersed in a book, when she went into a semi-conscious state and appeared to be oblivious of everything else.

'Sorry, what is it?'

'Do you still think about Dad a lot?'

'Not a lot . . . just regularly. I've got over the stage of thinking of things I want to tell him. It's more when I'm reminded of things we did together.'

'He *was* ill, wasn't he?'

'If you mean he wouldn't have left us if he hadn't been

ill, I don't know. There were some things he couldn't face – like loss of face itself.'

'It isn't hereditary, is it? Like cystic fibrosis?'

'Darling! Of course it isn't. He was going through a very bad time in his life, and he just couldn't cope.'

'He left us to cope, though, didn't he? Do you think he thought of that?'

'No, I don't think he did. What he did, he did on the spur of the moment.'

Amelia could never be sure if she was answering truthfully. She did not know if he had planned it. And if he had – for how long? He had been inscrutable, those last few weeks, as if he was gradually disengaging himself from them. But had that been intentional? She did not know, or want to know any more. But she understood that Josie still needed to talk about her father, and it was her job to listen, to reassure where possible, and field the questions as honestly as she could.

The relationship between father and daughter had been regularly punctuated by skirmishes, but just as Amelia had been inclined to think that one more sniper's bullet would ensure all-out war, they had suddenly resumed their normal protective father/loving daughter roles and Amelia, who had initially intervened and tried to keep the peace, realized that the bickering, teasing and snapping was more often than not initiated by Josie as if she were a cat sharpening her claws on a tree trunk – and that these sharp rows were somehow necessary to both her and her father, and that they both enjoyed the process.

Josie seemed satisfied for the moment and started on her essay on gang warfare in sixteenth-century Florence, writing furiously for a minute or two, then sighing and running her fingers through her hair and twisting the little gold sleepers round and round in her earlobes. Amelia read another few pages. Geoffrey's Lier had a far more honourable demise than Shakespeare's Lear; in this version Cordelia too was dealt a better hand, becoming Queen of Britain before eventually being imprisoned by her nephews and killing herself out of grief at the loss of her kingdom. Amelia wondered why Shakespeare had changed the story, at least as far as Cordelia was concerned. Things were becoming confusing again, with lists of kings with unlikely names rampaging across the pages – Cunedagius, Rivallo, Gurgustius, Sisillius and Jago.

'Mum?'

This time Amelia was more alert, her interest in Geoffrey of Monmouth waning.

'If Dad hadn't killed himself – would you and he still be together?'

'God help me!' thought Amelia, then aloud, 'I can't possibly know. I suppose that it is possible not, but, on the other hand, I think we probably would be.'

'That's very evasive. What does it mean?'

'It means that *I* never considered leaving your father before he died.'

'Ah.'

'What exactly is worrying you, Josie?'

'I'm not worried. There's no point in worrying about something that has already happened, is there? It's just that it is a year and a half now, and I still don't understand what went wrong.'

'Neither do I. Nick used to get muddled himself, sometimes.'

'We will manage, won't we?'

'Yes, we will. We've managed so far. Things can only get better.'

That was tempting fate with a vengeance. She suppressed the urge to leap up and touch the golden globes on the desk.

'Do you get lonely, Mum?'

'Yes. But I've got you with me and that helps a lot. I've also got good friends.'

'I won't be here forever.'

'I know that,' said Amelia, sliding her wedding ring up and down on her finger. She must have lost weight, it was quite loose.

'I'll go and start the supper now,' said Josie, who had written no more than one paragraph. 'Crumble first, and get that in the oven. Then the omelette. Are there any chives left, or have they been frosted?'

'No, I've got some under a cloche. And thyme, I like fresh thyme in omelettes.' Amelia laid down her book and stretched. On the one hand she was glad that Josie wanted to get at the truth and not construct an arbour of glorification around her father. History woven into myth, embroidered with fairy tale and fantasy, a pattern of Chinese whispers based on an already misinterpreted and misunderstood story.

'Only two or three more hours to get through,' thought Amelia, 'then I can go to bed and lie safe.' She would drift as usual, plotting the likely course of their futures, working out stratagems for improving things, and having her usual daydreams of fame and fortune, and more recently and urgently, sex.

That night Josie awoke from a nightmare in which she had been standing at the bottom of a Martello-like tower, only it was taller, seeming to stretch up into the air forever, and her mother had called out to her from the top window, before throwing herself out, falling in slow motion like a dummy in a film, cartwheeling through the air before crashing limply to the ground at her feet. She went weeping into Amelia's room, feeling urgently for her in the bed in the dark to make sure she was still there.

'Sweetheart, don't, don't cry so. You are safe. Get into

bed with me.' Amelia held her close, rocking her like a baby, and Josie eventually slept. But Amelia did not. In her mind's eye, her brain was a small shining globe, and thoughts moved through it as drifting dead leaves, from top to bottom, slowly and gracefully side-slipping as she tried to catch them. At other times the thoughts flew past fast across the space, from left to right, like swallows, and were as difficult to trap as the leaves. Her memory had become very selective after Nick's death, refusing to file anything that did not refer to some immediate need or activity. It was not so much that things were not retained, but that her retrieval system failed her when it came to finding the right file. She tried to recall her own father who had died when she was three – and could only summon up the itchy feel of his tweed jacket on her bare legs as he held her in his arms, and the stale male tobacco smell.

When Nick had died, she had woken up into a nightmare, not awoken from one; having, she thought, dreamed her way through life till then, through men, husband, work, baby, never really aware of happiness until the moment was past, whereas the unhappinesses had always been in the present tense. Josie, only seventeen, had everything to come. But what was 'everything'? She hoped that the nightmares would eventually cease. Josie had not told her what she had dreamt, but Amelia could imagine it to have been traumatic enough.

After Josie left for school the next morning, looking fresh and pink, Amelia went outside to collect the washing, hollow-eyed and paler than usual. The clothes had frozen stiff, making them impossible to fold up. The air was very still and the cold crept like corrosion up her nostrils and into her brain. The warmer, damper lull in the weather had been brief. A cotton nightdress gave a creaking warning of intent to shatter like a pane of glass as she tried to manoeuvre it into a more manageable shape. 'Men are launching probes into outer space and I still have to do the washing by hand. What I need is a mangle, not the Internet.' She carried the unwieldy pile into the house, where everything stood up straight on the floor, empty ghost shapes of jeans, socks and board-like pillowcases, refusing all attempts to bend them over the towel rail. The technological world had passed her by.

However she could afford a Christmas tree and would drop in at the farm shop to order one for next week – Josie would spend hours refurbishing the tatty little collection that had survived from Amelia's childhood, mending the hangers on the coloured glass balls, restringing little circles of beads. She put her gloves on, picked up the axe from behind the door and went out to split the logs. Her least favourite task, particularly in this cold, since she was always frightened that she might injure herself in a moment's inattention, but it was quite satisfying watching the wood cleave neatly down the middle, then again, making four out of one, filling the barrow steadily, but she was out of breath, unfit. She must give up smoking.

'Would you like some help with that?' said a voice from behind the threadbare hedge. She nearly sliced her foot off, and called out nervously, 'Who's that?', unable to see clearly through the scrappy hawthorn and privet. The figure moved down and came in through the lower gate, a tall young man with a deerhound in tow. Amelia could not immediately see if his hair was in a pigtail but she suspected it was, there not being so very many deerhounds kept on Romney Marsh.

'I'm Will Redding, Mrs Redding's grandson, from the house by the bridge,' he explained, holding out his hand.

Amelia relaxed her grip on the axe, and held out hers. 'I'm Amelia Sailor.'

'I know. I met a friend of yours, Mary Beaton, Dr Beaton.'

Amelia was thinking that she would love someone to take over the log-splitting, but couldn't really afford to pay anyone to do what she could do for herself, if she put her mind to it, but he saw the doubt on her face and said quickly, 'When I said "help", I really meant it.' He held out his hand for the axe, and grinned most engagingly. 'If you hold Cosima for me, I'll get it done in no time at all.'

So she relinquished the axe; angels did not appear too frequently on the Marsh, and this young man had every appearance of one, so she put faith before suspicion and went to put on the kettle, taking Cosima with her. The cat spat and hissed a great deal as Cosima lay like a heraldic hound before the stove. The sun came out, bright but mean on heat, and Will worked fast, splitting up two barrow-loads and filling the copper for her before coming indoors and having the coffee. She found out that he was house-sitting for his grandmother who was in hospital, that he had a degree in environmental sciences but had been unable to find a job since graduating last summer, and was now working part-time at a local garden centre.

'I spend more time selling garden ornaments, upmarket gnomes in fake stone, and goldfish than in dealing with plants. It's very dull.'

She sympathized with him, thinking what a vast improvement he was on poor Mikey. Thanking him, she invited him to drop in for a drink next time, when Josie would be at home.

On Friday afternoon Johnnie and Xenia set out to collect Rupert from school and attend the carol service. Xenia was wearing the red jacket with silver buttons, and Johnnie thought she looked pretty good. She had renewed her bright smile with scarlet lipstick and was wearing her strong, 'I'm-in-control' expression. They found Rupert in a state of lyrical excitement, leaping about his dormitory like a ten-year-old.

'Where's your friend Foxy?' asked Xenia, noticing that the bed next to Rupert's was already stripped down, and all signs of him removed. 'I've got your grown-out-of jacket here for him.'

Rupert assumed a serious look. 'I'm afraid he won't need it now.'

'What do you mean? I told his mother I'd hand it over at the end of term.'

'He's been given the heave-ho. He left yesterday.'

'No! But why?'

'He got drunk and climbed up the Christmas tree in the Buttermarket, but he fell off, and brought all the lights and things down with him.'

'Well, I'm not surprised he's been expelled then. I suppose the school had to pay for them to be replaced? You weren't involved in this, I hope?'

'Me? Never! If I'd climbed up the tree I wouldn't have fallen off.' Xenia and Johnnie shot glances at each other, but carried on with getting their son's trunk and other bits and pieces into the car, before walking together through the precincts to the Cathedral, taking the narrow little passage, so hideously haunted, known as The Dark Entry.

It was quite astonishing, thought Johnnie, how the pupils, in their stiffly formal uniforms of winged collars and black jackets with striped Victorian shop-assistant trousers or skirts, managed to look so wildly unhomogeneous when grouped together. Rupert had left his parents and joined a gangling, shuffling, bulging, wriggling mass, drifting untidily into their seats in the nave. Generation upon generation upon generation had been educated there, first by monks, then by priests, and now, for the most part, by laity.

The lights were extinguished and silence fell, the congregation ceasing their rustling and whispering. A cool, clear boy's voice soared out of the darkness, sending shivers down spines.

> 'In the bleak mid-winter.
> Frosty wind made moan . . .'

Christina Rossetti's ice-like words floated above their heads as if bringing the weather indoors with them, chilling those snugly seated in the warm interior. Then a single candle was lit, followed by others as the service of nine lessons and carols commenced, and the soloist was joined by the choir and the other participants, with increasing volume and enthusiasm as the service progressed, till the sounds filled the high golden vaulted spaces above with exultant joy, rattling the stained glass.

'Joy at being let out of school,' thought Johnnie cynically, able to smell the suppressed anarchic excitement amongst the pupils, the restless thrumming of energy as they sang their hearts out. Glorious descants climbed up out of reach into the Bell Harry Tower, surely stirring the bones of the Black Prince lying dustily beneath his gilded effigy and accoutrements in the Trinity chapel.

Then, almost too soon for Johnnie, but not soon enough for the pupils, it was all over. The choir and priests processed and the congregation rose to its feet, smiling self-consciously with emotion, twitching scarves, buttoning up overcoats, searching for gloves. Allie Snodland sat two rows back from Xenia and Johnnie and barged her way forwards as they passed down the aisle, pouncing on them.

'Hello! Xen, Johnnie!' she exclaimed enthusiastically, beaming, with much uplifting of eyebrows and enquiring looks at Xenia, as if to say, 'And how is the old man behaving?' Her own husband, a small and bumptious man whom Johnnie loathed, dressed in an overlarge and important navy-blue cashmere overcoat, clapped him on the shoulder, as high as he could reach, and started to talk loudly, before they had even emerged from the Cathedral, about a forthcoming skiing holiday with his family.

'What, not going this year? What a shame!' He and Allie and the boys were off straight after Christmas for two weeks, he babbled on and on, till Johnnie, a polite smile fixed to his lips and the carols still echoing beautifully in his ears, felt like smiting him.

Once they were outside he caught Allie subjecting him to a fond but considering look, which he did not understand. Damn the woman, he thought, recovering Rupert from the crowd. They greeted other acquaintances, admired the floodlit exterior of the Cathedral, had a quick word with Rupert's housemaster to ensure that he hadn't been involved in the Christmas-tree affair in the town and were assured that he hadn't. Back to the car, hurrying now as it was too cold to stand around any longer and Xenia was worried that they wouldn't be back by the time Edmund arrived. Johnnie asked her what on earth was up with Allie, staring at him like that, as if she was almost sorry for him.

'Nothing that I know of,' replied Xenia, guiltily, making a drama out of adjusting her seat, trying to avert further questions.

'Does she know something I don't?'

'When's Henry coming?' interrupted Rupert, saving Xenia from replying.

'On Monday, after lunch,' she said to Rupert, a little pink in the face, and glad of the dark.

Edmund's car gave a choking whine, and died, as it had on occasion recently, so, cursing, he retrieved his bag and headed for the tube, too impatient to fiddle about waiting for garage mechanics to turn up. At Charing Cross there was a train due to leave in five minutes and he fumed at the ticket office queue and then dashed across the concourse, scattering commuters and backpackers, flinging himself on to the train. He was lucky to find a seat and collapsed into it breathing heavily. An unpropitious start to the end of the Mimi affair, for that is how he now saw it, having last night taken a deliberately pessimistic view of the whole thing, and in an effort not to tempt fate had forced himself to believe that a) he would find that Mimi Taylor had gone away to Africa on holiday, or b) if she had not done a) would turn out to be a scraggy witch in a gingerbread house who would invite him in and keep him there forever. The Marianne occasion had alarmed him.

He was sitting next to a young man in an enormous Puffa jacket which took up more than his share of space and whose headphones gave out a continuous tsikety-tsikety noise. 'I hope he goes deaf before he's twenty-five,' thought Edmund irritably, shuffling his bag beneath his knees and wondering why the train had not started. His opposite neighbour was a bosomy woman in a tight bright blue suit and a lacy white shirt, which gaped between the buttons whenever she moved, exposing little leaf-shaped expanses of some pink undergarment. She wore quantities of gold jewellery: a teddy bear brooch on her jacket, a watch chain around her plump creased neck from which dangled a gold sovereign, gate bracelets on each wrist and several large rings. She bent to get her *Evening Standard* from a shiny black shopping bag at her feet, also withdrawing, after a scuffle, a tube of very strong mints. Still not started; he'd sprinted for nothing. He read the headlines of her newspaper which announced that Royal Secrets had been Stolen. He was astonished to find that there there were any left to steal and turned his attention to her neighbour. A man in a dark blue suit, with a red tie and hornrimmed spectacles, sat with his legs crossed and an appreciable amount of white, hairless leg showing above his black sock. He was doing the *Daily Telegraph* crossword with such velocity that Edmund suspected him of having cheated and peeked at someone else's answers during the day in order to impress people on the journey home. Edmund guessed he was an accountant and that he would get out of the train at Sevenoaks.

Across the aisle a girl with a haversack and suntan turned the pages of a paperback novel, the cover of which showed a mystical-looking woman rising from a fog, dressed in a sort of Iron-age bra and holding a sword aloft. The title, *The Aeons of Irima*, was emblazoned in large gilt letters, suggesting that yet another English graduate had taken a deep breath and gone severely downmarket. The woman in bright blue spent a great amount of time trying to unwrap her packet of mints, dropping small pieces of silver foil into her lap, then opening her mouth exaggeratedly wide to pop one in, flashing a gold tooth as she did so.

The train started with a jerk, and rumbled out of the station, over the Hungerford Bridge and the glittering Thames, wheels squealing on the tracks. A ticket collector came and went, an attendant with a trolley passed up and down and the woman opposite went on eating mints. Edmund, having exhausted the possibilities of his fellow-passengers, and not having brought a book with him, since he had expected to be driving down, dozed. He woke with a start at a station – peering out into the dark he could see it was Sevenoaks, and the crossword maniac had put on his coat and left. Halfway there. Mrs Minty was opening another packet. Her newspaper was now folded on the empty seat beside her. Edmund asked her if he might borrow it, and read first the book reviews, then the theatre reviews, then Brian Sewell opening another can of pretentious worms, gradually crushing them one by one under a gleefully sadistic foot. City pages, sport, and then the train was pulling into Parden, and Mrs Minty stood up, showering the floor with a snowstorm of silver paper, fighting her way into a yellow macintosh, smoothing on pink gloves.

Edmund had to change trains here, and catch the old diesel Marsh train. It was sitting waiting, engine chugging comfortably, when he eventually found the right platform. He had successfully stopped himself from thinking about Mimi since leaving London, but now, avoiding the seat with chewing gum on it and flopping down by the mud-streaked window, he was struggling. He could still see in his head the photograph of the girl in the hat, the face hidden. The heating didn't seem to be working, but the trip was only fifteen minutes or so. An old man, malodorous in a filthy black coat tied round the waist with bailer twine, sat nearby, muttering and clasping a sack. An elderly couple handed each other biscuits and played children's pass-the-time games. 'Now, let's do stations ending in A. You start.' 'Victoria' – 'Vindolanda' – 'I'm sure there isn't a station at Vindolanda' – 'Well, let's go on to B, then.' 'Widdicomb' – 'I think that has an E on the end – give me another choccy biccy.'

Edmund thought how neat and cosy they were and the woman crossed her ankles in their sensible visiting-London shoes and smiled at him timidly, a sort of half-smile, meant to engender fellow-traveller feeling more than conversation. Edmund felt that if he turned round sharply he would catch sight of Lewis Carroll's Sheep, knitting in the corner.

The train mumbled its way across the dark fields and little bridges, depositing him at the dark and unmanned Eeldyke Halt, where he went in search of a telephone. There was no answer from the farm, so he presumed they must still be on their way back from Canterbury. There were a couple of sheep in the weatherboarded waiting room on the platform, so he didn't fancy hanging around in there. It did cross his mind that they might wander on to the track, but there was no one to inform, and he wasn't going to chase them out. They looked contented enough where they were. No one else had got off the train with him, and he stood in the dark outside the disused Victorian station building, the icy wind whipping round his face and scouring the tarmac of the small car park. There seemed no point in waiting there and the Eeldyke Inn wasn't far up the road, so he set off on foot.

Having made contact with the farm, Edmund slid gratefully on to one of the chairs beside the coal fire, the seats of which had been buffed into conker-like glossiness by five generations of behinds. Seth was polishing glasses behind the marble bar and one or two groups of customers were in quiet conversation about manifolds and gaskets in the candlelit back room, a pleasant hum of sound rather than the Sunday-lunchtime cacophony. An outsize scarlet amaryllis stood on the bar, its two massive velvety flowers pointing in opposite directions like secret botanical listening devices. Tomorrow, somehow, he would have to give Xenia the slip and go to find Mimi. He'd asked Seth the whereabouts of Jarvis Cottage, and it was less than a mile along the road. He was very close, but he needed time to psych himself up, to prepare for disappointment. He tried out the plausibility of various sets of excuses. 'I really need to go for a walk on my own – business problems to sort out.' That sounded unlikely. He could however say he was going to spend the morning investigating Marsh churches? That would ensure that neither Xenia nor Rupert would insist on accompanying him. But he had no car – he would have to borrow one.

A gust of wind caught the door out of Johnnie's hand as he entered, banging it against the wall.

'Hello, sorry to keep you waiting. I think I might join you in a pint. I always like to get away while Rupert is being debriefed at the end of term.' He turned to Seth. 'What's good this evening?'

'Marshadder,' said Seth, 'the Norseman's Whore isn't ready yet – too lively. Shot the bung out this afternoon – look at the ceiling.' He pointed at the sticky hop-encrusted spray across the ceiling above his head.

'Right then, Marshadder it is.'

Johnnie sat on the other side of the fire and, leaning forwards, said quietly: 'I think I should warn you that Xenia's a bit on edge at the moment. Not quite herself. See if you can't try to cheer her up a bit, could you?'

'Is she in a rage with you? Another attack of the green-eyed monsters?'

'She's got absolutely nothing to be in a rage about,' said Johnnie gloomily. 'I've not done a damned thing. Anyway, some of the time it's the opposite. She's being over-solicitious, over-zealously wifely – I find it quite frightening.'

'Well, she must think you've done something – to her, that's always been the same thing as being guilty. Thank God she's not a JP.'

'Lucky says he's finding it hard to get on with his work because she's forever tracking him down and asking where I am. Says he daren't have a pee behind a hedge in case she's watching.'

'What about . . .' Edmund lowered his voice still further '. . . Amelia?'

'What about her?' Johnnie snapped defensively. 'I've told you already, I just like her occasional company, that's all. She's an interesting woman.'

'Yes, she is, isn't she? Did I tell you I bumped into her in London, by chance, a while ago? I bought her a sandwich.'

Johnnie felt Edmund was treading on his toes a little, and looked about, intending to get off the subject of Amelia as fast as possible. He spotted his copy of the *Ingoldsby Legends* on the shelf next to the bar.

'May I take this back please, Seth? I think it was left for me?'

Seth, in a lull now that he had served Johnnie and no one else appeared to need attention, was back in his seat, dozing.

'You needn't say "please" to *me* about it,' he said, without looking up. 'I didn't put it there, and I'm not going to take it away.'

Edmund felt this sounded very familiar, but couldn't place it for a moment. 'Nothing going on then?' he said to Johnnie, grinning. 'Amelia seemed rather interested in the *Ingoldsby Legends*.'

'I'm not satisfied that that is what Xenia is really going on about,' said Johnnie. 'It's all so unlike her. Banging doors, silences, and then the next minute dreadful fake jollity and vast meals. I simply don't know what she's going to do next.'

'You've really tried to get to the bottom of it?'

'Of course I have. But she looks at me as if I were Vlad the Impaler and says, "Absolutely nothing" in the sort of dead level voice that means there is absolutely everything.'

'Well, I think she is worried about Amelia – perhaps you could try appearing as reassuringly faithful as possible? I know she can be infuriating but she's obviously in distress about something.' Edmund finished his pint. It was so pleasantly warm in the pub and the place had an air of sanctuary about it of which he felt that Johnnie had more reason to be eager to take advantage than he had.

They returned to delicious smells in the hall, and Rupert's half-unpacked trunk on the floor, with Xenia rushing up and down stairs with armfuls of shirts and pants. Rupert was helping in a desultory sort of way, removing the odd book, or boot, and leaving them on the stairs.

'Uncle Eddie! Great to see you!' He rushed across to the door and stopped short of giving Edmund a hug, being fourteen now, so they shook hands and Edmund teased him about the pin-up stuck to the inside lid of the trunk, gave him a lottery ticket and propelled him into the kitchen to help his mother prepare the supper trays, for they were to eat by the fire in the drawing room. Edmund searched for signs of stress in Xenia, but found none, though she did look a bit tired. Supper was hot game pie, with a salad and potatoes, followed by bottled Victoria plums and cream. Rupert put on a childish voice, difficult since he was at the stage where it scooped up and down the scale with a surprising range of growls and squeaks, counting out his plum stones: 'Tinker, Tailor, Soldier, Sailor – Crackhead, Surfer, Dipstick, Brief!'

'Darling, do try and grow up,' said Xenia, piling up the plates.

'It's not something that one *can* try to do. It'll just happen.'

'We need to have a talk soon, about what you think you might like to do when you leave school,' said Johnnie, who had at last been reading his report and was not impressed.

'Oh Lordie! Lordie! I've not even taken my GCSEs yet! Give a man a chance.'

Rupert turned to Edmund, hoping to change the topic.

'Fancy a game of chess?'

'No, I'm a bit off chess at the moment.'

'Well, cribbage then?'

'Cribbage would be fine,' said Edmund, glad of something to keep himself occupied.

Xenia went off to finish the unpacking and Johnnie sat reading the newspaper, listening to *The Magic Flute*, and covertly watching Edmund and his younger son where they sat on the hearthrug, dealing out cards and manufacturing pegs from broken matches. Rupert resembled his uncle, with the same oval face and small dent in his chin, the same slightly upslanting eyes and thick dark hair. But one could see Rupert would be taller, like himself and Xenia, by the length of the thighbones and the half-grown gangliness of the arms.

'Aha! Two for doing it!'

'Ten.'

'Fifteen for two.'

'Twenty-one.'

'Twenty-six.'

'Twenty-eight.'

'Thirty-one for two.'

'Six.'

'Twelve – that's two for a pair and one for finishing!'

'That's pretty expert pegging!' said Edmund, counting out his hand.

Outside in the hall Xenia picked up the final pile of clothes and, spotting a book on the table, placed it on top, intending to take it upstairs with her and put it in the spare-room bookcase. The book slipped off with a thud, landing on one of its leather-edged corners, spilling out a piece of paper. She stooped to pick it up, and saw 'Many Thanks – very enjoyable – Amelia' written across it.

Proof, proof, she had proof! To Xenia, in her present state of mind, sharing books was, as Edmund had pointed out to Johnnie, tantamount to sharing a bed. She pushed the note back in the book with a shudder of distaste, and leaving it on the table, stamped upstairs, stiff with wrath. She sat on Rupert's bed for a while, suppressing her rage, recovering her poise. There must be no scenes, particularly not now Rupert was back. But she would speak to Edmund, find out if he knew anything and enlist his support. She put away the last pile of underwear and went back downstairs, banging shut the lid of the trunk with its offensive picture sealed inside till next term.

9

Breakfast next morning was unusually disorganized, with Johnnie getting up and down to answer the telephone and shouting up the stairs to Rupert to stop mucking about with his guitar and come downstairs at once, since his bacon and eggs were getting cold. Xenia shoved piles of Rupert's muddy sports clothes into the washing machine while mechanically feeding bread into the toaster, making twice as much as was needed. Rupert, when he appeared, started pleading to be taken in to Tenterden to do his Christmas shopping.

'I've really got to do it all today. I don't want to waste time trailing around shopping once Henry's here. Can't we just pop in quickly this morning? I've got my list and the money saved up and everything. I hate shopping – it'd be great to get it all done at once.'

'But I'm so busy this morning!' said Xenia, reluctant to leave Johnnie and Edmund on their own. 'We can't leave poor Uncle Edmund kicking his heels alone. I'm sure he doesn't want to come shopping.'

Johnnie said that he had to go out and check the sheep, and Edmund was welcome to come with him.

Edmund saw his chance and took it. 'Oh, don't worry about me. I thought I might take one of the bikes and go and visit a few churches. Need some fresh air after being stuck in the shop all week.'

The combination of bicycle and churches did it. Xenia acquiesced and so, that sorted, she went to get ready for Tenterden, and Edmund sneaked upstairs to get his precious carrier bag.

There was no sign of Johnnie after Xenia and Rupert had left, so Edmund pulled Henry's old bike out of the shed by the barns, pumped up the tyres, and set off, weaving about uncertainly for a few minutes until he got his balance. It was a long time since he'd ridden a bicycle. It was sunny, but the wind was still fiercely cold and he stopped to tie his scarf round his mouth. A pair of swans climbed the bank of the Royal Military Canal, stood there for a second before turning themselves into the wind and, after two short steps, launched themselves into the air, swinging low over the road in front of him, their powerful wings making a curious skweeching sound as they gained height and flew, line-astern, across the fields, their necks stiff and straight as sticks ahead of them. The sun caught them as they wheeled about and turned inland, breathtakingly white against the dark clouds on the horizon. In spite of a pre-dentist churning sensation in his stomach, Edmund enjoyed the actual riding, feeling his muscles stretching as they propelled him along, the air rushing past, the immense open spaces and vast skies around him. He felt freer out here, away from the hills and copses surrounding the farm, and a million miles away from the claustrophobic overhanging cliff faces of the London buildings.

The house, when he found it, was square, with dirty white weatherboarding, sitting close to the narrow road which divided the Romney from the Walland Marshes, slightly raised up on a bank, part of the old Rhee wall – the ancient sea defences. There was a blue painted gate with 'Jarvis Cottage' in chipped white plastic screwed-on letters. He knocked on the front door. After a second or two a voice called out: 'Use the back door. This one's been nailed up!' and then 'Who is it?', but he had already gone round to the lower gate, pushing his bicycle awkwardly through, and letting it fall to the grass.

His heart was thumping as he heard footsteps coming to open the back door, so that by the time it was opened he felt almost breathless with excitement.

'Mimi Taylor?' he started. 'I've brought you some papers . . .' but he was stopped in mid-sentence by the sight of Amelia Sailor, who stood there, smiling at him, pleased to see him.

'But Edmund, how lovely to see you again so soon!'

He was thunderstruck, and quite unable to leap the barrier of the names.

'But I'm looking for Mimi Taylor – does she live here too?'

'Mimi Sailor, if you like. Yes, that's me. I just don't get called that much any more. I dropped it.' She was staring at him, since he had gone quite white. 'Nick didn't like it – he thought it sounded fluffy.'

'Mimi Anderson?' He was blundering.

'Yes, that's my maiden name. Whatever *is* the matter?'

He stood there with his hair on end from the wind, his face registering mild shock – perhaps he had made a mistake and hadn't been looking for her after all, she thought, or perhaps I have soot all over my face, or my skirt's rucked up? Perhaps someone has changed my name without permission?

'Oh, I'm so sorry. Can I come in? It's very cold standing here.'

He followed her weakly into the low kitchen, where she stood with her back to the stove, leaning against its warmth.

'I'll try to explain. I just wasn't expecting to see *you*, but

I *am* pleased to see you, that it *is* you I've been looking for.'
She was slim-waisted and upright in her long black skirt.
He could not take his eyes off her, but held out the bag.

'These are yours, I think. Amelia, I am sorry. I must look
a complete fool . . .' She did not stop him. 'Look, it's like
this. Some time ago Xenia bought a trunk in an auction.
I found these papers in it and I've spent weeks trying to
find the owner, only there was so little to go on. Only
M.A. Anderson, on an exercise book. I've even been up to
Norfolk to try to trace her, you, I mean.' She was looking
at him strangely, still not sure what on earth he was talking
about. The woman he had practically fallen in love with on
the strength of a few edited scraps of autobiography stood
in front of him; the woman who had put such a gleam in
Johnnie's eye. Oh God. Johnnie!

'Shall we go into the sitting room, and sit down? Then
you can start again.' She led the way down a narrow
passage and he followed her, twice as aware now as he
had been in London, when she'd been bundled up in her
old corduroy coat, of the long neck, the shiny gold hair,
the slightnesses and roundnesses. She was, oh joy, shorter
than he was!

He started again.

'My sister wanted to throw all the things in the trunk
away. It's an old elm seaman's chest. But I found out who
put the chest into auction. It was Helen Strood's niece,
Marianne.'

At last a beam of recognition flitted across her face.

'Helen! Of course! She took my chest up with her the last
time I saw her, and lots of boxes of books and things. I had
to move to a much smaller place, and there wasn't room
for so many things. I'd got into a terrible muddle, packing,
and she came for the weekend and helped sort me out. It
was chaotic. She took it to Norfolk with her. But I spoke to
her, about three months ago. And I've sent her a Christmas

card, and why has she sold the chest? I was coming up to collect it in the spring.'

Edmund had clean forgotten that he might also be the bringer of bad news. He felt suddenly as a policeman must feel at the door of a stranger, a destroyer of peace. He took a deep breath.

'Helen died in a car crash, in the autumn. Her niece put it in the paper. I'm so sorry you didn't find out till now.' He could see the shock in the dark eyes before she turned away from him.

'Helen. I've known Helen since I was a small child. She's my oldest friend.'

Edmund wanted to go to her, to comfort her, but did not move.

'We didn't meet so very often, but we always kept in touch. I would have rung her on Christmas Day. We are both alone, you see.' She pulled a handkerchief out of her pocket and blew her nose. 'It's such a shock. I can't believe she's *dead*? She was one of those people who are always there, you know? You can rely on them to feed the cat, criticize one's work, rock the baby, stir the jam, make you laugh when you're in a moody . . . I can't believe I didn't know she'd died. Why didn't the niece tell me?'

'Marianne, the niece, gave me her address book. I started ringing everyone in it, but only got as far as F – if only I'd looked a little further.' He got the book out of his pocket, and looked under S. There it was, Amelia Sailor, but the address was different, although still on the Marsh. 'A Mr Fuller had bought some of your books – he had a book with M.A. Anderson written in it, and the Flower House address in Kettleham. So we went up there to try and find someone who knew you. In the end there was your Christmas card, with this address.'

'But what was in the chest? I can't *remember* where I put

anything. All my bits and pieces are farmed out to so many places, boxes, bits of furniture . . .'

Edmund held out the bag again, and this time she took it, carrying it over to the window and up-ending it on the table. She stared at the contents transfixed, before diving for the two Jiffy bags.

'Oh my God! My diary things!'

She swung back to him, her turn to look white and bewildered. 'I can't take all this in. Helen is dead. And somehow you have all my private papers?' Tears started to run down her cheeks and Edmund went up to her and put his arm round her shoulders.

'I'm . . . I'm so, so sorry. I didn't think it would be like this. I kept telling myself it'd go wrong, rebound on me, so as not to be disappointed. I mean, I forgot you wouldn't know about Helen's death, or of course you wouldn't have sent her a card. But I just can't believe it's you . . . the child in Lebanon . . .' He stopped, too late.

'So you've read these? You've read everything?'

The white was transfused with an angry red, affronted, embarrassed.

'I had to read them to find out who they belonged to. I am sorry . . .' The word now had meaning to it. He was, deeply, sorry. 'I haven't shown them to anyone else.'

'I should hope not!' She was angry now, furious with herself for being so careless as to have left them in the chest in the first place, furious that Helen, whom she had loved dearly, should have just vanished into thin air, the grave, limbo, hell, heaven, wherever she had gone, furious at being *left*, again.

To Edmund all this was both better and worse than he had imagined. He had been searching for a woman whom it turned out he already knew and had begun to like a great deal. But he had doubly distressed her by being an inept idiot and rushing round to her, forgetting about the wretched Helen. He should have telephoned her first, after all. But the name . . . Taylor. Tinker, Tailor, Soldier, Sailor. The old vicar must have been deaf and got it written down wrong. Even he, now he realized how slow he had been, should have made the connection between Mimi and Amelia Sailor, or at least tried it out.

Amelia had moved away and was staring out at the road. A young man with a large dog walked past, and waved, but she did not acknowledge him. Time stood still for so long it grew mould. He didn't want to leave her in such a state, not without explaining how he'd loved what she had written, how fascinated he'd been by these glimpses into her life, how fiercely he was interested in her. Amelia wanted him to go now, at once.

'Please – I want to go and tell Josie about this.'

'Josie?'

'My daughter – please go now. Please,' she said, her voice thickened with tears.

Edmund could not do other than leave at once. He rode the bicycle back to the farm, making slow and wavering progress against the wind, his eyes watering, bereft. The encounter had taken ten minutes and had seemed to take ten hours. Where did he go from this dismally low point? He pedalled on, tormenting himself till, off the flat lands and facing the struggle uphill, he had to dismount and push.

Having done some food-shopping in Tenterden, Mary Beaton drove past him on her way to drop off some things she'd been commissioned to buy for Amelia, planning to go on to put in a couple of hours' paperwork at the surgery. She glimpsed the handsome small face as she passed and wondered if it was just the cold or the steepness of the hill which had caused such a set, grim, thundercloud expression.

'Dear Amelia, what is the matter?' she cried as the door was opened and Amelia's tear-streaked face presented itself, and instead of merely handing over the sausages which Amelia had asked for, came in and held her hand, retreating with her to the moulting carpet with the cat, holding on to her and listening.

'And that's not all,' said Amelia, tears springing out again, 'I was so dreadful to him. He'd read the papers, you see. Diaries and things to try and find out who I was, he said.'

'Well, I suppose that's true. Wouldn't you have read them, if you'd been him?'

'Well, I suppose I might. It's just the thought that someone I don't know, well, don't really know, knows about me. My private past.' She got up. 'I may seem hysterical, but Helen's dead, and that's all that matters. So many deaths, and I'm still alive. I wish I could have gone to her funeral.'

'Where's Josie?'

'She's gone upstairs – a bit upset too. Helen was great with her. She was such a splendid talker and never took account of age. I expect she's left everything to her unsatisfactory niece, and the niece just flogged everything off. She couldn't have known that the chest wasn't hers to sell. I only met her once, the niece, a few years ago. She was one of those people who doesn't really understand anything – takes one literally all the time, if she took it in at all. A dull, closed, little person. I felt there was something trapped inside, like a pinched nerve. I should write to her, shouldn't I?'

'I've got to get going,' said Mary. 'Look, I'll see you tonight at the carol service, if you still feel like going. Then how about us going to the pub afterwards and having a drink to her memory, together. I can collect you, and drive you home.'

'All right. Thanks for the comforting. I seem to always be asking people for comfort recently. My turn next.'

'See you.'

''Bye.'

Amelia stopped sniffing, and took the papers upstairs to put them away, popping into Josie's room to give her a cuddle.

She remembered winter nights, sitting with the old type-writer, reading the old diaries, cataloguing and clearing up the already distant earlier life. The diaries had petered out not long after she had met Nick. She had been content then, and busy, but it was strange that one should so rarely rush to record the happy moments, but spend hours scribbling down the miseries. She would miss Helen badly. They had always been aware of each other as they went through their different lives, often crossing letters, and telephoning when the other was thinking about them.

She stood by the window, picking up sheet after sheet till she found a short letter from Helen, written when they were in their late twenties and, being both about their own business, had not seen each other for some time.

Dearest Mimi

I've been very bad recently and not got in touch with anyone – having been wickedly and totally absorbed in the new life with Derry. I say 'new life', since everything has changed so dramatically, although I'm still living in the same place. My recent past seems like mouldy cheese, a pile of dirty washing in the corner, like a stuffy doctor's waiting room full of sniffles and sprained ankles and anxieties. Now all at once, I wake up singing, cured.

Derry is there when I go off to work, and I *know* he will be there when I return. I'm certain you will love him. He's not unlike that man we once met at Salthouse, do you remember? The writer on the beach? We talk, we

argue, confirm, deny, assent, tell tall stories and laugh a
lot. And the sex is utterly wonderful. I can't believe my
luck. I had just settled down to be the archetypal English
mistress, gradually becoming dottier and more eccentric
as time passed. Well, I probably will continue to do so,
but Derry will be there to control the excesses and gently
guide me into buying the right jeans. I do miss you on
that account! As well, of course, on other accounts, such
as the time we got drunk together and quite out of order,
when my parents went to London for the weekend and
left us in charge of the house.

So there we are. Our spare room is ready and waiting
for your visit. It's mustard-coloured (the dingy French
variety, not Colman's). It is a mistake. And I thought it
would look so pretty with the green and yellow curtains.
I need your clear and generous hand with colour, so you
must come before I turn the house into a dun-coloured
Slough of Despond. Could you come for Easter? Derry's
book will be finished by then, he swears on the Bible,
and we can all rattle about the countryside visiting old
haunts. My mother says she's looking forward to seeing
you again very much.

All my love,

Helen.

Amelia slipped the letter back, and read another piece, by
her erstwhile self, wondering why, with her intelligence,
her brightness of vision, Helen should have been taken in
by such a shit.

It's happened – what we, and by now Helen herself
– had come to expect. Derry has pushed off and left
her. We agreed the first time we met him that there
was more than a trace of hubris in his character, and
although I could never think of one single reason for

disliking him, and indeed, always enjoyed his company, there was always a tiny reservation there, like a small weed in an otherwise immaculate border. It's easy to say this with hindsight, I know. His third novel was very badly reviewed, more badly probably than it deserved, and he seemed to blame Helen for it. At least that's what she thinks now she's functioning again. She was quite literally prostrated with shock when she first rang to tell me. I tried to enjoy reading the book when it came out, out of loyalty to Helen, but it's very, very patchy. So dense in some places, so incredibly thin in others, particularly when the first-person narrative comes to the fore. The person he invented comes across with a kind of narrow cruelty which he cannot have intended, from what I could make of the plot, and this made a nonsense of the chain of events. I never did like first-person novels, and there are patches in it which are almost certainly Helen's work. They stand out to me because I know her so well, and are, ironically, the only ones with any colour any sense of what kind of light there was, what temperature. Derry describes the physical features of places and people, their height and width and depth, but one is left with a curious formlessness, like trying to imagine the height of hills from the contours of a map. Out of perspective, no idea what time of day. I didn't notice this so much in his first book, which was an ironical autobiographical faction of the twenty-year-old Derry, and which was deservedly popular, carrying on at a great pace. The second book was good too, although he started with what appeared to be serious sociological intent, and then, thank God, got carried away by his own clever narrative, rather like Dickens in *Hard Times* (although not, obviously, in that class!)

Dearest Helen, thought Amelia. So many years of happiness measured out, then snip. Along comes Atropos with her shears. Is death easier to cope with, if life is seen as a preordained length of thread? One then need not ask, 'Why?' only, 'How long is your piece of string?'

She decided to go back to work for an hour or so, to cook the lunch, take Josie over to Ruffles for the afternoon, then go to the village carol service in the evening. She thought of Edmund's stricken face. Keep going. There is no alternative.

Edmund spent the rest of the morning lying on the spare bed amidst the lacy trimmings, reading. It took his mind off the mess he had made of his visit to Amelia. He should have – why hadn't he – why did he? He was reading a chapter of Robert Graves' *The White Goddess* which was sufficiently wordy and esoteric to make him concentrate very hard. He often used reading as a mind-cleaning exercise, knowing that he might be able, after a couple of hours, to rise up refreshed and clear-headed enough to face life in undimmed Technicolor. He was reading of the importance of proleptic thought in the creative process – the ability to leap over the methodological obstacles and come to a correct result, so often unobtainable by plodding through all the reasonable processes. Nowadays it would be called lateral thinking, he supposed, but it seemed an apt, if excessive, description of what he needed to do. He needed a new vision of Mimi, and in securing it would find he had circumvented the difficulties caused by his unwelcome intrusion. He'd had all the wrong ideas about her, having gained from her writings a picture of a woman needing some sort of help, his help. She had seemed at times to be floating, unsecured, and he had assumed that she needed an anchor . . . His ploy of distancing himself from Amelia by reading had not worked. It was apparent to him that it was he who was searching for the anchor of loving and needing to be loved, not Amelia. Well, he would just have to take himself to Amelia and try somehow to make amends. He got up, put away *The White Goddess* and caught his foot in the lace hem of the counterpane. Downstairs he could hear sounds indicating the return of the Christmas shoppers, and Johnnie's voice, rumbling in the kitchen.

Rupert whizzed past him on the stairs with a bag under his arm. 'Mission accomplished! Sorry, uncle Eddie.' He punched the air with his arm and disappeared into his room, locking the door against pryers. For his mother he had bought a Sabatier vegetable knife. For his father a novel by Derry Johnson, since he had seen copies of two other books by the same author in the drawing-room bookshelves and assumed that he was a favoured writer. For Edmund he had bought a bright green cup and saucer, breakfast size, from Webb's. He'd stayed in Edmund's flat on occasions after cinema or theatre visits and half-term treats, and thought the place needed cheering up, hating the stained beigeness of everything. Henry's present was a small shiny stone lion, about three inches high, which he'd discovered in an antique shop, whose chipped paw had allowed him to feel justified in bargaining the price down till the stall-holder had taken pity on him and let him have it for two pounds. Its face had a seriously silly, domestic-pussy expression, which had greatly appealed to him. Grandmama wasn't coming over from France this Christmas, so he didn't have to get her a present, and neither of his cousins were coming either, so he didn't have to deal with them. Cards would do. Very satisfied with his morning's work he put the presents in his shirt drawer and picked up his guitar.

Edmund spent the afternoon reading, and being interrupted by Xenia, who kept on asking him whether he fancied roast pork or lamb for Sunday lunch, whether he'd visited the Eeldyke church on his rounds that morning, since that was the church in the group of parishes which was holding this year's carol service, and whether he'd seen any more of Mary Portley-Tall over the last few weeks. Was he quite warm enough in this cold weather, she wondered, he could always have another duvet if need be?

He knew that reading near Xenia was like a red rag to a bull and put his book down.

'Xenia. Tell me. What's wrong?'

'Nothing, absolutely nothing.'

Edmund identified the same flat tone that Johnnie had detected.

'It doesn't sound like it.'

'There is nothing, absolutely nothing wrong.'

She felt there was no way she could put her feelings into words without sounding silly, although she had intended to tell Edmund about the book and the note.

'That's all right, then.'

He should have prised and poked, like Allie. She was expecting him to try harder and was annoyed by his lack of persistence.

'Shall I help you make the tea? Or you put your feet up, and let me do it anyway?' he asked.

'No, no. I've got things to do in the kitchen anyway. You make road-menders' tea.'

'OK.' He returned to his book, despairing of her. She felt he should have insisted.

That evening, wrapped up like Michelin men against the wind and the temperature inside the church, they entered via a treacherously slippery brick path, clutching at gravestones as they slithered backwards and sideways in the dark up the steep incline to the door, for the church had been built on a low mound rising up out of the Marsh. The interior was harshly lit and the air was arctic, feeling several degrees colder inside than it was outside. It had been individualistically decorated with a huge bowl of holly, pointily sparkling beside the pile of carol sheets; an arrangement of battered mauve chrysanthemums with Japanese pretensions stood on the font, skewered into an unlikely mossy log. Pretty little bouquets of berried ivy and some silver-leaved plant hung at the end of each pew and a vast florist's bunch stood handsomely to the side of the altar.

They took their seats modestly at the back, this not being their regular church and not wishing to take the familiar accustomed pews of those amongst the congregation who were regulars. The congregation had indeed been artifically boosted that evening, even allowing for the cheerful nature of the service. Phylly and Seth sat two rows ahead of them, surrounded by their family, glowing happily as they turned and welcomed those of their customers whom they had corralled into coming. These took up at least five pews, the would-be drinkers knowing that the pub would not open until the service was over and landlord and wife returned with the keys. The remainder of the worshippers were the local farming families and the few retired people who lived in the area, wedged solidly, like fudge, into their box-pews. Edmund read the printed sheet which had been handed to him at the door by a churchwarden, 'Worship Occasion for Advent with Carols', noting that the priest was now called a 'Leader'. When the 'Leader' appeared, he led in such a low voice that few could hear him, the densely packed people in their thick coats sopping up his voice like a sponge. The harmonium wheezed sadly as a white-faced old man, with whiter hair, pedalled ponderously. He seemed only able to play in time with his pedalling, so all the carols were taken at the same dead-march tempo.

The second carol was unknown to anyone, and after a few brave tries they all subsided into guilty silence, but there was an air of shy bonhomie as they lit their little candles in their cardboard drip-guards and Edmund feared for the safety of the lacquered hair of the woman in front as Rupert, struggling with the order of service and the printed carol sheet, wavered about, dropping little splatters of candlegrease all over himself and Edmund. During a quiet moment in the prayers, a hissing, burbling sound emanated from the vestry as an electric tea-urn was switched on. Edmund, head down, peered sideways, noticing an eighteenth-century lead plaque on the wall, commemorating the name of the plumber who carried out the releading of the roof, with 'all his jolly men', now all laid to rest in the mounded earth outside.

When the service ended everyone milled about drinking steaming tea and coffee and eating mince pies. Edmund wandered over to inspect the plaque in more detail, brushing against Amelia. She was with her daughter, he easily guessed, a taller, teenage look-alike of great potential beauty.

'I'm sorry . . .' they said together.

He took her hand.

She said, 'I was rude to you.'

'I upset you . . .' he said, wanting to talk to her urgently, but privately. He made do with asking if he could call on her tomorrow morning. He had not meant to sound so formal. Her face showed astonishment, then a smile came to her lips, flickering through her face like a leaf catching fire. What was it Charlie had called her? Incandescent. Not bad, for Charlie, who usually had a more *louche* vocabulary. She had liked the feel of his hand – cool, smooth, encompassing. That was all right then. She said she had a little work to do, but, equally with great politeness, that she would be delighted to break off for a while, say at eleven o'clock?

Had he been wearing a hat, he would have swept it from his head and bowed, but he had none, and so nodded agreement eagerly, retreating as Mary Beaton came up and stuck an arm through Amelia's.

'Coming for a drink now that an assignation has been made?'

'You were listening?'

'Couldn't help it. So sweet. Why didn't you ask him to join us for a drink?'

'No, he's with his family. I don't want to make things awkward for him.'

'Quite right. Stay in a stew all evening. Come on, both of you.' They followed Seth, who was rattling his keys suggestively, and joined the impatient queue which had formed outside the door of the pub.

'You do flash about,' said Mary.

'What *do* you mean?'

'First Johnnie, now Mr Edmund. No, I promise I'm joking!'

'You'd better be! You know Johnnie was never a serious proposition. I got an incredibly frosty look from his wife earlier on. If I'd shown any interest at all, he'd have run a mile.'

'I bet he wouldn't have.'

'What will you have to drink?' asked Amelia, laughing for the first time that day.

'In Helen's memory? I'll have a half of Bateman's, please.'

Josie wandered off with her drink to join some friends, and Amelia and Mary sat at a little round table in the back room, out of the reach of some dangerously inaccurate darts players.

'Now, tell me about Helen, since this is her wake. What did you do together, as children?'

'When we lived in Suffolk, we used to make a mixture of flour, sugar and water in a cup, and sit in an apple tree eating it with our fingers. We thought it was manna.'

'Drink up. Go on.'

'We used to go to the beach at Southwold – Helen's parents had a little beach hut there. It was shingle, by

the town, but if you walked up to the left it was sandy
– funny orange-yellow sand, and we'd walk miles, with
no one ever worrying about us, or so it seemed, but I
suppose we were actually under someone's eye. We pre-
tended we were angels, with white bath towels hanging
from our shoulders, tucked into the straps of our bathing
costumes. Helen once found this huge piece of carnelian
– that orange-red clear semi-precious stone? I was very
jealous because I never seemed to find any. There was a
shop in the town that sold carnelian jewellery, and I can
remember being told that it was the same thing as Helen
had found, and what was even worse – I stole it from her
when we went to bed that night, and hid it in my sponge
bag, but I felt so guilty that I got up early next morning and
put it back. I hadn't slept a wink all night.'

'Then what?'

Amelia knocked back her whiskey, and went and got
another one.

'It was pretty much an enchanted childhood, but it all
changed. Georges Fleury turned up and I went to live in
Beirut with him and my mother. Beirut's not a bit like
Southwold.'

'No, I don't imagine it is. So did you and Helen keep in
touch? How?'

'When we were six and seven, our mothers used to write
for us. Then we started on our own, and kept it up two
or three times a year. I saw her every other year, though,
because my mother used to bring me back with her to
England for a holiday – and Helen and I just took up
where we had left off last time. Helen grew a lot taller
than I did. She had the most wonderful elegant model's
figure you can imagine by the time she was in her teens.
But she was completely and utterly useless at showing it
off. She just didn't care about how she looked at all, which
was refreshing and infuriating at the same time.'

'Hold on – I'll just get one more half.' When Mary came back, Amelia made her promise to stop her if she got boring and started to ramble. 'Rambling, that's a lovely word, isn't it? Ambling with intent . . . intent to steal roses? It's the only thing I've ever stolen, apart from the carnelian. Helen and I stole them because we wanted to put them on Helen's dog's grave. They were apricot-coloured roses, and grew in Chesney Grove's garden. We went in with the scissors at six in the morning, a commando raid, and took five of them, one for each year of the dog's life.'

'What had it died of?'

'A surfeit of ice-cream.'

'No, really?'

'Yep, it was all Helen's fault. He was a very small dog.'

'Did you get caught?' asked Mary, imagining a cairn terrier rolling in agonies on the ground, stuffed to death with Walls' sixpenny tubs of vanilla ice-cream.

'I never got caught. But I often get guilty and confess.'

'Didn't Nick catch you?'

Amelia picked up the switch in meaning without pausing.

'No. I can truthfully say that I caught him. I chased and entrapped him. I was very determined. It was a mistake, looking back from here.'

'I got caught twice,' admitted Mary. 'They seemed so . . . possible? Now I know they were dreadful mistakes. I'm wiser now, and do the chasing myself, and I only chase men who are impossible. It makes life much easier. I can't really concentrate on work and look after a family, although I know lots of people who do. The trouble is I'd end up doing everything at half-strength, rather than one thing well. It's like these frantic women who give dinner parties of almost Victorian proportions, serving three-or four-course meals as if they were trying to keep up to the standards of their grandparents, only without the resources or the servants. And they do it after having been at work all day, or if they've got children they've been wrestling with recalcitrant toddlers all afternoon, making sure the silver's all polished and there are no dog hairs on the sofa and their fat husbands, who've probably already had huge business lunches, sit back and don't lift a finger to help except open the wine. The food is always all wrong, too ambitious, and the standard of conversation is appalling. I have to fight off sleep.'

'Come on! Not every one round here is that formal!'

'A lot of them are. It's like living in the eighteenth century.'

'There are times when I'd quite like to live in the eighteenth century. Look at this place, things have barely changed here at all.'

'Well, *we* wouldn't be in here then, sitting and drinking whiskey and beer. No, I love my life the way it is. Now.'

Ragged carol singing was going on at the crowded bar, and Phylly and her family were working hard. Some customers had wandered in carrying musical instruments and settled themselves down, tuning and wheezing and tweeting. Then they struck up 'The Holly and the Ivy', being joined by singers of varying degrees of tunefulness.

'To go back to the possibles and the impossibles,' said Amelia, 'I think, I know, that I married someone totally impossible out of wilfulness. I've had months and months of a strange sort of peace, like when the wind drops after a gale. But in spite of being able to get on with my work, I don't enjoy being alone. I miss being able to rush and tell someone about things, or show them what I've made, and listening to someone else talking, instead of to the endless voices in my own head. Josie is good company, but it's not the same. Do you mind being alone in the evenings?'

'Who said anything about being alone? I manage, but most of the time I'm too exhausted to care.'

'I think we ought to go soon.'

They sat and listened to the music for a while – things were hotting up and Irish drum and tin whistle were in concert with concertina and banjo.

'The reminiscing does good, I suppose,' said Amelia, picking the gutterings off a candle. 'And I love this place too. You never know what you're going to find or hear next. I've heard conversations that started off with raising goslings and ended up with the Big Bang theory. Anyway, thanks for the company – I was just hit hard, at a bad moment.'

Mary deposited Amelia and Josie back at their cottage, and then returned herself to her two-up, two-down red-brick farmworker's house in the middle of a field near Fingle. She locked the door behind her, took off her boots and turned off the light. She mounted the creaking stairs, pulling off her sweater, and met with some resistance as she tried to open her bedroom door, then it suddenly gave and she found herself facing Cosima in the dark, her tail waving thinly in greeting.

'Hello,' said a voice from the darkened bed. 'You've been ages so I thought I'd warm things up for you.'

'Will! You rat! You frightened the wits out of me. How did you get here, I didn't see your Gran's car?'

'Bicycled, with Cosima running beside me. But I'm not in the least tired.'

On Sunday morning, Edmund again found himself thinking of means of escaping the house without anyone knowing his business. Succour came in the form of an advertisement in the parish magazine for a charity booksale in Rye, which started at ten thirty.

'I think I might pop in to Rye, to have a look at this,' he said, waving the magazine under Xenia's nose. Then, 'But of course, I can't. I didn't bring the car.'

'Don't be silly – you can take the estate,' said Xenia.

Edmund thanked her without a shred of guilt. But Johnnie didn't seem to need a hand with anything, and Xenia was busy with pre-Christmas cooking. He wasn't quite sure why he had been invited down again so near to Christmas – she hadn't seemed about to unburden herself of anything of great import. He drove around a few lanes, killing time, reminding himself that to Amelia, however much she seemed like an old friend to him, he was a virtual stranger. Outside Jarvis Cottage he paused to take in the garden, where a few ancient apple-trees, leaning with the prevailing wind from the southwest, an overgrown raspberry patch and vegetable plot took up the north side, and a tangle of old farm machinery, rusted, forsaken harrows and trailers covered a large part of the south. Her workshed stood between the two and he found her still there, about to start a delicate bit of soldering.

'May I watch?'

'Of course, only don't distract me. If you stand there, you'll be able to see, but be out of my light.' She smiled up at him. 'I hope you don't mind? I really need to get this finished.'

She held the slim crescent of yellow gold in one hand and applied first borax flux, with a tiny paintbrush, and then little sequins of gold solder to the upper surface. She wedged the bangle upright between two charcoal blocks and lifted the already intricately formed lacing of gold, fingers very steady, and placed it on top. Then with the flux and the paintbrush she applied more solder and tiny beads of white gold into the pattern, holding her breath.

'Please God, it'll take all at once.' She lit her burner, and then her blowtorch from it, and glanced up at him. 'This is the make-or-break part of it.' She took a deep breath and, putting the rubber tubing from the blowtorch into her mouth, blew steadily and produced a large rosy flame from the nozzle, gently and evenly warming up the two component pieces. Then another deep breath, and Edmund was amazed at how long she could take in expelling it. She regulated the flame to a harder fiercer burn, concentrating it on the applied design, passing it up and down over the surfaces, till, magically, the solder suddenly ran brightly all at once and the top settled minutely down on the bottom.

'Alleluia!'

Edmund realized he had been holding his breath in agony in case something went wrong. She poked gently at it, testing it with a needle file, but seemed satisfied that it was all firm and now the two parts had become one.

'But it looks so dark. Does all that dinginess polish off?' asked Edmund.

'Patience. Wait a minute and you'll see.' She picked up the bangle, still hot, with tweezers, and dropped it with a little hiss into a deep dish of water which had a bluish tinge to it. 'That's hydrochloric acid solution. It cleans off the flux. I just leave it for a moment or two.' She leant back and wriggled her shoulders. 'Thank goodness that's done. Johnnie is supposed to be collecting it on Tuesday or Wednesday.'

She took the bangle out, rinsed and dried it and took it over to her electric polisher. Edmund felt quite dizzy, fascinated by the hot smells and her delicate skill, even more fascinated by the closeness of her. She held it under whirring brushes, tilting it this way and that, using a strange block of pink polish, then changed the brushes for a soft cotton mop-like thing. It started to gleam and he watched her intent, totally absorbed face, streaked here and there with carbon from the charcoal blocks, her beautiful filthy hands.

'May I see?'

She slipped it on to her wrist and held it out for him to look at. Her wrists were chicken-bone slim.

'It's very, very beautiful. Can I hold it, or will it spoil the polish?' It was still warm and surprisingly heavy, the raised and encrusted pattern had an ancient, wild and surging form – alive and moving – Celtic, Edmund thought, yet far from the tight and formalized knotted patterns he thought of as Celtic. 'The Mimi Anderson I was looking for was an artist, a painter,' he said.

'I changed horses when I was about twenty-three or four. I found this very satisfying, and more fruitful, in the financial sense. I love to work in the round; I did a bit of sculpture first, but that needed huge workspaces and I didn't have the money to rent them. So I started doing this. It's quite like sculpture, in a way, only in miniature.'

He transferred his attention from the lovely thing back to her, seeing that she was pleased with the close attention he had given to both the process and the result.

She held out her hand for it. 'I need to take it indoors with me, I have to sit and look at it, make sure I still like it!'

'But it's for Xenia?'

'Yes, but I have to like it too.'

'She'll think it's wonderful, it's so elegant.'

They were again in her gloriously parrot-coloured sitting room, which he had been too preoccupied to notice much on the previous visit.

'I wanted to apologize for the way I broke the news of Helen's death yesterday. It was thoughtless of me – I didn't mean to shock you. I was just so intent on finding you that I forgot that you wouldn't know, that I would have to explain what happened first. I was immersed in my own idea of what Mimi would be like and was a bit stunned when I found out she was you.' He drew a deep breath. 'Although, you see, I did want to see *you* again, anyway. I would have come sooner or later, and perhaps would have found out who you were, in time.'

'I have to admit that I hoped you would come too. You seem to have been very assiduous in your detective work.'

'I'm sorry I read your things. I felt sure that there would be a key there, somewhere. But you covered up your tracks very carefully indeed when you were writing. Not an address, not a name anywhere, nothing I could latch on to. Why *were* you so secretive?'

'I wasn't aware that I was being. I think that's just the way I function.'

'I can see now how you must have felt about the intrusion, invasion more like, of your life. I just wanted to beg you not to execute the messenger.'

She laughed. 'I dare say I can live with it. It was just embarrassing, that's all.'

'I wasn't some prurient peeping-tom, you know. I just enjoyed reading about you.'

'But you still don't know me, not very much more than I know you. Even if you have read everything.'

'I didn't actually read it all. I found you before I'd finished.'

'Did you tell Johnnie about this? I mean did you tell him you were looking for someone called M. A. Anderson?'

'Yes, I did, right at the beginning, but he didn't seem very interested. Why?'

'He would have known,' she said slowly. 'He knew Amelia Sailor was Mimi Anderson – look. Here's my business card. He had one of these when he ordered the bracelet.' Edmund took the little printed card and read: M. A. Anderson – jeweller, Jarvis Cottage, Eeldyke, Romney Marsh, Kent, and a telephone number. 'He's also seen the painting in the kitchen – that's actually signed Mimi Anderson. I think he's been rather unkind in not telling you.'

Edmund suddenly felt quite angry with Johnnie. The old bastard, he thought, the old dog-in-the-manger. He'd mentioned both names to Johnnie, now he came to think about it – he must have known. He said in a rush, 'I think he's been rather underhand with me. I think he may have thought he could keep quiet and keep you all to himself. Look, I would like to see you again, very much.' Steady, he thought, steady, don't rush.

'I think we'd better leave it at that, for the moment,' she said.

'For the moment, then.' He was staring at her too hard, and she had broken away, looking down at her feet, very still in her warm cave, surrounded by her books and oddities.

'I'm going back to London tonight, but I'll be down again at Christmas, and staying till the New Year.' He tensed himself up, preparing to put his foot in his mouth. 'Johnnie . . . ?'

She saw his drift immediately and tried to tell the truth, as she'd tried to do with Josie.

'I like him. It started as a friendship, and although I knew there was a bit more on his side, I did try not to flirt with him, or give him any reason to think there would be anything else. I was pleased to have some intelligent company, and flattered to have his attention, that's all. I hope he doesn't take it any more seriously than that. If you're speaking on your sister's behalf, she doesn't have a thing to worry about.' She was blushing.

'It's absolutely none of my business, but she's a very jealous woman, that's all, and I think she may have got the wrong end of the stick; actually I think she's swallowed the stick.'

'Oh dear. Can you reassure her?'

'I'll try. Meanwhile, can I telephone you? We could meet over Christmas.'

'I'd like that. But I've been invited to drinks there on Boxing Day, Josie too. Won't I see you then?'

Yes, he thought, but it'll be mayhem. And Xenia has asked you for the wrong reasons – I wouldn't presume to know what her reasons are, but they are bound to be the wrong ones. Aloud he said, 'I'll see you then – and I will ring before.'

'Goodbye, Edmund.'

She watched him from the window as he left – a neat small figure, coat swinging, a seemingly happier man. He turned and on the spur of the moment, seeing her watching, blew her a kiss. She notched him down a point as a romantic idiot, but felt a minute but distinct contraction of muscles somewhere deep inside herself – a tiny detonation of excitement. Now there was a truly possible man, clear-cut, simple in his dealings.

Edmund saw that he could not embarrass Johnnie by making him aware that his obstructiveness had been discovered. It had been understandable, given his undeclared interest in Amelia. He couldn't be blamed for trying to keep her to himself. However, having found Amelia, Edmund wasn't going to let Johnnie in on the secret, wanting to keep her privately in his head for a while longer. She'd been friendly, in a carefully controlled way. She'd accepted his apology, accepted further contact. What more could he ask for at this stage? The framework was there; he could work on it. He sang the rest of the way back to the farm. 'In dulce jubilo . . . o . . . o . . . o, Now sing with hearts aglo . . . o . . . o . . . ow.'

Johnnie was at the back door, unloading a barrow-load of logs. 'You were very quick. Nothing there to tempt you?'

Edmund had forgotten he was supposed to be at a booksale in Rye, and hastily explained that it had been a bit of a waste of time – nothing there but rubbish, but added that it was always worthwhile checking these things out.

He changed, putting on an old jacket of Johnnie's, and accompanied him in the Land Rover to feed the sheep, perching on the back with the hay bales. He was quite fond of the sheep, liking their patient, letter-box-slit eyes, and the oily smell of their fleeces. The wind dropped and a weak sun shone along their fluffy backs. He cut the twine with his penknife, splitting the bales into smaller book-like sections, teasing it up and scattering it to the sheep following behind as they drove along. It was good to be doing something practical, better than sitting worrying about how to proceed with Amelia. Phase one had been completed. Phase two was to convince her of his suitability as a second mate. He jerked nervously as the import of this thought hit him, nearly losing his balance as the Land Rover bumped back across the fields. 'Yes! Yes!' said alter ego, disconcerting him by being so positive and not slapping him down in its normal denigrating fashion. 'But,' it continued in a whisper, 'take it very, very easy. *Festina lente*. Don't hurry her – she is self-contained, perhaps a little stubborn . . . caution is essential.' He leapt off the back of the Land Rover to open a gate, getting back into the cab with Johnnie.

'I tried to get something out of Xenia. Not a sausage. As she says, "absolutely nothing". But I think it *is* Amelia she's worried about.'

'Thanks for trying,' said Johnnie. 'I'll take your advice and become her shadow over Christmas.'

Edmund nodded his head encouragingly.

Back in London that evening, Edmund was greeted by the usual tired smell as soon as he opened the door. The little pile of pages, the first two chapters of his book, sat reproachfully on the table, gathering London dust. He reread his description of the leading female character – his anti-heroine – and started to rewrite it in his head, transforming the tall dark woman into someone small, whose red-gold hair was curiously at odds with the deeply dark eyes. Amelia's eyes were not black, but a rich peat-colour, but he found to his dismay that any attempt to summon up her features dissolved each time he focused on a particular point, the nose, the chin, the jawline of the remembered image. Abruptly he closed the typewriter and shovelled the manuscript into a drawer.

10

Edmund was seriously worried about losing Amelia by being too pressing and kept himself from telephoning her during the week. The bookshop was furiously busy in the run-up to Christmas, which stopped him brooding on modes of approach. Tom Treasure was promoted to front-of-house, after his fingernails had been inspected, and Charlie and Edmund arranged to shut up shop from lunchtime on Christmas Eve till January the third. Charlie was looking forward to Christmas, having been invited down to stay with friends in Rye, and in his imagination had built up a brightly coloured glossy tourist-brochure image of blazing log fires and copious food, ancient beamed inns and dark cobbled streets. Tom was returning to his family in Cornwall, and was simply looking forward to sleeping a great deal. He was working full-time in the shop till Thursday, and then he was off, out of the hell-hole of his shared flat in Manor Park, out of the bookshop, out of university. He had sworn not to open a single book during his holiday, whether Russian or English, and had no intention of touching his essay on progressive thought in late Tsarist Russia either.

On Tuesday afternoon Edmund returned from a brief lunchtime respite of pint and sandwich and was just about to re-enter the shop when he caught a glimpse through the window of someone inside talking to Charlie. This caused him a flutter of anxiety. It was Marianne who leant against Charlie's desk, apparently writing out a cheque. He thought it most unlikely that she was buying a book, but what else could she be doing? Had she come to see him, or Charlie? Various pieces of possible unwelcome news flittered through his mind and he turned fast and walked up the street, pulling his ear nervously and bumping into ambling tourists. He had told Charlie a bowdlerized version of his trip to Norfolk, and had not informed him of his success in tracing Mimi. Wondering edgily what Marianne was up to but deciding reluctantly he had to brave it, he returned to the shop. She was still there, leaning her narrow little hips up against the counter and laughing. She turned as he came in, and gave him a look which he interpreted with relief, as much as one could interpret such an enigmatic expression, as non-dangerous. She looked considerably more animated than she had at any time on their snowbound excursion together, and Charlie's face was lit up like a neon sign, a flashing advertisement for over-stimulated hormones.

Edmund prayed that he had not been the subject of their conversation and put on what he felt was a welcoming grin.

'Hello, Edmund!' she said, returning his smile. 'Have you found your lady yet?'

'Almost – I really am hot on the trail now.'

She may have seen through his smile to the underlying anxiety, for she shot him another pacifying glance, which he hoped desperately he had correctly decoded and that she wasn't about to let any cats out of bags. He was sweating slightly.

'Oh, good. Well, I must get back to work,' she said. ''Bye, Charlie.'

''Bye, Marianne. I'll pick you up at seven thirty,' said Charlie, looking indecently pleased with himself.

She nodded coolly to Edmund, picked up the shop's little purple carrier bag containing her purchase and left, standing aside for a woman who was unsuccessfully pulling at the wrong side of the door, and who seemed to be mouthing things to Edmund through the glass. Marianne opened the door for her and Xenia almost fell through into the shop.

'Good heavens, Xenia! *Quelle surprise*! Have you been lunching?' asked Edmund.

'I should say I have been lunching. Yes, it's Good-Heavens-Xenia! Smudgie and I have had a wunnerful lunch at Wildfire's and now I'm ... I'm on my way to Charing Cross, but it seems to have moved.' Her voice, deep and booming, had a more than detectable slur to it, her legs were those of a newborn foal, struggling and straggling to its feet for the very first time. She put her bag heavily down on Charlie's desk and let fall several expensive-looking carrier bags.

'Why Charlie, how immaculate you look!' She leant across towards him in a slightly alarming manner, as if about to proposition him. 'I do hope wicked Edmund isn't working you too hard?' she said, in a voice both arch and patronizing. Xenia had never quite managed to remember that Charlie and Edmund were equal partners, in spite of the age difference, and she had on the two previous occasions she had met Charlie insisted on treating him as a minion, embarrassing both of them. She is definitely drunk, thought Edmund, wondering what other unbidden visitors were going to emerge to torment him that afternoon. He raised his eyebrows apologetically at Charlie, who was retreating timidly beneath Xenia's onslaught.

'Xenia, you must be exhausted with all that shopping,' he suggested. 'Have a chair, and let Tom go and get you a cup of coffee.' Customers were staring at Xenia with interest.

'How kind, darling. Yes, I would like to sit down. I feel a little strange.'

Edmund commissioned Tom to fetch black coffee from the sandwich shop and tried to elicit from Xenia the time of her train, praying that it would be soon.

'Three forty-five, I think. I'm not sure. I think I'd rather stay here and chat to gorgeous Charlie. But I really wanted to tell you something . . . what was it? Oh, yes. Mummy's changed her mind again. She *is* coming for Christmas, arriving on Friday. I do like that dark green jacket, Edmund. You look quite tidy for once. She only let me know this morning. Isn't that typical of her? Such a nuisance. Where's the coffee?' She let out an enormous, Channel-Tunnel sized yawn. Edmund dealt quickly with a customer, glancing at her nervously, wishing her voice wasn't quite so loud.

'How did you get here, from Wildfire's?'

'In a cab, of course! Why are you whispering?'

Tom returned with the coffee. He had guessed correctly that a plastic beaker would not be quite the thing for Xenia, and had bullied the café assistant into letting him take out a cup and saucer.

'Now Xenia, drink your coffee and then I'm going to walk you down to Charing Cross. I'm sure the fresh air will clear your head.'

'And what are you doing for Christmas, Charlie?' She dropped the plastic spoon, slopping her coffee into the saucer as she bent to retrieve it.

'I'm going to stay with friends, in your part of the world, in Rye. That's on the edge of Romney Marsh, isn't it?' Charlie looked happier now that she was ensconced further away from him.

'Oh, what fun! I do wish *I* could go and stay with friends for Christmas. But we are giving a little linchtime drunks party on Boxing Day. Why don't you come, and bring these friends? *Do!* Twelve o'clock. I'll give you the address.'

She scrabbled in her bag and produced a Harvey Nichols till receipt and a red lacquered fountain pen. Concentrating very hard, her tongue poking out like a child's, she wrote on her knee, digging the pen through the thin paper at intervals and making little splodges of ink on the skirt of her pink wool suit.

'There you are! We'll look forward to seeing you, won't we, Edmund?' She stood up uncertainly, cascading gloves and pink silk scarf to the floor.

'Perhaps we ought to go for that train?'

Edmund escorted her to the station as a constable steers an arrested suspect, wheeling her in and out of the crowds, waiting patiently while she bought a copy of *The Big Issue* under the impression that it was a bumper copy of *Harpers & Queen*, and almost man-handling her across the road at the lights at the bottom of the Strand, his hand firmly clutching her elbow. He got her into her carriage and folded her up into a seat.

'Now listen. You must not go to sleep and miss your station. Where did you leave the car? Parden or Eeldyke?'

'Eeldyke. It was Eeldyke.' She looked at him heavily, unhappily, as the high began to slide away from her.

'Good. Now I'll telephone Johnnie and get him to meet you. You really mustn't drive in that condition. I'll be down on Friday, and help you deal with Maman.'

Xenia leant back against the blue plush of the seat, and closed her eyes. He patted her hand, made sure she had her ticket, and left her, concerned. At least she had something to read. He raced back to the shop.

'Sorry to leave you in the lurch. I've never, ever, seen Xenia even remotely tiddly before, let alone pissed like that. I'll just phone Johnnie and get him to meet her.'

'What did she say she'd been doing?' said Charlie. 'Having a girls' lunch? It's obviously more fun than my lunches. What do you suppose they talk about?'

'Haven't you ever sat next door to a table full of Xenias lunching? They screech a lot, and cut each other to bits, very slowly, in tiny, carefully placed snips. It's very cleverly done, and then some of them tell dirty stories just loud enough to embarrass the waiters. Not that Xenia would join in that part of it, or even realize it was going on. She's astonishingly innocent.'

'Sounds a bit more sophisticated than throwing bread rolls, anyway. Do you think she meant the invitation?'

'I'm sure she did. I'm sorry she speaks to you as if you were ten.'

'I don't take offence that easily,' said Charlie.

'I saw you've made a hit with Marianne. What on earth did she buy?'

'Barbara Comyns – *The Vet's Daughter*. Yes, I think I've really cracked it this time – she's really easy to talk to.'

Edmund wisely shut up. He had been allowably flustered by both these visits, hating his private life running headlong into his business one.

He found it hard to concentrate. The flow of customers had eased and he needed to do some Christmas shopping. He had arranged to meet Hatty and Jerome at the bookshop at five thirty, for an exchange of presents, and intended to take them out for a drink and supper before they returned with him to stay the night at the flat. He squared it with Charlie, and then put his coat on again and braved the heaving mass of humanity moving up and down Regent Street in a multi-lingual, multi-coloured, chattering, moaning Mexican wave. His present-buying so far had been haphazard and eclectic, and this afternoon he found it difficult to remember who had been bought what. He saw several things he would like to give Amelia, and knew he could not. The most he could give her without seeming over-enthusiastic would be a book, but he was attracted variously by a tight green velvet jacket, then a fat little teapot with graceful spout and handle in turquoise blue, a red silk petticoat-thing, and an antique silver spoon, with bright-cut decoration, and the initials AM still softly visible through two hundred years of fervent polishing. He couldn't really afford any of them, which was lucky. He still had Hatty and Rupert's presents unsolved. Hatty he bought a bright green silk *choli*, the little short-waisted blouse that Indian women wear beneath their saris. It semeed cold and flimsy beneath his fingers, but the weather would change, summer would come and meanwhile she could wear it to go dancing.

Rupert? He'd forgotten the fourteenth birthday, and needed to make up. He recalled the pop poster on Rupert's wall. The Dark Entry, that was it. He pushed his way through the crowds; over-excited children, pulled along with their silvery-red helium balloons wobbling above them, wailing with tiredness and a surfeit of chicken nuggets, exotic-looking teenagers, with such quantities of makeup on their little faces as to look like refugees from a Kabuki theatre experience. Bewildered men, their arms stretched to new lengths by the weight of their purchases, trailing hopelessly after their frantic-eyed women, who appeared hellbent on doing just one more shop. The traffic was nearly static as he crossed the road beneath the gaudy street decorations, aiming for a ticket agency. He made enquiries and was immediately relieved to find that they *had* heard of The Dark Entry, indeed they had, and that the band was playing the Brixton Academy on January the seventh. He calculated that Rupert wouldn't have gone back to school by then, and found that the band were not so well known as to command ferociously high ticket prices, so he bought two. Rupert would undoubtedly have a friend he'd like to take with him. It was ten past five, time he went back to the shop.

He was pleased with himself at having solved everything so quickly. He passed a hot-chestnut seller as he turned into Leicester Square, and sniffed the evocative winter smell appreciatively. He was tempted, but he needed to do one or two things before the children arrived and hurried on up the street.

A roaring wind passed him, flipping him up with it – and then his eardrums exploded with sound and he could hear nothing more for an instant. He appeared to be on his hands and knees on the pavement, with half-cooked chestnuts rolling about him. Did hot-chestnut stalls explode? There was a strange silence. Was he deaf? Then, as he knelt there, still clutching the bag which contained Hatty's present, it started to rain, or so he thought at first, feeling warm drops on his hands. It was raining red and, confused, he looked up at the sky. Winded, he leant forwards and struggled to his feet. Slowly, slowly, sounds were filtering in: tinkling glass, the sound of bus and cab engines running, voices . . . and screaming. Upright now, and still facing the way he had been travelling, in slow motion, he put one foot in front of the other, but he seemed to be planting his steps in jelly. So slow. A pinkish mist filled his eyes, and something warm was dribbling down his neck. He knew the way. He turned the corner, crossed Charing Cross Road, plod, plod, plod, seeking markers for his progress. There was the lunchtime pub, there was the sandwich shop. People were staring at him, standing at their shop doors and leaning out of office windows. They loomed up at him, excited, frightened, shocked, offering help. He pushed the door open and saw Charlie's face, white with fear. He collapsed untidily into a heap on the floor. Safe.

They said he could go home, so Hatty and Jerome took him back in a cab, having first checked that he had enough money in his pockets to do so, since they had spent all theirs shopping. An exaggeratedly large bandage was wound about his head, shading his eyes so that to see properly he had to hold his chin up like a guardsman beneath a bearskin. What was under these dressings was not quite clear, but he had been told that he had lost the tip of his right ear, and had stitches put in a cut on the back of his head. He had been very lucky, he was told. They were superficial cuts caused by flying glass. Edmund was grateful that he did not have a television. He had no wish to see the carnage that had taken place behind him that afternoon. Jerome told him that miraculously no one had been killed, but that twenty people had been injured by the bomb, mostly by flying glass, and that the police were incredulous it had not been worse. He wondered what had happened to the chestnut vendor, and then turned his mind away from the thought, unable to cope with it.

Jerome went out and got a takeaway from an Indian restaurant and they sat close together on the sofa, eating it. He felt incredibly high, now that he knew what had happened. His children were pressed close to him, feeding him comfort. Hatty made a lot of phone calls, but Edmund stopped her before she rang her grandmother in France. He didn't want her worried when there was so little wrong with him. His ear hurt, but the only thing he could remember with any accuracy was the sight of the half-roasted chest-nuts, rolling about him on the cold grey pavement. Charlie telephoned to see how he was and to tell him not come in next morning.

'No. I will. I'm all right, really I am. A bit euphoric. Hatty says that's post-shock syndrome, relief at being alive. I didn't see any of it, it all happened behind me, and I didn't look back. I'm being fed quantities of chapatis and rogan josh, and whiskey and sympathy, by the children. Thank you for mopping me up. Is the floor ruined . . . ?' 'Shut up,' said Charlie. 'Go to bed and get some rest.' His voice was constricted by an emotion curiously akin to that of a mother finding her child safe after losing it in a department store. 'OK. I'll see you in the morning, if you must. But Tom and I *can* manage, you know. I expect it'll be a quiet day.'

When he had time to think, taking full advantage of his children's loving concern, and sitting propped up in bed with extra pillows, a cup of tea steaming in his hand, there seemed nothing to think about. He had been lucky. He had escaped being killed by a bomb. End of story. Tomorrow his ear wouldn't hurt. Life was sometimes in very bad taste. Things would be calmer in the country.

He lay in bed next morning later than usual. Only the possibility of Jerome getting into the bathroom first and becoming immovable forced him up to bathe and shave. It was tricky shaving with the ridiculous mono-earmuff of bandage stuck to the side of his head. He edged cautiously round it with the razor, wincing as he passed over the spreading bruise on his jaw. He had no recollection of having hit it on anything when he'd been blown over. Drying his face, he fell naturally to wondering what kind of man could resort to murder for the sake of an idea, but he knew that all men could. But only those inflexible enough to invest their action with a kind of divine right, would. Then there were those who believed that they always had God on their side. This led him to think unfairly of Xenia, whose unfounded certainties dismissed any form of rational discussion. He had believed both Johnnie's and Amelia's refutations, but Xenia's fears were obviously quite real to her, and therefore needed attention paid to them . . . He hoped she would be so busy over Christmas with the family all present that she would have no time to brood. He was going to look monumentally silly, with all this bandaging. Perhaps he would be able to take it off for Christmas lunch? He'd been told to go to his local surgery for the dressing to be changed and to have the stitches out later, but he wanted to look under the bandage and find out how much ear he had lost. The nurse had said 'a bit' of ear, but how much was a bit? He'd made a weak joke about having to wear his earrings on the other side, but had been thinking that if he'd known it was missing he would have searched for it amongst the chestnuts and taken it with him to hospital so they could sew it back on again. He telephoned the hospital where they had taken the casualties and enquired about the chestnut man – and was told he was comfortable.

The only other ill-effect he had was a sensation of being slightly outside his own body, as though he were standing beside himself – this was so strong at times that he glanced aside to see what he looked like and got that unfamiliar side-view of oneself that occurs in triple mirrors on dressing tables.

When he got to work he was amused and pleased by Charlie's fussing and Tom's awed glances.

'You must admit,' said Tom, 'it must take guts to just carry on walking back to work in that state, as if nothing had happened.'

Charlie, who was lovingly unpacking a blue leatherbound set of Trollope, admiring the clean gilt-edged pages, agreed.

'But I don't think he knew what he was doing. He seemed a bit confused. The bookshop is his safe haven – his home, almost. Getting back here was probably an instinctive reaction.'

At about the time the bomb had gone off in London, Johnnie had left to collect Xenia from the five fifteen train. It was dark, and the train was late. He sat there in the Land Rover, fuming and worrying. Edmund had given him the briefest of explanations, that Xenia was tired, and verging on the emotional, and should be met. He couldn't believe that she had got drunk. It seemed so very unlikely. But then all her actions had seemed unlikely, recently. However, he knew that having her mother around would put her on her mettle; he was himself looking forward to seeing Sofia again. The red lights on the level crossing started flashing and bleeping and the gates went down, indicating that at last something was happening, so he went on to the platform, scanning the lighted windows as the train came past, looking for Xenia. He saw her nodding in a corner, and opened the carriage door.

'Xenia, wake up! You're at Eeldyke!' He had to shout.

She jerked awake and stared at him, her face crumpled and vague.

'Come on! Pass me those bags. That's it. Out you come.'

Xenia emerged, peering into the dark in a tentative manner, swaying slightly.

'I stayed awake till Parden, then after I changed trains I just couldn't keep my eyes open any longer. I'm sure I brought the car this morning. Why have you come to meet me?'

'Because I had a phone call from your brother who seemed not a little worried about you. What have you been up to?' He heaved her up into the Land Rover with her shopping, having first cleared the seat of mud and a few stray sheep-feed pellets.

'Oh, just Harvey Nichols, and then Peter Jones, and then lunch with Smudgie. Then I went to Edmund's shop. I can't think why he phoned you. I'm perfectly all right.'

'Have you got your mother a present? That was the reason you went up in the first place.'

'I seem to have bought quite a lot of things. I can't remember if any of them were presents. I think I may have eaten something bad at the restaurant. I felt most peculiar when I got to Edmund's.'

'Not too much drink at lunchtime perhaps?'

'I never drink too much. I only had a couple of glasses of wine.'

'If you say so.'

*　　*　　*

The sun set before four o'clock and Amelia and Josie sat on the kelim rug in the sitting room, curtains drawn and lights on, surrounded by old scraps of pink, scarlet and yellow material, cutting little strips of this and that, to which they attached old beads with gold thread. The cat, her dark tabby markings resembling nothing so much as a sleeping python, not stripes, but whorls and circles of creamy grey amongst the black, dozed by the hearth, occasionally putting out a paw and patting a piece which had taken her particular fancy. Amelia had her bead box beside her, filled with the remnants of generations of broken necklaces. Here was Bristol glass, mock jade, amber and shining, deadly black jet. Here also were the remains of a child's plastic daisy necklace, gold-speckled glass from Venice and rosy-pink quartz from China.

They had considered their box of old tree decorations and sadly decided enough was enough – they had been repaired beyond repairing, a fresh start was required – and put them away again, unwilling to consign the lot to the dustbin. They had instead decided to make a votive tree, such as one sees in eastern countries, with strips of cloth tied to the branches, left there by supplicants as reminders to the resident saint of that particular place of their prayers and expectations. So instead of buying a tree, Amelia had taken a saw and hacked a dead branch from an apple tree and stuck it in the earth-filled green coal bucket.

Amelia hoped that Edmund would telephone and gave an involuntary little jump each time it rang, but it was always for Josie, her friends arranging an end-of-term meeting of the tribes. She found her own reactions irritating. Here she sat, a mature woman, nervously twitching, waiting for a phone call she wasn't even sure she wanted. Had she always vacillated like this? Vacillation implied there were choices to be made, but what choices had she ever made? As a child they had been made for her; then on growing up she had caught Nick's butterfly attention and it was she who had instigated their living together, their eventual marriage. But had there been a choice? How could one make a choice when one was so desperately infatuated that the steps she had taken had seemed completely inevitable, without alternatives?

She cut three strips of red cotton, sewed three blue glass beads to the ends and handed them to Josie to tie on to the twiggy makeshift tree. This time she should let someone else do the choosing, should the occasion arise, her previous 'choice' having been so unsound. Edmund Yearne had the look of someone 'possible', just as Nick had had 'impossible' written all over his forehead. Perhaps she should, with no further ado, let loose and throw herself in Edmund's general direction, hoping with all her will that he would be inclined to catch her before she fell. But would it be best, perhaps, to just wait and see what he would do? Passivity was not in her nature, but she could cultivate it.

'Pass the scissors,' said Josie, who snipped off a piece of gold thread. 'There, that looks simply amazing!' It did indeed. They were astonished at their own cleverness, and picked up the tattered flame-coloured remnants, put away the beads and went into the kitchen to make tea.

Later that evening, when they were preparing for bed, and making hot-water bottles, Amelia asked Josie what she thought of Edmund Yearne.

'Edmund Yearne? Yearne's an odd surname, isn't it? Yes, lovely little man, in a middle-aged sort of way.'

'Oh, damnation with faint praise. Didn't you think he was rather good-looking?' she asked hopefully, screwing up the stopper to Josie's bottle.

'Oh yes. And he'd left his Zimmer frame at home.'

'You rude little biscuit!'

'Well, you know what I mean. He's got wonderful old-fashioned manners, hasn't he? I thought he looked a bit

like a badger, I mean determined, solid, rootling about –
looking for someone to play with?'

Amelia had to chuckle. 'You *are* unromantic. Yes, though,
I think you are right about the badger.'

'Does this mean you're looking for someone to play
with?' asked Josie.

'Well, I suppose I might be. Would you mind?'

'No, I don't think so . . . but you wouldn't go off with
someone I absolutely loathed, would you?'

'No. If you absolutely hated them, I'd be bound to think
there was something crucially wrong with them that I
hadn't spotted.'

'I'm off to bed now,' said Josie.

'Goodnight, my darling. I think the tree's turned out most
surprising. Quite magical, don't you think?'

'Yes. It was a good idea. Perhaps some saint will listen to
our prayers.'

'What are you praying for? Passing your A levels? The
attention of Will Redding?'

'Not a chance – winning the lottery. 'Night, Mum. And
you don't look a day over thirty.'

Amelia cheerfully threw an oven glove at her.

When she got to bed, Amelia sat up with an old tar-
tan blanket round her shoulders, listening to the news.
She heard about the terrorist bomb in London which had
exploded near Leicester Square. Amongst the injured was
a chestnut seller who was still in hospital but was said to
be comfortable. He had apparently escaped serious injury
by chasing after a youth who had stolen a bag of chestnuts,
just before the bomb went off, but staff at the hospital said
he did not intend to press charges.

'And so, horror strikes the streets again,' said the news-
caster, his voice heavy with the seriousness of the news
item, 'and the people of London, happily going about their

Christmas shopping, are subjected to yet another outrage. A Sinn Fein spokesman said this evening that the injuries caused were regretted and talks will continue in Dublin tomorrow . . .'

Amelia wondered what 'comfortable' meant, in hospital parlance. Was it meant to indicate a lack of pain? The word 'pain', she had noticed, was very rarely mentioned amongst the medical fraternity. She had been asked, when giving birth, whether she felt any 'discomfort', and she had hit the nurse with her useless gas-and-air mask. And sworn at her, but apparently such behaviour was not uncommon, except in films where women puff and groan a little and then give sweet Madonna-like smiles, while their 'birth-partners' leap around as exultant as if they had done it themselves. She herself felt that the fathers involved should be a million miles away from any childbirth. There are some things one should do in private and that was definitely one of them. Having fought so hard to get rid of male dominance in the field of obstetrics, all these wretched women were doing was letting them back in on the scene to try to take over again. One should not be asked to produce a work of art with people leaping around yelling advice. Her mind was off on a ramble.

The paraffin stove was flickering. The comforting, little circle of blue flame was sending out warning yellow flashes that indicated it was getting low on oil. The image of the roast chestnut man, lying cut and damaged in hospital, kept returning. She got reluctantly out of bed to turn off the stove and thought, 'He hasn't phoned yet. But I will see him on Boxing Day in any case.' She saw herself in the long-mirrored wardrobe, huddled in her blanket, a tear in the hem of her nightdress where she'd caught it on a bramble while chasing sheep out of the garden. She also wore a pair of thick red arctic fishermen's socks. Not a very enticing sight. Her reflection was foxed and misty and there was not enough light to see her face clearly, but she already knew about the wrinkles, tiny creeping furrows by her eyes, the softening of the chin, which had once been so severely pointed. But her body, that wasn't too bad at all. Nothing seemed to have drooped the last time she'd been warm enough to stand still and look at it, except that her breasts seemed to get further apart each year, as if they were trying to escape under her armpits. She laughed, and did not care. Her hair showed only the slightest signs of grey and she had very few stretch marks. She was lucky. She jumped back into bed and turned off the bedside light, lying there in the rustling dark, thinking about Edmund.

A fox barked destructively beneath the window and she heard it with pleasure, for she was warm and snug in bed. The sound of the fox's unearthly harsh yelps gradually decreased as it went on its way, down across the silent moonlit fields, where it sniffed about Phylly's locked chicken shed and had to make do with remembrance of meals past.

11

At mid-afternoon on Christmas Eve, Sofia Yearne arrived at the farm, waiting in the car for Johnnie to come round and open the door for her, emerging in her grey fur coat with a flourish of still-graceful legs. Her hair, Xenia noticed, as she and the boys came out to help with her luggage, was dyed a new strong russet colour which it had never been before she had gone grey.

'My darling – 'ow wonderful it is to be 'ere again. Careful with that! It is the presents. *Mon Dieu*! 'Ow cold it is 'ere. I 'ope you 'ave the central 'eating on full, Xenia? Give me a kiss, Rupert. 'Enry, 'ow *wonderful* you look! *Très branché*. I adore the purple shirt.'

Xenia growled inwardly. She had spent half an hour trying to get 'Enry out of the purple shirt and into something less obtrusive. She had also been severely annoyed by the length of his hair when he had returned from university and now it was tied back in a short thick ponytail; she had told him that he looked like a barman.

'I must go upstairs and change. Xenia, darling, come with me and tell me everything.' She put her hand on Xenia's shoulder; being, if anything, slightly taller than her daughter once, she had not lost much height with age. 'My sweet – you look a little tired. I 'ope this is not too much for you, all this entertaining. I promise to be very good, and not annoy you at all.' She swept up the stairs with them all in tow, struggling with the luggage. Xenia stayed to help her unpack, unzipping little bags, hanging up dresses.

'Ah, such a pretty room. I am always so comfortable 'ere. And do you still 'ave all those naughty books?'

'What naughty books?' Xenia paused with a skirt and hanger in her hand, perplexed.

'Oh, you know, the little shelf of pornographic ones – quite amusing, I thought, to 'ave them there, to entertain your guests.' She took off her coat and threw it on the bed, and patted her outrageous hair, piled up on her head like an Edwardian dowager's. She unstrapped a suitcase and commenced pulling things out, leaving Xenia to study the bookcase in a puzzled fashion.

'These, do you mean?' asked Xenia, picking out a copy entitled *Les femmes s'amusent* by someone called only 'Victorine', and *O . . .*' I never noticed them before. But surely, not pornographic?' She had turned a gentle pink, trying to remember who had stayed in the room since her mother was last visiting, almost a year ago. Edmund, of course, but who else? Would they have noticed them? She opened the first one at random and read: 'Clothilde lifted her great spreading skirts up to her naked waist, and lowered herself voraciously onto . . .' 'Oh, Mummy!' She banged the covers together. 'How did these get here? Rupert could have found them.'

'I'm sure 'e 'as,' said her mother, busy putting out little bottles of creams and lotions on to the dressing table.

'But it's disgusting. I won't have them in the house. Why didn't you tell me when you were last here?'

'Because it never occurred to me that you did not know what was in your own bookshelves. They 'ave been there for a long time. I expect it was a kind thought of Johnnie's. Such a thoughtful man!'

The pink cheeks turned fuchsia. Her mother had succeeded in wrong-footing her, however unintentionally, in
the first five minutes of her visit. It had to be Johnnie who
had put them there, imagined them well-hidden from her.
But it was possible they had been left behind by poor
Edmund, or a guest. Surely not Edmund?

She gulped and helped Sofia, who seemed to have
brought a great quantity of clothes for such a short visit.
She would take the books downstairs and burn them on
a bonfire when her mother had gone. And how could *she*
read such things, at her age?

Sofia changed into a long grey velvet skirt, the hem
encrusted with embroidered acanthus leaves, and a matching
cashmere sweater. Her bangles and bracelets clinked on her
thin wrists, seven gold on her right arm and seven silver on
her left.

'*Bon*. Now I am ready. Let's go and have a look at your
magnificent tree. When will Edmund be 'ere? I am looking
forward to my tea, so much.'

Xenia was almost numb with annoyance, but had forgotten that she had to break the news of Edmund's mis-
hap.

'There is something we have to tell you,' she said, as she
followed her mother down the stairs. 'He'll be here soon
and we didn't want you to have a shock.'

'Shock?' Sofia swung round on the stairs, an enquiring
look on her face, which gradually turned to fright as Xenia
hesitated.

'It's poor Edmund. He's had an accident. Only superficial
cuts, but a lot of bandages, apparently.'

'*Comment*? Bandages? *Tell* me. What has happened to
my boy?'

'Darling, there really is nothing to get steamed up about.
He's quite safe. There was a bomb in London this week,
and he got caught in the blast. But he says, truly, there is

nothing the matter with him except a few little cuts. He's driving down. He'll be here quite soon.'

'But why wasn't I told when it 'appened?' Sofia's variably accented English suddenly became clearer and sharper, Xenia noticed, thinking, of course, this is going to be all my fault. She tried to lay the blame where it should have lain. 'Edmund told me not to fuss you with it. Come on, let's go and look at the tree.'

Sofia turned and carried on downstairs, a little hurt. She adored Edmund, could not bear to think of anything dreadful happening to him; he had had more than his share of unhappinesses in his life. She turned again to Xenia, stopping so suddenly that Xenia almost fell over her.

'Is it 'is face? I couldn't bear it for 'im. 'E 'as, you both 'ave, such beautiful faces.' So many aspirated H's were beyond her.

'No, it's just the back of his head, and his ear.'

Sofia recovered herself a little, admired the tree enormously and gradually settled down in the drawing room with the boys while Xenia went to prepare tea-trays, set out an apple cake and warm mince pies. She was still upset by the books, dirty books, in her house. She had indeed been unnaturally innocent at school, had married young and had led such a sheltered life since then that even the most lightly erotic works would have seemed to her grossly indecent. Her ignorance and prudishness, quite a novelty to Johnnie in the sixties, had amused him at first, then had merely become something which he had to accept that he could not alter. She did not want to know. Her friends found her naivety hilarious, but suspected that it had to be simulated; after all, no one could be quite that ignorant – or could they? In any case, it was a great laugh.

She filled the milk jug, put the kettle on the hob and wondered miserably whether Johnnie had lent such books to Amelia. She felt quite sick at the thought of it. The dreadful Amelia would shortly be coming to her house, at her invitation, and she could not, without letting Johnnie know that she knew all about their nasty little goings on, stop her coming. She returned to the drawing room, asking the boys to go and make a start on decorating the hall.

'The holly's in the kitchen, by the back hall. Where's Johnnie?'

'Gone off to move sheep from Home Field to Hilly Foxes. He's taken Meg and Flit, he won't be long. It's getting dark.'

''Enry 'as been telling me all about this exotic Manchester – I never imagined it to be so exciting,' said Sofia, leaning back on the Kaffe Fassett needlepoint cushions which Xenia had spent an inordinate amount of time stitching on winter evenings, carefully following the intricate pattern of greeny-blue cabbage leaves. She was very proud of them, and would have done more of the same pattern, only Johnnie, fearing his drawing room was being turned into a vegetable patch, had suggested she did something different next time, butterflies perhaps, and she had not been able to find a pattern for these.

Out of habit, Edmund drew up at the back door and sat in the car for a moment or two, needing to compose himself. The house was a dark block, the chimney belching out grey-blue woodsmoke against the darkening navy-blue sky. The lights were on, making an asymmetrical pattern of yellow lit panes against the bulk of the walls. He had tried to restrain himself from fantasizing, from imagining what would, what might, transpire at his next meeting with Amelia. He had been honest with himself about the success of their last meeting. She had said 'for the moment'. Well, that moment was over now, and another was about to begin. Another moment that he might very well have not been alive to see. He was intolerably impatient for more of her company, greedy for her to the point where he felt he could not sustain the formalities of family – the greeting and the hugging – the friendly Uncle Edmund and dutiful son performances – for his mind was so set on one thing that any amount of time not spent with her had become almost unendurable. But endure it he must. He must give her time, not let his head gallop ahead of their tenuous relationship. He planned to sneak off and use the farm office phone to call her as soon as he decently could.

There was a great deal of yelling and shouting going on in the kitchen when he came in through the back hall, hanging up his coat and hat on the old wooden pegs, patting the poor old dog, wondering why it had never been dignified with a proper name, like Horatio or Beowulf. The house had leapt into life as it had every Christmas since the first farm house had been built in the 1600s. He suspected it of hoarding a vast essence-of-Christmas breath of woodsmoke, stuffing and Chanel No 5 and exhaling it, year after year, on Christmas Eve, in great gusts of nostalgia. The smell of hot mince pies floated in the air above the heads of his nephews, who raced howling like small children, bellowing with laughter and mock rage, round and round the kitchen table, leaping over chair seats and knocking apples and clementines from the huge bowl on the dresser. Henry became entangled in the pile of holly by the back door, slipped and crashed full-length to the tiled floor at Edmund's feet. He did indeed, as Jerome said, look different. But it was, surely, a fairly surface difference; a thinner, paler Henry, who seemed however to be fit enough and in cracking good humour.

'Oh shit! Uncle Eddie! My word, you do look sick! Are you OK, really OK?' He got to his feet and gave Edmund a bear hug. 'Sorry about the chaos. This little turd just shoved some holly up my shirt and patted it. I was trying to get my own back. I think I've got an instant tattoo. Look!' He lifted his shirt and there on the white flat stomach was a small prickling of red spots.

'Rupert! What a miserable trick. Where are the parents?'

'Drawing room. Gran's holding court. We just came out to get the holly done in the hall. Shall I take your bag up for you? You're in the yellow bedroom. Gran's got the wifty lacy one.'

'Yes please. I'd better go and pay my respects to Gran.'

'But you haven't told us about the bomb!' said Rupert. 'Was it horrendous? Did you go in an ambulance? Have you lost your ear completely?'

'No. I haven't. Only a little piece. I've had a peep under the bandages and it's got stitches in it, which itch. It looks more dramatic than it is.'

He went off, closely shadowed by Rupert.

Sofia was still seated on the sofa. Her face, no stranger to the plastic surgeon, had a wide-eyed innocent look, but her expression conveyed not only unlikely youth, but concerned motherliness. She rose up and advanced, clanking her bangles, across the carpet, bending to kiss him.

'Darling boy! I 'ave been in a positive fever about you since Xenia told me what 'ad 'appened. I 'eard about the bomb when I was still in France, of course, but one 'ears about so many.' She put a finger lightly to his cheek. 'Such a shocking bruise! But I can 'ardly see you under all that dirty bandage. I shall 'elp you remove it after tea. I spoke with Hatty on the telephone and she tells me you walked all the way to the shop after it had happened. Crazy boy! What were you doing in Regent Street? Is Liberty's still there? That would be an 'orror, to lose Liberty's.'

She sat down again, pulling him with her and held on tight to his hand.

'*Maman*, Liberty's is quite safe. The bomb was in Leicester Square and caught me on my way back to the shop. Now let's forget all about it. I know I look very silly, and I'd love you to help change the dressing this evening. How was your trip?'

'Oh, dreadful. So many awful people and those seats are so close together, no room for one's legs.' She stretched hers, drawing attention to their great length.

'But, I sat next to this charming undertaker, and I'm 'ere now, and not at all tired.'

'I think you mean underwriter, *Maman*?'

'Perhaps. 'e 'ad something to do with Lloyds.'

'Then he's probably an undertaker as well.'

Xenia sat in her little chair by the fireside, looking tense and watchful, while Johnnie sat relaxed and benevolent opposite her. Edmund admired the great dish of silver foliage and orange-berried gladwyn before she drew his attention to it, trying to gain a few brownie points to heighten his stock with her, ready for the moment when she found out about him and Amelia. He adroitly manoeuvred the conversation round to his mother's garden at Nîmes, admired her skirt, asked her what she'd been reading recently and whether she'd seen any good films, and then moved on to her disgraceful neighbours, the Déligondes. He behaved exactly as a good son should, and she expanded with delight and approval and regaled everyone with the doings of the Déligondes' niece, Ségoulène, who had rushed off and married a Belgian footballer.

'She is of course *enceinte*. Marie-Ange is hysterical with rage and Georges is speechless. I mean to say, a Belgian!' Being a Belgian was far worse to her than being a footballer. Rupert and Henry arrived with the tea, and Sofia bit into one of Xenia's mince pies with uninhibited relish. 'Now that, that is delicious. All the way over on the plane I was dreaming of your mincy pies, Xenia darling. I look forward to Christmas so much.'

Xenia relaxed a little. It was hard to be cross with such a genuinely appreciative woman, although she was still on her guard against further embarrassments. After tea, Edmund made his excuses and said he had to go and wrap up presents, borrowed some scissors and ribbon and disappeared. He sneaked across the hall to the office next to the kitchen, shutting the door behind him and picking up the phone. He dialled the number at the bottom of the Christmas card Amelia had sent Helen. It rang for a long time, but when she answered she sounded as if she was laughing with her mouth full.

'Hello? So sorry, let me swallow this piece of toast. There, that's better.'

'Amelia?'

'Sure is! Danged cat has jest run off with the lairst biscuit. I'm so sorry – Josie and I have been watching *Stagecoach* on Mary Beaton's televison, and can't stop riding shotgun.' She paused. 'That is Edmund, isn't it?'

'Yes, it is.' He stopped, realizing that he would have to explain at some stage about the bandages. He was going to look ridiculous, confronting her in this lot; perhaps it would be better to take them off, and hope that the ear didn't look too repellent and she wouldn't notice at first the narrow shaven strip at the back of his head. But she was still laughing, so he thought he'd leave it till later. She had a lovely deep amused chuckle. Josie was screeching in the background.

'We are a bit out of order, I'm afraid. Mary had a bottle of damson wine and we've drunk it all in one go. It's fearfully strong, and I can't remember how we got back here.'

'I rang to wish you Happy Christmas, and to make sure you weren't going to chicken out of coming over on Boxing Day. I really *need* to see you, Amelia. But I can't get away. I'm going to be wrapped tightly in a silken cocoon of party games and food until then.'

'I'll be coming, and Josie too, I expect. I'm going to be very brave and meet your fierce sister face to face.'

'She's not very fierce at the moment. My mother is over from France and it takes all Xenia's energies to keep one step ahead.'

Amelia had calmed down now, and was telling Josie to keep quiet or go away and stop listening in.

'Edmund?' Her voice sounded softer, less jokey. 'I'm looking forward to seeing you again, I really am.'

'So am I. Very much. I was expecting you to be different, to put me off. I've been thinking about you a lot. I was scared of being pushy.'

'I've been hoping you would ring, ever since you left.'

He put the receiver down quietly and peered out of the room. The hall was empty. He tiptoed upstairs and wrapped up his presents. Then, facing the dressing chest mirror, he gingerly unwound the bandage round his head in order to inspect the damage properly. The ear muff came away with it, and there was the ear, looking rather red, but with neat stitching across the bottom like a tiny zip-fastener. He bore a faint resemblance to a farm animal that had had its ear clipped for identification purposes, but he didn't care. She *wanted* to see him. He ran downstairs again carrying the packages and set them about the base of the tree.

In the drawing room Sofia was beating Rupert at Spite and Malice, which game she had taught Edmund and Xenia when they were children. Later on that evening, after a light supper, they all trooped out to Midnight Mass, returning with wrinkles ironed out and light hearts – except for Xenia, whose interior being remained deeply creased.

Christmas morning dawned icy-white, a thick hoar frost decorating every twig of every hunchbacked hawthorn tree, every blade of dead brown grass, and clinging to the backs of the sheep in the fields, the tips of their creamy yellow fleeces shining with an unearthly whiteness. It was stone quiet – the wind had dropped, no traffic moved along the lanes, no birds sang, no beasts dared open their mouths.

Amelia sat up reluctantly. The rising sun shone watery pink through the gap in her curtains and the frost ferns on the inside of the window. It was a red sun, so deep a red that there was little brightness to it. Amelia felt the weight of one of her scarlet woollen socks, bulging and knobbly, stuffed to bursting point, across the bottom of the bed. Josie had made her a stocking! She got out of bed and lit the stove and crossed the landing to Josie's room, her feet wary against splinters in the rough floorboards.

'Darling, are you awake? I've found your stocking! Why don't you come and open it with me. It's no fun opening presents on one's own.'

'Mmnnh.' Josie's head appeared from beneath the mounded blankets.

'Come on!' repeated Amelia impatiently. 'It's Christmas morning. I've got presents for you too, and it's getting late. I'll go and make us some tea and bring it up so we can have it in bed while we're unpacking the goodies.' She disappeared again, and Josie padded across to the other room, while Amelia in a flurry of quite childlike excitement stoked the stove, boiled a kettle and fed the cat the unlovely mixture of fat from pork chops, gravy and mince that was its Christmas treat. She put half a dozen chocolate digestives on the tray, stuck a spring of holly in the teapot spout and whisked upstairs again.

'Oh bliss! I love chocolate first thing in the morning.' Josie munched, watching Amelia start to explore the contents of the stocking. Out first was a ball of purple string, then a chocolate heart wrapped in pink tinfoil, a clementine and three walnuts whose shells had been painted gold. Then a bottle of calendula handcream, a tiny phial of scent, L'Air du Temps, of the type given away as samples. A metre of green velvet ribbon, a yellow sugar mouse with almond ears and string tail, a fat orange candle, and a box of Black Russian cigarettes. Then a brass thimble, a fine-point drawing pen, three 2B pencils and a tube of cerulean oil paint. Finally there was a pair of green socks, printed with Persian carnations.

'Josie! I haven't had a stocking since I was six. It's the best thing you could have given me – I love it to death!' She gave her daughter a kiss. 'Move over, the cat wants to get in on the act. I've got to reach under the bed for your presents.'

She pulled out a large squashy package done up in newspaper with large red Urgent stickers all over it, and a little scarlet box tied up with gold thread. The squashy package contained Josie's velvet hat – The Velvet Hat. She squeaked appreciatively and put it on – her unbrushed hair sticking out at angles beneath it, the resemblance to the Mad Hatter being emphasized by the fact that Amelia had written out a ticket to stick in the hatband, which read 10/-6.

'I love it. I love it. I love it! Thank you, Mum. Now what's this?' Inside the red box was a pair of of gold earrings fashioned as tiny daisy plants, with cabochon amethysts as centres for the flowers. Josie adored these too and tried them on immediately. She stared at herself in the hand mirror Amelia produced, very, very pleased with what she saw.

Downstairs they breakfasted on fried potatoes and bacon and snarling black coffee with loads of sugar. There was ice on a mug of water left overnight in the sink. Josie lit the fire in the sitting room, and Amelia filled all the stoves and trimmed their wicks. Mary telephoned.

'This is an imposition, but I have a feeling you wouldn't mind being imposed upon today. Will Redding, who says he knows you, is at a complete loose end after he's visited his granny in hospital this morning. I found out he was going to be on his own all the rest of the day. If I bring extra pud and more wine, could he come and have Christmas lunch with you as well? He's very charming.'

'Yes, I've met him. Of course you can bring him,' then suddenly suspicious, laughing, 'He's there with you now, isn't he?'

'Well, yes. He's just about to take the dog out for a walk. But you are a pig! You've guessed!' She became serious. 'You must not tell a soul, though. You aren't having any other visitors, are you? He's not my patient of course, so that's all right, but I don't want any wagging tongues.'

'Of course, I'll be silent as the grave. Josie will have her nose put out of joint a bit. She rather fancies Master Will.'

'So does the entire female population of Romney Marsh. But they're all too late. I've got him, for the moment anyway. It isn't serious though, the age difference is mind-bogglingly awful. Meanwhile, I'm ecstatic'

'We'll see you both at one o'clock then. The goose will easily do four people. I'm just about to start cooking.'

Amelia felt a pinch, just a pinch, of envy which she could not quite suppress, but she made stuffing, scrubbed and cut up the potatoes, putting them on the stove to parboil, thinking of Edmund and wondering what tomorrow would bring. Josie, still in her hat, fished out a jar of redcurrant jelly and then a pot of Amelia's garlic, ginger and plum chutney.

'Would this be good with goose, do you think?'

'It's good with anything. Let's get the table laid, and the goose in the oven and go out for a walk round the fields at the back, while it's still sunny.'

She had a pair of green candles which looked pretty in the old faience candlesticks with chipped feet. In the drawer where she kept her drying-up cloths, butter muslin and greaseproof paper, she had waiting a set of thick white damask table napkins which she brought out for the occasion. Josie polished the glasses till they sparkled and they then set off, wrapped in as many clothes as possible, to enjoy the Marsh at its most magical, just to get a feel of the day, Amelia said. The white fields stretched ahead, glittering. A jack snipe flew up, and Josie ran ahead, crossing a ditch in a great balletic leap, her legs flying out fore and aft so she appeared to float for a second.

'I just had to do that. I suddenly have a surfeit of optimism.'

'Good, so do I.'

But it was too cold to stay out long.

'I'd like some more coffee, and I'd like to have one of my decadent ciggies. Let's get back,' suggested Amelia, whose nose had gone blue. Their mood was verging on the euphoric, and even the discovery of a dead fox by the hedge did not dampen it.

'How sad! But he's very handsome, isn't he?' Josie said, examining the sleek tawny fur, admiring the pointed mask. They knew it would be impossible to bury him, the ground being too hard to dig. Best to leave him to the crows and other carrion eaters. Amelia supposed he must have been hit by a car.

'Come on. Leave him now. I've got to go and turn the goose over and the sitting room fire'll go out if we aren't quick.'

Josie got up from her stooping position over the fox. She had been feeling his thick coarse fur which, ruffled by the slight breeze, gave an appearance of fluttering life.

'The wind's changed, gone round to the east. There's cloud coming up over there. Perhaps it will snow?'

'So there is. I don't want to be snowed in but a little sprinkling would be quite acceptable, on Christmas Day! Winter seems to have set in dreadfully early this year. Come *on*, Hat!'

The house had warmed up nicely while they were out,

and the smell of roasting goose wafted about the kitchen, to which was added the smell of Amelia's Russian tobacco and a little dash of the scent which had been in the stocking. The potatoes went into the oven, along with stuffing balls and small sausages and bacon. They opened a bottle of wine and toasted each other as they waited for their guests.

'Here's to us, and absent friends.'

'Here's to us!'

'Who's like us?'

'Damn few!'

'This is so much better than last Christmas, when we were living in that horrid little shack of a cottage in Fingle, and we were both so sad,' said Amelia, thinking that Josie had not seemed too unhinged by the fact that Mary Beaton had got there first with Will Redding, had seemed to think it quite a giggle. Josie had in fact been seriously pissed off for at least ten minutes, but she admired Mary's panache and although she had been surprised that anyone over thirty-five could possibly be attractive to someone of Will's age, 'wasted' on her, she thought, and although Mary did look very young for her age and rode a motorbike, she would have to rethink things.

There was a furious rat-tatting at the door, shrieks and shouts of 'Happy Christmas! Happy Christmas! Look, here you are Amelia, this bag's full of South African white and this is the Australian red, and here, tarara! is the pudding! Will, where did you put the beer? Oh, I see, in the middle of the floor.' Mary took the tinfoil off a green Wedgwood leaf dish and there was a miraculous, dome-shaped pudding, dark brown and dangerous, with cartoon icing dripping from the top and a sprig of holly stuck in it.

'It's ounces and ounces of bitter chocolate, butter and chestnut purée with oranges and a glass of brandy. It'll kill us all!' said Mary, satisfied with the applause it produced.

The final preparations for the Great Feast gathered momentum. Potatoes were turned, goose basted, wine was drunk and Will proved to be a sturdy butler. They ate slowly, with the greatest satisfaction, gales of laughter and Party Poppers, their pastel streamers trailing from the beams of the ceiling, startling spiders and deafening death-watch beetles. The remnants of Will and Mary's home-made crackers littered the floor; these had been a great success, having a horticultural theme, their ends tied with green garden string, their contents green paper hats and brightly coloured packets of seeds. Mary had handwritten the jokes on slips of pink paper, all strongly agricultural in flavour, and all quite unsuitable for children.

Afterwards they collapsed in a heap in the sitting room, Mary and Will lying flat out on the floor in front of the fire, devastated by the combination of goose and chocolate. By common consent they remained comatose for a while, before Amelia and Mary bestirred themselves sufficiently to go into the kitchen and try to make some order amongst the wreckage. Amelia tackled the worst of the washing-up, thinking that if she had to wait much longer to see Edmund she'd go spare. When Johnnie had called to collect the bracelet he had suggested that Edmund might like to meet Mary, that she had been invited to drinks too, with the object of introducing them. She relayed this piece of information to Mary while potting up the goose fat and giving the carcase to the cat outside in the garden.

'Good God! It *is* the eighteenth century. I told you so. Serious match-making, no less. Anyway, Mrs Sailor, I do believe the gentleman in question is spoken for, is he not?'

'I think indeed he might be, Mrs Beaton.'

'What, no indecision? No demurral? No blushes? I do believe you've cracked it!' She threw the drying-up cloth into the air. 'Now let's go and play cards or something. I'm on call from midnight on, so I can't have anything more to drink. Then we could all go back to my place for tea, I've got this silly film on video that Will wants to watch, called *Beetlejuice*, and Josie'll like it too. It's a mocky-rocky horror film.'

The rest of the afternoon passed lazily, with cards and a manic version of vingt-et-un, for which, there not being enough matches in the house to use as chips, Amelia had produced a packet of sultanas. Josie would have won had she not eaten all her winnings as fast as they came in.

'Right, let's go and watch the film, and I can drive you back afterwards,' said Mary, heaving Will to his feet. She had been pleased that Josie had accepted the situation, and that she had not appeared too alluring in her velvet hat. It was dark now, and as they opened the back door the first few flakes of snow drifted into the kitchen.

Amelia watched the film in a happy haze, tipsy enough to find it excruciatingly funny and to stop her wondering how Edmund was faring with his family. But the snow was settling fast, and they had eventually to drag themselves out of the warmth and head for home. It being Christmas Day, no gritters had been out on the roads. There was no traffic at all.

'Goodnight, dearest Mary. Thanks for bringing us home. Take care of yourself, with Will, I mean. Don't get hurt,' Amelia whispered as they hugged on the doorstep.

'I won't, I'm a tough old boot. But he is lovely, isn't he?'

'Yes, very beautiful, and almost unnaturally thoughtful for someone his age. I liked the way he helped you into your coat, and made sure you'd got sacks and a spade in the car, as if we were in the Grampians. I hope the snow doesn't stop us going to the Whitbys' tomorrow.'

At the Whitbys', the day had passed in a fashion so well-ordered as to be regimentally boring. Christmas breakfast was at nine o'clock on the dot, with Sofia grumbling in a dressing gown of supremely sumptuous terracotta-coloured velvet. She had at least managed to refuse to get dressed for the occasion. Xenia had the order of the day pinned to the wall. At ten thirty, everyone was to get ready for church. At a quarter to eleven, they would leave for church, after the geese had been put in the oven. At twelve fifteen they would return to the house and have drinks in the drawing room. There was a general rebellion led by Henry and Rupert about going to church, since they had attended Midnight Mass the night before.

'But, we never, ever, go to both. It's ridiculous!' said Rupert.

'No, not again!' said Henry. 'We'll have to sit through the vicar's Christmas sermon. It's the same one, every year. Listen, I can tell you how it starts. 'When I was a little, little boy, I lived in a small, small ever-so-poor-and-humble house, next door to a great big enormous manor . . .' I think the text is 'Blessed are the meek for they shall inherit the earth,' but he isn't meek at all. In fact he's got the most rampant chip on his shoulder about the people in the great, big enormous manor.'

'I don't think chips can be rampant,' said Rupert pedantically. 'I think chips should be huge, or heavy, or marble, perhaps.'

'I quite agree with you,' said Johnnie. 'It *has* been the same sermon for the last three years. I think he imagines he's communicating with the children in the congregation, but he only succeeds in patronizing them and infuriating everyone else. I'll give you three to one it's the same sermon this year. Any takers?'

Xenia was looking dangerous. She had planned that they would all go to church, and go they all would.

Sofia took the bet, and put a pound coin on the hall table in token of her sincerity. Xenia glared at them all as if they were recalcitrant children, and Johnnie decided a bit of mollification was needed and frowned at the boys and his mother-in-law, warning them of a serious rupture if they did not do as they were told. So they went, and sat through the first part of the service with mounting hilarity, breathlessly waiting as the heavy vicar mounted the rickety pulpit and leant forward to speak.

'Blessed are the meek . . . Now when I was a little, little boy . . .'

Rupert bent double and had to be pushed down by Edmund on to the dusty floor of the box-pew, out of sight of the rest of the congregation, muffled. To judge from their reaction, there had been gambling in other houses that morning. Edmund swore he saw money change hands.

Sofia looked annoyed. 'So I lose my pound,' she whispered to Johnnie. ''Ow could 'e do it again? Is it to tease us?'

'Shsh!' said Xenia, but Johnnie was smiling and shaking his head in exasperation.

Edmund's thoughts drifted off once the sermon had started and the excitement was over. It had been the only excitement of the morning, since Xenia had stuck rigidly to their parents' rule of Christmas presents not being opened until teatime. It had been there on the timetable, he had noticed. One o'clock, lunch. Five o'clock, tea and present-opening. Followed by drinks at six, supper at eight, and she had even put 'Eleven o'clock – *bed*', underlining it as though it were the most important item of the day. Perhaps it was for her. Glancing at Johnnie, who was in a depressed state of sleepiness, his head propped up so that he appeared to be listening to the vicar, he wondered how they got on in bed. It had crossed his mind before that things had not been as smooth as they might have been between Xenia and Johnnie, long before her present bout of insecurity and jealousy-provoked fits of sulking. But it must be very difficult, being married to someone with Xenia's temperament.

Although it was to a great extent her own fault, he loved and felt sympathy for her as she sat there, neat and apparently attentive, watching the vicar's fat chins wobbling loosely as he proclaimed his childhood meekness. Xenia's timetable was only an aide-memoire, interspersed with cooking reminders such as 'make cheese straws' and 'poach salmon'; it was a rather touching testimony to how much she cared that things should run smoothly; but surely she had gone completely over the top now, forcing everyone to come to church. Their mother was in any case Russian Orthodox, in so far as she was anything, and had been severely put out at being frogmarched to church like a child. They were all being treated like children so that she could keep to her blessed timetable. Was she in fact becoming slightly deranged? He could not see Amelia anywhere, although his eyes had passed up and down the pews ahead of him and he had even twisted round during the numerous risings and fallings as the service wended its way through the unfamiliar intricacies of Rite Z, or was it W, or even Y? It certainly wasn't the prayer-book order of service and seemed uncommonly lumpen in its vocabulary. He had not really expected to see Amelia – she had not struck him as being a church-goer. He had no religious beliefs himself, since having them seemed to entail, amongst other things, a belief that mankind was somehow able to swing events in its own favour through supernatural means and this appeared to him to be patently untrue. Neither had he seen any signs of meekness leading to anything other than the meek being trampled underfoot. 'For they shall inherit the earth.' He could understand that better if it had said 'for they shall inherit heaven'. Xenia was the least meek person he had ever come across.

The vicar was drawing his sermon ponderously to a close,

having wondrously lost the thread of his argument. Someone should do something to stabilize the pulpit, thought Edmund, or the meek would soon be flat on his face on the gravestones of past local worthies, who were also unlikely to have been very meek, judging by the size and beauty of their monuments. He supposed that going to church provided people with ritual, and that ritual gave people time to order their thoughts and concentrate on things other than their own immediate needs. Which was why there had been so much uproar when the forms of services and wording had been changed, leaving everyone flustered and lost, and denied exactly that peace and certainty which they had come to partake in and enjoy. He could not really understand it. Here they all sat, like members of a club at an annual general meeting (and he disliked both clubs and committee meetings), waiting for the chairman to proceed to the part of the agenda which listed any other business. The incongruous Calor Gas heaters hissed sibilantly in the background. Great fidgeting was taking place.

'In the name of the Father, and of the Son and of the Holy Spirit . . .' It was finished at last, and they rose to sing again, feet ice-cold, fingers stiff.

Lunch was wonderfully cooked, amazingly all eaten up; wine flowed, and any attempts at discussion of anything was headed off by Xenia, who even stalled her mother in mid-sentence, just as she was vehemently refuting Johnnie's comment that Britain would quite likely become a republic soon.

'I think that very, very *un*likely,' Sofia was saying. 'What on earth would the British 'ave to talk about? It is in the interests of the media to sustain . . .'

'Johnnie!' said Xenia, suddenly and loudly, 'have you wound up the hall clock?'

'Good God! Xenia!' said Johnnie, exasperated. 'Have you been reading *Tristram Shandy*?'

'No. I just wanted to know if you'd wound up the clock. Is *Tristram Shandy* one of those revolting books you keep in the spare bedroom?'

There was a long silence.

Johnnie at last made sense of what she'd said, and looked helplessly at Edmund, who, unable to stop himself, gave an embarrassed and guilty grin. Henry said he didn't see how anyone could plough through all of *Tristram Shandy* and that none of it matched up to its first page. Rupert said he hadn't seen *Tristram Shandy* in the bookcase last time he'd been looking for something exciting to read, and then Xenia banged down her fork and, leaving her Christmas pudding, the table and her family, stalked out of the room.

Sofia also rose, as if to go after her, but Johnnie told her to please sit down. They would finish the meal.

'I don't see why we should have our conversation censored, do you? I'm bloody well not going to have everybody's Christmas spoilt by her autocratic behaviour. Now, Sofia, what were you saying?'

Of course it was impossible to continue the conversation, and they all made excuses for Xenia. How tired she had seemed, and overwrought by little things.

'I've finished now,' said Sofia. 'I'll make the coffee and take it through, and the boys will clear the table and stack the dishwasher, yes? Good. I'll just go and find Xenia. She needs a little calming, per'aps.'

Edmund doubted her ability to calm instead of inflame and offered to go instead, but Sofia insisted. She wished to get to the bottom of things, she said. Something must have caused this '*petite crise*'.

She returned with the coffee, saying that Xenia was fine, and would be down shortly, but she looked a little thoughtfully at Johnnie.

Xenia did reappear in time for tea, which Sofia and Edmund prepared. She had her unseeing smile on her face, said she was sorry she'd had to go and lie down, perhaps she had been a little tired. It was time to open the presents. A fire had been lit in the hall and they sat around it, the boys ferrying presents to their owners. The tree sparkled prettily in the corner. Edmund was the happy recipient of a navy-blue cashmere sweater from Johnnie and Xenia, which was a good thing, since the navy-blue cashmere sweater they had given him last year had worn out. He was terribly pleased with Rupert's green cup and saucer and looked up to thank him, but intercepted Johnnie's anxious hopefulness as Xenia unwrapped the gold paper from a little box and took out from its little burrow of scarlet tissue the bracelet.

'Here, let me slip it on for you,' said Johnnie, 'your wrist fits sideways through the gap – see? Like this.'

'Johnnie . . . I . . . it's gorgeous.' She seemed taken aback.

'I had it made specially for you,' said Johnnie proudly. She looked back at him, mercifully appeased and happy with it, he thought, and gave him a kiss on the cheek.

She showed it round to them all, and Edmund feigned surprise and admiration. It gave him a strange feeling to see it after having watched its construction and knowing the delicacy of the process. Now it rested on Xenia's arm as if it had always been there. Sofia was most intrigued by it, and kept asking Johnnie where he had commissioned it, but he was jokingly evasive.

'But the workmanship is exquisite, and such a strong design.'

She was quite envious. It would have made a nice addition to her own collection, but she knew it was too good to be worn as one of a group and needed to be seen on its own.

'Thanks! Thanks, Uncle Eddie. You're a magician!' Rupert waved the tickets about. 'Look, Henry! The Dark Entry!'

Henry had been unimpressed by the music of the band when he'd been at school, but had been friendly with its members and was now very interested indeed having discovered that knowing them personally had a certain cachet at university amongst the cognoscenti of such music. He hoped Rupert would give the spare ticket to him.

Xenia was both pleased and worried by her present. She could see it was unusual, special in some way she did not understand, and checked the hallmarks, gratified by everyone else's raptures. It did look good on her wrist, fitting snugly, the mysterious design gleaming up at her; she would not normally have worn such an obviously modern piece, preferring things to be less conspicuous. But it was heavy, solid gold. Gold – gilt – guilt. The words unfortunately dripped through her mind in sequence. Could it be a guilt present? It was quite out of the ordinary for Johnnie to give her jewellery: he had bought her rings when the boys had been born, but nothing since. Why now suddenly ignore her modest Christmas list and spend so much money? She spoiled her own pleasure in the gift by starting another agonizing tallying up of the signs of unfaithfulness, but meanwhile checking her list, poaching the salmon, making mayonnaise and counting the little pastry cases ready for tomorrow's party.

12

The snow was not thick enough to hinder them from getting to the party, so after breakfast Amelia and Josie set about their clothes; Josie pressing black jeans and picking the odd cat hair off the black jersey which Amelia had lent her. She would naturally wear the black hat, making a neat minimalist outfit to which she would, unfortunately, have to add the boots she wore to school.

Amelia was in a slight panic, at a loss to know what to wear, knowing what she would like to look like, but so financially strictured had she been recently that she hadn't bought anything new for over a year. She pulled from her cupboard a creased little green velvet jacket, a bit tight round the upper arms, but worn without another layer beneath, it would just fit. She expected the Whitbys' house would be well heated. Steaming the velvet over the kettle worked magic, and she shook out the creases, thinking that Edmund, whose attitude to dress had seemed casual to the point of negligence, would surely not be too critical. The coral skirt which came from Barnardo's in Parden would smarten it up considerably but she was anxious in case the previous owner of the skirt would be at the party and recognize it. Shoes! She hadn't thought of shoes. Josie watched her shuffling through the hoard at the bottom of the cupboard and pounced.

'What about those? They're so old-fashioned they've come in again. They'd look just right with that length of skirt and they're exactly the same colour as the jacket.'

'But the heels!' wailed Amelia. 'They're so scuffed – but I suppose I could paint them. Would they dry in time, do you think?'

'Of course they will. Use thick poster paint and spray them with fixative.'

'Brilliant. I'll go and do that now.'

After half an hour's fiddling she'd got the right shade and painted them, leaving them to dry on the stove. She washed and dried her hair, snipping a few loose ends and blow-drying it till it sat thick and wavy about her face. Then with great care, the paint appearing dry, she sprayed the heels of the old shoes with a can of matt artwork fixative; it smelt a bit gluey, like lighter fuel, but that would soon evaporate. They looked pretty good, she thought, as she slipped her feet into them. The snow would surely ruin the paintwork so she would have to carry them, go in Wellington boots till reaching the front door and then change quickly.

Josie put on her gold daisy earrings and made up her pointy little face. Since Will was temporarily unavailable she was in search of a replacement fantasy man and intended to stand out in the crowd – surely not all the guests would be geriatrics? The earrings looked cool. She might be able to get a commission for her mother. She took one final look in her mirror and saw the beginnings of a zit on her chin, panicked and applied more foundation over it but with any luck it wouldn't come to a head till the evening.

She went and stood in the door of her mother's room, a fashionable waif, posing and waiting for approval, while checking out her mother's makeup.

'Do your eyes properly, won't you?'

'Why, don't I usually?' Amelia asked, thinking that she looked perfectly all right as she was.

'No, you don't usually bother. Go on. Eyeshadow, that greeny-gold one. Pencil, mascara. The lot. If you've got it – flaunt it.'

'Bossy cow. All right, here goes. But won't I look a bit overcooked for lunchtime?'

'No. It'll look perfect,' said Josie, exasperated.

She watched as Amelia bent towards her mirror again, and did as she was told. She really looks quite startlingly good, thought Josie, with satisfaction.

'I'll go and scrape the snow off the windscreen. We ought to be going, soon. It's midday.'

'Right, I'm ready as I can be.'

Amelia nipped into the sitting room and gave the Arabian brass globes a quick polish. 'Come on! Come on! Some good fortune needed here. I want to like him, but I'm frightened of being disappointed. And I don't want to do any catching. I want to leave it to him. And I *don't* want another quick affair.'

She did not notice that her shoes left little reversed horse-shoe prints of green across the floor as she left the room.

They had to drive very slowly, as the roads were worse than she'd anticipated. They leant forwards, willing the car up the slope, thankful not to meet anyone coming down as it was quite narrow. The Whitbys' house was not visible from the road and the lovely cream-painted lines of the eighteenth-century front surprised them both when they came upon it suddenly. There was a muddle of cars and banks of snow in the drive, Johnnie having brought round the tractor with its snow plough earlier in the morning and attempted to clear as much space as possible. Amelia managed to park where she felt there was no opportunity of being boxed in, in case she needed to make a quick getaway should things turn out to be too much for them.

'Oh look! Two Rollers! I didn't know it would be this grand. I thought Johnnie Whitby was just an ordinary farmer, like Ruffles' Dad,' said Josie.

'He is just an ordinary farmer. But they know all sorts of people, so you mustn't be put off. You look absolutely fine,' she added, divining the source of the panic in Josie's voice. She left her old coat in the car and smiled with a confidence she did not possess as an elegant couple arrived behind them, just as she was leaning up against the doorway, changing out of her Wellingtons and into her painted shoes on the doorstep.

They went together into the hall with its huge blazing fire and the hubbub of talking and laughter coming from the drawing room. Already the gathering was spilling out into the hall where Rosy Pressing and her daughter stood in charge of the drinks, wearing black dresses and with beaming pudgy faces. She liked a good 'do', did Rosy, and she summoned up a certain frenetic energy for the occasion which was lacking when she went about her usual work in the house. Amelia smiled at her, having seen her in the village shop on numerous occasions, and Rosy smiled back in a conspiratorial manner, poured them both brimming glasses of hot punch and leant forward to say: 'You'll find Mr Johnnie in the drawing room.'

But Amelia wasn't looking for Johnnie.

Josie momentarily shrank back behind Amelia as they stood in the doorway. The noise was intimidating as forty-odd people with no inhibitions about the sound of their own voices brayed information at each other.

Edmund had been fielding sympathetic questions about the state of his ear and was lurking in the drawing room. Xenia had been popping in and out of her kitchen, anxiously scanning the new arrivals for signs of the great whore of Babylon, and getting her glass refilled by Rosy. Her trips in and out had become less frequent now she was embarked on getting the hot food ready, Edmund noticed. He also was vigilant for Amelia, but it is doubtful if it was the same person they were expecting. Sofia had been talking to a supremely uninteresting lawyer with a passion for rhododendrons.

'When we first moved here from Surrey,' he said, drawling condescendingly as if he had now reached Ultima Thule and found it wanting, 'I was appalled to find that so few people grew them. But I have, with great difficulty, and quantities of peat and acidifiers, induced them to grow.'

'But that is very cruel of you. They will never be 'appy 'ere. They will always be poor, struggling things in this alien soil.'

She caught sight of a woman with red-gold hair, standing wavering by the door, noticed the searching look on her face. A small woman, but with style, in spite of being a little down-at-heel, with dignity, looking for someone. Behind her was a tall girl in black from head to foot, unmistakably a daughter. She saw the scanning gaze flash into a smile, the dark eyes widening at first with pleasure, and then she put her hand to her mouth and the pleasure turned to concern. Sofia turned swiftly to see the object of the look.

'But, that is what I so enjoy, *making* them grow. You don't like rhododendrons, I can see,' said the man, trying to get her attention again.

But that attention was on Edmund, pushing his way through the guests with more haste than care, apologizing to left and right as he nudged hot punch on to the carpet and trod on patent leather toes.

'I think they are very beautiful, in Surrey. Per'aps you should return there where you will 'ave more success. It is sadistic to try to grow them 'ere.'

Edmund was taking the woman's hand, bending forward to kiss her on both cheeks, and greeting the daughter.

He was standing there, still holding her hand, making a charming exhibition of himself.

Well! she thought. At last he is interested in someone. I must meet her in a moment or two.

The rhododendron man seemed taken aback. Sadism was not something of which he was used to being accused, neither did he see how it applied to a plant lover, which he fervently believed himself to be. He tried again. 'My other great interest is bonsai.'

'Then you are definitely a torturer, a foot-binder!'

She smiled sweetly at him, and he discovered at last that he was being teased. He was wrong.

'You will excuse me, I think my son-in-law needs to speak to me.' She turned away and swished off in her soft silk skirt, leaving him feeling culpable of some unknown crime.

'Johnnie? Excuse me a moment – who is that – the pretty woman to whom Edmund is so obviously attached?' She nodded her head in the direction of the doorway. Over the heads of the crowd Johnnie saw Amelia talking earnestly to Edmund, who was bent towards her, trying to hear over the football match roar that was developing now in the hall as well as the drawing room. What did Sofia mean by 'attached'? Had Edmund found out who she was, at last? He looked hard and long at his brother-in-law's body, bent, now his attention had been drawn to it, protectively, proprietorially, over Amelia. They certainly looked better acquainted than he would like and a small seed of jealousy germinated, but he contrived to crush it.

He turned back to Sofia. 'Her name is Amelia Sailor.'

'But, my dearest Johnnie, your wife is convinced that *you* are 'aving an affair with 'er! She told me yesterday, after a lot of trouble. I did not believe 'er, and now I see I was right to disbelieve.'

'Keep your voice down, Sofia! Yes, you were right to disbelieve. For once and all, I have *not* had an affair with her.' He had lowered his voice and speaking directly into her scented ear.

'Why not, then?'

He stared at her. Was she suggesting that he should have? She was Xenia's mother, for goodness' sake.

'Because of Xenia, of course.'

'It is precisely because of Xenia that I asked. I know you 'ave a difficult time with 'er, you are good to 'er, but she is very, very *difficile*.'

'Sofia, I can't stand here talking about this in public. Someone will hear.'

'I don't see 'ow. I can 'ardly 'ear you myself. But take me over now, and present me.'

Reluctantly and slowly, Johnnie got his wits together and made a path through for her.

'Hello, Amelia, and Josie. How good to see you both. Did you have much trouble getting through the snow? Sofia, may I introduce Amelia Sailor and her daughter Josie? Amelia, this is Madame Sofia Yearne, Edmund's mother.'

Sofia's eyes were sharp and enquiring, alight with an almost gloating interest.

'*Maman*, Amelia speaks excellent French, so you may give up the struggle for a little while, and relax.' This was unfair of Edmund, since Sofia had no trouble with English, nor indeed with Italian or Russian, but she was delighted to hear that Amelia was bilingual, although as the conversation progressed, she found it hard to place the slight accent.

Edmund braced himself to explain to Sofia the tale of his discovery of Amelia, since Johnnie had so meanly kept his secret. He described his difficulties with such pathos, his discovery – almost as if she were a new continent – that she lived only a few miles away with such delight that Sofia was enchanted. Johnnie tried not to grind his teeth.

'But this is really a most extraordinary story – that you

should 'ave been so close, 'ad lunch with 'er and not suspected. You 'ave been very slow, Edmund!'

I'd have been a lot quicker, thought Edmund, if old Lothario here had come clean.

Sofia was searching Amelia's face, for signs of affection returned, and was almost satisfied. They need time together – then all will be well, she was thinking.

Henry passed by with a tray of little choux buns filled with crème fraîche and caviar, and was waylaid by Edmund.

'Henry, dear Henry. This is Josie Sailor. She says she remembers you from reel-parties when you were children.'

Henry stared at Josie with dawning recognition, but he was rather short on gallantry.

'I should say I do. You used to lie on the floor and see if the boys who were wearing kilts had anything on underneath!'

'Henry!' said Johnnie, growling at his elder son's lack of tact.

However Josie did not even blush. 'Well, yes. I remember. But I was only ten, and very curious.'

Henry thought she was considerably more interesting now than she had been then, but wasn't going to show it, just yet.

'I've got to get round with these. Would you like one before I go and throw them to the starving elephants?'

'Yes, please.' She took one and popped it in neatly between her painted lips.

'I'll catch you later on, when I've done the duties.'

She nodded as coolly as she could, thinking that he looked quite promising.

To save her from an imminent interrogation from his mother, Edmund asked Amelia if the necklace she was wearing was one of her own, one she'd made, explaining to Sofia that she was a talented jeweller and had made the bracelet which Johnnie had given to Xenia.

'Yes, it is one of mine. You like it?'

'I think it's lovely, but I've just been talking to someone who is looking for something original as a twenty-first birthday present for his daughter. I have a feeling he'd be tempted by something like that. Come and meet him. His name is Gavin Wallace and he's an astronomer. You come too, Josie. He's one of these people who has enthusiasm for so many things he's always interesting.' He shepherded them away, leaving Sofia and Johnnie feeling, for different reasons, like cats who have had their recently caught and as yet unplayed-with mice removed from them.

Gavin Wallace was an ascetic-faced man in his fifties, wearing a fashionably cut plum-coloured jacket with an extravagantly embroidered waistcoat, which delighted Amelia, since it was embroidered with the constellations in silver, with a border of silver flowers which would have done credit to the Tailor of Gloucester's mouse assistants. He examined the necklace with care, enquiring about the casting of the small acorns, eggs and birds with which it was hung, asked for her card and said he was sure they could come to an understanding. She was immensely relieved she had been optimistic enough to bring the cards. The room was becoming overstuffed and hot, upholstered with soft wool Jaeger suits, navy twill blazers, hand-tailored grey flannel, country tweeds, Laura Ashley velvets and unfortunately amusing Christmas-present silk ties. Rupert zig-zagged through carrying a jug of punch, and paused beside them.

'Would you like a refill?'

'Yes, please. You must be Edmund's other nephew?' said Amelia.

'Yes, I'm Rupert. How did you guess?' He filled her glass solicitously.

'I think you look rather like him. Did you have a good Christmas? Lots of interesting presents?'

'Oh yes, but the best was Uncle Eddie's. He came up with tickets for The Dark Entry. That's a brilliant band who used to be at school with my brother. I've met them all, of course, when they were in the sixth form.'

'Heavens! How exciting! So I can tell my friends I've had my glass filled by someone who knows Kieran Gaffikin, can I?'

Rupert looked at her with admiration. Josie became further interested in Henry.

'Not many people know that,' Rupert said, meaning that not many people her age knew that.

'Josie likes them too, that's how I know.' Rupert looked at Josie and was smitten. Here was the perfect person to take to the concert. She was older than him of course, but then some girls liked younger men. He'd have to think about it since there was Foxy to be considered, languishing at home in disgrace in Sussex, in need of cheering up.

Charlie Parrott appeared at Edmund's elbow.

'We made it! The roads are appalling – it's taken us an hour to get here from Rye.' Edmund stared in disbelief at his companion. Marianne had returned to haunt him again. She looked stunning, in tight black trousers and a soft jade-green leather jacket. She put her hand on Charlie's arm, and it occurred to Edmund that perhaps she was as nervous of him disclosing something untoward as he was of her. He managed a brotherly smile, introduced them to Amelia and Josie and Gavin Wallace. By common consent they all moved out to the less crowded hall and Edmund led the new arrivals to Rosy Pressing who was dispensing drink at high speed and managing to keep an eye on everyone and everything, storing it all up for a later recounting at the village shop, her face positively twitching with interest.

'Thank you Rosy, now give me a jug of punch and I'll take it round,' said Edmund, glancing about for someone to whom he could introduce Marianne and Charlie. He rejected old Major Snargate and Allie Snodland, who were discussing the iniquities of the Parden Planning Department and then lit on Ted Spirit, the science-fiction writer who was now deep in conversation with Sofia.

'*Maman*, you have met Charlie before, and this is his friend Marianne who was so helpful to me when I was looking for Amelia.' He turned to Marianne. 'You may have seen the television adaptation of the book, *Troic and Zilda*?'

Delayed by the snow, but undeterrred by their search for what they knew would be a good party, people were still arriving. Battalions of boots lined the walls of the hall, melting snow making little puddles of water on the flags. Regiments of coats were flung across the banisters, empty glasses lined the windowsills. He hated to leave Amelia for a second, but felt bound to do some more handing round of food and clearing of glasses. Light-minded, confused by the chaotic choreography of introductions and the noise, he headed for the kitchen to collect a tray. He hadn't set eyes on Xenia since the first guests had arrived, but he found her in the kitchen, dragging a tray of salmon patties out of the oven, hair limp and dress decorated with a spray of mayonnaise up the sleeve. He would have to let her meet Amelia soon – hoping that his explanation would take the heat off Johnnie.

'Just rounding up a few glasses for you, Xenia. Rosy's running low. Shall I take that food out for you, and put it in the hall? Rupert and Henry are doing a grand job waitering.'

'Rupert may be, but Henry's disappeared upstairs with a girl in a stupid black hat.'

'Oh, Josie Sailor.'

She looked flushed and her eyes were a little unfocused.

'Why don't you go and enjoy your party, Xenia? It's going so well. I'll get someone to come and take over here.'

'No, no! I've got to finish the hot food. And Rosy's brought me in a glass of wine.'

'That's punch, Xenia, not wine. It's Johnnie's maxi-strength brew.'

'I am not drunk – that's what you're saying, isn't it. You think I'm drunk?'

'Don't shout at me, Xenia! I merely said to watch it. It's very strong.'

Edmund took a dish of patties and returned in search of Amelia, whom he found talking to Mary Beaton, standing beneath the Millais portrait of Johnnie's great-grandfather, a bewhiskered young Victorian gentleman leaning against the gate to Hilly Foxes field, a bunch of primroses in his hand and a delicate, adoring spaniel at his feet in the green, green grass. *When* was he ever going to get a chance to talk to her alone?

Johnnie passed him.

'Where is Xenia? She should be out here with her guests. Some people are starting to leave and she's hardly even said hello to anyone. Why can't she just leave the damned food on the tables so that people can help themselves. I told her to get in caterers, but she will *insist* on doing it all herself.' He disappeared into the kitchen.

Sofia detached herself from an elderly judge who was ranting on about poisoning rats.

'No good at all. They're super-rats now. Doesn't have any effect on them.'

She followed Johnnie, meaning to offer a hand. She'd never heard so many ridiculous conversations in her life and thought she might get a minute's peace in the kitchen. Amelia introduced Mary to Edmund.

'Oh, but I remember you very well. You are the motor-biking GP who arrived at the Eeldyke pub just as Johnnie and I were leaving. Have you been working over Christmas, or did you manage a decent break?'

'I was on call from midnight last night till just now. Not too bad, really. One attack of indigestion, which the family took to be a heart attack, one broken ankle caused by someone falling off a table, or so he said. One genuine heart attack, but I managed to get the air ambulance helicopter in for him. And one croupy baby. Considering the appalling weather it was quite quiet.'

Edmund's eyes were straying to Amelia while Mary spoke. She was laughing at something Charlie had said, throwing her head back so that the necklace tinkled round her throat. Her skin was very pale as it disappeared into the deep V-shape of the front of the jacket. It was just as well he had not bought her the one he'd seen in London – a pretty coincidence that she had chosen to wear just what he would have chosen for her.

'You've known Amelia for a long time?' he asked Mary.

'At least four years. She was my first patient when I joined the practice, and we've been good friends ever since. She's been through a rough time since Nick committed suicide,' Mary said in a lowered voice, as if warning him not to muck her about any further. He wanted to ask what Nick had been like, why she thought he'd done such a thing, but Amelia was too close, and he could ask her himself, much later, if there was a later. They were interrupted by Allie Snodland who boomed into them, almost pinning Amelia to the wall.

'Mimi, darling! How are *you*?' she emphasized the last word as if Amelia, who was looking trapped, had already enquired about her own health. She was one of the people whom Amelia had known before Nick died, and who had drifted away on the tide of omission afterwards, and Amelia did not much care for her and her delving curranty eyes.

'I'm not contagious anymore, if that's what you mean,' Amelia said, hearing her own belligerent voice with astonishment. The punch must have been stronger than she'd thought. Allie did not know how to take this and was momentarily aware that she was being attacked, but was saved by Sofia's appearance.

'I've come to find an 'elper, Edmund. Xenia is a bit tired, but she will not stop putting things in the oven. I tell 'er everyone 'as 'ad enough to eat. She will not listen to me.'

'I'll come and help', said Amelia, thinking this would be as good a moment as any to set about dispelling Xenia's preconceptions about her.

'Me too', said Mary. Edmund took Marianne's arm. 'Come on, Charlie, come and meet Nigel Hogarth.' Nigel was the local celebrity, an actor steadily in work, a patient, gentle person with a scarred cheek and pitted skin who specialized in playing unpleasant thugs. Charlie followed. He had been impressed by the beautiful house and had spotted a set of George Vertue's 1830s *Picturesque Beauties of Great Britain* in the drawing room, which he rather hankered after.

By the time Edmund got back Sofia had taken Amelia and Mary into the kitchen, and he galloped off to protect her, leaving Allie with the rhododendron man who had resurfaced, searching for a fellow fanatic to enthuse with. He'd met his match in Allie, who shared the same level of intense passion, for azaleas, and could bore for England on the subject. A few people were beginning to leave, worried by the prospect of further snow, and were saying goodbye to a harassed-looking Johnnie who hurried back to the kitchen ahead of Edmund.

The beautiful painted cupboards hung open, there was water on the floor, and eggshells, and a large piece of fruit cake on which someone had put their foot. Johnnie had hold of Xenia's arm and was pleading with her to sit down for a moment. Xenia's eyes focused on Amelia and narrowed.

'Xenia,' said Edmund hurriedly, 'this is Mimi, the person whom I've been searching for all these weeks.' He was trying to throw her off the scent, and wondered why he so often thought of Xenia as some kind of dog. Allie appeared behind him.

'Hello, Xen. Where have you been hiding yourself? I told you in Canterbury, remember . . . this is Mimi Anderson . . .'

'I know perfectly well who she is,' Xenia said, venomously, her eyes snake-like, and Edmund hastily took Amelia's arm as if to emphasize the connection between her and himself, not Johnnie. Raucous male laughter came from the hall. Haw, Haw! HAW! Xenia took in the gesture, and snarled, 'I suppose you and your daughter will try to seduce Rupert next?'

'Xenia!' Edmund said, appalled. 'Don't be unpleasant and idiotic! We've just come to help – to give you a break.' Johnnie was looking stricken, Sofia quite shocked.

'I *know*! I know who she is, and I know what she's up to. She's trying ruin my life. Take everyone away from me! She's had Johnnie and now she's taken Edmund.' She was clenching the table top, her knuckles white. 'Her little tart of a daughter has gone off somewhere with Henry!'

Amelia, inspired by the punch, waded in. 'That's utter balls! You're completely off the mark and totally offensive! I wouldn't have come if it hadn't been for Edmund, and *only* Edmund.' Then, thinking desperately that there might be other reasons for the onslaught, 'Didn't you like the bracelet?'

Xenia looked at her wrist, where it shone gracefully, as if she had never seen it before. 'What has the bracelet to do with you?'

Sofia interrupted. 'Johnnie commissioned it from 'er. For you, specially. Didn't 'e tell you?' This was so untimely as to be seriously late.

'You did what?' Xenia screamed at Johnnie. 'You mean *you* made this . . . this . . . ?' she shrieked at Amelia. She scrabbled at the bracelet, trying to drag it off, succeeded and flung it to the floor, where it rolled beneath the kitchen table, clanging to a halt encircling a mislaid hard-boiled quail's egg. Allie couldn't wait to go and tell someone that the Whitby's were having an almighty row and headed for the hall, missing seeing Xenia picking up Rupert's present, the Sabatier vegetable knife, and lunging at Johnnie with it. Johnnie sidestepped smartly and made a grab for her arm but missed. The knife sliced across Amelia's collarbone, chinking harshly on her silver necklace. Sofia shrieked, leapt forward and captured the flailing arm and slapped her daughter hard across the face. In Edmund's eyes it happened simultaneously in slow motion and at high speed. So fast, like running, running to stay in the same place; Xenia was the Red Queen, gone horribly wrong and murderous. He flung his arms around Amelia, who was clutching the wound, blood welling up between her fingers.

'Oh Christ! Amelia! Someone stop her before she does any more damage!'

But Xenia had already dropped the knife and Mary stepped calmly into the middle of this little tragedy, took a quick look at Amelia's cut, tore some paper towels from the wall and told Amelia to hold them tight against it. She then looked at Xenia, limp and sobbing, still pinioned by her mother.

'I'd get her out of here and up to bed,' she said in a light conversational tone, as if discussing the removal of an overtired toddler who had outstayed its welcome with the grown-ups. Johnnie scooped her up, and staggered with her to the back staircase, just off the rear hall, but the old dog, convinced that Johnnie was about to do something unspeakable to the only person who had taken any notice of him over the past few weeks, and perhaps confused by old age and the smell of human blood, barred his way, growling, and as Johnnie tried to push him away with his foot, fastened his toothless jaws firmly round Johnnie's ankle.

'Get this bloody animal off me!' shouted Johnnie, shaking his leg and banging Xenia's head against the wall as he tried to climb the old staircase. No one took any notice and Mary went outside to fetch her bag, shutting the main door to the kitchen, a trifle too late, since the screaming and shouting had silenced the nearby guffawing guests who were now being given a blow-by-blow account of the scene by Allie. Rosy Pressing was looking wildly excited. The noise level abated in time with the spread of the news that all was not well with the Whitbys. Sofia was looking a lot older.

'Amelia, my dear Amelia. Sit down here. So lucky your friend is a doctor. Does it 'urt very much?'

'No. Yes. I don't know. I feel silly. I know it wasn't aimed at me.'

Edmund sat beside her at the cluttered and sticky kitchen table, holding her against him. This is nice, she thought, suddenly feeling sleepy.

'I'm a fool,' said Edmund to Sofia. 'I should never have let Amelia anywhere near her. None of us realized that she was getting into such a state. Not just today, but for weeks. It's been building up. There seems to be a lot of blood. Where *is* Mary? Do you think we need an ambulance?'

'Right, first things first.' Mary reappeared. 'I've told everyone that Xenia has been taken ill, and that it's snowing hard enough to warrant them all thinking about getting home. It is two thirty, and they've all had their money's worth. Why don't Edmund and Mrs Yearne go and join them and do the goodbyes and how-delightful-it's-been-to-see-you-agains, while I get on with this?'

Sofia left, but Edmund stayed put, not wanting to leave her until he'd found out the extent of the damage. Mary mopped up efficiently and Edmund felt slightly faint, which he hadn't when it had been his own blood last week.

'Look, it's not very deep at all. You've got a charmed life.

It could have been your throat. It's glanced off the necklace, very lucky. I'll stitch it, I think. OK?'

'I've never had stitches before.'

'I'll be so quick. I promise. I'm excellent at embroidery.'

Amelia knew this to be untrue, but laughed weakly at the old joke.

'What's happened?' Josie appeared at the door and took in the group by the table and let out a melodramatic shriek. 'Oh Mum, Mum! What's happened?'

'Nothing darling, a little accident with a kitchen knife – I'm fine. Mary's dealing with it. Make us all some coffee, would you sweetheart?'

Charlie also appeared, but hastily withdrew when he saw Mary bending over Amelia, preparing to stitch the cut. Edmund was about to explain to Josie what had happened, but this was harder than expected. 'My sister has just stabbed your mother' sounded a bit sensationalistic. Perhaps he should leave it to Amelia, whose explanation had seemed sufficient for Josie.

'I think I'll go and rescue Charlie and Marianne. Don't move. I'll be back in a minute or two.'

Sofia was in the hall doing her duty. 'Goodbye. Drive carefully, won't you? So sorry Xenia 'as 'ad to retire. Gastric flu, we think. Goodbye.' She improvised unwisely, not considering that the guests might be alarmed, having consumed quantities of Xenia's home-prepared food.

'Well, well. There seems to have been a bit of an explosion, I hear?' said Charlie, who had been collared by Allie.

'A bit worse than that. My sister completely lost control of herself and tried to stab her husband, only she got Amelia instead, but mercifully it isn't too serious.' Edmund found that his hands were trembling.

'God! It's all very Russian and emotional, isn't it? Is she really all right?'

'Yes. But we are feeling a bit shaky. Look, it would be

best if you and Marianne left now, if you see what I mean. There's a wonderful little pub about four miles down the road, if you fancy taking your chances in the snow. The Eeldyke Inn. I'll tell you all about it in the New Year. By the way, how was your Christmas with the friends in Rye?'

Charlie looked a bit evasive. 'Not quite what I'd thought it would be, actually. The farmhouse is a building site, unfinished, and Chris and Philomena are at each other's throats every five minutes; babies crying, untrained dogs all over the place.' He grinned. 'This all seems very civilized by comparison. I'll be quite glad to get back to London. I find the country overstimulating. Come on, Marianne, stop eating all the leftovers.'

Marianne gave Edmund a kiss. 'Perhaps you will get snowed in, tonight?' she said demurely. Edmund watched her leave holding on to Charlie's arm, then bending to pick up a handful of snow and threatening to rub it in his face. They seemed very friendly indeed, and he wondered what magic Marianne had wrought on Charlie. There was clearly nothing he needed to worry about on that score.

Ted Spirit was leaving too, and saw Marianne getting into Charlie's car. 'Lovely girl, that. So interested in my work. She reads a lot of my kind of thing. She thought the TV series based on *Troic and Zilda* wasn't quite up to the book.'

Major Snargate had joined forces with the judge, who was still on the topic of rats. 'You need one of my daughter's Jack Russells. Splendid little chaps! Kill them off faster than they can breed.'

'Yes. But I still think sitting there, waiting for them in the shed with the old rat gun is more fun.'

Allie had been refused leave to visit Xenia, even for a little minute, and had left in a huff with her confused husband. Rosy Pressing and daughter were rushing about the drawing room, setting it all to rights. Rosy had not caught the gist of the row since she had been in the drawing room at the time handing round a plate of miniature chocolate éclairs, but she knew something tremendous was up.

Edmund raced back to Amelia, who was sitting calmly, almost as if nothing had happened, talking to Henry and Josie. From upstairs they could hear Rupert playing his guitar.

'I think I should drive you home now. It seems best to leave Sofia and Johnnie to sort out Xenia. It's about time Johnnie looked after her.'

Mary was packing up her bag, sipping coffee. She picked up a blood-stained tea-towel and threw it in the dustbin. Already the kitchen was being returned to its former *House and Garden* immaculacy. The crumbled fruit cake and egg-shells had been swept up, the floor seemed to have been washed, the table cleared.

'Yes. I would like to go home. Josie's supposed to be going to Ruffles' tonight. But I don't think she can, if the snow keeps up, and anyway, I'll have to leave my car here.'

'I could take her. Is it far away?'

'No, only a couple of miles. Come on, Josie. Edmund is going to drive us home.'

Josie lingered with Henry after the others had gone out into the hall. 'No one will tell me quite what happened. It's ridiculous.'

'I don't know either, but I think Mum got rather drunk. She's never done that before,' said Henry,

'Oh, mine often does; well, not drunk, exactly, but definitely tiddled. We have quite a laugh sometimes. But I don't understand how she managed to cut herself.'

'I didn't know she had.'

'She's got this gash on her shoulder. I watched Mary put stitches in, she was incredibly neat. Do you think your brother would sell us his Dark Entry tickets?'

'Not a hope in hell, not an ant's chance in a Grand Prix.'

'Rupert said he heard your parents having a row.'

'Just don't know how to behave, do they?'

'I'd better go. Your uncle's giving us a lift home. He seems very keen on Mum, doesn't he?'

'Your mother's very attractive for someone her age. Perhaps they'll get it together? I'll call you, and let you know what I can find out.'

'Great, see you then.'

Edmund saw the little green hoofprints on the hall floor where Amelia's shoes had come into contact with damp patches from the melted snow. He wondered what they were – leprechauns? Once the final guests had departed and the Pressing duo were vacuuming the drawing room carpet, Sofia disappeared upstairs to see her daughter. The hall looked desolate in spite of the Christmas tree, the fire having burned right down; a serving dish with three little salmon patties sat on the white tablecloth amidst the empty glasses and punchbowl. There were several pairs of boots left behind by the front door. When Amelia changed into hers, Edmund was delighted to see the cause of the green footprints and by the time they had been joined by Josie they were laughing about the shoes, trying to cover up the awfulness of the scene in the kitchen.

13

Having been extremely drunk, Xenia slept heavily for some hours, watched over alternately by Sofia and Johnnie, both of whom were deservedly wrestling with a certain amount of guilt. Sofia felt guilty because mothers are always prone to, but Johnnie was visited by this irritant emotion not primarily because of his failure to understand the depth of his wife's distress, but because he had, by default, obstructed Edmund and Amelia's meeting. Xenia had not been the only victim of her own jealousy – Johnnie had suffered too, and could not get it out of his head that given more time, he could have overcome Amelia's scruples had not his wretched brother-in-law marched round his Maginot Line of silence and invaded his territory. That his wife had attempted to stab him had been a most horrible surprise and he was greatly shaken by it, although he was not displeased by the uncharacteristic show of her feelings for him. He could see that he had to renounce all thoughts of Amelia. Edmund had gone off with her, and had not returned.

Sofia busied herself with organizing the household and minimizing Xenia's explosion. She paid Rosy and her daughter and sent Henry off to drive them home. She brought Xenia coffee when she eventually woke up at seven o'clock and, disapproving of allowing people to shirk responsibility, gently told her the details, in case she had forgotten what had happened, and sat with her while she cried. She also noticed that Edmund had not returned, and was pleased. He was better out of the way and in any case, she and Johnnie could manage Xenia till they could see if any further action was required. She knew of a good nursing home in East Sussex that dealt in just such cases. A couple of weeks' total rest and Johnnie's constant attendance would do wonders for her, and then Johnnie should take her away on holiday for a bit.

Meanwhile Josie had wisely decided not to enquire any further into the incident although she was fairly convinced that things were being kept from her. As soon as they had reached Jarvis Cottage she rushed to telephone Ruffles, her mind now on other things.

'You're off the hook!' she said to Edmund, grinning. 'Ruffles' Dad has a four-wheel drive Jeep-type thing, and he's going to come over and collect me. You will be all right now, Mum?'

'Perfectly, darling. But *please* put some warm clothes on and take a blanket with you.'

After the warmth and space of the farm, the cottage seemed icy and cramped. Edmund made Amelia sit on the sofa and put her feet up, but she was hyped up and restless, watching him relight the fire, mentally measuring the pleasing ratio of width of shoulder to narrowness of hip as he knelt by the hearth at work with the bellows. She hoped that Josie would be fetched soon before he decided to try to get back to the farm, hoped that he wouldn't leave at all and remembered that having him sitting firmly beside her in the Whitbys' dishevelled designer kitchen had been very pleasant indeed. He had felt both frightened and angry for her then – she'd smelt it overriding his own particular male smell, which she'd found decidedly attractive.

'I don't feel comfortable like this,' she said. 'I want to wash and change into something warmer. The jacket is ruined anyway – look, the material's cut on the collar, and it's got bloodstains on it. Perhaps wearing green *is* unlucky.'

Edmund sat back on his heels. 'I was wearing a green jacket too, when the bomb went off. I think it's more likely to be a fortunate colour, since we've both survived. Hatty took mine to the cleaners who think they can restore it.' He got up, put his hand up to his ear out of habit, and then let it drop back. 'Do you know – I wanted to buy you a green velvet jacket I saw in London, as a Christmas present?'

She went upstairs, leaving him to stoke the fire and watch the snow, falling steadily now. It would soon be dark again. A red Jeep-type thing drew up outside, and hooted. He could see a man in a flat cap at the wheel, blowing on his hands, and a girl sitting beside him, who waved. Josie found her mother wriggling awkwardly into a thick jersey, green again, to flout fate, wincing a little.

'Can you manage? Does it hurt?'

'No, I'm fine. I really am. You go off, and ring me tomorrow.'

Josie gave her a hug and disappeared, clattering down the narrow staircase. She poked her head round the door to say goodbye to Edmund.

'I'm off now. I know you want to be alone with her. You'll take care of her, won't you?' Her voice had a trace of a giggle in it, a little teasing. 'What a couple of old crocks! Both of you all stitched up. Bye, then!'

'Goodbye, Josie,' said Edmund, thinking what a dear, wicked person she was, glad that she could happily trot off and pursue her own ends. She barely knew the Whitbys, was uninterested in their domestic dramas except in the fact that it had somehow affected her mother, whom she could now see was unharmed.

Over the last few days Edmund had been so concentrated on his growing desire for Amelia that the sudden violent disruption of the afternoon had shocked and disconcerted him far more than his narrow escape in London. He was, however, still thinking that he must hold back and give her a chance to get to know him, though she had not seemed uncomfortable with him holding on to her in the kitchen. He didn't believe he'd ever feel comfortable in that kitchen again.

'I was thinking,' said Amelia, coming back into the sitting room, 'that I seem to attract violence, or rather that it follows me about. Not necessarily violence done to me, I don't mean that, although that has happened once or twice, but that violent things seem to happen around me too often.'

Edmund recalled that she had witnessed an assassination as a child, and shivered. 'That doesn't mean it always will,' he said comfortingly. 'Things change, all the time. This might be the last occasion.'

'Yes, I suppose there is a chance of that. So, here we are, both alive. Are you very worried about your sister?'

'To be truthful, I'm more worried about you. I think Xenia will get better, now she's let off steam – only that is a trivial way to think of what she did – I think she probably needs professional help, but I doubt she'd agree to that. Poor Johnnie. Perhaps we ought to do graffiti on all the walls round the farm . . . 'Johnnie Whitby is almost innocent, OK?' I don't know anything about nervous breakdowns – they don't run in the family – and she's only been drunk once recently to my knowledge. But she's always been a very buttoned-up, strait-laced sort of person, constipated by her own precision, forever trying to keep tabs on everyone, organizing them, bossing. No one can keep up to her standards. I think she felt she had lost control of us all, and so lost control of herself.'

'Will your mother be able to help? I thought she was wonderfully funny.'

'Funny?'

'Yes, didn't you hear her telling everyone as they left that Xenia had been taken ill with gastro-enteritis? Then she got bored with saying gastro-enteritis and told the last two to leave, the two old boys who were bent on exterminating rats, that Xenia had conjunctivitis.'

'I expect they all left worried that they were going to catch something. But my mother is one of the people who Xenia has never been able to control. They don't get on at all. When my father died, Xenia moved in on her, ordering her to do this and that, sell her house, come and live with her and Johnnie. Sofia escaped to France as fast as she could. She visits us all at Christmas and we all go over to see her whenever we want. The children love going to stay with her, but I haven't been able to go as often as I'd like. She has a wonderful brother, Uncle Serge, who lives in Paris. I always drop in to see him when I do get over. He lives in their parents' old flat and he's an expert on icons and on pre-revolutionary Russian art.'

'What an interesting family you have. I've only got Josie now, and Aunt Margaret in Galloway. And there's Nick's mother, who still blames me for his death. I honestly don't think I had anything to do with his death. I suppose you've heard the story from Johnnie, of what happened?'

'Only partially, as I've come to expect from Johnnie. All I know is that he killed himself. Do you know why?'

'I think it was just as he said in his note. Boredom. He was frustrated by failure and bored with responsibility. I hate to admit this, because of Josie, and such things can run in families, can't they? But it became clear to me about five years into our marriage that he was mentally ill at times. Nothing you could put a name to, no syndromes, just depression of a peculiar sort. When one is married to a depressive, one tends to think that one is to blame for their depression a lot of the time, and they of course don't try to put one right, the opposite in fact. There were good times, of course, but it's getting harder and harder to remember them. In the same way that you've only just realized there was something wrong with Xenia, it took me ages to pin down Nick's problem. You've made your sister sound like an emotional terrorist.'

'Poor Xenia. But that *is* what she is. Do you know she practically forced us to go to church yesterday? In spite of us all having been to Midnight Mass the night before, to please her. None of us is religious by nature, and I can't seem to get on with the present Church of England at all – it seems to have become an uninspiring sort of club.'

'I went to the carol service because I thought you might be there. That's using it as a club, isn't it? But I like the marking of the seasonal changes, old pagan festivals dressed up as something else. I think they're more important than people think. But I must admit I've never fitted in to any clubs. A bit like Groucho Marx, you know?'

'That you don't want to belong to the sort of club that would let you become one of its members? Yes, I know what you mean. I found out after my wife Sylvestra had left that I had left a club I didn't even know I belonged to. Within a year the other members were all frenziedly matchmaking, desperate to get me to rejoin, as if I'd be subversive if I didn't, or else they didn't know what else to do with me.'

Edmund didn't feel that the conversation should be taking this turn at all, but seemed unable to stop himself.

'Why did you break up – can I ask?' Amelia had been about to ask if stabbing was a genetic trait in his family, but stopped just in time, but not before Edmund had divined what was on her mind.

'It wasn't violence on my part, I promise you,' he said, alarmed. 'Sylvestra left me because she had fallen in love with someone else. Which means that she had fallen out of love with me before she met him, I suppose, or she wouldn't have been looking, would she? She did have one or two flings before, but I didn't think they were serious. This one was and I stupidly didn't take too much notice until too late. People often ask if one has got *over* an event such as a divorce or a death. I don't see how one can get *over* it. The word has the wrong spatial connotations, don't you think?'

'You could always try going round instead. I got round Nick's death in the end, although at the time the event itself had taken on the proportions of Ben Nevis. I refused to take the blame, and had to work very hard, and Josie being there helped too.' Amelia felt the dressing over the cut on her collarbone and looked straight at Edmund, seeing how anxious and tense he was. 'There is a difference, you know, between over and round. Over implies an effort, uphill. Through is the same, tunnelling in the dark. But round, well that's just by-passing, circling, bending the rules a little. I don't want to, can't, I mean, forget life with Nick, nor what he did. But I don't have to let it take part in the present.'

'Since I found your papers I've thought about Sylvestra less and less. This is the first time I've thought about her since I last saw you.'

'You've come round then? Am I that diverting?'

'I think I have. And yes, you are.'

'What would you like for supper?' she said.

'I don't know what you've got. Something childish, I think. Scrambled eggs on toast? Eggy bread?'

'What the hell's eggy bread?'

'Shall I show you? I'm beginning to feel quite warm now, and very hungry. Have you got any jam, or marmalade?'

They went into the kitchen together. Outside in the dark, Edmund's car had all but disappeared. Snow had come in under the ill-fitting door in a little white drift, unmelting on the brick floor, like caster sugar. He took the loaf of bread she gave him and cut four thick slices, beat up three eggs in a wide blue china bowl and added a little milk and a pinch of salt. He had a frown of concentration on his face, his thick eyebrows drawn together. 'Now, see. You put the slices to soak in the bowl. They have to be really sodden, all the way through. Keep on turning them, top to the bottom. Then you get a large bit of butter. Butter, butter, where's the butter? Ah, I've got it. Big frying pan? Got that too. Then you get the butter hot, as if you were about to make an omelette, and you throw in the bread . . .'

The delicious smell, the sizzling sound. Amelia suddenly felt quite faint.

'Now, turn them over. Can I put my arms round you again, while the other side cooks?' He'd forgotten his resolution and reached round her waist from behind her, held her close, rocking her from side to side as she turned the bread.

'I'm not hurting your shoulder, am I?' he asked, anxiously.

'No. It's no worse than a cut finger. I think this is done.'

'Then quick! Plates and jam and sugar! It's called *pain perdu.*'

Amelia found that eating eggy bread with a man she now knew she fancied to death was an extraordinarily sensuous experience. She licked her jammy fingers, and Edmund, watching her with pleasure, thought she resembled nothing so much as an Abyssinian cat, completely unselfconscious, at peace with itself regardless of the havoc it had unwittingly caused around it. A cat returned from a fray, safe by its own fireside. She smiled up at him, clasping her arms round her knees, wondering what he looked like beneath the dark jacket and white shirt, with the tie askew.

'You must be cold, in your party clothes. I'll find you something warmer to wear.' He was cold, in spite of the fire. He'd been accustomed to Xenia's over-heated house, and was out of the habit of layering clothes just because it was winter. 'And I'm going to telephone Mary, to thank her. Back in a minute.' She disappeared again, leaving him wondering what to do, or what not to do.

Mary was unsympathetic to Xenia's predicament. 'She deserves an Oscar. I've never seen such melodrama, pure *Grand Guignol.*'

'Yes. The farcical elements didn't go unnoticed. But perhaps she hasn't had a lot of practice at throwing tantrums and didn't know how far to go.'

'She's gone quite far enough for the rest of her life. But are you OK? Is Mr Yearne looking after your interests?'

'I'm fine. He's just cooked me a delicious tea. And my "interests" are still untouched. But what about Xenia?'

'I've had a chat with her own GP, which I can't go into, obviously. You're not pressing charges, are you?'

'Good God, no! She meant to get Johnnie, not me,' said Amelia, appalled. 'Anyway,' she continued, 'I just wanted to thank you for looking after me again. I was quite scared you'd do blanket stitch, but I've just looked at it in the mirror and it looks very neat. I've put some marigold on it.'

'You and your herbal horrors! No, I know it's a good natural antiseptic.'

'It does make things heal up quicker. I don't want a huge scar. It used to be used by optimistic young women in an effort to restore their virginity. Did you know that?'

'No, it's a bit of information I failed to pick up in medical school. Sadly it's a bit late for both of us, isn't it?'

When Amelia had put the phone down, she scratched a little hole in the developing frost on the window with her fingernail, and tried to peer out. Still snowing. She ran upstairs again, to fetch a heavy grey fisherman's jersey for Edmund and returned to the pumpkin-coloured sitting room to find him going through her bookshelves, intrigued by the collection. He'd picked out Dorothy Hartley's *Food in England* and was leafing through it, wondering if the way to a woman's heart was through her stomach.

'I loved the *pain perdu*. What else can you do?' she asked.

Edmund thought he'd only thought the words: 'I'd love to make love to you, but not yet. We're both too shaken.'

Amelia laughed. 'All right then. I am a bit shaken. That's why I keep getting up and down.'

'What do you mean?'

'I mean, all right, not yet.' She hesitated and then laughed again at him. 'You didn't realize you had spoken aloud, did you?'

'I didn't!'

'You did. I heard you quite clearly.'

'Could I stay the night?' He looked doubtful, cautious.

'You could hardly do anything else, I think. The wind's getting up and the snow does drift here so badly.' As she spoke the wind was conjured to give a warning howl in the wide chimney. 'But you can't sleep down here. The fire will go out and you'll get hypothermia.'

Edmund's self-imposed restraint and Amelia's growing impatience passed each other in the street without recognition, then light dawned and they turned and waved.

'We could then, at least, keep each other warm?' he asked.

'I think that would be very practical.' She looked closely at him and saw that he was still very white. 'I believe you're more shocked than I am by all this.'

'I've been frightened half to death by the thought of losing you. And I think the bomb business has caught up with me. I keep thinking I can see myself out of the corner of my eye.'

'I can see you full on. You look like a man who's seen a ghost.'

'Come to me, then. I need you.'

And because it was he who had asked, chosen, she came and lay beside him on the sofa and they became inextricably involved, happily and painfully entangled, and quite desperate for somewhere more comfortable.

'You go up first, the fire's lit up there. I've got to lock the door.'

'Who do you expect to come, on a night like this?'

'You're right, I expect it would be rather difficult for anyone. We'll go together.' And in spite of the cold, the tangle of heavy bedding and not being able to take off their clothes without getting frostbite, and in spite of the bruises and stitches, they made love for a very long time, without once repeating themselves, tasting, testing and treating each other ecstatically, with infinite care and patience, till they fell into a pleasure-saturated state of sedation. The paraffin stove made a tiny fluttering sound and threw its little patterned light on to the uneven, bulging plaster ceiling. The wind moaned, as if saddened by the cessation of activity. Amelia slid her hand up Edmund's chest beneath his shirt, running along the sharp line of fur, and fell asleep to dream of badgers. Edmund dreamed of sitting naked on a beach with Amelia, in hot sunshine, eating, feeding her fingers of eggy bread, but she turned into a yellow cat and ran off with her tail in the air. He chased her all round the island, for that is where they were, but she was always a yard ahead of him.

'Edmund!'

'Mm.'

'Edmund!' The voice had more urgency to it this time, but was laughing.

'What's 'a matter?'

'You're holding on to me so tight I can't breathe.'

'I thought you'd run away.'

'Oh no, not me.'

He released her, reluctantly, slowly opening his eyes and staring at her in the semi-dark, eyes heavy-lidded. She stared back, the peat-brown eyes huge, pupils wide.

'Good morning, dearest man.'

'Where are you going?' She was sliding away from him, slipping out of bed. She stood there, wearing only her green jersey. He glimpsed the white roundness of her behind before she wrapped herself in a dressing gown.

'I have to go and feed the cat. I'll make some tea.'

'Bugger the cat. Come back.' He'd felt a twitch, a surge of renewed desire. 'But it can't be morning. I've only just fallen asleep.'

But she went after planting a kiss on his mouth. 'Keep my side of the bed warm too.'

He heard her footsteps on the creaking wooden stairs and the click of the inner kitchen door, her voice softly greeting the cat, clanking metallic sounds as she riddled the stove and poured in more coal. Then he heard her gasp.

'Edmund!'

He stuck his nose out of the bedclothes, feeling the bite of the air.

'Edmund,' she called out again. 'We're competely snowed in! It's halfway up the windows.' Edmund groaned and got out of bed but couldn't find his trousers, nor his socks. He dragged a blanket off the bed and wrapped himself up in it. This seemed awfully familiar. It was an odd coincidence that within a space of a couple of weeks, and after over a year's abstinence, he had made love to two different women while snowed in – but there was no comparison between them, between the two events, apart from the damned snow. His mind was full of last night, although he now considered it lucky that he didn't have chilblains on his private parts. He scraped ineffectually at the window. The ice was thick, but he eventually made an area large enough to look through. But there was nothing to see. Thousands of acres of snow, with just the odd black bush peering through it. The road, which he knew to be beneath the window on that side of the house, had disappeared. He stumped back to bed across the plank floor. He felt a sock, then another, then retrieved Amelia's tights and knickers, and his tie which looked as if someone had tied a reef knot in it. Amelia came upstairs with two mugs of tea and a can of paraffin. She filled the stove, and got back into bed with him, making him gasp as her icy legs touched his.

'I'll warm up in a second,' she said.

'Let me warm you up.' He stroked the bright hair, twisting his fingers into it and kissing her cold ear. Then he put his cup down, felt under the bedclothes and ran his hands up and down her thighs, warming them.

'Do you realize we've screwed each other silly and not even seen each other's bodies?' she said. 'Like a Victorian couple with all those voluminous nightshirts and dresses.'

'Well you're not seeing any more of mine till spring. You shouldn't have to live like this. It's like the Middle Ages.'

'I'm tough, and I got used to the cold when we lived in the other house. We couldn't afford to heat that either, it was too big. We used to wear our coats indoors, and two or three pairs of socks. I'm afraid I often go to bed in all my clothes. But this is exceptionally bad. It doesn't snow down here all that often – and it's certainly colder than I can ever remember. I don't see how we can get out at all. It's still quite dark downstairs because the windows are blocked up with snow.'

'Don't talk so much – is that nice?'

'Yes.'

'And this?'

'Even better. I suppose we could get out of the sitting-room window, that's on the other side of the house.'

'Who wants to get out? I'm sure there are bits of you that I haven't touched yet.' Edmund didn't feel it was an appropriate time to discuss means of escape.

They emerged breathlessly some time later, pink-faced and tousled and utterly happy.

'We didn't do that last night,' he said, looking a little surprised.

'I forgot to tell you how much I like it, but you do need to shave.'

'I didn't bring a razor. I didn't think I was going to be able to stay.'

'That was silly of you.'

'You don't understand, I was so scared of moving too fast and putting you off – you seemed so cool and self-contained, and you were very angry that I'd read your papers, if you remember. I felt so guilty.'

'Poor lamb. I did like you at once, really. I just didn't want to do any of the running at all. Just in case I'd made a mistake again.'

'And you think you haven't?'

'I don't think I have. No.'

At midday they got up and shared a bath.

'You could try shaving with this. I promise I've only used it once for my legs.' They'd warmed the bathroom first with one of the ubiquitous paraffin stoves, and she lay in the soapy water dreaming a little while he tried to remove the dark stubble. He turned away from the foggy mirror and watched her intently, savouring the ins and outs of her body, the breasts quite round and full, the small dark nipples, the light dusting of freckles on arms and shoulders, the ugly cut on her collarbone, even that he found attractive.

'You are beautiful, you know.'

She sat up self-consciously, splashing the wall, and began scrubbing her feet with a nailbrush, turning suddenly and giving him her set-afire smile. 'You don't mind the stretch-marks, then?'

Edmund couldn't see any. She rose, flicking water from her hands, and bent to show him, a little staggered row of pale silver streaks, just above the golden public hair.

'No, I don't mind them at all, so long as you don't mind me missing a bit of my ear?'

'Poor mutilated thing!' She reached out and put her arms round his neck as she stepped out of the bath. 'What I like about you is you're so three-dimensional – some men are sort of flat, have no depth to them. You are columnar, strong. Considering the amount of time you must spend poring over books.'

'Books are incredibly heavy and I spend more time heaving them about in boxes than poring over them.'

The room was full of steam, little runnels of water coursing down the inside of the windows coagulated and froze. They dressed quickly and greedily breakfasted on thick rashers of green back bacon and black coffee before attempting an escape from the house – the only exit being through the sitting room window. Edmund climbed out and passed logs back through to Amelia till the copper was filled and the dampest ones were stacked at either end of the large hearth, enough to feed a fire for at least three days. They lay in front of it, lazily talking, reading a little and since no one was going to be able to drive anywhere for the foreseeable future, drank two bottles of wine which had been unaccountably left over from the Christmas feast. The telephone was out of order, but Amelia did not worry about Josie since she would probably be warmer where she was. They heard on the local radio that large swathes of Kent were cut off but didn't greatly care, and lay snug, talking and talking.

'Tell me more of your marriage to Nick. You never wrote about him.'

'No, I didn't. In the early days it seemed that to commit

it to paper would destroy it. Later I was quite unable to be truthful any more, in case he read it and was hurt. We all expected too much from marriage. The romantic novels that girls read in those days, still do as far as I know, concentrate on the hunt, the banquet and then tail off. They never told us how indigestible marriage can be sometimes. I can only say that there were times when I was so bitterly disappointed that I couldn't bear it, and I'm sure he must have felt the same. We did both try, of course, to make things better, but we never managed to coincide in our efforts.' Amelia rolled over and propped herself up on a cushion.

'Tell me about Sylvestra.'

'The trouble there was that I only believed what I wanted to believe. I couldn't imagine that she was unhappy. It's easier to see now that I rushed her into it – marriage, I mean. I thought her emotional outbursts were just the way women were and didn't understand their reality. She needed excitement and admiration all the time. I just accepted her rages as part of our life together without trying to forestall them by behaving differently.'

'There won't be any real reason for us to have to do things differently, will there? We can go on just as we are – take it in turns to visit each other, have our cake, slice after slice and when that's finished, bake up another.'

'I think this is the first time in my life that I've dared to admit that I'm happy now, this minute.'

'Could I prick the bubble of your euphoria, just for a moment, and ask you to relinquish a little more of the rug. I've got one cold ear.'

'Happily.'

Edmund lay beside her in the dark that night, fully thawed out and thinking that middle-age could have the edge on youth in some respects, for one's optimism was by then tamed to sensible proportions and any delights that came one's way were seen as a glorious bonus rather than as rights. He turned to Amelia to see if she had any thoughts on the matter of rights, but she was sound asleep, breathing gently and regularly, her ivory-white face tucked into his neck. Breathing . . . The room smelt of paraffin warmth, of clean sheets and saltily of sex.

Two days later, when the roads had been cleared, Johnnie sat with Sofia in the pinkish teatime light of the drawing room, discussing Xenia's immediate needs. They had agreed, with her doctor's approval, that she should go to a nursing home for a couple of weeks, where she wouldn't be perpetually thinking of things which needed doing, and could have a proper rest, following which, Johnnie would take her for a holiday. Xenia, in a semi-sedated state, had vaguely agreed to the proposal. She was now standing on the landing in her nightdress, wondering if it were lunchtime or suppertime, staring at the crooked picture of the almshouses in the snow, unable to remember when or where she had bought it, while downstairs, Sofia was rising from amongst the cabbage-embroidered cushions, drawing a vast red cashmere shawl around her shoulders and saying: 'Well, that's settled then. I shall go and make arrangements for us to visit tomorrow to check whether it is suitable for 'er. It is a semi-religious institution. I 'ope she will like that.'

Xenia heard Sofia's footsteps in the hall, heard the tinkling of the bracelets as she dialled and her voice, muffled as if she were at a great distance.

'Allo? Is that St Cecilia's Retreat?'

Xenia's head began miraculously to clear. She knew that Johnnie was downstairs, planning a holiday for them both. She knew that Edmund had gone to be with Amelia. That, strangely, didn't seem to matter any more in the slightest.

She could see in her mind's eye the group of faces frozen round the kitchen table on the day of the party, shocked. With a slightly crooked smile she straightened the painting. She expected that they would all take her more seriously from now on.